THE DARK
UNWINDING

THE DARK UNWINDING

Sharon Cameron

SCHOLASTIC INC.

This book was originally published in hardcover by Scholastic Press in 2012.

ISBN 978-0-545-32787-9

12 11 10 9 8 7 6 5 4 3 2 1   13 14 15 16 17 18/0

Printed in the U.S.A. 40

First paperback printing, September 2013

The text type was set in Goudy Old Style.

The display type was set in OPTI Ceasar.

Book design by Elizabeth B. Parisi

FOR MY MOTHER,
WHO WOULD HAVE BEEN PROUD

Fish Toy

Mechanism Detail, Pendulum, and Flyrotational Stabilizer

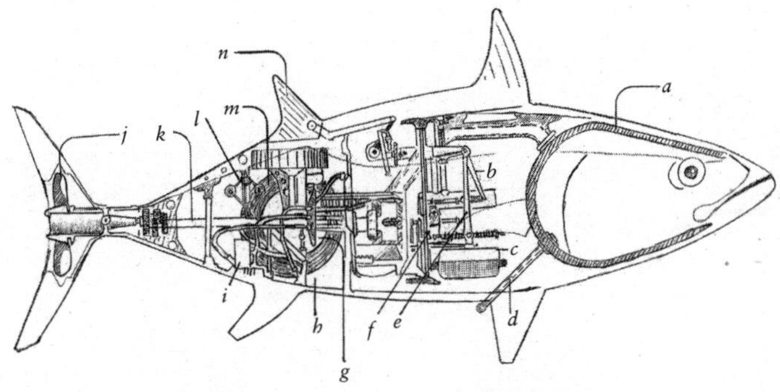

a. air flask
b. rock shaft
c. pendulum-bob
d. filling tube
e. pendulum
f. connecting rod & sleeve
g. valve manifold

h. engine compartment
i. valve chamber
j. screw drive
k. drive shaft
l. velocity governor
m. fly rotor (gyroscope)
n. actuating lever (fin)

CHAPTER ONE

June 1852

Warm sun and robin's-egg skies were inappropriate conditions for sending one's uncle to a lunatic asylum. I had settled this point four hours earlier, while miles of road slipped beneath the carriage wheels. The clouds, to my way of thinking, should have turned themselves black, should have rumbled and crashed, and flung needles of rain at the trees. But there they lazed, the errant things, like tufts of discarded goose down, shadowing the slopes of the passing moors. I removed my gaze from the window. The weather was most insensible.

Beads of sweat rolled down my neck, the empty seat across from me rocking with the wheels. The interior of the carriage was crimson and airless, like Aunt Alice's morning room, where I do the family accounts.

"Katharine," my aunt Alice had said. She was perched on the edge of the velvet settee, stroking the head of a round-bellied pug, allowing it to lap tea from her saucer. The dog's dislike of me was almost equal to his mistress's. "Katharine," she had said, "I've a job to be done, a job for which I find you most suitable."

Yes, Aunt, I'd thought. *I am always the most suitable for your sort of jobs. Is there a maid to be scolded, another necklace to be pawned? Or has my cousin Robert done something disagreeable in the potting shed?* I blew on the wet ink of the ledger book and laid down my pen.

"Your uncle Tulman, I am afraid, has become unbalanced in his mind."

I waited, wondering if I would now be expected to rearrange the workings of a human brain. Aunt Alice set aside the saucer and drew a paper from her bag. The dog whined.

"This letter is quite concerning. Not only has your uncle refused to see Mrs. Hardcastle, he has caused her to fear for her life. She was obliged to flee. She also says that your uncle has undertaken certain projects at Stranwyne, projects that are seriously depleting the wealth of the estate. This would explain, of course, the reluctance about any little increases to our own family income. If we are not active . . ." She cast a loving eye on her only son, sprawled on the rug like a man-sized child, his puffy cheeks round with toffees. ". . . then there will be nothing left for poor Robert when he comes of age."

I closed the ledger book. That our income might be increased by denying "poor Robert" his daily access to the sweet shop was a fact I kept to myself. My realm was confined to the ink and subtraction marks; I had no say in what made the numbers come to be. Not yet.

"I have seen my solicitor," my aunt announced. "And due to the . . . delicate nature of these matters, I am told that someone — preferably one of the family — must go to the estate, to bear witness to your uncle's incapacities. And without, of course, attracting more scrutiny or scandal than need be." She gathered up the dog and kissed it, glancing at me sidelong through her fringe of curls. "You, Katharine, are the soul of discretion."

I woke late to my danger. "But, Aunt," I said quickly, "surely you would wish to attend to such a matter yourself? It is our Robert's inheritance, after all." I was aiming for her weak spot, but she was far ahead of me.

"I am surprised at you, Katharine. Robert will be your sole provision in life once I am gone, so this concerns you far more than it does me, I'm sure." She cuddled the squirming dog. "And you forget that it is the season. I, of course, could never leave London in the season."

It was her unspoken words that silenced me. That I could have no hope of future provision beyond the charity of my fat cousin, and had no invitations to keep me in London for the season, were far weaker places than her love of money, and she knew it.

And so the carriage rattled onward to Stranwyne Keep, my trunk lashed to its back, a letter of introduction in my valise, instructions for declaring my uncle a lunatic tucked in my head. But I had given my situation and my cousin's inheritance some thought since that day. Aunt Alice might be sharp, but Robert was an idiot, and with a mind unlikely to improve under his mother's tutelage. If I could retain my position as keeper of the books, and with Robert of age, rich, and so easily manipulated, I might be able to create an independent world within the one I now inhabited, with an income that allowed me a certain measure of freedom. I had been tasting that freedom in my dreams for a fortnight. Fat Robert would inherit; I would make sure of that.

The driver hit a rut, and my teeth cracked together. I had bloodied my mouth twice before learning not to travel with my tongue between my teeth. Country bumps, I discovered, came at you by stealth. I planted my feet, leaning back against the cushion as the road tilted, and then the sun was extinguished and the carriage plunged down into a pool of midnight.

I blinked in the sudden blackness. Wind and storm I had imagined more suited to my task; apocalyptic eclipse had never entered my mind. I reached out with a blind hand, fumbling for the window latch, but it became visible to me again almost at once, lit by a harsh, yellow-white glare. I put my head out the window.

We were in a tunnel, half round and large, wide enough for two carriages to pass side by side. The walls and ceiling were bricked and curving, illuminated every few feet by an orb of glowing gaslight. The artificial sparks glimmered one after the other, on and on, dwindling away in the long dark of the tunnel.

"Driver?" I called. "Where are we?" If the man answered, then the racket of hooves, harness, and carriage wheels had not allowed me to hear it.

I shut the window. This was unexpected. I did not like the unexpected, and though every one of my seventeen years had taught me to tolerate what I did not like, I disliked it still. The gaslights streaked, blurring as they sped past my eyes. I counted three hundred twenty-six through the left-hand window before the carriage went dark, tilted, and emerged once more into the sunshine.

The road led onto a circular drive. Behind me was the mouth of the tunnel, opening like an expression of surprise from a knoll of gray-green moor grass, while before me rose a wall of brown stone, growing upward as the carriage rolled forward. Stranwyne Keep. The stone house came closer, filling my square of glass, windowpanes and casements and shrubbery passing by, and then I was jerked back against the cushions. We had stopped. I pushed down the latch and clambered out without waiting for the driver, bonnet and valise in hand.

Three rows of windows were stacked above those level with my eyes. Twenty-five or so in each row to the right, while to the left they were more difficult to count, the straight lines made irregular by insets and bays. About one chimney for every five windows was visible, and assuming that each floor shared, that would be at least four rooms to a chimney. My eyes roved the roofline. I could count thirteen chimneys at a glance. The place was a monstrosity.

I started at a touch to my elbow, but it was only the driver, a genial old man with a shock of gray hair and teeth to match. "Should I loose the trunk, Miss?"

"Yes, bring it down, please. Thank you." Gravel amongst weeds crunched beneath the man's feet, and for the first time I noticed the stillness, absolute but for the breeze and the birds. The arrival of the carriage had not roused the house. I marched up the steps, set the valise at my feet, took hold of a heavy iron knocker, and rapped.

Nothing happened.

The old man grunted, and I heard my trunk hit the ground with more force than I thought advisable for its contents. I wiped at the rust now staining my glove and knocked again.

"All right there, Miss?"

I turned. The driver was back in his seat, reins in hand, my trunk lying where it had fallen. *Coward*, I thought. I came down the steps and handed him a coin from my glove. He doffed his cap, chirruped to the horses, and I watched bits of gravel spray from the carriage wheels as he whipped the horses around the drive and disappeared into the hole in the hillside.

I walked slowly to the door in the returning silence, wishing I was back in the speeding carriage, rushing through the gas glare to somewhere else, a somewhere that was of my own choosing. Then I wondered how much of that glare was Fat Robert's inheritance being sucked away by hundreds of gaslights in a useless tunnel. I lifted the door knocker, and rapped again. When there was still no answer, I put my rusty glove on the latch and pushed. The door creaked, reluctant on its hinges.

I stepped into a tall and narrow entry hall. Curtains of deep rose damask covered the two long windows on either side of the door, tinting the flooding sunlight a hot, brazen pink, a shade mirrored by the paint above the wainscoting and the matting on the floor. The color was an assault on the eyes almost as the silence seemed an attack on the ears.

"Hello?" I called. My voice fell dead in the stale, pink air. I shut the door behind me.

A set of neat footprints in the dust-covered matting, feminine from their size and narrow heel, led away from the door, meandering amongst the haphazard groupings of sheet-clad furniture. There were none coming back again. I clutched the valise, and began my own set of footprints.

In the very back of the room, where the sunlight could not penetrate, a wide staircase rose into darkness, and beside the stairs was a door, light leaking from its edges. I opened this, and found a windowless corridor, gaslit and stifling. Door after door slipped past me, set in walls the hue of half-ripened cherries, a sense of suffocation growing as I moved deeper and deeper into the house. A closed door ended the hall, and behind it was another room, also windowless, a single chandelier throwing both illumination and shadow on nothing but clocks.

They were stacked on tables, on the floor, and covered every inch of wall. Old, new, intricate, and plain, gilt, brass, oak, teak, rosewood, and mahogany, and every one of them polished to perfection, shining in the dimness and glare. Those that were floor-standing were placed back-to-back or side-to-side, leaving narrow, winding paths through the jumble. One clock had the phases of the moon etched into its glass, another had tiny wooden figures that turned as the seconds passed, but they were all of them ticking, pendulums swinging, and at such different rhythms that I felt almost dizzy. I squeezed onto one of the paths, struggling to count as I maneuvered through the noise. The air was thick with the smell of oil and beeswax.

Something clunked to my left, heavy and metallic. I looked up to a tall black-enameled cabinet, my eyes following its pattern of gold-leaf paint to the cherub perched on its top, and above it, hanging from the ceiling, was a gilded birdcage. A stuffed bird sat inside, feathers jewel-bright in the light, the face of a clock forming the cage's rounded bottom. Cogs whirred as I stared, and the bird raised its wings with the rasp of a spring and one faint click. I turned, head swiveling. The birdcage had read five o'clock. All of them, every one of them had hands pointing to five. . . .

The cherub-topped clock boomed like a gong, the jewel bird sang, and an avalanche of bells, chimes, tolls, and whistles shook the floor. I covered my ears and fled through the clock maze, the valise and bonnet banging against my head, running for anywhere that was away from the noise. I pulled open the first door I saw, thick and on massive iron hinges, ran through, and had to use both hands to pull it shut again. The clocks ended their announcement of the hour, and the thud of the door and their last discordant clangs came back to me in a fading echo. I looked up.

I was in a room of stone, chapel-like with its vaulted roof, columned archways, and the hush that had descended after the clock chimes. Arched windows tinted the sun, this time not with cloth, but with the grime that coated their glass. I tried to slow my breath, cool air entering my lungs, my boots tapping an unwelcome staccato across the stone-flagged floor. I raised a hand and touched the nearest column. The surface was worn, pitted. This room was old, older by centuries than the others I'd walked through.

I had the oddest sensation then, with the chill of that ancient column soaking through my glove. It was like being turned the wrong way out, inverted, as if by running through the clocks I had somehow moved backward instead of forward, and to a place that did not want me. I dropped my hand. I could make no sense of my surroundings. I did not like that. A draft moved, a teasing whisper on the back of my neck, and again my boots rang a rhythm on the floor stones, ruining the quiet, their noise returning from the shadows with a soft, burbling giggle.

I spun on my heel, chest thudding, searching for a laugh that had seemed both before and behind me, and when I whirled about the other way I froze. A young woman stood not twenty feet away, plain, panting, and wearing my gray dress, staring back at me wide-eyed from a tall gilded mirror that stood propped against the wall. I let out my breath. I could see my boots, the valise, even my untidy hair.

I could also see two black eyes, glittering in a pale face that hovered just behind my shoulder.

I screamed, then clamped my mouth shut and turned, my shriek coming back to me, mocking. A little man sat at a table between two columns, a parson's hat the style of thirty years ago tilted on his head. The black eyes danced as he grinned, but now I could see that their sparkle was only glass, shimmering in the reflected light of the mirror. A crack ran down the porcelain of his face, twisting his smile. I stepped back. Whatever he was, the little man had not laughed.

"Where are you?" I called, eyes roving the emptiness. The columns held up a gallery, and on the far end, in the dim, top recesses, I could just make out a door. It was open, swinging slightly in the draft.

I set the valise at my feet, and smoothed my disarranged hair. Someone was alive and breathing in this house, if for no other reason than someone had to wind all those clocks. And that someone, I suspected, had just tried to make a fool of me.

I left the parson smiling at his table, my boots clacking to the far end of the room, where I jerked open a door and tromped down the salmon-hued hall behind it, bonnet swinging by its strings. I turned right, up a short flight of stairs, marched through a fuchsia room with more dust sheets, turned right again, and came to a choice: right, or left. A door slammed somewhere to my right so I went that way, skirt swishing against a carpet the color of faded sugar roses. I rounded the corner and flung open the first door I saw.

The inevitable color of this room was softened by smoke stains, peeling plaster, and a faint orange fire glow. Copper pans and braided onions hung from the ceiling, clouded by a fog of steam that blurred the outlines of the furniture. But I could see a woman, stout and in a pale blue dressing gown, standing with her feet apart before a stove that needed blacking. She had just clouted the child in front of her on the head with a spoon.

". . . will be taking you straight to the bad place for such lies, Davy . . ." She looked up then, and her mouth dropped open. "Well, who the devil are you?"

CHAPTER TWO

The child put two long-lashed, inky eyes upon me, grinned, took four steps, and folded himself onto the hearthstone. He carried a massive hare, brown-and-gray speckled, that settled into his lap like some sort of long-legged cat. Here, I thought, was my giggler.

"Well, who are you?" the woman repeated.

I held tight to the valise. "Please be so good as to inform my uncle that his niece, Katharine Tulman, has arrived. I'm afraid there was no one to meet me at the door."

The boy fondled the ears of his rabbit while the woman stared, her spoon dripping. Either she was hard of hearing, or her brains were as addled as my uncle's. Hoping for the former, I cleared my throat and spoke louder.

"Would you please have my uncle Frederick Tulman informed that his niece, Katharine, has arrived?"

"Who?" the woman squeaked.

I turned to the boy. "Could you take me to Mr. Tulman, please?"

The boy lifted those dark eyes to me again, his face curiously untroubled as he stroked the hare. He did not answer.

"But it's playtime," the woman said.

I turned again to look at her.

"Mr. Tully's at playtime. You can't go and be bothering Mr. Tully when he's at playtime."

I could not think of a suitable response to that. Steam spouted from a pot on the stove, and behind it I spied a kettle. "Is that Mr. Tulman's tea you are preparing?"

The woman gazed at me as if I were an insect that had just crawled from her pudding.

I raised my voice. "I said, are you making tea?"

Her eyes flicked once to the kettle.

I set down the valise, wondering if the entire household needed to be sent to an asylum. "Well, I should like some tea, thank you. I've been traveling since early this morning and find myself much fatigued. I'll have cream and sugar — half a lump, no more — and buttered toast, if you please." I came down three steps, pulled a chair from the table, and sat on it.

That broke the woman's trance. Her astonishment at my presence in the kitchen became open alarm. The spoon clattered to the floor, and she moved like a barrel on wheels to the table, her dressing gown flapping. She snatched the creamer and the sugar bowl, moving them away from my reach, eyeing my chair as if she might like to do the same to it.

I began loosening the fingers of my left glove, holding tight to my hand, to prevent her seeing its slight shake. So, I thought, this was her domain, her kingdom, and I had just invaded. Well, well. Everyone had something they valued. Aunt Alice had money, Robert had toffee, and this woman had a kitchen. What I valued was respect, and I intended to have it. I took a deep breath.

"As soon as you have begun the tea, please inform the housekeeper that I will require a man to deal with my trunk. It was left at the front doors. Have it taken to my room immediately, if you please, and you may tell her that I will do my own unpacking."

The woman released the sugar bowl and squinted. "Who the devil are you?"

"I might ask the same of you, ma'am, though I, of course, would never swear while doing so. I shall try to forget that you have. I repeat that I am Katharine Tulman, Mr. Tulman's niece. Obviously you have not been told of my coming. I take it you are the cook?"

The woman frowned. "I do for Mr. Tully. My name is Jefferies, Mrs. Jefferies." She watched me pull my fingers one by one from the other glove, then moved heavily to the stove and put the kettle to the heat, her eyes darting back to me every few seconds. "You're never . . . you couldn't be Mr. Simon's child?"

"Simon Tulman was my father, yes."

"Why, Mr. Simon couldn't have been near this place for almost ten years."

"Considering that he has been dead for sixteen, I would say it has been rather longer."

Mrs. Jefferies nodded in thoughtful agreement, her double chin disappearing and reappearing as she sliced bread. But I knew she was watching, to see what I touched. She skewered the bread on an iron fork and handed it to the boy. He held it over the flames without comment or instruction, the fingers of his other hand still fondling the contented rabbit. "And what would be bringing you to us now?" she asked softly.

I recited my lines. "I have come to Stranwyne to be Mr. Tulman's secretary."

"Secretary?" Her lips pressed together, and she turned back to the stove. I kept a guarded eye on the bread knife. "This'll be that Alice's doing, the little . . ."

Mrs. Jefferies mumbled on, apparently believing the whistle of the teakettle to be masking the rather offensive word she chose to describe my aunt. As I could not disagree with her, I turned to the boy. "Your name is David?" I asked him.

The child smiled, one deep dimple appearing in his left cheek, but he said nothing. I wondered how he was not miserable so close to the fire. The room was oppressively hot. He flipped the bread, exposing the other side to the heat.

"And do you often play in the unused portions of the house, David?"

His expression went blank, his attention all on the perfection of my toast, and I decided not to pursue the matter. The normalcy of being in a room with a woman who despised me had restored some of my common sense. There was nothing to be feared in dust sheets or a porcelain figure or an inordinate number of clocks. In any case, this boy was only nine, possibly ten. Perhaps he had not intended to frighten me with his laugh, or at least, not as much as he had. I had no wish for him to receive another rap on the head. "What is your rabbit's name?" I asked.

The dimple came back, but he did not answer.

"Bertram," Mrs. Jefferies said, slapping a cup of tea on the table. "We call the beast Bertram."

I stared at the hot tea, feeling a drop of sweat sneak down my back. "I take cream and half a lump, if you remember, Mrs. Jefferies."

Mrs. Jefferies grabbed the cream, poured a scant measure and set it away again, out of my reach, plopped a full lump into the cup and slid it to me, tossing the bread the child had finished toasting onto a plate alongside.

"Buttered, if you please, Mrs. Jefferies. And I wonder if you have given any thought to my trunk."

The child unfolded himself from the hearth, arranged the rabbit so that its front legs hung over his shoulder, and went silently through a door beyond the stove. I caught a whiff of cooler air and a glimpse of walled garden.

"He'll be getting Lane," said Mrs. Jefferies. "Lane'll fetch your trunk, though I'm sure I don't know what he'll be doing with it. We've nowhere to put you, you know."

As I was sitting in one of what must be a hundred rooms, I ignored this, took a sip of my tea, and bit back a cry. It was not hot; it was scalding. I set down the cup, noting that Mrs. Jefferies was not attempting to produce any butter. "When does my uncle take his evening meal, Mrs. Jefferies?"

"One hour, seventeen minutes. And Lord help us, Miss, if you're making it any longer than that."

I raised a brow. Then my uncle was an exacting man, like Aunt Alice. I looked to the window and the angling sun, and held in a sigh. "Well, perhaps you'd better take me to him now."

Mrs. Jefferies spread her hands on her wide hips, her chest heaving with a sudden agitation I could not comprehend. She lowered her voice. "I know what you've come for."

"Oh, I doubt that, Mrs. Jefferies."

"I know it well. And I'll be making it hard for you, Miss, just you mind that. I'll be making it as hard as I can."

I studied her with new interest. Graying hair, a broad nose, deep wrinkles around eyes that were faded and . . . shrewd. The woman's brains might be in working order after all. I stirred my tea, sucking on my burnt lip. Maybe it really would be best to see my uncle as soon as possible. If he was doing anything odd — which seemed a distinct possibility given Mrs. Jefferies's behavior — I might get what I needed at once, no need to stay at Stranwyne for even a night. There must be someone I could pay to transfer me to the coaching inn at Milton, and I could pay well; Aunt Alice had given me enough for a stay of two weeks, if needed. I felt my nerves calm at this plan, and I smiled at Mrs. Jefferies. She narrowed her eyes, and then the garden door opened.

The boy and the hare slid back into the kitchen, leaving a lean young man in a grease-stained shirt hanging on the door frame behind them. I guessed him to be about eighteen or so beneath the dirt on his face, gray eyes regarding me like two chips of stone.

"Well, Lane, what do you say to this?" said Mrs. Jeffries.

He hung there, lazy and tense all at once, like a cat, arms over his head, dark and sweaty hair just brushing the lintel. I wondered if he was leaving grease spots on the paint. "I'd say you burnt the porridge, Aunt Bit," he replied. His voice was very low.

Mrs. Jefferies made a noise of disgust and ran to the pot that was no longer steaming, but smoking, as Davy sat back on the hearth-stone, cuddling his rabbit. I met the gray gaze, and lifted my chin.

"I am Mr. Tulman's niece," I said. "I wish to see him without delay, please."

Mrs. Jefferies hissed from the vicinity of the stove, but the young man merely regarded me, a crease in his forehead. "It's Mr. Tully's . . ."

"Playtime. Yes, I have been made aware of it." I tucked my gloves beneath my arm, and stood. "Take me to him, please. Now."

Mrs. Jefferies sputtered as if she wished to spit out the fire. "He'll do no such thing."

I looked to Mrs. Jefferies. "Yes, he shall."

"You've no business giving orders in my kitchen, Miss!"

"And you, Mrs. Jefferies, have no business wearing a dressing gown at five o'clock in the afternoon."

The woman's mouth unhinged, and I glanced sidelong at the doorway. The crease on Lane's forehead had become a scowl, and the arms were no longer hanging, but crossed. That battle was lost. But I had no intention of remaining in Stranwyne for the night. I ran a finger over the sugar spoon, to irritate Mrs. Jefferies. "Then perhaps David will tell me where my uncle is."

"I'll reckon he won't." This comment came from the doorway.

I turned to the child and smiled. "David, take me to Mr. Tulman. And if you do, I'll have no reason to mention anything that . . . might have happened before."

The boy hugged his rabbit. The odd, blank look was there again.

"I'm sure Mrs. Jefferies would not be pleased if I told her what you did this afternoon. Just show me where Mr. Tulman is, and then I shan't have to." I held out my hand, but the child scooted backward, dangerously close to the fire, the rabbit clutched hard against his chest. Lane left the doorway and came properly into the kitchen.

"Stop it," he said. "You're frightening him."

My eyes widened slightly. Aunt Alice's servants usually just hung their heads or ignored me altogether; they certainly did not reprimand. But I only replied, "I am merely trying to make a bargain, not frighten him." I smiled again in Davy's direction. "Which is more than I can say for you, isn't that so, David?"

"What are you going on about?" asked Mrs. Jefferies.

"Well, David, are you going to take me to Mr. Tulman?"

The child stared, the seconds passing, and then without warning he convulsed backward, as if I had threatened him physical harm, bumping hard into the iron grate that held the coals. A shower of sparks flew up the chimney and I reached out a hand, but Lane had already scooped both boy and hare away from the flames.

"I told you to stop!" Lane yelled, the deep voice hitting me like a blow. He set the child on his feet, brushing away the cinders. "Why did you have to scare him like that?"

Silent tears were overflowing Davy's eyes, and my face flushed. I didn't understand anything that was happening, but after my experience in the chapel, the injustice of that last statement stung. I pointed at the child. "Why don't you ask him why he wanted to frighten me?"

"I can ask as many times as you want, you little idiot, but it won't do any good. The boy is a mute!"

My gaze went again to Davy. Other than the gasping breath, his crying was noiseless. "But if . . . he didn't . . ."

In my mind, I heard the soft giggle, creeping to me through the room of stone. I took a step back. "Where is my uncle?" I demanded.

"It's play —" began Mrs. Jefferies.

"Mr. Tully's in his workshop," Lane said, "on the other side of the estate."

"He's not . . . here?" I felt a tingling sensation pressing on my neck; it might have been horror, or it might have been my own hand. "Then who else is in the house?"

The faces looked back at me.

"Who else is in this house?"

"No one," said Lane, his arm still around Davy. "There's no staff, just me and Aunt Bit, and the workmen don't come near, not if they can help it."

I stepped back again. There was something not right here, like that laughter, and those silent tears. "Take me to Milton," I whispered. "I can pay."

"Can't do that."

I looked wildly about the kitchen. "Then let me ask someone else, I . . ."

"Makes no difference," Lane said. "You can't get back across the moors before dark." His dirty face was brown and smooth, like the stones on the front of the house. "And there's not another man or horse within half a mile."

CHAPTER THREE

The sun was almost down, but in the windowless corridor it might as well have been midnight. There was no gaslight here. Lane's back rose tall before me, only half lit by my guttering candle as he pulled the trunk along on some sort of flat wooden cart. He'd hoisted both trunk and cart up two flights of stairs without effort or speech, and he was silent still, our footfalls muffled by the roses woven into the carpet. He stopped abruptly, and I bumped into the trunk.

"Take your pick," he said.

I examined my surroundings. The corridor was relatively short, and I thought I could see six closed doors in the darkness, all on the left. On the right, there were only portraits, one for each door. *Like sentinels*, I thought. Lane stood with his arms crossed, offering neither help nor hindrance. I had no idea where I was, or how to get back to the kitchen. I opened the nearest door.

The windows were full west, catching the very last of the sun before the moor hills shadowed it. Squinting, I could just make out shelves with books, a large desk, and some very dusty lounges. Two more doors, one on each end, connected the room with its neighbors. Not a bedroom, then, but a library or a study. I shut the door, noting the portrait of a bewhiskered gentleman in a ruff that watched me do it, and went quickly to the far end of the corridor. I had not liked the thought of those inner doors. A corner room should have only one interior door, rather than two. I put my hand on the last knob in the hallway.

"It leaks," Lane said, startling the silence. "And that one, too." I had taken a step toward the next door. My skirt swished as I made my way to the opposite end of the corridor, to the other corner room. I put out my hand.

"Mice," he said.

I raised a brow, and grasped the knob anyway.

"In the bed," he added.

I dropped my hand and looked again at the corridor, this time not at the doors, but at the portraits. One door down from the library, the picture was of an old woman. I held up the candle to look at her. She was gray-headed, simply but elegantly attired in a lace cap, face as expressionless as the others, and yet . . . most women would not have had their wrinkles painted, at least not so realistically. I opened her door.

A massive mahogany bed stood not against a wall but in the very center of the room, hung with pale pink curtains of satin and velvet that fell perhaps eight feet from the canopy to the floor. Matching material cascaded from four tall windows, the last of the sunlight illuminating a thick rope of cobweb that linked two upholstered chairs with the wood-paneled ceiling. There was a connecting door on the left-hand wall, but on the right was only a wardrobe, heavily carved with faces and foliage, covering the wall from the corner to the marble hearth. No door.

"This one," I said, and I heard the wheels of the cart squeak as they entered the room. I set the candle on a painted dressing table and pulled aside one of the heavy drapes. Musty damp tickled my nose as I looked out on undulating hills, swaying grass, one or two trees, and a red-gold sky. No dwellings, not even a telltale pillar of smoke. I reached out a finger and touched the dust that lay soft and thick on the windowpane. I wondered if there was any regularity to dust, that if one could measure its depth, it would be possible to figure precisely how long it had taken to accumulate.

I dropped the drape and turned back to the room. The trunk was in the middle of the floor, the valise and my bonnet on its top. I ran to the door and looked up and down the hallway. I was alone.

I shut the door and leaned on it for a moment, then hurried to one of the heavy upholstered chairs and tugged, dragging it backward, making bumps and wrinkles in the filthy carpet. I pushed the chair up hard against the connecting door, gritted my teeth, and did the same with the other chair, wedging it tight against the door to the corridor. Recovering my breath and feeling somewhat better, I considered my stub of a candle. I ransacked each of the seven drawers in the dressing table, doing the same to a side table and an old trunk. I fingered the junked contents of many years before I found the polished box on the chimneypiece full of slender, white tapers, and in a ceramic jar next to that, a ring of keys. I had candles lit and the doors locked before the last of the sun plunged behind the hills.

The furniture was even darker in the flickering light, throwing high, hulking shadows against the walls. I looked at my hands, black with dirt, and then at my dress. "*Gray woolen worsted,*" I could hear Aunt Alice say. "*Nothing is more suitable. It will last forever, and never show dirt. . . .*" What the material never did, in my opinion, was flatter the wearer. But it would have to be decent for the journey back to London, a trip I was determined to begin no later than midday, just as soon as I had seen my uncle and gleaned the information that would ensure Fat Robert's inheritance.

I wiped my hands on the inside of my skirt, where the dirt would not show, then peeled off the skirt along with all three of my petticoats and tossed them over my trunk. I jerked a corset string and let that fall to the dirty floor, swinging my arms wide in the freedom of only a chemise and an underskirt, filling my lungs to capacity for the first time since that morning. I turned my attention to the massive bed.

I pushed on it once, knowing full well there would be no way to shift it, but I dreaded the thought of sleeping with all that open space behind my head. The coverlets seemed relatively dust free, thanks to the hangings, though they felt clammy and damp beneath my hand. Thinking of dry linens, I went to the wardrobe and tugged on a door. Locked. I took the ring of keys and inserted them one by one in the keyhole, the clinking of metal loud in the quiet, and on the sixth key, the lock clicked.

The door swung open, and a scented air, like lilies and cinnamon, wafted over me. I tilted back my head to stare not at linens, but at dresses, stacks upon stacks of them, lying on shelves that stretched from the level of my waist to the top of the wardrobe. Silks of lemon, lavender, and rosebud shone against the dark wood, dotted here and there by a white lawn or a winter-blue wool with sleeve lace the color of cream. There was nothing of yellow fog, sooty bricks, or suitability about them. Nothing of London. They were from another world.

A little ladder folded down and outward from the bottom shelf and, like a child who cannot resist a shiny toy, I pulled it out and climbed two rungs. I reached far above my head for a satin that was neither green nor blue but something in between, a shade I'd only seen once, in a painting of the Caribbean Sea. I pulled the dress free, watching it glimmer as it slithered downward in the candlelight, smooth as water in a stoneless stream.

A moan sliced through the air, so close to my head that I nearly fell from the ladder. But it was only the wind in the chimney, a noise I'd heard a hundred times. A breeze must be picking up outside. I stepped down, mesmerized by the shining dress. I knew I should go to bed. The next day would likely require all my wits, and sleep in this room could be long in coming. I knew all this, but I slipped the dress over my head anyway, tugging it quickly into place. I tied the ribbon sash, then snatched up the edge of the velvet drape and wiped at the grime on the dressing-table mirror, gazing at the blurry image.

The dress fit, not just marginally, but as if I had been measured for it by a seamstress. The waist was high, in the style of decades ago, edged with ribbon that ran up and around my neck. The skirt flowed in long gathers, needing no other decoration than the fabric, touching just at the toes of my boots. The boots looked shabby next to all that color, but I did not. I touched my skin, no longer drab as when next to the worsted, but ivory and peach. I yanked out my hairpins, setting the curls free, and saw glints of auburn come alive in the brown. I had never been beautiful, and I still was not beautiful, but this was . . . striking.

I hurried back to the wardrobe, folded up the ladder, and found a key that would fit the first drawer below the shelves. The chimney wind groaned again, a low, lonely sound that I almost did not hear in my excitement. The drawer was filled with shoes, delicate slippers of varying shades, and there was a box of long gloves as well, many pairs, ending well above the elbow, a bit yellowed, but sound. I kicked off my boots and wiggled into ivory slippers with blue-and-green flowers stitched on their sides and almost laughed. They fit perfectly. I would pin up my hair next, and leave ringlets that would fall about my face. I twirled once, listening to the swish of the blue dress, and put the key into the bottom drawer of the wardrobe, hoping for bonnets. I pulled open the drawer and thrust in my hand.

Something cold and soft surrounded my fingers, many somethings tickling my skin. And then I saw that it was human hair, dark brown and curling, gathered in silken bunches. The curls twisted, writhing, one upon the other, like dead things thrown into the same coffin. I jerked back my hand. The tresses filled the drawer, bound with ribbon as blue as a tropical sea, and in the flickering light I caught glimpses of color, glints of auburn coming alive amid the brown.

I leapt backward, one hand on my own red-brown curls, slamming the drawer shut with my foot. I backed away, the same suffocating horror creeping up my neck as when I'd watched the child cry silently in the kitchen. The hair in the drawer was mine; somehow it was mine. The moan from the chimney gained in pitch, and a wild wail, a screech like a wounded animal, sounded from just outside the window. I spun about, and another howl, and then another, pierced straight through my head, and with each came a deeper resonance, playing on the edge of my hearing, a noise whose source was nothing living. I threw myself at the bed, clutching my knees, fear pinning my back to the mahogany of the headboard. The lament in the chimney and outside my window fell away only to rise back up again, doubling its intensity. I shut my eyes, and for once let the tears spill.

When the clock pinged its seventh chime the next morning, I was at Mrs. Jefferies's table wearing my gray worsted, not one curl out of place, bonnet, gloves, and valise beside me, buttering my fourth piece of bread. The wardrobe was locked tight, the blue-green dress inside it, the chairs replaced and the coverlet spread neatly over the bed. Other than my trunk and some disarranged dust, the room, I hoped, would soon forget my existence. I wished I could do the same.

The kitchen door opened and Mrs. Jefferies, properly attired in calico and lace cap, entered and stopped short at the sight of me, a basket of newly pulled carrots balanced precariously on one hip. Her mouth fell open, and I held in a sigh. The woman's constant surprise was wearisome.

"You found the kitchen," she stated.

"Of course," I replied. It had, in fact, taken half an hour, but that was beside the point. I laid down the butter knife. The night may not have given me sleep, but it had given me a plan, and there was no time to waste, not if I wanted to spend the night in Milton. "Mrs. Jefferies," I said, "I believe I owe you an apology. My behavior yesterday was not what I could have wished. I was overtired from the journey, I'm afraid, and prone to upset."

She waited for me to continue, wary.

"But I think we can both agree that it would be best if I were to see my uncle at once. I cannot return to London without having done so, not without angering my aunt, and she will only send me again, or come herself. . . ." I was pleased to note Mrs. Jefferies's displeasure at that thought. "And once I have seen my uncle I can be on my way, this very afternoon, if a carriage can be found. This would suit us both, I think."

Mrs. Jefferies looked at me a moment. "There's sense in what you say," she said gruffly, "and Lane thinks the same. No use putting off what . . . can't be helped. He's coming to take you down to Mr. Tully as soon as . . . as soon as can be."

"Take me where, Mrs. Jefferies? Does my uncle not sleep in the house?"

The woman shrugged as she set the basket on the sideboard, running her thick fingers over the dirt that still clung to the carrots. "Most times he sleeps in the workshop. We've a little couch for him there, set up for the purpose. Mr. Tully don't like to be far from his playthings."

"Exactly what sort of 'playing' does Mr. Tulman do in his workshop?"

She shrugged again. "You'll see."

She went on picking through the carrots, making what I recognized to be a heroic effort to ignore my doings at her table. I straightened my back and said, "Do you have wolves here at Stranwyne, Mrs. Jefferies?"

She turned to stare at me, snorting. "Are you daft, Miss? There's no wolves in England."

I lowered my eyes to the buttered bread. She was right, of course. But it was the only explanation I'd been able to conjure for that unearthly wail in the air.

The door opened and then Lane was filling up the square of bright sunshine. He was clean, his skin the color of a heavily creamed tea. He stood silent, waiting for me. I folded my buttered bread in half and wrapped it in a handkerchief, then slipped it into the valise and picked up my gloves.

"You can leave the bag here," he said. "I've found a wagon for you. Your things will be in it when you're ready to go."

"And my trunk?" I inquired.

"That, too."

I stood, steeling myself for the unknown ordeal of meeting my uncle, the ordeal that would allow me to go back to London and pretend that none of this had happened. I turned to Mrs. Jefferies. "Well, good-bye then, Mrs. Jefferies."

The woman stayed hunched over the sideboard, her broad back to me. She did not answer.

It didn't come to me until I was out of the kitchen, feeling morning sun and dew both hot and cool against my skin, that Mrs. Jefferies had not intended to be rude with her silence. Mrs. Jefferies had been crying.

CHAPTER FOUR

Outside the kitchen was a walled garden, surprisingly well tended with neat rows of cabbage, lettuce, and beans, and one section showing freshly disturbed earth, where Mrs. Jefferies must have pulled the carrots. Once again I followed Lane's back. I caught a glimpse of a boy's brown head bolting away from me, into the safety of an iron-and-glass greenhouse, the legs of a hare flopping over his shoulder. I lowered my eyes to the crushed rocks of the path, my conscience pricking, until the path ended and Lane opened a door in the garden wall.

Then the moors were upon us, all tall grass, warm earth, and streaming sun. Wildflowers nodded, brightening the gray green with dots of yellow, and Lane, a red cap now on his head, took long strides down a well-beaten way through the swaying stems. I hurried to catch up with him, my wide petticoats an utter nuisance on the narrow track, setting flight to a family of linnets. Lane climbed a small hill and disappeared on the other side.

I stopped at the crest of the rise, already panting and my face pinked with the exercise. Beyond me a small river cut an arc through the hills, sparkling in the sun, and at maybe a half mile distant I saw a village, stone buildings and rows of cottages clustered together, with little strips of gardens in between. I frowned. Why hadn't anyone told me there was a town? If I could not have gotten to Milton, surely I could have found an inn here? I sectioned off what appeared to be a fourth of the village, counted the thatch peaks, and multiplied by four. Besides the larger buildings that were obviously public, there were roughly seventy-two dwellings before me.

The red cap was already at the bottom of the hill, rounding a bend in the path. I opened my mouth to call, and then closed it. I had no idea what Lane's surname was. "Mr. Jefferies?" I tried, remembering his reference to "Aunt Bit."

The red cap popped back around the bend, and then Lane was up the hill in seconds, springing like a cat. I pointed at the village. "What is the name of that place, Mr. Jefferies? I didn't realize . . ."

"The name is Moreau." My look must have been puzzled because he made a little rumble of impatience. "Not the village. Me. My name is Moreau."

"But Mrs. Jefferies . . ."

"Is my mother's sister. My father's family was French. Moors, probably, sometime before that."

I peered at him from beneath my bonnet brim. *Moors*, I thought. Then perhaps it wasn't just the sun that darkened his skin. I wondered if it was paler in the winter. I shifted my gaze back to the vista. "And what is the name of the village?"

Lane pulled the cap from his head, twisting it in his hands, his face curiously stormy. I waited until the silence grew thick, and at length he said, "It doesn't have a proper name."

I looked to the little town and back. "Why ever not?"

"Because it's not a village, it's . . . part of the estate."

My forehead creased. I was aware of no farm at Stranwyne, and if the little town housed servants, it was an incredible amount for a place so neglected. "And what, exactly, would bring so many people here?"

I watched in fascination as a muscle in his jaw popped in and out, in and out, until he finally forced out the words, "The gasworks."

I cursed my own stupidity. Where had I thought all that light was coming from? "My uncle has built his own gasworks," I stated.

The muscle worked in and out. "Yes."

"And where is it? I don't see the smoke."

"Beyond the rise, by the water. We've a strong wind here."

I nodded, my brain putting the pieces together like sums. "My uncle pays men to run the gasworks, and he built the village to house them. Is that correct?"

Lane crossed his arms. He would not meet my eyes.

"How many men are employed in the gasworks, Mr. Moreau?"

"Four or five, I'd say."

"There are more than seventy cottages down there."

The gray eyes shot to me, the appraising look I'd gotten the day before. "All right," he said, "it could be more like twenty."

"And how many men does my uncle employ altogether?"

He put the cap back on his head and stalked gracefully down the slope, utterly ignoring me.

"How many, Mr. Moreau?"

"Ask him yourself!" came the answer, yelled into a sudden gust of wind that would have taken my hat away completely had it not been tied beneath my chin. I gathered up my skirts and hurried down the path, leaving the bonnet to bounce against my back by its strings.

We walked a long way. Or rather, he walked; I ran. Down the path and through the village, past curious children milling before a schoolhouse and a staring woman milking her cow, past a loading dock at the riverside, and a barge full of coal. Dogs, wagons, donkeys, and men crossed our path, but especially men, talking, shouting, hauling loads, and generally conducting their business in a friendly way until they set eyes on me. My presence, it seemed, bred instantaneous silence.

Lane did not slow until we were well beyond the village and before the finest building I'd yet seen. Three stories of gray stone, slate-roofed, with two enormous brick chimneys spouting white smoke at the sky. Their shadows pointed at me like fingers. Lane turned the corner of the building and stopped at a door painted deep green. He pulled a chain, tinkling a small bell, and for the first time since our conversation on the hill, turned to look at me.

"Are you sick?"

I tried to speak, but found I had no sound. I was not used to running, and it was so unbearably hot beneath my dress; I clutched at the soaked fabric around my neck, panting. The door opened.

"Well, what have you done to her?" It was a cheerful question, from a man who was very proper, and very English, but the words were only an echo, spinning like the spots that swirled before my eyes.

When the spinning stopped, I found myself lying on a low bed in a corner of a dim, pink-plastered room. The curtains were closed but the windows were open, allowing a bit of breeze to pull the heat from my skin, while someone's wetted handkerchief dripped water down my temples. A face appeared over mine.

"Never known the sun to be so savage. Dashed odd. Are you feeling better?"

It was the man I'd heard before. Long blond side whiskers, neatly clipped, a brown coat and trousers of modern cut, with eyes that were blue, round, and peering down at me from a face that seemed younger, somehow, than the voice.

"Yes, I am better, thank you," I said, choosing not to relate the fact that my stomach was churning. I removed the wet cloth, and made to sit up. The young man straightened, watching with a frank, open stare as I tried to smooth my disarranged hair. My bonnet, I saw, was on the floor. "Where is Mr. Moreau?"

"He's just popped in on Mr. Tully. You're in luck, you know, it's nearly playtime. I'm Ben Aldridge, by the way. And of course we all know who you are, Miss Tulman."

I was about to ask why this was so when I heard shouting, indistinct at first, coming from a closed door a short distance behind Ben. I got quickly to my feet, arranging my skirt as the incoherent noise came closer. Aunt Alice had told me all about asylums, about the bulging eyes and drooling mouths, the human horrors that well-bred ladies paid their pennies to see. I straightened my back, heart hammering as the shouting became a bellow; it was just behind the door. I put out a hand for the back of a chair.

The door burst open, striking the wall behind it. I flinched, squeezing the chair back, but the doorway remained empty, nothing to be seen but the glow of a gaslight beyond it. I looked to Ben, questioning, and when I glanced back there was one very bright, very blue eye peering around the doorjamb. A short white beard appeared below the eye, slowly, and then a little man in a black dress coat eased into view, plucking at his jacket. He shuffled forward, as if he were being prodded from behind, his eyes on my feet, stopping not three inches from my person. I stood still, rooted to the floor. "Is it the one, Lane?" he whispered. "Is it her?"

Lane's low voice answered an assent, though I did not know where it came from; I couldn't take my gaze from the little man. The bright eyes dragged themselves up to me, as if in expectation of a demon or a gargoyle, and when they had lingered on my face for a fraction of a second, his hands darted out, snatching up one of mine. I gasped, but he only raised the hand to his lips, kissed it, then dropped the hand quickly, his eyes on the floor again, a sudden smile beaming like sun from an overcast sky. My own face, I am sure, was a study in astonishment.

"Simon's baby," he said, rocking on his heels. "Simon's baby girl. But you are too many, much too many to be Simon's baby girl. How many are you?"

"Seventeen," I whispered. He was still uncomfortably close.

"Lane!" he shouted. I jumped. "Do I have a niece of seventeen?"

"Yes," came Lane's voice from the door.

The old man relaxed. "Then that is as it should be. Lane always knows when things are as they should be. Where is your father, little niece?"

Lane spoke before I could. "Simon is gone away, Mr. Tully."

A cloud passed over my uncle, shadowing his sun. "I am forgetful. Too forgetful." He shook his head. "And you are very silent. I do not like silence. It leaves room for thoughts that are not nice. Tell me, little niece . . ." The bright eyes peeked up at me. ". . . do you like toys?"

Ben Aldridge watched with his hands in his pockets, his expression only curious. I looked to Lane, seeking guidance. "I am a bit old for toys . . ." I began uncertainly.

Lane's dark brows came down.

". . . but I do like them, of course. I'm sure I like them very well, indeed."

My uncle's sunshine burst forth again.

"Remember what I said about the lady not feeling well, Mr. Tully," said Lane. He leaned on the door frame, the gray eyes on me as he spoke. "Another day, perhaps."

I met his gaze, and defied it. "On the contrary, Uncle, I'm feeling quite well. I should like to see your toys very —"

"It is time!" my uncle shouted, again making me jump. He had gone stiff as a ramrod. He grabbed my arm, yanking me hard toward the door Lane blocked with his body.

"May I come, too, Mr. Tully?" This question came from Ben. My uncle stopped in his tracks.

"It isn't Saturday," he said, voice peevish. Then he let go of me and hurtled toward the door, as if Ben might give chase, or make a grab for his coattails. Lane moved aside for my uncle, and Ben gave me a halfhearted smile.

"I always hope he won't know if it's Saturday. Never hurts to try."

I moved to follow my uncle, but Lane shot out an arm, holding me back. He smelled of soap and, oddly, of metal.

"Touch nothing, and do not ask how they work." The warning in his whisper was clear.

"How what works, Mr. —"

"Do not touch, do you understand?"

My uncle's shout ricocheted from the doorway. "Hurry, Lane! It is time! You must make her hurry!"

Lane straightened, slowly removing the barrier of his arm. I walked past him, both irritated and puzzled, and entered a small corridor. My uncle's head popped out from the doorway on the left, blue eyes wide and looking for me. I followed him through it, and stopped.

The room was huge, even by the standards of Stranwyne. The lower walls were plastered, dotted round with bright-glowing gas globes, the upper spaces open brick and crisscrossed by pipes and ladders of iron, crawling upward to a ceiling too far in shadow to see. I became aware of a thrum in the air, a chug and throb I perceived not only with my ears but through the soles of my feet.

I took all this in quickly, the paint-spattered workbenches and the odd piece of metal or wood, two dingy pillows left on the debris-strewn floor. Then my eyes found the other end of the room, where they remained fixed, uncomprehending, as the gas globes lavished light onto a silent crowd. People, animals, and things I could not identify stood singly or in groups, caught in various occupations of sitting, standing, or raising a hand, the gas flame flickering over faces of porcelain and wax, all frozen in an unearthly tableau. I looked for my uncle and found him in an open space of floor, his hands clasped behind him. He was bouncing on his toes.

"Well, little niece, is it not splendid? Is it not right?"

The display was so bizarre it took the sense from my thoughts. I took a few steps forward, my eyes on a peacock, its feathers afire with turquoise, and my uncle came charging toward me.

"I think I shall show you this one!" My sleeve was yanked, and I found myself tripping awkwardly past the peacock, merging with the noiseless throng. I saw faces as I passed, painted smiles that reminded me of the little parson, and then my uncle halted abruptly before a child. She was seated at a pianoforte, eyes closed, life-sized though her instrument was miniature. Her wax hands lay gracefully on the keys, red-brown hair curling and waving from a blue satin bow. I bent down to look at her. She seemed to daydream.

My uncle knelt beside me, reaching his hand up and under the pianoforte. I heard a click, a faint whirr, and then sucked in a breath as the child's eyelids slowly opened. She blinked, the head cocked and turned, her body leaned forward, and the little hands began to play, each finger pushing down its key in perfect time. A minuet tinkled from the pianoforte. I sat down right on the floor, in a billow of worsted, my eyes locked on the little girl as she nodded and swayed, enraptured by the flow of her melody. My uncle sat beside me.

"Is it . . . is she like a clock?" I breathed. Lane made a deep noise from somewhere behind us, a reminder about the restriction on questions, but I could not help it.

"Clock?" my uncle said. "Oh, yes, yes. Like a clock. Clocks are fun, they should always be wound. But toys are much better."

I had heard of figures that moved by clockwork, but I had never imagined that such a thing could be so alive.

My uncle was plucking at his coat. "I'm thinking I shall tell you a secret. Should I? Shall I? I think I shall!" He leaned close to my ear. "Her name," he said loudly, "is Marianna."

My eyes darted back to the curling hair, glints of red beneath a bow that was such an odd color blue . . . a Caribbean blue. Then this child was my uncle's mother, my grandmother, whom I'd never seen. My hand lifted to touch the little girl's hair, to feel that it was real — I knew that it was real, I had seen it in the wardrobe the night before — but a rumble of warning sounded again from behind me. I put my hand in my lap. My uncle chatted on.

"Marianna says when people go away it is right to remember. I am quite forgetful, yes, too forgetful. But Marianna knows what should be, so I have to do just as she says, and so I remember. I made her not too many, so she could play and play and never make her fingers tired. People get tired when they are too many, and Marianna likes that kind of play. I like —"

"Uncle," I interrupted, "did you . . . make this?"

He pulled at fistfuls of his coat, shaking his head. "No. Not this toy. Not all the pieces. I just do the numbers and the pictures. Then Lane takes my pictures and brings back my pieces and I put them together until they are what they should be. But this toy did not come out of my head. No. It came from someone else's head, though they did not tell me how." The little figure of my grandmother paused and began her song again while my uncle's face brightened. "I'm thinking I shall show you what I'm playing with now. It's from my head. Every bit from my head. Lane? Lane! We shall show my little niece!"

I was pulled to my feet and trotted again through the menagerie, dimly wondering how many of the toys we passed were also people that had "gone away." Uncle Tulman chanted to himself while he pulled at my sleeve, a discordant accompaniment to the sweetness of my grandmother's music.

"Little first, big next. Little first, big next, little . . . wait!" I was jerked to a halt. "Lane!"

Lane appeared like an evening shadow.

"Backward, Lane! We shall do it backward! Big first, little next! Big first, little next! Come on, come on!"

I glanced at Lane's silent face, so strained that I wondered if he were in some kind of pain. But he followed my uncle, who bounded to the room's center like a child through the schoolhouse door.

Uncle Tulman stopped beside a large statue, maybe twice and half again my height, lying alone and on its side in a wide, bare swath of the bricked floor. It was a dragon, I saw, coiled like a snake around a thin white tower, the kind one might see in a book of fairy tales. I also saw why it was lying down. The bottom of the tower was narrow like a sharpened stick, coming to a point smaller than the palm of my hand. It could never stand upright on its own. A rubber tube came out of the bottom of the tower, connecting it to a hole in the center of a round, flat pedestal.

My uncle let go of me and ran to a metal wheel that hung on the wall. He spun it, and a hiss like an enormous teakettle came from the dragon. A softer *click, click, click* faded along with the hissing, until nothing could be heard in the room but the minuet, the throb below my feet, and a curious, humming whirr. Lane gave a gentle upward tug to the top of the tower. I thought he meant to lift it, but then the statue lifted itself, slowly and majestically, and without human effort. My head tilted upward inch by inch, watching it rise, until the narrow end had settled perfectly into the hole in the pedestal. Then the tower stood there alone, impossibly, balanced on a pencil point, the red eye of the dragon leering down at me from twelve feet in the air.

My uncle jumped up and down, clapping his hands, as a cloud of steam spewed from the dragon's nostrils, drowning the sound of the pianoforte.

"Is it not fun, little niece? Is it not just as it should be?"

My heartbeat thudded in my ears. I vaguely understood the workings of clockwork, how cogs and wheels could make my little grandmother move in ways that seemed a miracle. But this . . . it could not be real.

"Now the best part! The best part! Watch, Simon's baby!" My uncle made a run at the statue and shoved it, hard. The dragon teetered and I flinched, ready for it to fall, and it did fall, but inexplicably slowly, moving closer and closer to the floor as if lowered by a string. The dragon finally scraped against the floor bricks, scattering a few green scales, and then rose up again of its own accord, defying every law of nature. I stepped back, my hand at my throat.

"It isn't magic," Lane said from just behind me. He was sitting on top of an untidy desk, watching Uncle Tulman. "It's just a machine. I can't explain it, because I don't know myself. But it's just a machine."

"And . . . did you . . . help him make this?"

"I painted it."

I watched my uncle knock the statue down again, trying to regain my composure. "And how many other men does my uncle employ to help him make these . . . things?"

The gray eyes moved back to me and turned to stone. "Time to play something else," Lane said. He slid off the desk and went to my uncle.

I stayed where I was, my uncle talking incessantly of "little things" and "little things that become big things" while the air thrummed and the dragon whirred, all against the sounds of a simple minuet. But my mind was moving. Not only was there a gasworks, I thought, there were steam engines, and a foundry. There must be a foundry, for the metal, and . . .

And then I looked properly at the desk. In the midst of the jumbled papers was a drawing of the peacock, gears and wheels and things I did not understand traced out in a scrawling map of the bird's innards. I picked up the paper, peering at it in the garish light. Numbers mixed with letters moved like hieroglyphs along the page, a mathematical language I did not know. A cog clicked in my head.

"Uncle!" I called. "Uncle Tulman! Do you use numbers to build your machines?"

My question echoed and died against the metal and brick. I looked up. My uncle was staring at the paper in my hand, the blue eyes unblinking, blood burgeoning beneath the wrinkles of his skin. His arm seemed to twitch, and before I could move or even comprehend what was happening, something made of glass had flown from my uncle's hand and exploded, smashing into a thousand shards on the desk beside me. I stood there, dumbfounded, bits of glass sticking to my dress. The minuet played on, oblivious.

"No!" my uncle screamed. He was shaking, his red face something demonic. "No, no, no!"

Lane sprang forward, hands out. "Put it down!" he shouted over his shoulder.

I dropped the peacock drawing as if it burned, still staring, but not before Uncle Tulman had launched himself at me, arms outstretched.

A box of tools went spinning, mixing in a deafening clatter with the broken glass on the floor as Lane caught the old man in his arms and pinned him there.

"Go!" Lane yelled. "For God's sake, get out!"

My uncle flailed at the restraint, spitting words that were senseless, hands convulsing as they reached for me.

I fled.

CHAPTER FIVE

I ran through the green door and slammed it, shutting away the howls of my uncle and the vision of his grasping hands. I leaned against the door and closed my eyes, letting my knees steady and my lungs slow, attempting to bring order to my thoughts. After what I had seen in the workshop, the presence of an entire village was certainly no longer a surprise to me. If there were engines and gasworks and foundries, then there had to be carpenters, masons, and bricklayers to build them, and run them, and men to bring the supplies in, not to mention the vast amounts of pipe that must have been made and then laid. And all so my uncle could play his games. Amazing games, but games nonetheless.

I opened my eyes. Aunt Alice's solicitor had been very clear. Insanity could not only be proven by the testimony of family and the signature of a doctor, but also by gross misadministration of an estate. Considering what these "games" must cost, the only real question at Stranwyne Keep was if Fat Robert had any inheritance left to be squandered. But the solicitor would want to know just how many men my uncle was supporting. I would discover that, and put this place behind me. I reached for my bonnet strings, but they weren't there. No matter. I smoothed my hair instead, straightened my back, and made a beeline for the village.

The first cottage I came to on the main road was small, tidy, and made of whitewashed stone, red and yellow roses twining around the door frame. A girl perhaps two years younger than myself, hair tied gypsy-like in a kerchief, weeded in an herb garden that was wilting in the sun, while well past the back of the cottage an older woman — her mother, I supposed — was taking advantage of the heat by hanging out her laundry. I pushed open the gate, and the kerchiefed head snapped up.

"Excuse me. Could you tell me, please, how many men are currently employed in the —"

"I know who you are," said the girl. "You're that tart come to take away Mr. Tully." She smiled broadly, stretching her freckles. "My mum says you must be a hard-hearted so-and-so, but you ain't looking so very hard-hearted to me, or much like a so-and-so, but then again, you can't always be telling about these things, not straight off. I hear you were giving poor Davy a fright, but he's a strange one and no mistake, and I hear you've been wandering about the big house on your own. . . ." She leaned forward, saucer-eyed. "I think a body might go right off their rocker running about the big house on their own. What do you say? I'd do it in a second, given half a chance. How else would a body know what it's like to go right off their rocker? You could go a lifetime without finding out, that's what I say, so you might as well be taking the chance when it comes along. You ain't off your rocker now, are you?"

I blinked.

"Well, no matter if you are, there's a fair amount of it going around. I hear you've been in Mr. Tully's workshop. I pressed my nose to the window glass once, when I was a wee thing, but it upsets Mr. Tully to see noses squashed on his glass, so mostly we stay away. It's an awful thing to upset Mr. Tully. We —"

Apparently it was swim or drown with this girl. I chose to swim. "Excuse me," I said again, loudly. "What is your name?"

Her eyes grew impossibly larger. "Why, Mary, of course. Mary Brown."

"And you have lived in the village how long, Miss Brown?"

She chuckled. "*Miss* Brown! Listen at you! I've lived here six years, right from when they was putting up the cottage stones, and never been called nothing but Mary during one of them, though that never was so in the workhouse. I got called lots of things in the workhouse. My dad came first, don't you see, and my mum came after that, so my dad, he didn't know —"

I glanced once toward the back of the cottage. The girl was a fount of information, and I feared the matron that was currently pinning up someone's frilly underthings might try to put a stopper in the flow. "Miss Brown," I interrupted, "the day is very hot. Would you like to come and sit with me for a few moments?"

Mary's cheeks rounded. She flounced around the corner of the cottage, where a bench was nestled in the roses by the front door, and dropped herself onto it, smoothing her skirt, leaving smudges of black earth on the cloth. I sat down beside her and smiled. I would start small, in case my well had a mind to run dry.

"You said you've been here since the village was built, is that right, Miss Brown? And that is six years, you said?"

"Oh yes, Miss. Little Tom wasn't born when —"

"And before that, where did your family live?"

"Saint Leonard Workhouse, Miss."

"And how many of you came here from the workhouse?"

Mary's nose wrinkled, the freckles merging into a single mass. "I suppose I don't rightly know, Miss. You see, we —"

If this girl was not even aware of the number of her own family, I was wasting my time. "Perhaps you could guess, Miss Brown. A guess would suffice."

"Does that mean my answer don't have to be just so?"

I nodded, and her thinking continued. "Well, I'm guessing it might've been about three hundred."

I stared. "Three . . . hundred?"

"Oh, yes, Miss. Maybe more. We —"

"Do you mean to say that three hundred people came to the Stranwyne estate from the Saint Leonard Workhouse?"

Mary chuckled heartily. "Oh, no, Miss! Don't be silly. Of course not! We wasn't all from Saint Leonard's! There was lots of different workhouses, mostly London, I'm thinking, though I can't remember that much about it, being a wee thing, though I do remember the stink, and Mr. Babcock, when he banged his silver stick on the table and when he —"

"Who is Mr. Babcock?"

Mary looked surprised. "Why, Mr. Babcock, Miss, the solicitor!"

I tucked the name away for future reference.

"Mr. Babcock's the one to come and get us, of course! I'd gone sneaking into the big room, you see, looking for my mum, as we weren't allowed to see our mums or dads at Saint Leonard's, and my littlest brother, he was that unhappy about it and I wanted to tell my mum so, and Mr. Babcock, he climbed right up on the table where they was dishing the porridge and banged it with his silver stick, saying any able man wanting to earn better bread could come and get in line. And my dad did that, and got his name wrote down in a little book, and he got my mum, and my mum got my brothers and me before they could sell us off and now my dad steers the riverboats."

I looked away while Mary paused for breath, observing the daisies that grew along the cottage path. I had been inside a workhouse once. A sooty pile of ill-laid brick that gathered poverty to itself and imprisoned it there, breeding misery that no bag of Robert's cast-off shirtfronts could have possibly alleviated. I found Mary eyeing me critically.

"I'm surprised you don't know all that, Miss. They teach it in the schoolhouse."

I ignored this slight on my education, and said, "How many would you say live in the village now, Miss Brown?"

"Well, I can't say as I know, having never counted it on my fingers, and having never had that many fingers to do the counting. I've the proper number, as you'll likely have noticed. Having extra fingers is a thing people mostly notice right away. Now for the Upper Village, you'd need fingers and toes to be keeping up with all of them, as the babies have been growing up and having babies themselves, which is the way of the world, as I'm certain you'll have —"

"Wait . . ." I frowned, trying to sift through the nonsense. "You said 'Upper Village,' Miss Brown. Is that where we are now?"

"Lord, Miss! Don't you even know where you're sitting? This is Lower Village, the new one! Upper Village is that way . . ." She pointed toward the river. ". . . downstream near half a mile, I'd say." She shook her head, kerchief ends waggling. "For being Mr. Tully's niece and all, you surely don't know much, though I suppose it ain't your fault if you're not very —"

"And is Upper Village as big as this?"

"Didn't I say the babies have been having babies, Miss? Upper Village has been here a good long time. We're the newcomers in Lower Village, that's what they're calling us, the new —"

"More than three hundred?"

"More like six, I'd reckon. Their babies won't be remembering the workhouse. . . ."

I had heard enough. I stood. "Thank you, Miss Brown. I do appreciate your talking with me. You've been most helpful."

Mary's eyes grew wide, and her mouth opened, but I turned and walked away, past the nodding daisies, through the white gate, and down the road, thoughts traveling in a circle, like a problem of division that has no end. I passed more cottages, many of them, and a small church with a cemetery. I heard the clang of a blacksmith's forge, and a mother calling for her child. I saw sheep dotting the pasture, made my way through a flock of honking geese, smelled someone's baking bread. Nine hundred people. I wondered if my father could have known of all this. Aunt Alice, I was sure, did not. Robert's gravy-spattered shirts might be given to the poor of the workhouse, but his inheritance never would.

My feet found the path snaking over the rise, and the blowing grasses rustled against my skirt. When I explained all that I had seen to the magistrate, Uncle Tulman was going to be put in an asylum. The law protected the inheritors of land. The estate would go to Fat Robert, and until Robert was of age, that would put Aunt Alice at the helm. I stopped walking. And when Aunt Alice was in charge, she was going to turn them out, every man, child, and Mary Brown of them.

The knowledge took firm hold while I stood on the path. They must have all understood what my presence here meant, from my first step over the threshold. Life at Stranwyne hung by a ribbon, a ribbon that was currently tied to my hand. I gathered my skirts and hurried up the slope, knees still weak from the last time I'd run up and down this hill. Lane's reticence and hostility were no longer a mystery to me, or Mrs. Jefferies's tears, or even the insults of Mary's mother. Nine hundred people would go back to the workhouses, or worse. And yet, whatever might be left of Fat Robert's dwindling inheritance could not be frittered away. It must stay intact. If it did not stay intact, then I would be left without the smallest hope of independence. I would die by degrees, smothered in the crimson of Aunt Alice's morning room.

I looked up. I'd missed the turn to the kitchen garden. Stranwyne towered tall and brown on either side of me, throwing heat onto both cheeks while a stiff breeze whipped at my hair from behind. I entered a curving stone passage, house above and on either side, then stepped through an arch. There was the circular drive, the mouth of the tunnel straight ahead in the distance, to my right both land and house falling downward with terraced levels of rose gardens. A wagon was to my left, before the front doors of the house, my trunk corded onto its back and a boy lazing in the seat, waiting to take me away. Back to London, to Aunt Alice, her solicitor, and to the magistrate.

The wind had loosed many of my curls before the boy saw me, standing statue-like before the archway. He jerked upright and doffed his hat, but I did not acknowledge him. I stood, rooted to the ground like the weeds beneath my boots, because the path was no longer clear before my feet. The boy stirred, the reins held loose in his hands. A mighty gust of wind rammed my back, and I strode quickly to the front doors and grasped the latch.

"You may put away the horse," I said over my shoulder, "it will not be needed. Not today."

The latch rust was gritty, but the metal beneath it was shaded and cool, like the chilled stone of the chapel room. The memory of that soft laugh moved through my mind, echoing from nowhere, slithering across its walls, joined by the resonance that had wailed in the dark outside my window. I spun on my heel.

"And when that is done you may go to the Lower Village and bring me Mary Brown."

"Lord," Mary said, eyes sparkling. We had just hauled the trunk up two flights of stairs, into the corridor of the portraits, and opened the door to the bedchamber. "I never saw nothing half so grand, nor half so dirty. I . . ."

She chattered on in a way that rivaled my uncle while I stood in the doorway, a sense of unreality spreading numbness through my veins. Scant hours ago I had left this room thinking never to return, and yet here I was, and now it had a name. It was Marianna's room — the blue of the ribbon and the auburn hair had shown me that — and the room itself no longer frightened me. It was what lay outside of it that made me tremble. I shut the door and turned the key in the lock, gazing at Mary dubiously. I had brought her here out of cowardice, really, to avoid being on my own. Now that I had her, I didn't quite know what to do with her.

"Miss Brown . . ." I began.

Mary turned to me, hands on hips. "You must be calling me Mary. A body who's gone and been pushing a trunk up all them stairs in a haunted house should be calling them that helped with the pushing by their Christian name."

I chose not to puzzle through this logic. But Mary's face was friendly, such an unusual expression when someone had their eyes on me, and she had been such a wealth of information before. "Mary," I said, "I . . . I was wondering. Last night, when I was sleeping in this room, I heard a . . . noise, and . . ."

Mary leapt onto the bed and propped her chin on her hands, rapt.

"Rather like . . ." I bit my lip.

"Chains?"

I shook my head.

"Whispers? Creaks? Footsteps where there weren't none?"

"More like . . . a howl."

Mary's nose wrinkled. "Good Lord, Miss, you don't ever mean a trogwynd?"

I looked back at her blankly, mind full of ogres and evil spirits. Mary's face fell.

"But a trogwynd is just . . . wind, Miss! Coming with a strong breeze north, and we've often got a strong breeze north. Ripping strong. My dad says 'tis an old word, and that the wind must've been making noise through the hills around here for a long, long time, but with Mr. Tully's tunnel, 'tis like God blowing on an empty bottle of ale, that's what my dad says. . . ."

I closed my eyes. Wind. I'd been hugging my knees like a child over wind. Mary began wandering about the room as she talked, peeking behind curtains and opening cabinet doors.

"He says that's where the house was getting its name, too, says it's meaning 'strange winds' or some such nonsense, though that ain't the way a body goes about talking now. You'll have to be hoping for some better luck soon, Miss, or there'll be nothing to be telling your grandchildren, and what a shame that would be, don't you know, to get old without . . . Oh!"

Her squeal brought me running. She had opened the connecting door, the one I had blocked with a chair the night before, and behind it was a room devoted entirely to private functions. The floor and even part of the walls were smooth marble, impervious to water, and an enormous tub, a tub one could almost lie down in, stretched across one end of the room, a faucet hanging over its edge. The faucet was attached to a tall cylinder, pink roses painted on its side, a little door near its base with a cast brass flower for the knob. I tugged on the knob and saw soot inside, and some ashes. Then this was to heat the water. One could have a warm bath, and with no need for a kettle or running back and forth between the bedroom and the kitchen.

Mary, meanwhile, stood enthralled before what my aunt would have termed a "convenience," though it was unlike any I had ever seen. Another water cylinder perched high on the wall, with a chain hanging down from it, a little tasseled pull dangling from its end, tantalizing. Mary's brown eyes met mine, and I shrugged. She took hold of the tassel, grinning hugely, and pulled.

A loud and sudden gurgle made me start, and a rush of orange-brown water poured into the convenience. Mary had leapt all the way to the far wall before she came cautiously forward again.

"Oh, the water's poisoned, Miss! That's a shame, that is."

I stared at the water, regretting the long and uncomfortable trek to find a chamber pot that morning. "Wait a moment. I have an idea." I went to where yet another faucet protruded over a basin and turned the handle. The water ran a deep orange for a few moments, lightened to the color of mud, and then cleared. "See, it's not poisoned, the pipes are just . . ."

But Mary was not listening. She was on her knees, peering upward beneath the basin. "But where does it all go, Miss? Where does the water go?"

I had no answer.

Mary was like a trogwynd herself, I discovered, making noise and pushing those around her at all times. She found a basin and torn rags — from another room's curtains, I suspected — and commenced scrubbing the various tables and shelves, and even the wooden sections of the floors with vigor. I pulled down the filthy bed curtains and dragged them through the bathing room and another small chamber to the library I'd seen the day before. I threw the bedclothes over a piece of old rope Mary had filched from beneath a mice-ridden mattress, then beat the dirt out of them with a tatty umbrella. It felt good to hit something hard. I counted the rhythmic *thwack, thwack, thwacks* against the heavy pink cloth, filling my mind with numbers and dust until there was room for nothing else.

At dusk the windows were open, the curtains hung and the linens turned out, and a fire burned in the hearth, driving away the damp. The temperature had dropped with the sun, so Mary and I sat together before the hearth and candle flicker in the darkened room, faces dirty and hair mussed, finishing the bread, cheese, and tea I had raided from the empty kitchen along with some kindling and a few lumps of coal. I stared into the embers, half-drowsing in exhaustion, lounging in a mental haze that hid away the thoughts of such things as inheritances and workhouses and the porcelain faces of people who had died.

"You ought to go home, Mary. Your mother will be worried," I said, forgetting that the whole reason for summoning Mary in the first place was because I'd not wanted to sleep in Stranwyne alone.

"Don't be silly, Miss," said Mary, her mouth full. "I already told her I wasn't coming back tonight, and I was right to tell her that, don't you see, 'cause if I had been coming home after all, then she'd have naught but a surprise instead of a fright, while if I didn't come home she'd —"

"But why," I interrupted, something I now did more often than not, "did you think you wouldn't go home?"

Mary's voice was pitying. "Now how could I go and be your ladies' maid from my own bedside, Miss?"

"My maid?"

"That's right. They said you'd come all by yourself, and that means you didn't have one, and that means you'll need someone to be doing for you, and I know all about the doing of such things. My mum was laundress in a big house once, and the lady of that house had a maid, and the maid told my mum, and my mum told me all about it, don't you see?"

The candle flames stirred with the air from the window, and my protest flew away like the fleeting idea that had created it.

"Anyhow, 'tis time for your bath. Ladies get bathed regular, my mum says, even once a week, and I couldn't think to shirk my duties, Miss, not for a sixpence. 'Tis a grave thing," Mary sighed, "to be taking care of a lady."

Mary must have already filled the cylinder and shoveled coals from our fire through the little rose-petal door, because in less than two minutes I found my foot sinking deep into a pool of deliciously warm water. I slid into the tub all the way to my chin, experiencing a luxuriance I'd never imagined. The small aches of unaccustomed walking and work were coaxed away, and I allowed myself to be lulled even deeper into lethargy. Dimly I was aware of the creak of boards and the stamp of boots in the hallway of the portraits, just the thickness of a wall away from me, and then a fist banging on the bedchamber door. A deep voice shouted words, two of which I thought might be "Mary Brown."

"You can go your own way, Lane Moreau," Mary piped from the bedchamber. "My lady is having her bath and can't be bothered by the likes of you. She'll be taking visitors in the morning, and if you ain't a visitor she's wanting to see, you can be leaving her your card, if you've a mind to, and . . ."

I sank lower, letting my ears fill with the odd hum and rush of sound that was water, and many minutes later, when I slithered upward again, the commotion was gone. But as the water drained from my ears like consciousness, I was aware that the boards in the hallway were creaking, very quick and very light, as if slippered feet were stealing their way down a dark, rose-covered carpet.

CHAPTER SIX

A sky of watered ink hung above me as I shut the kitchen door and put one foot into the soft earth of the garden, avoiding the noise of the gravel path. I had woken in the predawn well rested, and with a head that was calm, the dim and whirling thoughts that had so troubled me yesterday now ordered and stilled. Whatever Aunt Alice chose to do with any information I gave her was neither my responsibility nor my sin. And she would find out in some fashion, whether from my lips or others. Better for those lips to be mine, especially if I wished to be kept in charge of the books. Being kept in charge of the books was as essential to my own future freedom as finding out just how much of Fat Robert's inheritance might be left. Therefore I had slid my feet from beneath the sleeping Mary, curled protectively across the foot of my bed, and stolen the dress she had left thrown over a chair. I tied her kerchief around my head as I hurried through the dew-dampened garden. At least the width of the worsted would not immediately point me out as a stranger and an enemy.

The Lower Village was sleepy, lanes deserted and dock quiet, the occasional call of a cock or milch cow only adding to the stillness rather than breaking it. I approached the green door of my uncle's workshop and very slowly pushed down on the latch. It did not open.

I stared at the door, surprised at my own surprise. I don't know why I had thought my uncle's workshop would be unlocked, open for just anyone's perusal. I hurried around the corner, seeking another entrance. The building was much larger than it looked from the vantage point of the road. There were no other doors on the workshop end of the building, but on the river side, there were two wide ones for the delivery of coal, I perceived, and another beyond that, all of them locked. I checked the sky, paler and with one bright star shining just above the dawn. I went to the nearest window, and it pushed upward.

I thought for a moment and, after a quick glance at the deserted riverbank, scrambled headfirst onto the window ledge, swung one leg through and then the other, and landed lightly on the other side, brushing bits of dirt and crumbling paint from Mary's skirt. And that, I thought, was one thing I would not be telling Aunt Alice. I looked around.

An enormous engine rose ten feet above my head, quiet now and partially obscured by a brick wall, tubes of polished copper and brass running out of it and along the walls. But I was looking for papers, not pipes. The numbers were so unbelievable, proof of my uncle's expenditures might save me a certain amount of trouble and explanation. I moved across the soot-strewn floor and found a door with a short hallway behind it, two doors to the left, two on the right, and one at the end, which I recognized as leading to the little sitting room with the couch, where I had entered and left the day before. Silently I opened the second door on the right, and slipped inside my uncle's workshop.

I was not alone. On the far end of the room, beyond the rows of Uncle Tulman's toys in the faint glow of the gas lamps, a man had his back to me. He was in his shirtsleeves and waistcoat, leaning over what looked like a trough that ran the length of the wall, something I had not noticed the day before. The man whirled about as if I had shouted, and the expression of dismay on his face softened into a smile of recognition. It was Ben Aldridge. He put one finger to his lips before turning back around, and I came noiselessly through the room to stand by his side. The trough he stood before was full of water.

"What are you doing, Mr. Aldridge?"

"The same thing as you, I expect, Miss Tulman, but I'd be most obliged if you would keep your voice low. Your uncle is asleep in his sitting room, and the walls do echo."

I eyed him speculatively. "Do you often come into my uncle's workshop without permission?"

"Only every blooming chance I can get, Miss Tulman." He grinned, blue eyes twinkling in a sun-reddened face, making him somehow, just as yesterday, seem younger than his voice. "I am a student of science, and there is more knowledge in this workshop than in all the scientific brains at Cambridge."

"Have you attended Cambridge?"

"I am a graduate."

I must have looked surprised, because he said, "How unfortunate it is to never be believed when I say that. I grew the side whiskers, but it doesn't seem to help." I smiled in spite of myself, and he laughed quietly. "I came here three months ago, Miss Tulman, after my graduation, to visit my aging aunt, the last of the old servants other than Mrs. Jefferies. My aunt had already died, I am sorry to say, but I stayed on, hearing at first the rumors of what this room contained, and then finally being admitted to see the marvels for myself. I wish to learn of them. But your uncle, I'm afraid, shares knowledge most reluctantly."

"So you sneak in, in the middle of the night."

"One does what one has to. I go to take up a private teaching position in just a few weeks' time, so my opportunities are not unlimited." He leaned on the trough, his sleeves rolled up and arms dripping wet, like a boy playing boats on a pond. "And what has brought you here so early, Miss Tulman? I heard your visit yesterday ended rather badly."

"Ledger books," I replied, "the estate's accounts."

Ben said nothing, but his smile disappeared. He stared pensively into the water, and after a time said, "Tell me what you think of this."

He plunged his hands beneath the surface, breaking the reflection of the gaslights into rippling sparks, and out came a metal fish, some two and a half feet long, painted a luminous green and blue. "Your uncle calls this object a toy, Miss Tulman. And, indeed, the action of swimming, though clever, is no great mystery. The fins wave, the tail swivels, the casing does not allow the leaking of water. And like a fish, when this toy swims, it does not sink, and nor does it float. That all is simple mechanics. But this fish also holds its course, not just in forward motion, but in depth. What, Miss Tulman, gives this machine the ability to swim parallel to both the surface of the water and the surface of the earth?"

I ran a finger over the slick blue fin. "It looks too heavy to do anything but sit on the bottom."

"Ships much heavier than this sail the oceans every day." It was the challenge of a schoolmaster.

"But they are wood," I protested. "This is different."

"Ah! But at this very moment the emperor of France is building a ship completely encased in iron, Miss Tulman, an iron ship impervious to cannon fire, and he expects it to float very well. But you are right, this is different, because this fish does not float or sink like a ship. It swims its course underwater in a straight line, right, left, up, or down. How I long to know how it would fare against current or in surf! I would take it apart if I did not fear my own inability to put it back together again, and the loss of your uncle's hard-won favor."

I watched him place the fish reverently back in the water.

"We live in a fantastic age, Miss Tulman. At the edge of a time when nothing will be denied us, not the moon or stars or even life itself. Your uncle is a genius. It would be . . . a crime, you know, to lock it away, to let it rot in a lunatic's cell."

"That is not my choice," I said. "I only do what I am . . . compelled to, just as you." Suddenly I felt very tired. "But all knowledge aside, do you not think my uncle is a danger to others or even to himself?"

"No, I can't say I believe that. He is easily upset, and he has his own set of rules that he feels compelled . . ." His gaze slid to me on the word. ". . . to follow. His works are like his own children. He is protective of them, frightened of having someone take them away. He finds it extraordinarily difficult to trust another human being. It has taken me weeks to be allowed in this room on two consecutive Saturdays, and then I still cannot ask questions or even see Mr. Tully's drawings." He turned to look at me again. "He trusted you almost immediately."

I thought of my uncle's face the last time I had seen it. "I doubt that is the case now."

"You should try again, Miss Tulman, indeed you should. As I shall keep trying to understand this fish."

"If you come in here when my uncle is asleep, Mr. Aldridge, why do you not simply find the drawings for this fish?"

"Because they do not exist, or do not exist that I know of. No more than the drawings of that dragon you saw yesterday exist." He smiled again. "Mostly your uncle finds written plans unnecessary. His drawings are for the foundry, and are generally piecemeal or incomplete."

"And what about ledger books, Mr. Aldridge?"

He frowned slightly. "It would surprise me greatly if your uncle has ever kept a ledger book in his life." He wiped his hands on his trousers. "We should be bobbing off, Miss Tulman. Mr. Tully's guard dog will be along soon."

"His guard dog?"

He took my elbow, steering me to the door. "Surely you've noticed your uncle's guard dog? Dark, moody, and prone to an angry expression?"

I smiled at this description of Lane, but removed my arm. "I'll risk a few more minutes, if you don't mind. I haven't done what I came to yet."

Ben's brows lowered for a moment, but then he smiled and inclined his head. "I hope to see you again, Miss Tulman. And . . . do be careful."

I gave him a small curtsy in return, wondering who he was warning me against: Lane, or my uncle.

My perusal of the desk with the jumble of papers proved unrevealing. The peacock drawing — which looked complete to my untrained eye — had been replaced, and the bits of broken glass swept away, but there were no books, no records, nothing to indicate how much of Fat Robert's inheritance was being spent, or how much of it might be left. But someone had to pay the men, order the coal, buy the base metal, and likely a dozen other things that had never occurred to me. And I doubted very much that it was my uncle.

I stepped out of the workshop. There were voices in the engine room, male voices, and I heard the scrape of a shovel on a brick floor. I had dallied too long. I tiptoed down the hallway, pushed soundlessly on the sitting-room door, and peeked inside.

Early shadows had collected like cobwebs in the corners, and on the little couch where I had rested yesterday lay my uncle, a blanket pulled up to his chin, breathing deep and slow in his sleep. Lane was stretched long on a blanket on the floor, his arms behind his head, conveying the readiness to spring even while in the depths of slumber. Beside the couch, on top of a cabinet, sat my bonnet.

My fingertips had just touched the brim when a voice said, "What are you doing, Miss Tulman?"

I started, my hand jerking back of its own accord. Then I snatched up my hat and turned around. Lane was on his bare feet, hair tousled and chin shadowed, his voice rough with sleep. "I am getting my bonnet, Mr. Moreau."

"You didn't come down here for your hat."

The gray eyes bored back into mine, but this time they were not like stone. They were wild, unpredictable, like a storming sea. I opened my mouth to protest, and found I had nothing to say.

"Why didn't you leave?" he demanded.

My gaze darted to my uncle. Lane was not shouting, but he was not whispering either. He crossed his arms.

"He'll not wake," Lane said, "not after he's been upset. Why did you send away the wagon?"

"I'm not obligated to tell you anything of —"

"Yes. You are."

I clutched the hat to my chest. My uncle had moved slightly, a corner of his tucked blanket now hanging loose to the floor. "I have only come for my bonnet," I whispered. I turned away and hurried for the green door.

"It doesn't match your dress!" I heard him call, the latch clicking shut on his words. I stood on the doorstep, blinking in the dawning sun, resentment rising slow and hot into my face. None of this was my doing, the result not my responsibility; I had settled that firmly with myself on Marianna's mattress. Lane Moreau had no right to show me such open contempt; as Mr. Tulman's niece, I was due his courtesy, at the very least. In London such insolence would have had him packing his bags. I lifted my chin, pushed down the latch, and marched back through the door.

Lane wasn't there. The room was silent but for the breathing of my uncle. I crossed the room slowly and looked down on him. He wasn't just beneath the blanket, I saw, but cocooned in it, the tight cloth only just moving against his intake of breath, the dangling corner carefully tucked back in. The white hair was wild, and yet his face was peaceful, trusting, like a swaddled child.

I smelled cooking from the garden, and when I entered the kitchen, Mrs. Jefferies, wearing a starched apron and with her hair combed and pinned, looked up from a sizzling pan. Her brows rose, at Mary Brown's dirty skirt, I supposed, but she kept her remarks to herself. The table was set for four and had a cloth upon it.

"Are you expecting company, Mrs. Jefferies?"

"I thought we'd sit and have a proper breakfast, is all. Unless you'd rather not, of course." Something like hope momentarily crossed her face. "Lane will be along soon."

I remained silent. A meal with the two of them was not likely to be a pleasurable experience, but I had a feeling it was wise to take food at Stranwyne when offered. I eyed the fourth plate. "Will my uncle wake in time for breakfast?"

"Mr. Tully don't come to the house to eat," Mrs. Jefferies snapped, "and when people are going and getting him upset, he's . . ." She stopped the rise of her voice. "I hear he's a bit peaky this morning, that's all. The other plate's for Davy, of course."

I had not noticed until then the brown head and tattered jacket in the corner by the fireplace, Bertram placid at his side. While Mrs. Jefferies busied herself with the pan, I set the bonnet on the table and went to the hearth. I bent down, reaching out one finger to stroke the rabbit, but Davy scooped him up and scooted quickly in the ashes of the hearthstone, putting his back to me. I knelt down.

"Davy," I whispered, hoping the noise of the cooking would be enough to fill the ears of Mrs. Jefferies. "I want to tell you I'm very sorry that I frightened you. I was quite frightened myself at the time, so I rather think I know how it felt."

His back hunched, hovering over the rabbit, but other than that, he did not acknowledge me.

Lane came, dark, silent, and with no mention of our previous conversation, and ten minutes later I was having the oddest breakfast of my life. Mrs. Jefferies served bacon, ham, tea, toast with marmalade, and a kidney pie in a room that tinkled with the clink of cup and plate, while fairly crackling with a strain that was more sensed than heard. I hardly cared; I felt as if I hadn't eaten properly in a fortnight. I polished off a second plate, four pairs of eyes watching every raise and lower of my fork, three of those pairs wishing me rather more ill, I fancied, than not. The rabbit, surely, could have no opinion in the matter. When I finally sighed and set down the utensil, Mrs. Jefferies cleared her throat, and looked hard at Lane. He broke the silence.

"Aunt Bit and I have a right to know what . . ." Lane stopped himself and, like his aunt earlier, adjusted his tone. Politeness, it seemed, was the new policy of the morning. "We would . . . appreciate knowing your plans, Miss Tulman."

"Can you tell us . . . how much time we're likely to have?" Mrs. Jefferies added. Her voice was trembling.

Now I understood the breakfast and even the tablecloth. I made lines in it with my fingernail, counting the stripes. The moment was upon me, and I did not know what to do with it. At length I said, "I cannot tell you my plans, because . . . because I do not know them myself."

Lane leaned forward in his seat. "Then you are undecided."

I made more stripes. There was nothing to be undecided about. My plans were clear, or at least they should be. But there was still so much that I did not understand, even the simple fact of whether Robert would inherit a fortune or a derelict pile of stone that came with nine hundred paupers. And the sight of my uncle's sleeping face, my father's only living brother, my only blood relative besides Fat Robert, had unsettled me.

"Then agree to a bargain," Lane said quickly. "Wait one month. Thirty days until you go to your aunt, and after that, tell her what you will."

"And what will change after one month, Mr. Moreau?" I looked him full in the face. "I could go back to London and tell them that Frederick Tulman is a respectable old gentleman on the verge of a peerage, and my aunt would still find out the truth in time. Nothing will change."

"I know it," he replied. "We've all known it, one way or another. The relatives will come, the law will come, Mr. Tully will die. It cannot last, unless . . ." The gray eyes met mine, his face expressionless. "But you could buy us time. Maybe years, even. You might come to think that worth the lie."

I bit my lip. He could not know the slow suffocation those years would be to me. But then a new thought occurred. What if Fat Robert did have a sizable fortune? Aunt Alice was cunning; she could hide the extent of it from me, if she wished. And now that this idea had presented itself, it seemed quite clear that this would be exactly what she would do. No matter what might happen in the meantime, I would have to go back to London, and doing so armed with that particular piece of knowledge would be greatly to my advantage. Mrs. Jefferies dabbed her eyes while Davy's round hand caressed the rabbit.

"If I were to agree to this plan," I said slowly, "then you would have to tell me everything. Nothing secret and no more hiding, whether it helps your case or it hinders it. I cannot . . . make a decision without the facts. And in return for your candor, I would give you one month. Could we agree upon that?"

Lane leaned back in his chair, dark brows furrowed, arms crossed. He nodded once.

"Then I think I should start by spending the afternoon with my uncle, in his workshop."

"No," he said immediately. "Mr. Tully doesn't mean harm, but he just doesn't . . ." Lane's jaw set. "The workshop is Mr. Tully's, and Mr. Tully sets the rules. He won't allow you back in it."

My own brows came down, and Mrs. Jefferies put a hand on Lane's arm. "Davy says to let her." I looked in surprise at Mrs. Jefferies, and then at Davy, silent as always, his small hand rubbing the long ears of the rabbit, his large eyes on Mrs. Jefferies. "And Mr. Tully, he did take to her. . . ." Mrs. Jefferies shot me a glance, as if there was no accounting for taste. "Maybe it's for the best."

"I won't have him upset," Lane said. He looked at me. "In the workshop, we abide by Mr. Tully's rules. If he won't allow it, then he won't allow it."

"Davy says not to worry," Mrs. Jefferies said. My gaze darted back to Davy, brows raised.

Lane flung his napkin down onto the table. "Fine, then."

"Thank you," I replied. "And sometime before tomorrow, if you please, I will also require the address of a Mr. Babcock."

Mrs. Jefferies's shoulders slumped, and Lane's gray eyes narrowed at me appraisingly. But despite the ferocity of his gaze, I had the feeling that somehow we'd just shaken hands.

CHAPTER SEVEN

I sat on a cushion on the floor of the workshop, watching my uncle, kept silent by both my fascination and fear of offense. I was back in the worsted — after a tirade from Mary that would have impressed my aunt Alice — and Uncle Tulman had not only accepted my presence, he had welcomed it, to everyone's shock, as if previous transgressions had never taken place.

Now Lane stood at a worktable, supposedly painting a small square of wood, but with his stony eyes on me like a mother hen's on a hawk. Spending the afternoon with my uncle would not really further my purpose, I knew that; it might even hinder it were I to trample again on some enigmatic rule. But people, in my experience, could be sorted like numbers: evens, odds, groups that could work together, and others that could not. My uncle was someone I could not sort at all. I did not like that.

Lane's brush tapped against the paint jar, and Uncle Tulman sat cross-legged on the floor, leaning over a wrinkled sheet of paper, making alternating numbers and shapes that captivated and yet meant nothing to me. A gaslight gave a soft pop, just audible over the engine hum. My uncle jotted two sets of three numbers on the paper, one upon the other, drew a line, and wrote four numbers beneath, all in the space of a breath.

"Uncle," I said, "do you multiply in your head?"

Lane shook his head fiercely at me in warning, but Uncle Tulman looked up, as if surprised to find me there. "Simon's baby!" he said. "Why aren't you playing?"

Lane's brows came together, and he looked to his paint, his expression now confused.

"I'm just watching today, Uncle," I replied carefully.

"Simon watched me play," Uncle Tulman said. "We did clocks."

I considered this insight into the father I'd never known, listening to the pen dip and scratch. After a few moments I asked, "What is twenty-five times fifteen, Uncle Tulman?"

"Three hundred seventy-five." The pen blazed across the page, scrawling a depiction of interlocking wheels. It took me several seconds to discover that my uncle was correct. I glanced at Lane. He was still, gazing at his paintbrush.

"Fifty times one hundred twenty-five?"

"Six thousand two hundred and fifty."

"Two hundred fifty times three hundred?"

"Seventy-five thousand."

I had been choosing numbers I thought I could do in my head, but Uncle Tulman was answering before I could begin the first step. "Four hundred eighteen times eight hundred and six?"

"Three hundred thirty-six thousand nine hundred and eight."

"Nine hundred forty-two times seven hundred and three?"

"Six hundred sixty-two thousand two hundred and twenty-six." Uncle Tulman's beard spread wide. Different numbers, letters among them, appeared in rows beneath the drawing. I had the same feeling as when I'd watched the dragon tower rise into the air. What was before me seemed impossible, and yet, there it was.

"Seven hundred seventy-four —" I began, but all at once Uncle Tulman crushed his papers to his chest and leapt to his feet. I flinched.

"Playtime is over!" he yelled, and before the sound of his words had gone there came a knock at the door, three times, very precise. Lane set down his brush and put the lid on his paint. My uncle glanced back and saw me, still sitting on the floor cushion, and began plucking unhappily at his coat. Papers drifted to the floor like slow-falling rain.

Lane spoke up quickly, his voice low and calm. "She can have the green cup, Mr. Tully."

"The green cup! Yes, yes, the green one. I was forgetting!" My uncle's agitation evaporated. "Come in!"

Mrs. Jefferies came through the door, still in her cap, pushing a tea cart that rattled over the floor bricks. I wondered where she had gotten tea things. I hadn't noticed them in my uncle's little sitting room. Lane whispered from behind me.

"Scoot around. That's Mr. Tully's spot. And it would probably be best if you didn't speak."

Not inclined to disobey, I moved hurriedly and my uncle Tulman dropped to the floor where I had been, though I could not see what marked that place from the others. Mrs. Jefferies laid a clean cloth right on the floor bricks, as if we were having a picnic, and proceeded to produce toast — buttered, I noticed — hot tea, and a honey pot from the cart. She poured the tea into white porcelain cups, each with a different color stripe painted near its rim.

"Yellow for Lane, rose for me, and now green for you, little niece! Green is for special," said Uncle Tulman. "That is the way things should be. Do more numbers, Simon's baby."

I saw Mrs. Jefferies's eyes dart quickly to Lane, questioning, but he only lifted a shoulder. I amused my uncle by asking him to multiply or divide whatever random numbers entered my head while Mrs. Jefferies stood against the wall, frowning, watching every sip I took of my tea. I wondered if it bothered her that I was touching these dishes, as it had in the kitchen, but I resisted the temptation to play with the honey spoon. The tea was very good. Orange, maybe. Warmth, strong and sweet, flooded right through my middle, radiating outward to my fingers and toes.

I had finished my second cup and only half my toast when all at once my uncle shouted, "Teatime is over!" Lane set down his cup, his spoon at careful angles, and the sight of the dark brows and tan skin, more suited to Spanish armor and flagons than yellow-striped teacups, made me want to giggle. I put a hand over my mouth, surprised at myself, but then again, I didn't much care. I felt happier than I had in weeks, years even. Uncle Tulman leapt up from the floor, snapped his arms stiff at his sides, and looked me in the face, unblinking.

"Good night!" he shouted. "Good night!" he said to Lane in the same manner, and again to Mrs. Jefferies. Then, as if released from a spring, he ran to the workshop door and slammed it behind him. Mrs. Jefferies put her hands on her hips and turned to look down her nose at me.

"Were you giving that Mary Brown a bedroom?"

"What?" I said, my eyelids heavy.

"Mary Brown. Were you telling her she could sleep in one of the bedrooms? She's been moving furniture and cleaning like the devil up there all day."

I yawned. "I think Mary Brown should have a bedroom wherever she likes." I stretched my limbs and smiled brightly at Lane. He looked startled.

"Well, you just tell her to be staying out of my kitchen," hissed Mrs. Jefferies. She cleared the tea things, muttering, while I got to my feet, brushing off my dress, my fleeting gaze fixing on an iron ladder that ran up the wall, past the gaslights, and up into the dimness of the ceiling. One would be able to see the entire workshop from up there. The benches, the toys, the top of Lane's head, like a bird, hanging from the sky like a bird . . .

I realized my feet were walking, that I was already halfway across the room, my hand reaching for the first rung. I grabbed a handful of my skirt instead, forcing my feet to stop. What was I thinking? Of course I could not climb the ladder. What an absurd thing to consider. Lane was stacking Uncle Tulman's papers and putting away the paint, so I swung my arms while I waited for him to finish, still with a handful of the worsted. *Swish, swish, swish,* went the cloth, like dancing. When Mrs. Jefferies began to push the loaded cart, I flitted through the workshop door, away from the temptation of the ladder, and turned toward my uncle's sitting room and the green-painted door.

"Not that way," Lane said, once again just behind me. "If Mr. Tully says good night after tea, he means it. He'll be sleeping by now."

Mrs. Jefferies came with the rattling cart, and I watched Lane pull down a large lever-shaped switch on the wall. One by one, the gaslights dimmed, popped, and went out, and he turned a key in the lock of the workshop. *Ben Aldridge must have a key, too,* I mused. I rocked back and forth on my heels. "What's in here?" I asked, reaching for the nearest door latch.

"Nothing," Lane snapped, immediately softening his tone. "Nothing. It's just my room, that's all."

"Oh," I said, smiling hugely. "Mustn't touch, then."

Mrs. Jefferies had pushed the cart down the hall to the door on the left and was unloading the tea things into a basket sitting on the floor. Lane opened the door and a black space yawned behind it. "This way," he said. I peeked around his arm. A stone staircase wound down below the floor.

"Take the basket back to the house, love," said Mrs. Jefferies. "I'm off to see to Davy." Lane nodded, and she bent him down to place a loud, smacking kiss on his cheek, throwing me a look of sheer malevolence as she did it. I stifled my giggles. Lane took both the basket and the kiss without comment, and then gestured to me, indicating the staircase. I stepped down into the darkness, clinging blindly to the rail, feeling Mrs. Jefferies's eyes on my back as I descended.

About halfway down, the light grew, the air cooled, and at the bottom of the winding stair I found myself in another tunnel. Sconces of gaslight were set on a twisting, wrought-iron letter S, like in the carriage tunnel, but this time there was no curving brick. The lights were connected by pipes tacked onto huge squares of rough-hewn stone, and the ceiling was much lower, uneven. Water dripped, the burning lamps hissed, and Lane's footsteps came softly down the stones while I twirled my dress, swishing as I looked around. "Is it old?" I asked when he reached the bottom of the stairs.

"Yes. Older than the house, even, except for the chapel. It led to the brew house, once upon a time." He adjusted the basket handles and began walking. I skipped after, hurrying to keep up with his voice. "Mr. Tully uses it to go back and forth, when he goes back and forth at all, but that's only on Thursdays now." He glanced over his shoulder. "You ought to use this way, too. It would be better, I think, if you didn't walk through the village. Not on your own."

I wondered vaguely why this might be as I trailed my fingers along the damp wall, counting the gaslights on each side as we passed. *Twenty-one, twenty-two, twenty-three* . . . The pitch of Lane's voice was so low and resonant in the tunnel. I wanted to hear it again. "Tell me about pink," I said.

After a few moments, he replied, "Aunt Bit says her mother told her that Mr. Tully would cry and cry as a baby, and bang his head against anything hard, so that they had to sew pillows to cover all the cradle wood. The only place he calmed was in his mother's room, and that was . . ."

"Pink!" I guessed.

"That's right. So Miss Marianna had the whole house painted or papered that way, every room. I don't think Mr. Tully's brothers liked that much." Lane paused. "Did your father . . . did he never speak about Mr. Tully, then?"

"I've never talked to my father. He was dead before I could've." I hopped over the puddles, waving my arms for balance. "But you can bet your buttons Aunt Alice doesn't know."

Lane nodded. "Miss Marianna spent her life keeping Mr. Tully hidden."

"Oh, I reckon Uncle George just didn't have the courage to tell her," I said. "I wouldn't have, if Aunt Alice had been my wife. She's a nasty old so-and-so." The flames in the gas globes seemed to jump and twist, like sparks. Two hundred and sixteen dancing sparks. I smiled, and then I realized that Lane had paused and was half turned to me.

"There's not much that any of us wouldn't do for Mr. Tully," he said. "You should remember that." He was another darkness in the tunnel, a lithe shadow amongst the shadows of the gas glow. Then he adjusted the basket and walked on, and I came after him, my dress swishing. *One hundred thirty-three, one hundred thirty-four, one hundred thirty-five . . .*

I realized he was climbing another set of stone steps, ducking through a low door at their top. I did the same, and we were standing on the far end of the chapel room, near the hearth. I looked back and saw a square of wall standing open, the stones a thin ruse mortared onto a heavy, thick-planked door. Lane shut it, and the door disappeared into the wall. "The people who built Stranwyne Keep must have been Catholic, I think," he said. "Rich Catholics, in need of a quick way out."

I stood still, panting a little, breathing in the scent of old stone. The room was much darker than when last I was in it; the sun did not penetrate the windows. The mirror stood a few feet away, to my left, and then I glimpsed the parson, smiling from his little table, his cracked face leering in the dim. I stared, my gaze caught as if in a net. I took a step forward, tripping a little over my skirt.

"Careful," Lane said. Then for the first time, I heard him chuckle, a very throaty sound. "Do you know who that is?"

I shook my head, still moving forward, my breath coming hard. The walk must have been longer than I thought. My head was light, spinning.

"It's Mr. George," said Lane. "He thumps the table and scolds when you turn his key, or he did before he got broken anyway. Mr. Tully dressed him like a parson because he said George was always telling him what to do." Lane laughed again.

I inched forward, staring at Aunt Alice's dead husband, the echo of Lane's laughter moving loud and soft, loud and soft around the walls.

"And all because I found that parson's hat," he said, "blowing across the moors. . . ."

Loud and soft the laughter echoed, and I could not tell whether the sound was inside my head or out. The room swam, and the porcelain sneered. Fear tickled, snaking up my back.

"Then the coal shipment was delayed and we couldn't run the engines and Mr. Tully got upset, and well, it was best to move it out, before anything else got smashed. . . ."

The parson grinned, and I saw the smaller cracks that ran outward from the large one on his cheek, spiderwebs of breakage spreading over the pale face. The creeping fear coiled around my neck, squeezing out my breath.

"Mr. Tully said a chapel was the proper place for a parson. . . ."

Laughter slithered along the walls, but I could not move or look away. I could not feel the floor beneath my feet. The parson's cracked gaze glittered black into mine as I stood there, heart beating in my ears and throat, suffocating from lack of breath, unable to break the spell of my stare. And then, very slowly, the eyelids came down, and the glass eyes blinked.

I ran, pushing past Lane, fleeing headlong through the chapel and into the corridor, away from the broken, blinking eyes, every rational thought sucked away into the void of terror that was now my mind. I stumbled through my turns and up the two sets of stairs, careening down the hall of the portraits until I had twisted the knob to Marianna's chamber. I flung the door shut behind me, panting, my hair unpinned and the rose-spattered walls turning circles around my head. I saw Mary straighten from the fire she'd been building, and then I watched her straighten up again, and again.

"Oh, Lord," her voice said. The words echoed in my ears. "She's gone and gotten tipsy. Tipsy . . ." I heard her repeating. "Mum told me about such things. There now, don't fall, Miss. I'll be taking care of you. . . ."

I let her hands tend me, her prattle fragmenting into meaningless sounds as she put me to bed and pulled the blankets up to my chin. The trogwynd blew that night, howling outside the window. I clung to the coverlets, shaking and sweating, as if they might keep out what haunted me, watching the bed curtains writhe in their own phantom breezes before sleep took the visions away.

CHAPTER EIGHT

I stayed late in bed the next morning, waving Mary away when she tugged at my blankets and brought me tea. My memories were uncharacteristically muddled, vague as if seen through steam, though I was certain I remembered Lane and the tunnel, and something about the chapel, and the parson's eyes.

I turned on my side, letting my head sink into the pillow. I had never believed in the infamous "overwrought nerves" of a female, though I had certainly found it a convenient excuse once or twice. But last night, I conceded, could have been nothing else. The strangeness of my surroundings, the heaviness of the choice I would be forced to make, it all must have overwhelmed me. I knew I could not have seen that broken parson blink, and therefore, logically, I had not seen it. That was very simple and very believable in the normality of the morning sunshine. I threw back the covers, my limbs tired and heavy, and went to sit at the dressing table.

I looked at myself while I worked out the knots in my hair, through glass that was now clean and shining. It was not the reflection, I decided, of someone without a firm grip on their faculties. I ran the brush down the length of my hair, all the way to the ends that touched the cushioned bench, and was pinning it all up again when I noticed a small square of paper lying on the floor. Someone had slid it beneath the door. A large hand had written:

MR. ADOLPHUS BABCOCK, SOLICITOR
WODEHOUSE, BABCOCK, AND KNOTTS
15A NORTH AUDLEY ST., HANOVER SQUARE
LONDON

Lane was keeping his word, then. What he had made of my bizarre exit from the chapel was beyond imagination. And mortifying. I put it from my mind. "Mary!" I called.

The shaking of the floorboards told me Mary was on her way through the connecting rooms before the door to the bathing room burst open. "I'm that glad to see you awake, Miss. Are you —"

"Mary, how do you receive your post, here?"

"Post? Do you mean letters, Miss? 'Cause if you're meaning letters, we get them off the riverboat, Miss, or put them on it, though most of us don't have anybody on the outside to be writing to, if you —"

"When does the boat leave?"

"The letter boat leaves late morning on Thursdays, Miss, like always. What do you —"

"Is today Thursday?"

"Yes, Miss. I —"

"Then fetch some ink, quick as you can, Mary. I need to write a letter, and I don't want it to miss that boat. But bring a cup of hot tea first, if you will. I'm sorry, but the one from earlier has gone cold."

"I'm certain it has, Miss. I'll go double quick. Likely you've got a head fit to bursting, if you don't mind me saying, but I've got some tea put back special in my room, so as not to always be running down to the kitchen. Mrs. Jefferies don't know what's what, she don't, so I'm doubting she'll miss it, and then I'll be finding the ink."

She tore out the door, nearly careening into a chair in her effort to hurry. I went to my trunk to rummage for paper and pen, wondering just why Mary would think I had a headache.

When I stepped down the path to the Lower Village, Mary running fast ahead for the letter boat, the first man I saw spat at me. Or rather, he spat at the ground, but the act had been deliberate, his eyes on my face. I walked on, pretending not to have seen, though we both knew I had. Lane and Ben Aldridge were deep in conversation before the green-painted door, their talk stopping abruptly when I approached.

"Good morning," I said, and pushed past into my uncle's sanctum before either could reply.

My uncle wasn't there, and neither was he in the workshop. The room was empty and dim, with none of the engines running; it was quiet enough to hear the gas hiss. I pulled off my bonnet, wandering past the tools and benches to the far end of the room, to my uncle's menagerie. I touched the head of a monkey, the fur real and coarse, then let my fingertips brush over the woolen jacket of a towheaded boy holding a top. The glass eyes stared back at me, expressionless. And he didn't move. Not one of them moved. Of course they did not, but I was relieved all the same. I wondered if I turned the boy's key if he could spin the wooden top; I wondered if he was my father.

"You shouldn't be in here," the low voice said, echoing against the walls. I had known Lane wouldn't leave me on my own for long, but the tone made me bristle. Or maybe, another part of me warned, it was my own embarrassment for my inexplicable behavior the day before. I ran my hand over the boy's hair. Real, of course.

"Where is my uncle, Mr. Moreau?"

"It's clock-winding morning. He'll come when he's finished. Why did you —"

"And at what time, precisely, will that be?"

He took a moment to answer. "Half past one."

"And since we are both aware that he will not arrive a moment sooner or later than his set time, that gives me nearly three hours, Mr. Moreau, to do as I wish."

"She's right, you know," Ben interrupted, his head poking through the doorway. "There's no point in keeping her out —"

Lane's voice was sharp, cutting Ben's words. "The workshop belongs to Mr. Tully, not her!"

I took my hand from the boy's head and spun around.

"And might I remind you, Mr. Moreau, that neither this workshop, nor anything else at Stranwyne, actually belongs to you. I assume you receive your wages here, just like everyone else?"

A dead silence followed this, and I stood motionless, struck by a lightning bolt of guilt that shocked me from my head to my feet. I had heard Aunt Alice use those very words once, while sifting through a housemaid's personal belongings. Lane's gaze of granite examined me for one more heartbeat, and then he turned, slid past Ben, and after a few moments I heard a slam and a harsh jangle, as if the little bell outside the green-painted door had just been flung to the ground. Ben shook his head.

"You are correct, of course," he said. "But he will not forgive you for that. Not readily."

I turned back to the boy with the top, my eyes stinging. I knew full well that Lane considered himself more family than servant to my uncle, and that my uncle felt the same; the only real question was who considered himself the father and who the child. I pressed a finger against my temple. I might be many things, but never, ever had I thought I could be like Aunt Alice. "Mr. Aldridge, I'm . . ." I steadied my voice. "I am glad to see you this morning. I wonder if you happen to know who is in charge of paying the men? I would like an introduction, if at all convenient."

Ben spoke from the workshop door. "There is a committee in charge of things like that, one for each village, I believe. But feelings being what they are, I . . . I don't know that a meeting with any of them would be pleasant, or indeed even wise, Miss Tulman. Not at the moment, at least."

"I see," I whispered, thinking of the spitting man. I may not have had Mary's headache before, but my head was pounding now. "Then please feel free to look about the workshop, Mr. Aldridge. Take out the fish, if you like. I don't think Mr. Moreau or my uncle will be back for some time."

"Miss Tulman, could I interest you in a walk beside the water?" Ben didn't wait for me to respond, but came across the room. "You seem flushed, and the wind is much cooler on the path. I'm sure it will do you good." He smiled down at me, offering his arm. "Come on, then."

"Thank you, Mr. Aldridge. But . . . would you mind giving me a moment to . . . to put on my bonnet?"

"Of course. I'll wait outside."

As soon as the workshop door closed I took a deep breath, thoughts and feelings churning in random disarray. This would never do. What difference could it possibly make if the servants, or the villages, or every soul on the Stranwyne estate thought badly of me? Hated me, even? It would not change what I had come to do. But it did make a difference. To me. And it would have been so much easier if it didn't.

I stepped out of the workshop, wiping my cheeks, my mind on the way a gaze could change from storm cloud to stone, and paused. The hallway was wrapped in silence, heavy and thick like dust. The door across from me stood slightly ajar. "Mustn't touch," I heard myself say, and saw again Lane's jerk of discomfort at the sight of my hand on the latch. I listened for another moment to the quiet, to the reckless curiosity now buzzing through my head, to the breath of temptation whispering along my neck. I hurried across the hall, and slipped inside the door.

Sunshine flooded through two open windows, muslin curtains swaying in a breeze that was both hot and fresh. The room was simple, with walls of plain gray stone, iron pegs driven in where spare shirts and a jacket hung. A pair of darned socks lay on the floor, boots sat askew by the bed, rumpled linens and a depression in the mattress showing where a body had recently been. I looked quickly away from this, heart thudding, and gave my attention to the other end of the room.

A workbench stood there, but there were no paint spatters, only some small, sharp tools, metal filings, and an amber substance that I discovered, upon touching, to be beeswax. And then I found the shelf. On the wall above the bench stood a row of little figures, miniature and gleaming in silver, the polished surfaces reflecting dully in the light from the window. There were perhaps a dozen of them — horse, stag, hound, and owl — beautifully crafted, and each drew my eye and held it, not just with the intricacy of its design, but with the story it told. The wolf bared its teeth, body tense, hackles rising in threat, and then the owl seemed to catch sight of me, twisting its head. I touched one finger to a falcon, wings out and back in a plummeting dive, feathers ruffling in an imagined wind. The metal seemed alive almost in the same way as one of Uncle Tulman's toys.

My eyes drifted downward, and I saw a square of white plaster on the workbench, the impression of a sleek, winged form in its middle. I picked it up, touching the indentations, running my thumb over the painstaking cuts of each individual feather. Splashes of bright, hardened silver dotted the plaster on one end. My gaze darted back to the falcon. Lane had made these things, carving them from wax to make a plaster mold, and pouring molten silver after that. I pictured the way he must look when alone in this room, the gray gaze neither angry nor cold, only sure and calm, carving delicate wings, telling stories to himself with a single object. It was a vision I could not reconcile with the way he looked at me.

I set down the mold carefully and took a step away from the workbench. Now I knew exactly why Lane had not wanted me in this room. I had seen something that was far more personal than an unmade bed or some discarded clothing. I had glimpsed a private piece of his soul. And it would be for what I'd seen, not for what I'd said, that he would never forgive me. I ran quickly back into the empty hallway and let the door click shut behind me.

I found Ben waiting outside, as promised, and we strolled the path beside the water, beyond Lower Village and the busy docks. He had been correct. A cooler breeze blew here, soothing my head.

"I wonder if you realize, Miss Tulman, what a feat of engineering you are looking at?" I followed Ben's gaze as it swept over what I had been calling the river. "This is a man-made canal, very clever, though it predates the current Mr. Tulman by centuries. There is a water gate at the head, where it branches away from the river . . ." He waved a hand. ". . . maybe a mile or less behind us, so the canal can be drained for repairs and what have you, and look at this. . . ."

He indicated the stretch of water we were approaching. The path we walked was steadily descending, but the canal remained at the same height, rising farther and farther above our heads, held in place by a dike of stone.

"This wall protects the entire lower portion of the estate, and has done so for more than two hundred years." Ben grinned at me apologetically. "You will have to pardon my enthusiasm, Miss Tulman. But I have been fascinated with this canal ever since I was a child."

I tried to put an answering smile on my face, to not seem sullen and out of sorts to the one person who was actually doing me a kindness. I groped for a subject. "I believe you said your aunt was the housekeeper here at one time, Mr. Aldridge?"

"Yes. Old Daniels. My father's spinster sister."

"And did you visit her here?"

Small lines crinkled at the corners of his eyes. "Why, I lived here, Miss Tulman. For two years."

"Really?"

"In the Upper Village. It was very new then, built around the old servant and farm cottages, and the workshop was just being constructed. I never saw Mr. Tulman, of course. Only certain people had run of the big house. Miss Marianna was gone by that time and keeping house servants was rather difficult. But Old Daniels stayed on. And Mrs. Jefferies."

"Then you knew Mr. Moreau?" The idea of Ben and Lane being children together seemed strange to me. But then again, I was learning there was much I didn't know, perhaps about either of them.

"I only knew him a little. He was five years younger, and even then your uncle's keeper. Not that Aunt Daniels would have allowed me his company in any case. I'm sure he . . ."

My obvious surprise made him pause, and his smile broadened.

"Why, I would not have been allowed his company because his father was a French soldier, Miss Tulman. Jean Moreau had fought with Napoléon Bonaparte all the way across Europe, right to the French defeat at Waterloo. Not a few in the village had family blood poured out on those battlefields, so you can imagine the sentiments. It's a wonder Miss Marianna allowed the man here at all, really, but she always was one for doing things her own way, or so my aunt Daniels said."

"But these ill feelings do not seem to be present now, Mr. Aldridge."

Now they are all reserved for me, I thought bitterly.

"Very true. Perhaps as time went on and Jean Moreau was gone they forgave the son the sins of the father. But that change would have been after my time. My own father was at sea with the Royal Navy — protecting the coasts from those 'dirty French frogs,' to quote Aunt Daniels — and it was relative to relative for me, until I was sent away to school. So only a short stay, I'm afraid. Though I never forgot it."

I digested these things as we walked, a small barge moving along the canal above my head. It occurred to me to wonder how a French soldier could have come to live and marry on an English estate. It also occurred to me that if the housekeeper Daniels was the unmarried sister of Ben's father, then Ben did not bear that father's name. But perhaps it was an indelicate matter to mention. Ben pointed ahead.

"And here are the gasworks, Miss Tulman."

I looked up to see a handsome brick building on the canal bank, the coal smoke from its chimneys borne high and aloft in the wind, and then to the storage structure beside it, a familiar sight to one who had spent all her days in London: round, red-bricked, and metal-domed, utterly dwarfing the first building in size. The metal dome ascended slowly within tall wrought-iron supports, rising little by little if one watched carefully, pushed upward by the pressure of the gas vapors inside it. I watched as I walked, realizing that the ground beneath me had also risen. The canal wall was gone, and we were once again on the same level as the water.

"G'day, Ben Aldridge."

I turned to see a wizened old man leading a cow down the path. He was gap-toothed and grinning until he met my gaze. Then his wrinkles turned downward and he looked right through me, as if he had come across cast-off entrails or horse dung, something too vile to be taken notice of. I looked away.

"Good day, Mr. Turner," Ben replied gravely, hands behind his back. I watched the slow-moving water, listening to the cowbell move away down the path. "This circumstance," Ben said, "is not one in which I'd like to find any sister or acquaintance of mine. Are you . . . certain, Miss Tulman, that you wish to do what you've come for?"

I closed my eyes briefly. "I always do what I have to, Mr. Aldridge, no matter how unpleasant." Thirty days I had agreed to; I had twenty-eight of them left. "I think . . . I'll go back to the house now, if you don't mind. The heat, you know."

"Miss Tulman," he continued, as if I had not spoken, "if you find yourself in need of help, or advice, I am always here."

I pressed a bead of sweat from my temple into the sleeve of the worsted, hoping my silence would not be taken for lack of manners. Responding to kindness was something I had no experience with.

When I crested the rise, I saw Mrs. Jefferies at the bottom of the slope, leaving through the door in the garden wall. She had her basket over one arm, and with the other made sure the garden door closed slowly and without noise behind her. Then she glanced left, right, and left again, and hurried straight out into the empty grass of the moors, at a surprising speed for so stout a woman, never once looking to the top of my hill.

I was glad to see her go. I trotted down the slope, through the door, and into her cabbage patch. After much pulling and soiling of my hands, I had managed to twist a new cabbage from its leaf bed. I placed the cabbage on the steps to the greenhouse, where I trusted a boy with a rabbit might easily discover it. If I had to spend twenty-eight more days here, then I would not allow those days to turn me into the likes of Aunt Alice. No matter what I had to do at the end of them.

CHAPTER NINE

The next day I was back in the workshop, the steam engine humming through the floor, Uncle Tulman huddled in his usual position, hunchbacked and cross-legged on a floor cushion, his papers now blackened with jottings of numbers. Lane was at the workbench, painting in silence, the gray eyes never once piercing mine.

"Do you think I might play today, Uncle?"

My uncle looked up, his joy bubbling. "Oh, yes! You must! You must, indeed, little niece!"

That got Lane's attention. The brush stopped moving, paint dribbling down it. "Why, Mr. Tully?" He looked as if he hadn't meant to speak that thought aloud.

"Because she likes it, just as she likes clocks! My little niece is very good at clocks, she knows just the right way to wind them."

I got up from my place on the floor. "Shall I help Mr. Moreau paint, Uncle?"

"Yes, yes! But let him show you how, niece. Show my little niece, Lane, so she can do it the right way. Lane always knows the right way." He went happily back to his scribbling while I approached the bench, trying to seem friendly. The paintbrush was already moving again.

"He let you wind the clocks," Lane said. But I knew it was not really a statement; he was demanding my answer.

I kept my eyes on his paintbrush. I had stood for a long time after leaving that cabbage for Davy, thinking of my twenty-eight days, the garden breezes pushing me this way and that before I picked up my skirts and ran through the house to the clock room. There I'd stood once again, this time just outside the doorway, watching my uncle. He'd been chattering as he wound, happy and lost in his own ticking world until he whipped around, the beard spreading wide, his shout of "Simon's baby!" ringing out over the noise of the clocks. We took turns after that, counting the revolutions of the winding keys, my uncle clapping when I did it right. But it wasn't until I was tiptoe on a stool, stretched full length to wind the birdcage clock, that I saw my uncle was no longer counting. He was waiting, eyes closed. The little bird whistled and the clock beside us boomed, the first chime of the noon hour, one clang in a cacophony of sound that made me drop the key and cover my ears. Uncle Tully jumped to his feet, laughing and waving his arms as if the noise were something he could swim through. "Listen, little niece!" he'd yelled over the din. "They are telling us when! Listen to the clocks tell us when!"

"He let you wind the clocks," Lane's low voice repeated, breaking my reverie. I looked up to see the gray eyes now fully on me, dark brows down, and realized I had been smiling. I settled my expression, lowering my eyes back to the paint.

"Yes, he did. The essential thing was to note how many times the winding key should be turned, and to always be turning clockwise before the reverse. We made short work of it, and . . . I think my uncle enjoyed himself very much."

Lane's paint went up and down on the wooden square, his fingers moving the brush in long, expert strokes. Here was someone else I could not sort. I did not like that. I thought of the silver falcon and the intricate cuts on its ruffling wings, and wondered what other skills Lane chose to hide from the world. The silence stretched long.

"Well, are you going to show me how, then, or shall I just stand here?"

He set down the brush, jaw tight, and handed me a piece of wood identical to his. It was very light. "What is it?" I asked.

"A dragon scale. A few got knocked off during your little demonstration the other day, and need to be fixed." He gave me a brush, and I dipped it into the green paint. "The 'essential thing,' as you say, is to leave no lines in the paint. If there are lines, then Mr. Tully will have to count them."

I nodded. I understood that sort of frustration. I began on the square of wood slowly while Uncle Tully talked to his papers, trying to be careful of my dress, though I didn't really care whether the dress had paint on it or not. I wished I didn't care if Lane were angry with me or not.

"Mr. Moreau, would you be available Monday afternoon to take me to the Upper Village? I have not seen it yet."

Lane painted on without answering.

"I hope you haven't changed your mind about our agreement?" I prodded.

"You're the one who seems changeable. One moment you're having a conversation, the next you're running out the door."

I took a long breath, and soldiered on. "I was thinking perhaps Monday might be convenient, after a morning spent at the waterside. Monday, I believe, is the day my uncle sets aside for trying new things, and I was able to point out to him yesterday that seeing his fish swim in the canal might be interesting and could even inspire further improvements. Mr. Aldridge is eager to observe this, too, I believe. They were both quite . . . excited by the idea."

Lane's voice momentarily lost its slight inflection and became very proper. "Then I'd have Mr. Aldridge take you on a village tour, Miss Tulman. That would be more suitable, I'm sure. And of course, I'm certain you understand that I have my duties to attend to."

It was a not-so-subtle slap. "Of course," I said, eyes on my dragon scale. "That will be most suitable, indeed."

"It is time!" shouted my uncle suddenly. I sighed and set down my brush. There were sixteen lines in my paint.

It was night, the sky was studded with stars, and I stood barefoot on the path beside the canal, the wardrobe of Marianna's bedchamber before me on the bank. The water was bright blue in the starlight, a tropical blue, and though I walked on dirt I could hear the faint groan of floorboards beneath my feet. I approached the massive wardrobe. The carven faces covering its doors and edges were whispering to one another, soft creaks of discussion, and they were discussing me. Then the door on the left swung wide and I saw the black closet-like space behind it, while on the right the wooden eyes of an openmouthed nymph turned toward me. "Misssss," she hissed slowly, and the mahogany face became that of Mary Brown.

"Lord, Miss, wake up!"

I sat bolt upright in Marianna's bed, my nightgown twisted around my legs. The windows were dead dark, the wardrobe door stood a little way open, and Mary Brown's eyes were two pools among freckles in the light of an upheld candle.

"You've a visitor, Miss! And Mrs. Jefferies says . . . oh, you'll never be guessing who it is!" Mary's nightcap shook as she bounced. "Mr. Babcock!"

In fifteen minutes I was dressed and hurrying down a corridor, wide-awake after a short argument with Mary about my boots. They'd been found in the bathtub, caked with drying mud, a circumstance Mary insisted that I had caused by straying off the path at the canal bank, when I knew perfectly well that I had done no such thing and had left them beside the bed in respectable condition. I could not fathom why Mary would not just admit that she had borrowed my shoes. I had, after all, borrowed her dress. But she was still annoyed as she hustled me down a hallway, barefoot, while I limped along, pinched in her too-tight boots. "Where are we going?" I whispered, speaking low only because the corridors were dark.

"Drawing room!" she said, turning confidently to the left to patter down a set of stairs I was unfamiliar with. I wondered just what else Mary had been doing with her days besides cleaning my room.

We entered the drawing room by the stairs at the back of it, the grand stairs in the room I had thought of as an entry hall on my first visit, but it was the only thing about the place I recognized. The dust was gone, and so were the dust sheets. The color of the walls was softened in the dimness, the furniture grouped and arranged comfortably, gleaming and polished in the light of a crackling fire. The other thing this firelight illuminated was the ugliest man I had ever seen.

"Miss Katharine Tulman," the man said, coming forward and extending a hand. He was short and rotund, with a misshapen nose, large jowls, and a head too small for his body. "I have been wishing to meet you these many years, and now, at last, my wish has been granted. I am a lucky man." He kissed the hand I put into his, bowed, and gallantly offered me a seat. I sat on the edge of the chair, trying to contain my astonishment, tucking Mary's unpolished shoes beneath my skirt.

"I am very glad to meet you as well, Mr. Babcock," I said carefully, "though I cannot say the wish has been years in the coming. I have known your name for less than a week."

"Ah," he said, settling his roundness into the depths of the chair opposite. "The Tulman men have a distressing tendency to short life, an affliction that has removed anyone who might have enlightened you to my particular nomenclature, I'm afraid. But I have known your name, my dear, since you were born. I was present, in fact, on that auspicious day, the day you entered this world and your mother left it." He shook his jowls sadly. "Joy and pain blended, Miss Tulman, joy and pain blended."

I thought about this. "I take it, then, that you are the Tulman family solicitor."

"Quite right."

"And yet you are not Mrs. George Tulman's solicitor."

"No." He smiled affably.

"And you represent the interests of Stranwyne Keep, and have done so for many years."

"Yes."

"Then perhaps you can explain to me, Mr. Babcock, how between eight and nine hundred people live and work on this estate, brought largely from the workhouses of London? My uncle, I believe, did not instruct you to do this."

The drawing-room fire settled in a cascade of sparks, and Mr. Babcock laughed suddenly, uproariously, his chins shaking. "Forthright! Down to business with no muss or fuss. I like it, indeed I do!" He chuckled. "Yes, Miss Tulman, we do have a problem, do we not? A pretty little problem, not unanticipated, but tricky all the same. Alice Tulman has undoubtedly gotten wind that her son's inheritance is perhaps not what it was and has sent you to begin the process of putting a stop to it. But those monies are being replaced, Miss Tulman, they are being replaced!"

"I cannot see how that is so, Mr. Babcock."

Mr. Babcock sat back and regarded me, fingers interlaced over his round belly, his rather ridiculous expression hooding eyes that were hard and bright inside the folds of his face. I was glad, suddenly, not to be on the wrong side of this man in a courtroom. He began with, "I'd like for you to consider your grandmother, Miss Tulman. A brilliant woman, peculiarly placed. In charge of the Tulman estate, not in name, perhaps, but in practicality. And she had three sons, the youngest two estranged from her, and the oldest, the heir of Stranwyne, a son who was — who is — special, a son who would never be capable of managing the estate he has inherited. A son who —"

"Mr. Babcock," I interrupted, "you said the money was being replaced."

"Patience, my dear. I do not stray from my point so easily. You are not averse to hearing facts, I assume?"

I shrugged a shoulder, and he continued.

"The problem your grandmother faced was twofold: how to provide for this special son's needs before her death, and how to provide for this son's needs after her death, when her other two children were not . . . understanding, shall we say."

"She was afraid my father or Uncle George or Aunt Alice would have Uncle Tulman put in an asylum."

"Precisely. So Miss Marianna concocted a plan. An original plan from an original mind. She proposed to create an estate that did not depend upon the interest of an enormous sum put back in the customary so-and-so percents, but a working, thriving place that could produce its own yearly income, while at the same time securing that particular environment so important to the well-being of her child. It was an enormously expensive endeavor, but with the goal of eventually bringing the family reserves back to their original level. Sadly, Miss Marianna left this earth before her plan could be fully realized. And as both —"

"Mr. Babcock, how is the money —"

Mr. Babcock held up an authoritative finger. "And as both Simon and George followed their mother to the grave not long after, I, Miss Tulman, have carried on the work in your grandmother's place. However, if Mr. Tully were to be proven unfit, if someone else was to be put in charge of the estate, someone . . . unsympathetic to your grandmother's vision, then the whole plan rather goes out the window, does it not?"

Mr. Babcock leaned back in his chair, and now that I could speak

I chose to be silent, amazed at my grandmother's attention to Uncle Tully, and the utter lack of it for her other two sons or their children. But I was wrong there, I realized. The Stranwyne estate was entailed, and would always pass intact to the next Tulman male. Fat Robert was protected. It was I who had been left with nothing. I returned my gaze to the solicitor.

"Did this plan of my grandmother's include emptying the workhouses, Mr. Babcock?"

Mr. Babcock smiled broadly, tapping his lumpy nose. "All me, I'm afraid. We had a gasworks to build, workshops, kilns, engines, and pipes, too; stone and wells to be dug; then schools to build, churches, and many, many cottages. Men must be hired. Why not hire those most in need of the work? Two birds with one stone, Miss Tulman, two birds with one stone! And a grand thing it is, too. Remarkably successful."

"And how . . . sympathetic, would you say, was my father to this plan?"

Mr. Babcock's smile left him. "My dear, I shall be honest with you. Simon Tulman was undecided on this matter, and the death of his dear wife, and then his mother — with whom he never reconciled — just after, preyed on his mind considerably. It is a serious thing to feel abandoned by a parent, even when that parent intends no such thing. But it is my personal belief that he would have sanctioned my actions in the end. George Tulman, being of a very different temperament, was kept deliberately in the dark."

I imagined my aunt's face when she heard this story. How quickly she would be calling for her maid, handing me the yipping dog, tying on her bonnet, hurrying off through the yellow fog to her own solicitor's office, her thin mouth pressed tight. She would try to have Mr. Babcock sued for this affair, or even arrested, but something told me she could not. Mr. Babcock was clever, a man who knew his business. I lifted my eyes to the solicitor. His fingers drummed comfortably on his round belly.

"Questions, Miss Tulman?"

"How close is the estate to rebuilding its reserves?"

Mr. Babcock lit like a candle. "We are sustaining already! Mostly from the exports of porcelain figures, hand-painted, very desirable, and we are doing well with custom decorative iron, and brass. . . ."

"How close, Mr. Babcock?"

"Five years," he said.

Five years. And I had the distinct feeling this might be erring on the side of optimism. The fire settled again in the gleaming hearth, and I heard the discordant chiming of the clocks come faintly through the walls. Four on a Monday morning. Mr. Babcock had ridden through the night and pulled me from my bed to have this discussion, and for the first time it struck me that he could not be responding to my letter. At best that letter could only now be arriving in London. Someone must have written immediately upon my arrival, and Mr. Babcock had come like the wind. Mrs. Jefferies, perhaps? I wasn't sure, but she had certainly known he was coming; the drawing room had been cleaned. Once again I found the shrewd eyes studying me.

"What do you want from me, Mr. Babcock? You didn't ride through the night to explain my family history."

"No indeed, my dear." He settled back in his chair. "You are quite astute. I hope to engage you in a game of subterfuge. I want you to keep Alice Tulman out of Stranwyne."

"For five years," I stated.

"Until our little plan has come quite to fruition. When Robert is of age he will begin receiving his allowance, as stipulated. This has been planned for and might well keep things quiet for a time, and when all must become known, well . . . in your grandmother's own estimable words, profit speaks louder than a parson. We are only in need of time."

"And how, exactly, would you expect me to keep my aunt away and in ignorance?"

He chuckled. "That question is beneath you, my dear. You would lie, of course. You would tell her that there is not the first crumb of provable evidence that your uncle is not in full control of his faculties."

"And when she wishes to climb into a carriage and see for herself?"

"She will receive a letter that the entire estate is experiencing an unfortunate outbreak of typhus. Or cholera. Very catching. Very nasty."

I raised a brow. "And when your quarantine is over?"

"If the bug to visit Stranwyne persists in biting, Alice Tulman will receive a most flattering invitation to spend a few months elsewhere. There are ladies your aunt would puff like a peacock to be associated with, ladies who live on the other side of England and owe me the odd favor or two. We need time, Miss Tulman."

I bit my lip. He was asking me to spend five years in Aunt Alice's morning room, playing a game of hide-and-seek, a game that could end in no other way than with me being found. And when all was discovered, Aunt Alice would take her revenge, I could depend on that. I would be cut off completely, with no way to support myself.

Mr. Babcock sighed. "I would ask you to think on this, Miss Tulman. I can see from your face you are not favorably disposed. But do consider, my dear, no matter how we all got here, that the villagers of Stranwyne do not deserve to be turned out of their homes. And neither does your uncle belong in a lunatic's cell, merely for the crime of being created differently from his fellows." He rolled his bulk out of the chair. "And now I am off. It has indeed been pleasant to meet you."

I looked up in surprise. "You are leaving at once?"

"Indeed, this very moment. Court is in session tomorrow at midday, and I shall have to change horses several times if I've any hope of being in it. I have spoken to Mrs. Jefferies, and she has informed me of the current arrangement. I will return before your thirty days is up, to understand your intentions. Send word, if you've need."

I stood. "Mr. Babcock, I have one other question for you." He paused, one arm reaching awkwardly behind him in an effort to pull on the jacket. "Do your fees come out of Stranwyne's reserves?"

I had thought he would be offended, but he nodded approvingly as he struggled into his coat, smiling as he did up the straining buttons. "Really, my dear, you are strikingly like your grandmother. I hope, very much, in more ways than one." His face darkened. "But do believe me, Miss Tulman, when I say that choosing allegiance in favor of your aunt would not be . . . advantageous to your person, that such a choice would cause you rather more harm than good. That is sound advice. It should be attended to."

Mr. Babcock bowed, but I did not return the curtsy; I was trying to decide if I had just been threatened. He moved toward the door, but turned back to me before he got there. "And upon my honor, Miss Tulman, I have not taken a fee for my services since the day of your grandmother's death."

And with that he whisked a hat onto his head, and the front door slammed. I sank back down into my chair, surrounded by the emptiness of an enormous room in an enormous house, listening to a carriage rattle fast down the drive.

CHAPTER TEN

I brooded over the dawn from Marianna's window, polishing Mary's shoes, thinking of what the misshapen little lawyer could have meant by doing me "rather more harm than good." He was trying to frighten me, I decided, and all for the sake of my grandmother. Mr. Babcock had said that my grandmother and I were alike, but I could not see how that could be. I had never inspired love or even admiration in another human being, much less unshakable loyalty that endured beyond the grave. What kind of woman must she have been, and why had I been the one chosen to tear down everything she had struggled to build?

I sighed, put away the cleaning cloth, and stretched. Now that Mr. Babcock was gone, I was extraordinarily tired, but there was no point in going back to bed. I tiptoed into the bathing room, setting Mary's boots beside the connecting door. Mary had carved out a place of her own by dragging a small stove and bed into the tiny chamber between the bathing room and what I called the library. I hoped she was asleep in it, and that finding her boots clean would end our little disagreement. Slipping on my own boots, which I'd found polished by the same door, I went into the corridor, past the portrait of my guardian, and down the stairs. It was our morning for trying the fish in the canal, and I stood for a moment at the landing, wavering: left to the kitchen, the gardens, and through the Lower Village; or right to the chapel, the parson, and the tunnel.

Deciding that my grandmother would not have been a coward, I turned right, walking briskly, though I would not run, my back rigid through the silence and chill of the parson's chapel. I measured my steps through the tunnel, climbed the stairs to the workshop, through my uncle's sitting room, and stepped into the sunshine, letting out a breath of relief.

The sky was hazy with a hot sun behind it, water thick in the air as well as between the banks of the canal, where my uncle, Ben, Lane, and Davy waited for me beside the loading dock. Work had been stopped and the area cleared of people, an amount of bother I had not bargained for when I suggested the idea; I had forgotten my uncle's inability to be near a crowd. But Ben was giddy with an excitement that was infectious, and even Lane, sprawled back on his elbows in the grass, seemed unusually relaxed. Davy had one hand on the grazing Bertram, his head on Lane's knee.

"Miss Tulman!" Ben called, beckoning to me from the water's edge. "Come have a look at this!" Uncle Tully stood a little way in the water, soaking his pant cuffs, holding the fish while Ben wound some type of thin rope or string around the tail. Ben was being very careful to tie the knot without touching the toy. "The string will make sure our fish does not go to its final resting place on the bottom of the river," he said as I approached, "and this . . ." He shook a thin wire that now stuck up and out from the fish's back, brightly colored flags tied at every few inches. ". . . this will show us whether our little fish maintains its depth."

I smiled at his sun-pinked face and scraggling whiskers, and turned to my uncle. "And how are you this morning, Uncle?"

Uncle Tully leaned close to my face, keeping a tight grip on the fish. "Splendid!" he yelled, making me jump. I heard Lane's chuckle.

"I am very glad you are so splendid, Uncle," I said, recovering myself. "Everyone should always be so splendid."

I had not meant much by that statement, had hardly even thought of what I was saying, but Uncle Tully's face became quite serious as he looked at me. "You are right, Simon's baby. I think that you are right. People should be splendid, all the time. That is what Marianna said, and you said it, too. That is right. Just so. People should be splendid if we can make them. It is very true, little niece. You said it, and so did Marianna."

I gazed into my uncle's bright blue eyes, thoughtful, as Ben said, "There!" and finished his knot. "Now, Miss Tulman," he continued, "if I could ask you to go stand on the dock? We will set the fish swimming right at you, and when it approaches I will pull on the string to slow it. If you could catch the string and help me remove our fish without dragging it through the mud on the canal bottom, I would be most grateful."

"Of course," I replied, and took my place at the dock. Lane observed, brows down, on the alert as my uncle walked with Ben down the canal, Ben with the length of string, my uncle splashing through the shallow water of the bank.

When they were far down the canal I saw Uncle Tulman wade in up to his waist, his coattails floating. I waved from my designated perch, and Ben held the string from the bank, ready to run along beside the fish's course. Lane moved Davy's head gently from his knee and stood, using the red cap to shade his eyes. Uncle Tully placed the fish in the water, bubbles and foam streaming upward, and I could just hear Ben call, "One, two, THREE . . ."

Uncle Tully released the fish on the count of two, and it took off in a streak, the thin, flagged pole sticking up like a fin from the water, moving so quickly that Ben lost hold of the string almost immediately. The flag came at me in a straight line, running free.

"Catch it!" Ben cried.

I scrambled to my knees on the boards of the dock, arm toward the water, but it was hard to move in the tight sleeves and petticoats. The bubbling streak blew beneath me. I snatched at it, overreached, and would have gone headlong into the canal had hands not grabbed my waist and pulled me upright again. A splash came from the other side of the dock, and I tried to turn my head to see even as Lane was setting me on my feet again. Davy's sodden curls popped up from the water, arms extended upward as he struggled to hold the whirring fish. Ben splashed in, took it from him, and stilled the mechanism.

The hands around my waist were very warm. I felt the heat of them leave me as Lane took two steps across the dock, reached over, and pulled Davy up and out of the water, which I was relieved to see was not deep. "Well done," he said quietly. Davy stood dripping on the wooden platform, his dimple showing.

"Did you see it?" Ben was saying to me, his eyes wandering lovingly over the fish. "Two flags out the entire run. Not a change in the depth! Perhaps a longer string next time, wound around a wooden bar, for grip, and a bit of a head start . . ."

"No, no, no, NO!" Every head turned at the bellow, and I saw my uncle come charging up to the dock, arms out, face red and fingers clutching, drips of water flying out behind him. Lane moved toward my uncle, but I stepped in front of him, hands on hips.

"Stop that," I said sternly. And Uncle Tully did. He froze in his tracks, his face going slack. "Mr. Aldridge didn't want to take your fish away, he just wanted to keep it from being lost." I took the wet fish from Ben and placed it in my uncle's arms. "It makes me quite unhappy to see you act so, Uncle Tully, and it is certainly not splendid."

His forehead creased as he stared at the wet metal in his hands. "It makes you unhappy?"

"Of course it does."

My uncle thought about this for a few moments before he looked up, his eyes very wide. "Then I shan't!" he shouted.

I smiled at him then, and his returning look was so childlike, so utterly trusting of me, that I experienced a twist of pure, hot hatred for my aunt Alice.

Uncle Tully moved off slowly toward the workshop, muttering to himself as he cradled his fish, until about halfway there, seeming to suddenly recall that he was in an area usually crawling with people, he broke into a dead run, careening around the corner toward the green-painted door.

"That was wonderful, Miss Tulman," Ben said, "I can't thank you enough for the opportunity. Just fascinating . . ."

"Yes, well done," the low voice said from behind me, very quiet, and I felt myself flush. I was quite certain he was speaking to something completely different than Ben.

"I'm going to try to follow up on my advantage, I think," Ben said, mostly to himself. "It isn't Saturday, but perhaps Mr. Tully would allow me to come . . . after all . . ." He wandered off after my uncle, still talking, lost in some kind of mechanical dream.

I turned around to find Lane grinning at the dripping boy beside him. "Well, Davy," he said, "you're something of a hero now, aren't you? I think you've earned a reward. How would you like to go rolling?"

The dimple jumped out again.

"Go on and get dry, then, and I'll see you there."

Davy scooped up Bertram and trotted off toward the village. I looked back at Lane, wanting to ask, but found the gray gaze already on me, appraising. He put his hands in his pockets. "You are showing unexpected talents, Miss Tulman. I wonder how far that streak might go."

I lifted a brow. "I'm quite certain I am equal to anything you might have in mind, Mr. Moreau."

He grinned at me then, and I could not decide what that smile meant. It was not approving, or encouraging, or even particularly friendly. I might have called it wicked. "Well, come along, then, Miss Tulman," he said.

I straightened my back and followed, spirits sinking under the sudden apprehension that what I had just agreed to was some sort of revenge.

I stood with Lane in near darkness on the far eastern end of the house, in a wing that followed the terraced gardens and the contour of the land right down a hill. We waited at the bottom of three consecutive stairways, before two massive doors that were closed, the one high window blocked by vegetation and allowing only the barest sliver of daylight. The silence pressed down, warm and uncomfortable.

"Davy'll come soon," Lane said. "Bide your time."

I peered at him through the shadows. I had not complained of the wait.

"You sway back and forth when you're impatient," he explained.

I stilled my rocking feet, a little embarrassed, and looked the other way, wondering what other things about me Lane might have stored up in his head, ready to pull out and use at a moment's notice. I was certain he had brought me here to frighten or humiliate me in some way, but he'd done nothing alarming, or at least not yet. I tried to fill the awkward space. "Were you born in England, Mr. Moreau?" I had been curious on that point ever since the day he mentioned Moors, and my conversation with Ben Aldridge.

"Yes. On the estate. I've never been off it, actually."

"Really?" I glanced at him, surprised.

"I walk out beyond the tunnel sometimes, and a ways down the river. I reckon that's off the estate." He took off the red cap, twisting it in his hands. *And that is what you do,* I thought, *when you are uncomfortable.* "My dad only came to England after France lost the war and Napoléon was exiled. We spoke French at home until he died, but I have never been there. To France, I mean."

I wondered where he could have seen a wolf, to make it so real. "Would you ever want to leave here, to see another place?"

He paused, the red cap going still. "I would like to see the sea. But I'd always want here, I think, to be coming back to."

There was nothing I could say to that. We stood for a minute or two, and when the silence again became too uncomfortable I said, "You don't sound all that French, Mr. Moreau."

He shrugged. "I can sound as French as I need to. My dad insisted on that. Didn't want me going back like an Englishman, I suppose."

"To France, you mean? Why would your father want to send you back to France?"

"Why, to carry on the cause of the Bonapartes, Miss Tulman. What else?"

I could see his sly grin in the dim, waiting for my reaction, but I only said, "Your father remained loyal to Napoléon, then?"

"When the news came that the new president of France was none other than the nephew of Napoléon Bonaparte, my dad stayed up all night shouting *'Vive Napoléon le Grand'* and drank himself to the floor with smuggled French wine. So, yes, Miss Tulman, I would say he did."

I pretended to examine my dress, thinking what it must have been like to grow up the son of a man who fought on the wrong side of Waterloo, but then Davy's head suddenly appeared right in front of me, Bertram with him. I jumped.

"Where did you come from?" I gasped. Lane laughed, and Davy just dimpled.

"Davy knows the house better than I do," Lane said. "It's a country all to itself, isn't it, Davy?" He mussed the boy's damp hair, and went to tug on one of the closed doors. Davy set down the rabbit and pulled on the other, and then both doors slid backward into the wall. A pale bit of light was on the other side, and a set of stairs the full width of the opening, maybe ten feet across, falling down into the gloom. "Wait here," Lane said, and both he and Davy trotted off down the steps, Bertram's ears flopping as he hopped after Davy.

I rocked back and forth until I heard gas ignite, and light blazed up the stairwell.

"All right," Lane's voice echoed. "Come down!"

My feet stepped downward thirty-two times, and when they stood on the polished wood at the bottom of the stairwell, I could only stare at what was about me. I was in the largest room I'd ever seen, larger than the chapel or the workshop. The lower walls were pink, of course, the upper walls all mirrors trimmed with gilded scrollwork. But it was the chandeliers that were the wonder, eight of them marching down the length of the room, each at least the width of my own bedchamber at Aunt Alice's, glowing and glimmering with hundreds upon hundreds of individual gaslights. The giant mirrors doubled and tripled the blaze, throwing sparkles from every wall.

Lane came from the other end of the room, and my breath caught in my throat. He was not walking, but gliding, like a ghost or a spirit. He placed one hand on the banister and slowed to a stop.

"What is it?" I whispered.

"A ballroom. And almost completely underground. See up there?" He pointed to a glass-and-iron cupola that rose upward from the center of the ceiling. "That sticks right up into the gardens. Roses are growing over our heads, or at least they do when anyone tends them, and at night when the lights are lit, the garden glows, too. Mr. Tully thought of it, so we could have a ballroom and a garden, and work for the carpenters and the gas fitters and the foundry. We made the chandeliers ourselves. . . ."

"I mean, what are on your feet?"

The smile from the canal bank returned, and he held out his arm. A pair of metal shoe soles, wheels fastened to them, dangled from his hand. "Skates," he said. "Like for ice, only with wheels instead of blades. We roll in them. Sit on the stairs, and give me your feet."

My eyes widened. "You must be joking."

"Now, wait a moment, what was it she said, Davy?" Davy came whizzing by on the skates, Bertram, like a rag doll of a bunny, flopping unperturbed in his usual position. "Oh, yes, now I remember." Lane raised the timbre of his voice. "'I am equal to anything you might have in mind, Mr. Moreau.'"

I sat down hard on the stairs and stuck out my foot. Lane's grin grew larger as he pulled the leather straps of the skates tight over my boot tops. Then he glided effortlessly away, backward.

"Well, up you go," he said.

I tried to stand, but my feet flew out from under me and I sat down again on the stairs, much harder than I had the first time. Now I understood his bit of revenge, but I did not intend to let him have it. Davy zoomed by, the noise of his rolling loud on the wooden floor of the ballroom. Lane beckoned.

"Use the banister to get upright and find your balance, and when you've got it, give one foot a slide to the side, then do the same with the other. Come on. It's easy."

I struggled upward and stood, teetering. Cautiously I pushed one foot to the side. The skate rolled, and kept rolling. In three seconds I was flat on the ballroom floor, lost in a pile of skirts. I stayed there, and Lane's wheeled feet stopped right in front of my face.

"Do you want to quit?"

"No." Though I'd said it through my teeth.

"Good. Because you haven't really tried yet. Come on." He helped get me to my feet, where I wobbled like a toddling child, clinging to his arms. They were surprisingly warm, as they had been at the dock, the muscles tense beneath my fingers. "Do what I said before, but in short steps, picking up each foot when you're done. Show her, Davy."

Davy wheeled a half circle and changed his direction, slowing his pace so I could see the rhythmic push and glide of each foot. I watched, and when I looked back up again it was to see Lane's mocking grin very close to my face. I clenched my teeth and pushed one foot, and then the other, one and then the other, clutching his arms with a grip of iron. We went a few feet and I stumbled, tripping so quickly I nearly knocked both of us down.

"I don't know what I'm doing wrong," I said. My temper was aflame, though I was trying not to show it.

"Me neither," Lane said. "I can't see your feet under all that. Think about balancing, hovering right over the skates, and the rhythm of the wheels against the floor."

I set my jaw and tried again, pushing one foot and the other, wondering how I'd gotten into this mess, one and the other, pretending I was floating, flying just above the skates, back and forth, side to side. . . .

"Look up," he said.

I raised my gaze from my feet. I was halfway down the ballroom. "Am I doing it?"

"Yes. And a right little fool you look, too."

I was delighted. "Let go. I want to try it by myself!"

He released my arms, turned expertly in mid-stride, and continued his movement frontward as he watched. I pushed with my feet and instantly fell forward, landing on my hands and knees, where I got a close view of the sparkling reflections on the polished floor. I felt the air move as Davy went by. "I caught my skirt in the wheel, that's all," I said, waving away Lane's hand. I got to my feet and held out my arms, fighting for balance, and then I was off. One, two, three, four strides, and my speed picked up. I could actually feel a wind in my face, and the tickling hum of the wheels traveled up my legs as I flew down the ballroom.

"I'm rolling!" I yelled. "Look! I'm rolling!" I craned my neck behind to see if Lane and Davy were watching, but I could not find them. And the next thing I knew, I had slammed into something that was hard and soft at once, smelling faintly of metal and paint, and knocked myself to the floor. I had skated right into Lane, who had put himself there to keep me from crashing headlong into a mirrored wall.

"Ow," he said mildly. Once again he pulled me to my feet, holding my arms until I steadied. "Perhaps a little less speed, Miss, until you've learned to stop?"

"I want to do it again," I said breathlessly, and I looked up into a smile that was only teasing now, not mocking, stretching the tiny stubble of an unshaven chin. But the gray eyes above mine were different than I'd ever seen them: calm, soft, without storm or stone, a glassy sea, just as I'd imagined when I discovered the falcon. And inexplicably, they were looking at me.

Heat spread through my chest, blooming like a hothouse flower, and I pulled away both my gaze and my arms, only just keeping my balance. What was I thinking? Had we been in London, the impropriety of this situation would have taken every shred of my good name with it. But I had not even considered such a thing, not here. Stranwyne was a place unto its own, as Lane had said earlier, with rules that were not the rules of the rest of the world. I felt the blossoming pink reach my cheeks at the thought of what my aunt and Mrs. Hardcastle would have said on the subject. And then I felt a tug on my skirt.

Davy was there, holding out a hairpin. My hand flew to my head. Curls were everywhere, loose and spilling all down my back. I took the pin and hurriedly stuffed it into my hair.

"Don't bother," Lane said. "It will just come back down again." I peeked up to find the inscrutable gaze still there, now resting on my hair. He held out an arm. "Hang on and I'll go beside you this time, and teach you how to stop."

I looked at the extended arm, at the skin like creamed tea below his rolled-up sleeve, thinking of the warmth I had felt before beneath my hand. I let my hair go free and took the arm. Aunt Alice was not here.

We rolled the length of the ballroom again and again, and each time I went faster, my wild hair flying, the sparkling of the gas lamps blurring in the mirrored reflections. And sometimes I closed my eyes, the better to feel the exhilaration of the wind.

CHAPTER ELEVEN

The first time I opened my eyes, I could hear Mary's voice, but the face I saw was Aunt Alice's, her thick fringe of ironed curls stretching and constricting over features that changed their shape like candle flame. I watched her face bubble and melt, spellbound, until she reached out and grabbed my arm. I tried to pull away, but the nails gripped my flesh like claws. She put my hand into another hand, and I looked up to see Mr. Babcock. He wore a judge's white-curled wig and, smiling like a predator, raised my hand to his lips as if he would kiss it. "No," I cried out. "Stop!" But he did not stop. He bit me, slowly, sinking his teeth deep into my hand while Aunt Alice dug in her claws. I shut my eyes against the pain.

The next time I opened them I saw Marianna's bedchamber blazing with light, every candle lit, voices buzzing and humming with words I could not understand. And some extra sense, some feeling only just awakened, was telling me to run, that I must flee, that I had only seconds to do so. But I could not run, I could not even move, my arm was trapped. I screamed and fought, terrified, writhing in panic, and cold hands held me down, pinning me to the floor. I screamed again, and the voices changed their tone.

And then I wandered away, calm and quiet, my fear forgotten. I padded through the dark corridors, the creaks and groans of the floorboards now familiar to me, through the empty kitchen and into the garden. The moon was full, riding high through tearing clouds, and I felt the gravel of the path bore gently into my bare feet. I was wearing Marianna's blue dress, and in that dress I could move, fly, flit like a ghost through the warm grasses, all the way to the Lower Village. The village was quiet in the dark — deathly quiet — and I felt mud between my toes. I went shadowlike to the green door, through the sitting room and to the workshop, and then I knew. The mud was in here, too. I lifted the giant switch, the gaslights hissed, and I beheld a massacre. Dismembered arms of shattered porcelain, broken legs, cracked faces and cogs and wheels, all mixed into a jumbled wash of dirt and silt. They were ruined, all of them gone, never to be wound up again. I sank to my knees in the filthy pile, a mass burial gone awry, and cried as if it was me who was broken, who was lost. My crying echoed through the empty workshop, and I cradled the sodden head of my grandmother in my lap.

When I woke, someone was singing, very soft, humming gently beneath their breath. Late morning sun laid yellow beams on Marianna's carpet, and the coverlets on the bed felt heavy, weighing my body down into the mattress. I sighed, and a woman, a stranger, was suddenly looking down on me.

"Awake, are you?"

I blinked at her slowly. "Am . . . I ill?" I whispered. My voice was hoarse.

"If you call coming off a bad drunk being ill, then maybe so."

I frowned, confused, and then the door to the bathing room opened, and Mary came out with a pitcher of water.

"Oh, Miss! How are you feeling, then?

"I'd say she's got a head fit to split like a ripe melon," said the woman.

"I don't have . . ."

"Mum!" Mary cried. "I've been telling you, just because my lady was tipsy once don't mean she was tipsy twice! She's just been sick, is all, as anyone with eyes can see. Here, Miss, have some water."

I sat up, grateful to take it, steadied the glass with my hand, took two sips, and fell back against the pillow. My hand was bandaged, I saw, slight red stains showing through the layers of cloth. I touched it, remembering the preying smile and sharp teeth. "Mr. Babcock . . . bit me," I whispered.

"Don't be talking rot," said Mary's mother. "You were so daft with drink you bit yourself."

"Mum!" Mary protested. "My lady was sick, I tell you! She never did such a thing last time she was tipsy!"

"Mary," I said shakily, "I haven't been . . . I haven't had spirits since I came to Stranwyne, not even a glass of wine."

Mrs. Brown whished some disbelieving air through her nose while Mary sat down on the edge of my bed, her freckles wrinkling. "Are you certain, Miss? I would have sworn on my own dad's Bible that first time that you . . ."

"Not once, Mary. I swear it." She looked back at me dubiously. "Just tell me what happened. Please."

She sighed. "Well, 'twasn't long before midnight when . . ."

"Wait . . . start before that." I was having trouble recalling last night at all.

"You came in a bit later than your usual time, Miss, remember? Your hair was all down and your cheeks was rosy and you were as chipper as them little larks that dart through the grasses . . ."

My hair was down. Lane's arm and rolling in the ballroom. I remembered that.

". . . and I asked what you'd been doing and you said I wouldn't believe it if you told me . . ."

Another disapproving "whoosh" from the other end of the room.

". . . and I had your bit of supper waiting and you got into your gown and had your tea and a think before bed, just like usual." Mary turned to her mother. "My lady always depends on me to know just what —"

"Mary," I said again, trying to steady my voice. I remembered nothing of this, not even leaving Lane. "What happened after that?"

"Well, I'd gone to my own room, you see, to be sewing on your dress . . ."

Had I asked Mary to sew a dress? I didn't remember.

". . . and I heard talk coming from your room, real loud, someone yelling 'Wheeeee!' as if they were having the jolliest of times, and when I came running the voice was you, Miss, dancing about in your nightgown, and when I asked what my lady was doing, you said, 'I'm a fish, Mary, and I fly!' and then you went quiet, and . . . 'twas like you had a fit, Miss. You stared off into the mirror, and then you lifted up your hand as if you didn't want to, like, and you bit it, good and hard, and yelled something fearful while you did, and I tied you to the bed and ran double quick and got my mum. She knows the curing of many a thing."

Disjointed memories crawled through my mind, incongruent and certainly unreal, only they did not feel unreal. I remembered the smell of rancid mud, felt the grit of shattered porcelain in my hand. I thought of the parson blinking his broken eyes, and for the first time in my life I was truly frightened, not of what might be around me, but of what might lurk inside my own head.

"You tossed your guts at about four in the morning, Miss, and you seemed to quiet a bit after that. . . ."

"Mary," said her mother, "go and fetch me a kettle of hot water, and I'll make the girl some of my special tea. A real lady's maid might've thought of that already."

Mary leapt off the bed and ran from the room.

"A good girl, that," said Mrs. Brown, "though a bit lacking in sense." She came and stood over me, hands on hips. "'Tis just you and me here, Miss Tulman, and I think you'll find that unlike my eldest I can hold my tongue when needed. So, time to confess. Where is it? I've searched the room, and why ladies would go and keep old hair in a drawer is beyond my imagining, but I haven't found it, and I'll admit that you're cleverer than me. But it's best to get rid of it, Miss. I'm guessing you didn't enjoy your little indulgence much, in any case. The screaming terrors don't strike me as being all that pleasant."

"The wardrobe was unlocked?" I said stupidly. I thought I had locked away my grandmother's things, and hidden the key beneath the doily on my bedside table. But then again, I couldn't be sure of anything I had done, or not done, recently. It was an unfamiliar, horrible feeling.

"Come now, Miss. Before Mary gets back. Let's have done with it."

"Mrs. Brown, I swear to you, I have not even seen a bottle of spirits since I came to Stranwyne. I've drunk nothing but water and tea." To my embarrassment, tears formed in my eyes. Mrs. Brown sighed.

"All right, if that's the way you're wanting it. But . . ." She leaned forward over my prostrate form. ". . . let's be laying it all on the table. If you're telling me the truth, young lady, then there's something wrong, something bad wrong, something that's beyond my herb garden and tea brews. I've let Mary stay in this madhouse 'cause she's silly, and 'cause there's no harm in knowing what the enemy is up to, anyhow. Mary couldn't hold her tongue if it begged her. But one way or the other you're poison, young miss, and I won't have my girl a part of it. She's silly, but she's my girl, and I won't have . . ."

Mary came back in then with the tea things, and Mrs. Brown straightened, crossed her arms over her ample bosom, and said no more.

Mrs. Jefferies brought me a tray in the evening. I was dressed, my hair neatly pinned, seated in a chair before the fire, watching the hearth flames. I was thinking of other girls my age, the ones I saw preening in the park, carefree with their parasols and organdy and doting papas. Why had life singled me out for drudgery and isolation, and to be the instrument of others' unhappiness? But my one boon, my saving grace, had always been my own mind, where I was free, where I could do as I would, without interference. And now that was being removed from me as well. I had seen the parson blink. I could admit that now. It wasn't real, but I had seen it just the same, like the phantasms of last night, like the calm expression in a pair of sea-gray eyes. And I had my own teeth marks in the back of my hand. I had looked, unwinding the bandages and comparing the shapes in the mirror. Perhaps Uncle Tully and I were not so different after all.

"Well, buck up, then," said Mrs. Jefferies. She set down the supper tray hard, making the dishes rattle. "I daresay it can't be as bad as all that. You ain't dead."

I almost smiled. For Mrs. Jefferies, the words had been kindness itself. Mrs. Jefferies backed away to stand against the wall, and I realized she was going to watch me eat, to look out for her precious dishes, I supposed. I examined the tray. Bread, tea, and a steaming soup, dark, but smelling of chicken and onions. Then I saw a white square envelope next to the bowl.

"Oh, it's for you all right," Mrs. Jefferies said, following my gaze. "Came on the noon boat."

I knew the handwriting well. Feeling as if I could sink no lower, I took the envelope, and slit it open with the butter knife.

My dearest Katharine,

Your lack of communication in this unfortunate circumstance is both surprising and distressing to me, as you were given explicit instructions on how and when to write. I must assume that your letter has been misdirected, as your disobedience in this matter would be an offense most grievous. Write instantly with the particulars of your uncle, that I may put an end to this sad business as soon as possible. The season is full this year, demanding much of my time, and there are many matters about the house that await your attention.

Fondly,
Mrs. George Tulman

I could hear the querulous voice coming straight at me through the ink. I sat up suddenly in my chair, letter still in hand. Mrs. Jefferies might be a difficult woman who disliked me, but she had spoken truth to me just a few minutes since, a truth I had never seen. I was not dead yet, and at this moment at least, in full control of my mind. And I had more than three weeks until I went back to Aunt Alice's, twenty-two days out of prison. There was no reason on earth to squander that time. I could do anything I wanted here. I saw that Mrs. Jefferies was watching me, her face bewildered. I sat back in my chair, crumpled Aunt Alice's letter, and threw it on the fire.

CHAPTER TWELVE

The next morning I was already in the kitchen, an apron pinned over the worsted, when Mrs. Jefferies brought the early garden breeze in with her through the door. I ignored her gaping and said, "Good morning, Mrs. Jefferies. Did you have a pleasant sleep?"

She closed her mouth and hugged a paper-wrapped parcel — meat, by its stains — to her chest, her eyes narrowing as they watched my hands move about the table.

"I've made a bit of porridge. It's on the back of the stove. Has Davy had his —"

"What do you think you're doing?" she interrupted.

I looked up, feigning bemusement. "I am slicing cucumbers, Mrs. Jefferies."

"And where were you getting them from?"

"The cucumbers? From your garden, of course." I tipped my slices into a waiting bowl. "Do you have any more cream, Mrs. Jefferies? Ah, I see that you do. And what about lemon? I am very partial to dilled cucumbers with lemon." Which is why, I felt sure, Aunt Alice had particularly forbidden them to be served. I dried off my hands, careful to avoid soiling the bandage on my right, and sprinkled salt over the contents of the bowl. I intended to eat cucumbers with dill every day I remained at Stranwyne. "Well, not to worry," I said to the silent Mrs. Jefferies, "I'll send for some lemons with the next boat. Should I get a pound, or perhaps two? Two, I think. They'll go nicely with the tea."

I put a cloth over the bowl, set it in the larder, and allowed Mrs. Jefferies to stare while I wiped down her knife. Then I unpinned the apron, hung it on a peg in the corner, and smoothed my escaping curls. "Well," I said brightly, "don't forget about the porridge then, Mrs. Jefferies. I daresay it's still warm."

I left her standing in the kitchen, in the same position she had assumed when entering it, and went to find Mary. We had plans to discuss.

That afternoon in the workshop I asked, "Do you count your years, Uncle Tully?"

It was playtime, and I was watching my uncle from a billow of worsted and a cushion on the floor. Lane stood at his workbench, a lean shadow in the gas glow, silent as he painted the last of the dragon scales with the cleaning sponge I had brought him. I had felt oddly reticent when handing him that sponge, not daring to look up and see what expression might be in the gray eyes, examining his boot tops instead as I explained my idea for using the sponge to paint without lines. The low voice had only thanked me, very polite, the Lane of the ballroom no more a reality than the ruined workshop I had also seen and touched. I was not surprised.

"Count years, little niece?" my uncle finally replied. He was using a hot iron pen to knit together two bits of brass with molten metal. "Oh, no. No. I do not count years. Seconds are very good to count, but never years. There is too much waiting for the next one."

I smiled at him. "Well, I like to count years, Uncle. When they're my own. Soon I shall have been alive for eighteen of them."

"Two nines and three sixes, or nine twos and six threes," Uncle Tully said.

"That's right. And my birthday is also the eighteenth day of July, in the year 1852. That is three different eighteens, Uncle Tully."

"Three eighteens is fifty-four." The iron hissed, and wisps of lead smoke trailed into the air as he set the iron back in the little coal brazier that kept it hot. For the first time that day the gray eyes shot me an inquiring glance, a glance that moved from my face to the bandage on my hand. I slid the hand inside the folds of my dress.

"And that's why I am having a party, Uncle Tully. For eighteen. Would you like to come to a party?"

His white eyebrows drew together and his mouth puckered, as I'd thought they might. I said my speech quickly, before he could decide to become upset.

"Let me tell you all about it. Mr. Moreau shall be there . . ." I looked to him hopefully, but the dark brows were together, eyes down. ". . . and Mrs. Jefferies, and Mr. Aldridge, and Davy, Mary Brown, and myself. We shall have a splendid time. . . ."

The brass Uncle Tully had been working with clattered to the floor. "Mary Brown?" he said. "I don't know Mary Brown. I don't know. . . ." I bit my lip. I had completely forgotten that my uncle would not know Mary. Uncle Tully's head shook back and forth, and oddly enough, Lane's was doing much the same, indicating that I should stop. But I did not stop.

"I am so sorry, Uncle. I was forgetting. Mary Brown cannot come. Mary will go somewhere else. So that means Mr. Moreau, Mr. Aldridge, Davy, Mrs. Jefferies, and me. And I thought we'd have our little party in Miss Marianna's rooms."

I watched the agitation on my uncle's face fade to indecision. He picked up his little brass assembly.

"You like it there, don't you, Uncle? And you could play if you wanted, and we'd all be happy."

His gaze jumped up to me, suddenly alert. "Would you be happy, little niece?"

"Of course."

The bright eyes went wide as they searched my face, looking, I supposed, for my happiness. "Then we shall do it," he pronounced, a little too loud, "for eighteen!"

I looked back into my uncle's smile, something inexpressibly sweet in my chest. I had thought it would take long to convince him to step away from his routine, from the things that made him safe like one of Lane's cocooning blankets. I had been ready to coax, cajole, wheedle, and even bribe him. Never once had I considered that he would do it just for me. "Look, Uncle," I said impulsively, "you have made me happy already." And I leaned over quickly and kissed him once on the forehead. Uncle Tully stiffened, the wheeled toy clattering back to the floor.

"Playtime is over!" Uncle Tully shouted. He sprang to his feet and ran from the room, slamming the workshop door.

"You really do have a way with him," Lane said in the resulting silence. His tone had been amused, but his face was still brooding as he looked down at the green paint staining his hands.

"Is playtime over?" someone whispered. I turned from my place on the floor to see Ben Aldridge. He slid through the workshop door like a sneak thief. "I thought I heard the sitting-room door shut."

"Mr. Tully was frightened away by a surprise bit of affection," Lane said, going back to his paint.

"Really?" Ben's gaze moved to me with interest. "Would you enjoy a walk to the Upper Village, Miss Tulman? I believe you haven't been there yet, and I am well acquainted with the general sights." He smiled.

"Oh," I said, flustered. I was not used to having my company sought. "That is very kind of you, Mr. Aldridge, but I think perhaps it would not be . . . wise." Public opinion being what it was, such a visit was likely to be unpleasant rather than not.

"Tosh," Ben said lightly. "Do come, Miss Tulman. You can observe the happy scenes of my childhood."

"Well . . ."

Lane said, "I'd have thought you'd want to be in the workshop, Ben, while you had the chance." He held up the last dragon scale to the light, examining its flawless finish of paint.

"One can't be working all the time, can one?" Ben turned back to me. "Do you need your bonnet, Miss Tulman?"

"I'll be locking up when I leave," said Lane.

"You do that, then." Ben's face was cheerful.

I looked from one young man to the other, one a thundercloud, the other sunlight. There was something in the air, a strain that made me uncomfortable. I gathered my skirts and scrambled to my feet. "I'll just wait in the hall, shall I, Mr. Aldridge?" I slipped out the workshop door before either one of them could answer, and quietly closed it behind me.

Lane's voice drifted through the door, low and angry, though I could not fathom why, and Ben's retorting words were sharp. And then a soft creak across the hall caught my attention. Lane's door was opening, very slowly, and I saw a frizzing gray bun and an expanse of calico through the ever-widening crack. Mrs. Jefferies was tiptoeing from Lane's room, backside first. She held down the latch until the door was fully shut, releasing it slowly to avoid the click, then turned and started violently at the sight of me.

We stared, both of us waiting for the other to speak, and I watched her broad face redden as something clutched in her hand went deep into an apron pocket. She straightened her dress.

"Is playtime over?" she said finally, her small eyes looking everywhere but at me.

"My uncle has gone to his sitting room," I said. Lane's voice rose, the words muffled through the walls of the workshop, and Mrs. Jefferies's head darted up at the sound of it. My gaze strayed pointedly to the door behind her.

"Socks," she said suddenly. "For the mending." And with that she barreled off down the hallway, wisps of hair trailing, and shut the door to the tunnel stairs behind her.

I stood for a long time in the hall as the argument in the workshop dissipated, listening to the chug and thrum of the steam engines through the floor. I wondered what Lane and Ben had disagreed about. I wondered if Lane trusted his aunt. I knew I did not.

Ben came out of the workshop, his cheerfulness unchanged, and took me down the hall and into the engine room. A blast of heat hit my face as soon as the door was opened, and the noise of the huge machine was not just a pulse in the air, but a racket that excluded all other sound. Five men stoked the two great ovens of the furnace, shoveling coal and arranging it in the red-hot glow. Bare backs bent and straightened with their work, and they were without faces, nothing but masks of burlap sacking where their heads should have been.

Ben took my arm and marched me awkwardly forward and, as before, work stopped instantly at the sight of me. Soot-ringed eyes, only just visible through slits in the sacking, matched my stare. The lack of facial features made them seem grotesque, and somehow inhuman, like men before a hanging. One man doffed a very dirty cap as I passed, masked face expressionless, sweat running freely through the grime on his chest, and then a whistle shrieked and a thick vapor of white steam appeared from the valves overhead. The men jumped to their work as Ben hurried me through the cloud and the double doors, and then I was in the open air, the canal flowing placidly back to the river.

"My apologies for taking you through there, Miss Tulman. But it's the closest route to the canal path, and it doesn't do to disturb your uncle when he has gone to his sitting room."

"Of course," I murmured. I could hear excited talk and the scrape of shovels against the floor from the doors behind me.

"It's the heat, you know."

I looked up at him, head cocked.

"The masks. That heat would melt the whiskers right off your face. Or my face, I suppose I should say."

I smiled vaguely at his joke. Those faceless men still had my mind on some half-forgotten nightmare. Ben offered his arm, and we started down the canal path. There was a slightly odd smell about him, acrid. "How far is it to the Upper Village, Mr. Aldridge?"

"Perhaps half a mile, or a bit more." He looked at me in sudden concern. "Are you up to the walk, Miss Tulman? I could find someone willing to lend us a cart."

I smiled in earnest at that. "I think you would find that no one here would be willing to lend me anything, Mr. Aldridge."

"And you might find that you are wrong, Miss Tulman. Word of your agreement to thirty days is now common knowledge in the villages. And as you have not yet left the estate, and have sent no letters to a woman named Alice Tulman . . ." His eyes crinkled at me. "Don't look so surprised. This really is a small place, you know, and any movement of yours is of the utmost interest. But sugar, Miss Tulman, as opposed to vinegar, is now considered the optimal method of influencing your decision. If you should still wish a meeting with the committees . . ."

I shook my head. The details of the business didn't matter so much anymore. I was certain that if I insisted upon knowing the true numbers, Mr. Babcock would tell me. Whether he had meant to frighten me or not, he was no friend to my aunt, and he had made it perfectly clear that there must be some money left by running across England in the middle of the night. But I did not want to think about this. I had twenty-one days to not think of it. "Tell me about the Upper Village, Mr. Aldridge," I said. "I understand they make porcelain."

Ben talked happily of clay pits and kilns while we strolled, and I glanced at him sidelong. Had I been on a London street, I thought, this walk would have been a thing of significance. Ben was not rich, nor was he well connected, but he was educated, pleasant, tolerably handsome, and able to earn a respectable living. His every move and every look would have been dissected by Mrs. Hardcastle and those other ladies who came to my aunt's ritual Wednesday tea, studied just as scientifically as Ben himself studied Uncle Tully's fish. That is, of course, had I been a young lady in organdy in the park. But I was Katharine Tulman, and had this been London, this walk never would have happened. Ben Aldridge would not have asked, and Aunt Alice would never have allowed it if he had. What she would have made of my jaunt in the ballroom with one of the servants was more than I could imagine.

We passed the stone wall that held the canal high over our heads, the gasworks, and then the canal met the river again and we were in the Upper Village. It was an orderly, neat place, larger and more established than the Lower, buildings of brick and stone, and little alleys branching outward from the High Street like veins. Lampposts of gaslight lined the streets, a wrought-iron letter *S* forming the cross-brace, and the tall cones of the pottery kilns smoked a little ways in the distance.

I craned my neck as we entered the gentle bustle, looking this way and that, astonished as men raised their hats to me, and women dipped once. One little girl even ran from her door with a bun wrapped in a cloth, still warm, stuffed with currants and raisins.

"Sugar," Ben whispered, chuckling at my expression. Mrs. Brown nodded once to me, a basket of herbs on her arm, and we passed another church with its cemetery, a small market, and a public square with a pump, where children stood in a line with their water buckets. I imagined this place after Aunt Alice had had her way, empty and deserted, weed-ridden, color and vibrance all sucked away, and continued my walk through the High Street in silence, feeling like a destroying angel.

"And this is the infirmary, Miss Tulman," Ben said, indicating a new stone building with a roof of slate. "For the sick, or mothers . . . Ah, Mr. Cooper! Good afternoon. May I present Miss Katharine Tulman to you?"

A wiry little man in a dusty black coat stepped down from the infirmary door. He eyed me warily, adjusted three heavy-looking leather-bound volumes beneath one arm, tipped a fraying top hat, and then took off down the street, his gait reminding me of a twitching spider. I turned to watch him go.

"Well, almost all sugar, Miss Tulman," Ben sighed. "Mr. Cooper is our resident surgeon, and current head of the Upper Village committee. Plucked from a workhouse by Mr. Babcock, of course, after he paid off a tidy sum of Mr. Cooper's gambling debts, if the rumors are true. But the villages needed a surgeon. Should any sickness occur outside his expertise, a boat is sent for a physician in Milton, a personal friend of Mr. Babcock's. The teachers for the schools have come in much the same way as Mr. Cooper, and there is even a parson who . . ."

A warm hand slipped into my bandaged one, and I found Davy at my side, Bertram on his shoulder. I smiled at him, but he tugged at my hand, yanking my arm, trying to pull me in the opposite direction.

"David," Ben said sharply, "let go of Miss Tulman this instant."

Davy pulled at my sore hand, his eyes wide and dark.

I leaned down and whispered, "What is it, Davy? Is something wrong?"

He looked up at me and went still, his dark eyes boring into mine, straining, it seemed, to put thoughts into my head. I straightened, unsure of what to do. Davy steadied the bunny and tugged again. I winced, and glanced once at Ben. His usual amiable expression had been replaced by stern disapproval. I leaned down again.

"Davy, I'd like to finish my walk with Mr. Aldridge now. Why don't you come with me? Would you like that?"

Davy did not let go of me, but instead of pulling he went still again, his eyes now on his bare and dirty toes.

"Come along, then." I moved experimentally, to see if he would follow, and he did. We walked slowly down the street together, an unexpected pleasure budding at the feel of the child's hand in mine. "I believe you were telling me about the parson, Mr. Aldridge," I said over my shoulder. Ben was close behind, catching up.

"Yes. I was going to say the parson gives a rather inspiring sermon, now that his thirst for drink cannot be quenched."

"And why can't his thirst for drink be quenched?" I adjusted Davy's hand. The child was sweating.

"Didn't you know, Miss Tulman? Spirits aren't allowed, not in either village. Not that a little doesn't come in, here or there, of course." I caught his look, and the way it darted quickly away from me. "But the villagers are wary of rule breaking. The benefits of living here are too good. So any little excesses that might occur are not . . . encouraged . . ."

Ben did not finish his sentence, his gaze deliberately taking in the opposite side of the street, and I experienced a humiliation just as unanticipated as the pleasure of before. Obviously he thought these words applied particularly to me. What had Mary or her mother been saying about my little "excesses"? I said the first thought that came to my head, to cover my confusion. "I wonder, Mr. Aldridge, if you ever had occasion to see my father at Stranwyne?"

His forehead wrinkled. "I don't believe I did, Miss Tulman. Forgive me, but when did Mr. Tulman die?"

"Fourteen months after my birth. At sea." The street was increasingly deserted, lined with dwellings now and little cowsheds and gardens. Davy's head leaned into the bunny that rode on his shoulder, but other than the pressure of his hand, he made no sign that I was there.

"Was your father with the navy, Miss Tulman?"

"Oh, no. He was a merchant. His ship foundered in a storm."

"My father died at sea as well. So we have that in common." Ben turned and opened a little white gate, and I saw a path leading to the twenty-fifth building on our left since entering the High Street.

"And here is my own cottage," he said, sweeping his arm across the view, "or my aunt Daniels's, I should say, rest her soul. The childhood home that is mine once more. At least until I take up my teaching position in September."

I studied the modest little house at the end of the path, limecoated and thatched, much older than the other buildings of the village. A garden wild with untended color rambled off to one side, its edges mixing with the grasses of the lawn, and one of the windows was open, propped with a boot. I wondered if anything inside that place would show me something of Ben's soul, as Lane's room had done.

"Won't you have a cup of tea with me in the garden, Miss Tulman? The flowers have persisted in blooming past all neglect, and it's really rather . . ."

"Davy?"

He was pulling my hand again, this time straining backward with the effort, staring not as if he would tell me something, but in that blank way I hated so much to see. I stumbled forward, Bertram squirmed, and then all at once Davy dropped my hand and was off like a shot, away across the High Street and into a wooded area that must eventually lead back to the big house. I watched him run, rubbing my hand as he disappeared among the trees.

"That boy takes advantage," Ben said. I looked back at him inquisitively over my shoulder. "Don't think me harsh, Miss Tulman, but David is a very intelligent child. He knows just what he is doing."

"He is also a mute child, Mr. Aldridge."

Ben shrugged. "They had the physician out here to look at him, you know, and he could find no malformation or physical trauma that would cause David to not speak. And yet the child is allowed to do as he pleases, to run wild."

Ben shook his head while I brushed away some of the dirt Davy had left on my hand, frowning. There were other traumas in the world besides the physical.

"Come and help me put the kettle on, Miss Tulman. We'll have our tea in the garden, as I suggested, shall we?"

I looked back to the woods. Davy's behavior bothered me, though for different reasons than Ben's. He had not seemed willful or rude to me; he had seemed frightened.

"Thank you very much indeed, Mr. Aldridge, but I think I should go after him. Or at least let Mr. Moreau or Mrs. Jefferies know that something is wrong. But I do appreciate the tour of the village."

Ben inclined his head, but I did not turn to go. "Mr. Aldridge, would you . . ." I paused. How did one invite a young man to party? Not like this, more than likely. I took a breath. "I would like to invite you to a little celebration, in honor of . . . my birthday. In a little more than two weeks' time. You will . . . be here, still?"

Ben's brows rose slightly, though whether from surprise or the awkwardness of my invitation I wasn't certain. "Why, of course, Miss Tulman. I am honored."

I smiled in relief and waved as I hurried away. When I looked back he was still watching me, but there were no laugh lines around his eyes.

CHAPTER THIRTEEN

I stood on the last rise of moorland before I descended to the house, turning circles in my own footsteps, shading my eyes from the setting sun as I looked for Davy. I went to the garden, the greenhouse, the kitchen, and even peeked into the dimness of the chapel and the ever-grinning parson, but I did not find him or Mrs. Jefferies. Mary had chicken with new potatoes and my cucumbers waiting for me, along with a fair dose of chatter, most of which I was not listening to while the room slowly darkened into night. I was lost in my thoughts until I took a sip of my tea and flinched.

"You've forgotten the sugar, Mary," I said, interrupting something she was saying about the ne'er-do-well exploits of a village girl.

"Oh, no, Miss! Wasn't you listening? I told you, it went bad, and I had to be throwing it out. I —"

"Sugar doesn't go bad, Mary. You don't mean it had . . . vermin?"

"Are you meaning bugs, Miss?" Mary began polishing a candlestick with gusto. "'Cause if you're meaning bugs, I don't know what sort of maid you're thinking I am, to go and be letting bugs crawl into a lady's sugar. I'm certain there ain't a bug in the world that wouldn't be scared of crawling into my lady's sugar, on account of being squashed. Now I meant to be borrowing more sugar from my mum, but I had so many things going 'round and 'round in my mind, what with parties and such . . ."

"Mary, do we have any sugar?"

". . . though my mum says I oughtn't to be saying 'party' at all, but 'function.' 'Tis a 'function,' Mum says, or some other such . . ." Mary's hands went still on the candlestick and she looked up suddenly, discovering I had spoken. "What, Miss?"

"Mary," I said slowly. The mention of her mother had reminded me. "There is something I want to say to you, that we must be quite clear about. You must never, under any circumstance, relate private matters about your mistress, not even to your mother. It is essential that a lady be able to . . . trust that her affairs will not become the affairs of an entire village. Is that understood?"

Mary's mouth was a perfect circle. "Why, Miss! I never did such a thing! I swear it!"

I grimaced. Likely Mary had not even realized it when she did. "I'm sure you didn't intend to, Mary, even if —"

"But I never said a word about my lady being tipsy! It was never passing my lips! Not once! What do you take me for, Miss?" Mary's freckles were blending into a tinge of angry pink.

"As long as it never happens again, Mary." I waited for her to speak, but she just polished the silver as if she wished to rub it into oblivion. "Do we have any sugar?" Mary frowned into her reflection. "Never mind, then. I'll just run down and get some from the kitchen."

"Well, I'm thinking you should, Miss, if you're wanting it that bad." She picked up the next candlestick. "Lord knows I've got enough to do."

I sighed and lit a candle, careful to choose a holder Mary had not yet polished, and slipped out the bedchamber door.

The corridor was dark, as usual, my candle throwing light in a scant semicircle on the carpet. I caught a glimpse of the portrait of my guardian and held up the candle to have a better look at her. I wasn't sure exactly why I thought of her as my guardian, but her presence outside my door was a comfort. Maybe it was just that her face struck me as the epitome of sense. I turned away, thinking that I should remember to ask someone who she was, when footsteps, very light and very quick, moved away from me in the darkness, toward the stairwell at the end of the hall.

I froze, fear tickling the nape of my neck as the footsteps pattered softly down the stairs. The laugh in the chapel came unbidden to my mind, but then my back straightened. Someone was in the habit of running about Stranwyne; I wanted to know who it was. I crept along the hall, glad that I had not bothered to put on my boots, and tried to peer down the stairs, but it was utterly dark beyond my candle. I hesitated for a moment, then blew out the light.

Blindness fell down like a blanket. A floorboard groaned to the left beyond the landing; my hand found the rail and I hurried down the stairs. I put my foot close to the wall on the ninth step, to avoid the squeak, realizing that whoever had gone down before me had known to do that as well. I turned left at the landing, and listened.

Not a rustle of cloth, not even breath. But my eyes were beginning to adjust to the darkness, and I could see a door about halfway down the corridor slightly open, the door that connected this section of the house with the rest of the central block. I moved swiftly down the hall, the floorboards groaning, wondering what might be waiting at the end of the corridor, watching me come. The open door swung slightly in the draft, and I stepped through.

I was on a wide landing with railings, almost circular, at the head of a set of stone steps, a sort of grand entrance to the private apartments of the house, a place I had mused might have once been outdoors. Thick stone showed through the peeling plaster, and there was no gaslight here. But the newer room just beyond had a gas sconce lit, a little dust-sheeted morning room, and the glow threw light at the bottom of the stairs.

Down I went, my stockinged feet silent on the stone, through the morning room, and around to the back corridor that led to the kitchen. The kitchen fire was out, but at the next corner, light of a different color leaked around a closed door, flickers of soft yellow and orange. I put my ear to it and listened, then opened the door.

Candles were lit, leaving the gas sconces dark, the flames shining on ornaments that had been crammed onto every surface: china plates, a silver candelabra, crystal, bronze statues, a painted screen, and other jumbled things I could not immediately identify. Yellow brocade glimmered on two matching settees, and the room was clean, sparkling even. I could smell soap and polish beneath the wood and coal smoke.

I wandered amongst the tables, one or two odd chairs, and a marble-topped bench, then approached the hearth. Two upholstered chairs faced each other before a small fire, a table set between with an elegant little supper of bread and carrots and fowl upon it. Steam still rose from the plates. I looked about the empty room. A small wooden door with a window, probably leading to the garden and badly in need of paint, was in the far corner, and I noticed that the walls were plain, no moldings or decorative relief, the floor beneath the thickly woven carpet made of flagged stone. This was only a workroom of some sort, maybe even a buttery. The brocaded furniture, carpet, and fancy ornaments must have been collected and brought here from other parts of the house. I looked again at the ready meal by the fire, sat down on the settee, and waited.

I counted the statues, organizing them into male, female, and animal in my mind, numbering the inoperative gas lamps while the steam from the plates began to fade. There must be a dozen ways into Stranwyne if someone was determined to get in. Perhaps there were villagers using the building to their own purpose, not as afraid as they were purported to have been. But surely Mrs. Jefferies would be aware of this room?

When the hearth flames had settled into an orange ember glow, I rose from the settee, lit my own taper, and blew out the other candles one by one. I left as quietly as I had come, took a few steps down the hall, stopped, turned, and went back into the room of the ornaments. A book lay displayed on a table beside the door, thick and embossed with gold, a painting of a jungle scene complete with snake and stalking cat on its cover. *Travels in South America*, the title read, and then I saw that next to it stood a silver wolf, teeth bared, the same wolf that I had seen in Lane's room. I shook my head, picked up the book, and took it with me as I went to procure my dish of sugar. I stole softly back to Marianna's room, seeing nothing more alarming than dust, hearing no sounds beyond the swish of my own skirt.

I was in the garden the next morning before the sun was fully over the hills, sitting on a small stool between the cabbages and the greenhouse. This time I knew what I was waiting for, and it was not long until I saw it: a tattered blue jacket, brown curls, and a lump of speckled fur, coming wraithlike from the garden door. I let him get close before I spoke.

"Davy," I said softly.

The child jumped as if I'd shouted, and made to run.

"Wait," I called, then softened my voice. "Wait. I have something for you."

Davy slowed and then turned, his curiosity getting the better of him, his large eyes locking on what I held out. It was the currant-and-raisin bun from the day before.

"And I've something for you to look at while you eat it." Still holding out the bun, I slowly pulled the book from the bag at my feet.

I sat that way for some time, arms aching from holding out the book and the bun, Davy staring at them both, undecided. Then he adjusted Bertram on his shoulder and came lightly toward me, his bare feet leaving no marks in the foliage and grass. He tugged on my arm, looking once toward the garden door.

"Do you want to eat it somewhere else?"

But he neither nodded nor shook his head, just pulled. I snatched up the bag and followed the tug on my sleeve through the door, off the path, and straight into the moor grasses, wildflowers brushing the width of my skirt. The birds jumped and twittered.

"Where are we going?" I whispered. I don't know why I whispered, and I don't know why I asked, because he was not going to answer. I followed him up and down the gentle swells, tripping over the hummocks, until we had climbed a small hill. But the hill had no summit. It was like a shallow bowl at its top, hollowed out smooth with short grass yellowing from the lack of rain, a large, flat stone standing up like a finger at its center. The grasses grew tall around the edges, and when Davy sat beside the stone, Bertram in his lap, I knew the only creatures in the world he was not hidden from were the birds of the air. I came and sat on the grass beside him. Bertram hopped down to graze.

"Is this your place, Davy?" I asked, more to fill the silence than to know his answer. I handed him the bun, which he tore into eagerly. "Is it a secret place? Shall I not tell?"

His large eyes looked up at me over the bun, wide and serious, and I stared into their blackness. They were very expressive eyes, like windows of nighttime, and somehow I was sure that Davy would not want me to tell.

"All right, I shan't, then," I said, answering as if he had spoken. "Not unless I know you wish me to. Is that a bargain?"

He took another bite of the bun, his gaze dropping to the book in my hand. I set it in his lap, and he turned the pages slowly as he chewed, stopping often on the pictures, which were vivid: tropical birds of fantastic colors, monkeys, and the depiction of an open-mouthed crocodile, water dripping from jagged teeth. He lingered long on that one.

When the bun was gone, I said, "You were frightened yesterday, Davy, and I don't know why." His eyes darted up, instantly fearful.

"You don't have to tell me," I said immediately, "but I wish I could know. Would you like to learn how to read and to write down what you want other people to know?"

He looked again at the book, silent, one brown finger on the picture of the crocodile.

"And if you knew how to read," I coaxed, "you could know what this book is telling you. See this word?" I moved his hand aside and pointed. "This word says 'crocodile,' and the rest of the words tell what the crocodile eats and how it behaves. Would you like to be able to read that?"

I could see nothing but the top of his brown curls, bits of leaf sticking out of them.

"Look," I tried again. "I've brought paper, and a pen, and ink." I drew them out of the bag. "Let me show you." I opened a small copybook to a blank page and uncorked the inkwell. I set the ink beside the stone, dipped the pen, and wrote a large letter *D.*

"See," I said, "this is the first letter of your name. There are twenty-five more letters, and when you know them all you can mix them up to make as many words as you wish. And when you know the words, you can copy them down yourself and tell whatever you'd like, and all without talking. Here." I put the pen in his hand, guiding it to a slight dip in the inkwell and back to the page. "Try the letter *D.*"

We sat there, breeze sighing as the sun became a yellow ball to heat up the grasses, Davy's hand hovering above the page until the ink began to dry. I helped him dip the pen again.

"Don't worry if it doesn't turn out well," I said. "Just try."

But still he did not touch the pen to the page. I put my hand on his, thinking to guide him, but he leapt up from my touch as if stung, sending the pen flying and nearly knocking over the ink. He hurried across the little dell and snatched up Bertram, holding the rabbit close, as a low voice from behind me said, "What's all this, then?"

I twisted around. Lane was there, the red cap on his hair, a rifle in one hand and a brace of dead pheasants in the other. He laid down the birds and the gun and stepped into the little bowl of land as I faced forward again, feeling guilt for I knew not what. Lane folded his length down onto the ground, leaning back against the stone, once again reminding me of a cat, dark and sleek. "Well?" he said again.

I lifted my chin. "I thought perhaps Davy could learn to read, and to write, so that he could . . . so that he . . ." I left the sentence unfinished.

"I see," Lane said, and picked up the open book on South America from the ground. Davy, fear evidently gone, came and sat down beside him, trying to imitate Lane's lithe stance against the rock, an impossible and slightly comical task for a boy with a short, round body and a bunny in his lap. I discovered the gray eyes on me, hard and accusing. "Is something funny?"

"No," I said, straightening my face.

Lane frowned down at the book for a moment, then leaned close to Davy. "Do you see that crocodile there? Do you know what it'll do if you try and touch it?"

Davy looked up into Lane's face, dimpling, and reached a tentative finger toward the picture.

"Bite off your hand!" Lane yelled suddenly, snapping the cover shut as if the book would eat the child's finger. Davy's hand jerked back, and his dimple deepened at Lane's laugh. My brows went up. Males were strange creatures.

When they were done amusing themselves by pretending that the book would consume pieces of their limbs, I said, "I was wondering, does Mrs. Jefferies sleep in her own cottage at night?"

Lane's brows came down. "Aunt Bit? Of course she does. Davy with her." Davy's dimple faded, and he stroked his rabbit.

"I was wondering because last night I heard footsteps in the corridor, and then . . . someone had a fire lit and a supper made in a room downstairs, just around from the kitchen. The room had been cleaned, and furniture and ornaments had been moved from other parts of the house. I thought perhaps your aunt would know." I couldn't mention the wolf, of course, but I watched for Lane's reaction to this information. There wasn't one.

"Aunt Bit had one of her headaches and went to her bed early last night," he said. Bertram hopped out of Davy's lap, and Davy got up and followed him to the edge of the dell. Lane frowned as he watched him.

"And there have been other times . . ." I said, forcing out the words. "The first day I came. Someone was in the chapel, and they . . . laughed. I thought people from the village might be . . ."

"And you're sure you really heard it?"

The gray eyes were on me again, cold and sparing me nothing. Had I heard someone laugh? Was I certain of that now? There were so many things I'd thought I'd seen, and hadn't. I tucked my bandaged hand into the billowing worsted and looked away. I could not answer.

"Which room is it you saw?" he asked eventually.

"Three doors down from the kitchen, around the corner." I wished I'd gone back there this morning, to be sure. How I loathed myself for not knowing. I watched Davy offer a spray of wild onions to the rabbit while a sudden breeze waved the grasses.

"Just what is it you're up to, Miss Tulman?"

I looked at him, still leaning back against the stone, and though his position had not changed, I could easily perceive that he had. He was coiled and tense, ready to spring. "What do you mean?"

"You know exactly what I mean. What are you doing with Mr. Tully, winding clocks and painting things and spending all that time in the workshop? What are you doing with Davy in this hollow? What do you hope to gain by it?"

I looked down at my skirt.

"You're still going to turn us out, aren't you? Can you deny it?"

I held silent. What could I say?

"You are going to turn us out. I don't care what Mary Brown runs about telling the whole village, you're going to send every last one of us to the streets. And you'll take Mr. Tully, too, and when you do, it'll kill him. You know it will. You know it the same way I do. You might be the only other person in the world that knows it like I do."

His words were soft and measured, like velvet-covered blows. I closed my eyes against the pain.

"You know it, and yet you smile and kiss his forehead and plan a party. A party, for God's sake! And what are you doing strolling about with Ben Aldridge and letting little girls give you gifts? What are you doing here at all?"

I held my breath, tears threatening my eyes. I wanted to tell him that none of this was what I would have chosen. That I was having a party because I'd never been to a party, and that it was helping me forget what was to come. That I was exchanging my uncle's life for a scrap — maybe less than a scrap if I could not trust my own mind — but if a scrap was the only life I was likely to have, then I would have to take it, no matter what came after. The outcome for Uncle Tully would be the same either way.

But of course I said none of that. I breathed and opened my eyes, feeling sore and bruised inside, watching my hand clutch the worsted. Davy sat on the edge of the dell, Bertram in his lap, while Lane's jaw worked in and out, in and out.

"Aunt Bit says Mr. George left his wife a great deal of money," he said suddenly, "and that you live in a fine house on a London square. She says there are shops and museums and theaters, and people packed like sausages so that you could never be done with the exploring of it."

He waited for me to confirm or deny. I only whispered, "I have never been to a theater, and I have never . . . explored London."

"You're telling me you go chasing footsteps through Stranwyne in the middle of the night, but that you've never wandered out your own front door?"

That was very true. I bit my lip and said nothing.

"All right, then what do you do there?"

I could have said I keep the ledger books for Aunt Alice and organize her receipts. That I write letters to her bill collectors, dust and tend the fire, and pluck the dog hairs from her dress. That I keep track of the housemaid's movements and go to market when we must discharge another cook because the wages have been spent on baubles for my indigestive cousin. That I have lived so many of my days cramped in one crimson room with a woman who despises me that it's no wonder if I was going mad now. But I said none of that either, though Lane's low voice answered, "I see," just as if I had. I looked up and saw that Davy was gone.

"We tried to teach him to read and write, you know," Lane said. "But he wouldn't learn. I think he could learn, but he wouldn't. I reckon he doesn't want us to know what he's thinking. Aunt Bit seems to know though, and without him having to tell her."

I remembered that certain expressiveness in Davy's eyes, and wondered if, with practice, I couldn't do the same. The wind ruffled my hair.

"Please lie for us," he said. "Just for a little while."

The softness of the request — a request I could not grant — hurt me so much more than his anger had. Again I held my breath. But then his tone changed.

"What happened to your hand?"

I tucked the bandaged hand back into the folds of my skirt, but Lane reached across the space that separated us and grabbed it out again. He held it up in front of me.

"Untie it," he said. I shook my head, but he slipped the knotted end over my fingers and unwound the ribbon of cloth, my stomach growing sicker as each fold fell away. The ugly scabs stood out red against my skin, individual marks in a half oval. He turned my hand over, and gazed at the corresponding set. "You did that yourself, didn't you?"

I shook my head again, but it didn't matter. He flung my hand into my lap and stood. "If you've got one good deed left in you, use it for yourself, Miss Tulman. Get rid of it, before you hurt more than can be fixed with a bandage."

He picked up the rifle and pheasants and was gone over the lip of the dell, leaving me with the blowing papers of the copybook. I let the tears come. It was horrible to be considered a drunkard, but the truth was so much worse that part of me thought I should probably be grateful. But I wasn't grateful.

I let myself cry until I quieted, breath shuddering as I gradually became aware of bird wings and hot wind and rustling, and when I opened my eyes Davy was sitting on the edge of the little hollow, his chin on his knees. He came silently across the dell, picked up the book about South America, and settled cross-legged before me. He looked intently at the pages, eyes darting, and after a few moments, paused. Before I knew what he was about he had found the pen, got ink on its end, and put it to the page of the book. Then he dropped both book and pen and flitted away, disappearing over the edge of the dell.

I picked up the book from the grass, sorry to see such a nice thing ruined, and looked at what he had done. It was the acknowledgments page, giving credit to the artist who had created the pictures, a Mr. David Woolsey, but now the *David* had a thin black line traced below it.

I closed the book carefully and looked up at the empty dell. Davy could read. Both Ben and Lane had been right. Davy was not incapable of sharing what might be in his head; he was merely unwilling. And I was not going to be able to change that. Or anything else. I gathered up my things and hurried from the little dell.

CHAPTER FOURTEEN

I went back to Marianna's room and locked the doors, refusing to come out even at Mary's nonstop insistence. I told her I did not feel well, that I did not wish to eat, that I would sleep, and it was long before she gave up and left me in peace. But I did not sleep. I sat in the stuffy room, staring as the sun moved slowly across the wallpaper, until the light finally dimmed and disappeared. What foolishness to think I could have this time, that I could pretend none of this was happening. Ben might let me, and Mary, and Uncle Tully could not comprehend, but Lane and his aunt were not going to stand for it. And how could I blame them? What would I do with an erratic, inexplicable girl bent on taking away everything I loved?

At length I did sleep, however, and when I woke the next day the sun was slanting from the very top of Marianna's windows. It must have been going on noon. I moved quietly about the room, not quite ready to face Mary's questioning, and finally sat down at the dressing table. My hair was wild where I'd slept with the pins in, the shadows beneath my eyes showing through my skin.

I opened the drawer to find my brush, but it was empty. Mary had put my hair things in the left drawer instead of the right. I ran the brush through my tangles and pinned it all up again before moving everything back to the correct drawer. I had slept in my dress and it looked it, but I didn't much care. I unlocked the door to the corridor and made my way silently to the kitchen.

It was amazing, I thought twenty minutes later, how a bit of bread with butter and milk could change one's outlook. I hurried back up through the twisting corridors and stairs, and gave my customary glance to my guardian before I turned the knob and walked into Marianna's room.

But I was not in Marianna's room. I was in the library, with the cobwebs and the dusty lounges. I stood in the dirt and shut the door behind me, a sense of wrongness and confusion making my head spin. I allowed the whirling to still, then took careful steps through the filthy room. I would not go back to the hall, would not check the location of my guardian's portrait. It did not matter. I tried to open the connecting door, the one that led to Mary's little bedroom, but it was locked. I knocked lightly.

"Mary?" I called.

The door flew open. "Lord, Miss. You gave me a fright! Whatever are you doing coming through here? I keep this door locked, you see, 'cause you can never tell what might be coming through a door, though locks don't keep out the things I'm worrying over, Miss, if you understand me. Not that I've seen the first —"

"I just fancied a look at the library, is all. How nice you've made your room, Mary."

Mary's freckles stretched with pleasure. The little stove was polished to a bright shine, fresh curtains hung at the windows, and a quilt was spread over the bed. None of it was pink.

"I just needed a bit of different, you know, Miss. That one color can wear on a person's nerves. Now what in the name of heaven's been the matter with you, Miss?"

"I . . ."

"I mean, how can I go and be a proper lady's maid with the doors all locked? That's a barrier to my job, that is. And some of us has got work to be doing, if other people are going to up and decide to be giving a party. There's —"

"Mary," I said, firmly enough to stop the flow, "I've decided that wasn't such a good idea. It was . . . silly of me, to think —"

"What are you talking of, Miss? 'Tis only what young ladies are supposed to be doing, that's what my mum says, and, Miss, if you don't mind me saying, it better be you or it's nobody."

"Mary . . ."

"Now I know what you're about to be saying, Miss, 'cause I've been thinking it all out for myself, and unless you're thinking of inviting every lass from Upper and Lower, which couldn't be fitting . . ."

"Mary," I sighed.

". . . or unless you're thinking that you and Mrs. Jefferies is making up a party, then I don't see how you can be doing it. My mum is none too sure of you, begging your pardon, and things being what they are, I can't be tramping down there to tell her you're inviting young men to a party in your own bedroom." Mary's eyebrows were straight up her forehead. I was a bit stung.

"But that was only because of Uncle Tully! His mother's rooms are the only place . . . I mean he wouldn't be . . . It's difficult to explain, but it doesn't matter because —"

"I know it, Miss, I know! That's why I was thinking about the library, then, what you just came through? That would've been part of the old mistress's rooms, and there'd be nothing improper in —"

She stopped abruptly, head cocked to one side. A knock was coming faintly to us through the walls. We moved through the connecting doors to Marianna's room just in time to hear it again at the bedchamber door. Mary clapped her hands together.

"Visitors!" she hissed, her eyes alight. "Quick, Miss, stand over there!"

She jerked my sleeves once to straighten them, then pushed me toward the hearth. When I'd regained my balance, she patted her hair once and flung open the bedchamber door.

"Good afternoon, Mr. Moreau," she said.

My eyes widened, both at the name and the voice that had said them. Mary's imitation of my accent had been quite credible. I moved into the sight line of the open door and saw Lane standing, red cap bunched in his hands, looking slightly bewildered. Just behind his head hung the portrait of my guardian. I turned back to the hearth.

"I . . . wondered if . . . Miss Tulman might like to go rolling," I heard his voice say. "In the ballroom."

Shock and surprise made my forehead crease, sending shivers of uncertainty to dance along my spine. I looked over my shoulder, careful not to focus on the portrait, and found the gray eyes already on me, expressionless, just letting me decide. Mary turned from the door she still blocked with her body, her round eyes also seeking mine. I studied a hole in the carpet. I wasn't certain I wanted another conversation with Lane; I was still aching from the last one. But he had requested, not insisted, and I had never stopped wondering about how much of our last trip to the ballroom had been real.

"All right." I steadied my voice. "You may tell him yes . . . that I . . ."

I looked up to see that Mary's eyes had grown rounder as she gazed at me, her head jerking once to the side as if she'd experienced some sort of spasm.

". . . that I would and . . ."

Her neck spasmed again, eyes growing larger.

". . . and Mary shall . . ." Mary gave one more jerk of the head toward Lane. ". . . shall accompany us, of course."

Mary sighed in relief, then slammed the door in Lane's face. She grabbed me by the arms and sat me hard on the bench in front of the dressing table. "Fix your hair, quick!" she whispered, "and I'll be doing your dress!"

"Just a minute!" I called through the door. "Mary," I said, holding my voice low, "my hair is fine, and don't make such a fuss. He only wants . . ." Actually I had no idea what he wanted.

"Don't be daft, Miss! I've never once been seeing Lane Moreau knock on a girl's door, and there are plenty who wouldn't have minded if he had, no matter what their papas had to say about a Frenchman. . . ." She paused. "Or maybe because of what their papas had to say . . . but anyway, if he did come knocking, they'd be brushing their hair when they was bid!"

Mary ran like a demon for water and a cloth while I capitulated and opened the drawer on the right side of my dressing table. My hair things weren't there. "Mary, did you move the hairbrush?"

"I didn't move it, Miss, you did. Remember? It's on the left, now." She dipped a cloth in the basin and began sponging frantically at the wrinkles in my dress. I opened the left-hand drawer without comment, took out the brush, and tried to better arrange my hair. Mary's breath whooshed from her nose and she slapped away my hand.

"Stop trying to pull it all back so! What's wrong with you, Miss!" She pulled loose a small piece of hair, one of the wisping curls that so vexed me, and to my horror, snipped it off, cheek length, with a pair of scissors. My mouth dropped.

"Hush!" Mary ordered. She snipped five more times, and when she was done, hair lay all over the dresser, a match of what was locked in the wardrobe drawer, and I had a few twining curls around my face. "Now come on!" she said, and shoved me off the bench.

I let the wind set flight to my newly cut curls as we glided down the floor of the ballroom. It had taken a few minutes to regain my previous skill, but soon my feet remembered themselves and kept me upright. Mary sat at the bottom of the steps, having refused Lane's offer of skates, stating her lengthy opinion that putting wheels on one's feet was the "devil's own foolishment." She propped her chin in her hands and gazed at the sparkling lights instead. Lane showed me how to lift one skate and cross the other, so that we could roll in wide circles around the edge of the ballroom without need for changing direction. Other than that, we did not speak.

We were making our seventh circle in this way, and I was concentrating on the feel of my speed when Lane said, "You didn't go to clock-winding."

I glanced at him sidelong. I knew he had brought me here for a reason, that he must have something to say, but this was not what I had expected.

"Mr. Tully was upset," he continued. "And then you didn't come to the workshop, and he was upset again. He didn't have playtime."

"He didn't?"

"No." Lane had his hands in his pockets, gazing straight ahead as he rolled, the dark hair blowing as if in a storm. "Mr. Tully hasn't missed playtime since his mother died, that's what Aunt Bit said. I told him you were resting, that you didn't feel well, and then he was afraid you were 'going away' and wouldn't get to count your years. He had a tantrum over it. I had to wrap him in his blankets so he could sleep."

I did not know how to respond to this, so I said nothing. We began our ninth circle. The roar of the wheels reverberated around the ballroom.

"I shouldn't have spoken my mind the way I did," Lane said. "My temper is too hot, and I let it get the better of me."

"It's no matter," I replied, rolling on a little faster. I didn't want to hear him apologize; how could I have expected him to think differently? He caught up to me easily.

"Come back to the workshop. Have your party. Mr. Tully needs those things now, even if . . . no matter what happens . . . after that."

I bit my lip. Now he wanted me to pretend as well. Surely that had been a failed experiment. But for my uncle . . .

"Will you come?"

I caught sight of our reflections in the passing mirrors. Lane was watching me, waiting for my answer, his jaw tight, the muscle working in and out, in and out. I nodded my assent without meeting his eyes, and he put his hands back in his pockets. We made our twelfth turn in silence, passing Mary, who now lay full length on the steps, eyes closed, arms tucked comfortably behind her head.

"I reckon," Lane said at length, "that you must feel it's . . . a wrong thing, to lie to your aunt. . . ."

I made a noise of disbelief at that, and he reached out and yanked me to a stop, pulling me around to face him. "Then why won't you lie? Why? You understand him! Better than I do in some ways and I've had the running of him since I was a boy. If you won't do it for us, then for God's sake do it for him!"

His voice rang against the wood, glass, and gilding. I waited for the sound of it to die before I spoke. "My aunt will find out the truth and take Uncle Tully away no matter what I tell her. And Stranwyne, too. And if she finds I've lied to her — when she finds I've lied — she'll leave me to the streets without a thought." I pulled my arm away. "I can't keep Uncle Tully out of an asylum, and I can't keep the villagers out of the workhouse. The only person I can possibly save is myself." I pushed my wheels against the floor and rolled away from him. I was no Joan of Arc. His voice came from right beside me.

"You needn't always live with your aunt."

"She is my guardian. She'll hold my purse strings until she dies."

"Have you no inheritance of your own?"

I shook my head. He swore softly, and we began our fourteenth circle.

"Then you will marry."

Again I shook my head. It had been made plain over the course of too many years that there was nothing in or about me to draw the attention of a man. Even now it was so. Lane had only brought me here to get something he wanted. Perhaps he had come to the same conclusion as the village: sugar, instead of vinegar. He reached out and pulled me to a stop again, gently this time. I turned my face away.

"Lie for him," he said. "Please, Katharine."

I could not answer; there were no answers to give, but I also couldn't breathe. It had seemed so natural when he said my Christian name, thoughtless even, and yet never had I heard it spoken in such a way. In his voice, my name had almost been . . . beautiful. My eyes were drawn upward, slowly, and then I was drowning in a gaze that covered me like a calm gray sea, a look I'd seen only one time before and told myself I'd imagined.

"Just say you'll think on it," he said. "We don't have to talk of it again. But say you'll think on it, and that you'll come back to the workshop. For Mr. Tully."

I nodded, still mesmerized, and he took both my hands in his, pulling me to the center of the ballroom. I did not resist.

"I'm going to teach you how to spin," he said. "Davy showed me, he . . ." But he loosened his grip on my right hand, which I had not bothered to bind up again. "Did I hurt you?"

I looked down at the red-marked hand he still held, pale against his tan. "No," I whispered. "It's healing."

"Good. Then we're going to spin."

"I don't think I can."

"It's easier than the other things you've done. All you have to do is hold on." A hint of a smile showed at the corner of his mouth. "But you really do have to hold on. Turn your feet like this and cross your arms. Don't let go now!"

His long fingers encircled my wrists, my pulse beat a staccato against them, and I could feel the warmth of him stealing into me. I hung on as he began to skate sideways, picking up speed, until I looked up and said, "No, wait. Stop!" He slowed instantly, forehead creasing. "You're going the wrong way around."

He relaxed back into a grin and rolled the other way, turning clockwise, swinging me in a circle, and soon we were swinging each other, faster and faster, until the lights were a blur and I knew I could not hold on and would go flying across the ballroom. I shrieked, and Lane slowed our speed as Mary sat upright with a start.

"Again?" he asked. I nodded, a smile spreading over my face as he tightened his grip. The way his eyes stood out against his skin fascinated me. And then I didn't care that he was pretending, if I was making a fool of myself, that he was my uncle's servant, or if every single bit of this was false. I wanted it anyway.

We spun until I shrieked with delight and a little fear, and then again, and again, always stopping just before I lost my hold. I was dizzy, breathless with laughter, and all my carefully combed hair had come down.

"How could you have done this with Davy?" I gasped. "Surely he couldn't hang on? You're too heavy."

"Oh, it's different with Davy, to be sure." Lane leaned over, whispering in my ear. "Davy goes air borne."

My eyes widened even as I laughed and tried to get away, but his grip was too strong. "Don't you dare," I warned him.

"Ready?" he asked, grinning like a dark and very handsome devil. "I'd hold on tight, if I were you. . . ."

And he spun me again, though he never let my feet leave the ground.

That night in Marianna's room, Mary was working the tangles back out of my hair when she said, "Do you speak French, Miss?"

"French? Only a very little, Mary." A very little.

"Enough to be writing letters in it, Miss?"

I winced as she pulled the brush through a tangle. "Goodness, no. I've never written a word in French in my life. Why do you ask?"

"Oh, somebody was sending letters in French, and I told them it wasn't you, and I was right, don't you see?"

I did see, indeed. Ben had mentioned before that the letters were being watched closely. I would have watched them, too, if I lived in the village. "Mr. Moreau speaks French, Mary. Maybe it was him."

"Fancy you knowing that, Miss." I caught her face looking smug in the mirror, and she leaned close to my shoulder. "You know I think you're right canny, Miss, to keep him guessing like that."

I turned to look at her, and her eyes widened innocently.

"You know what I'm meaning! To not be telling him right out that you won't be saying nothing to your relations about Stranwyne! To keep him wondering, like. 'Tis a lesson to me, on how to string your young man along. . . ."

"Mary." I turned fully around on the little bench, and she stopped brushing, waiting for me to go on. Obviously she had not been napping on the stairs. "Listen carefully to me. Mr. Moreau only wants —"

"I know, Miss, he —"

I held up a hand, and Mary clamped her mouth closed.

"I don't need you spreading such talk about the village. He merely wants something from me, that's why —"

"To lie for us, I know, he —"

I looked at her again, and she put a hand over her mouth.

"He wants something from me, that is why he took me to the ballroom today, no other reason." Lane had told me once that he would do anything for Uncle Tully, and I was certain that was true. He was trying to manipulate me, most likely. Would hate me, probably, before all this was done, but for now I would taste the sugar, if for no other reason than I could not resist it. But when I looked into Mary's freckled face, her hand clamped over her chin to ensure her own silence, my conscience pricked. It was one thing to pretend because one wanted to; it was another to serve lies to someone who had no idea what they were getting. "Mary, you do understand that I told Mr. Moreau nothing but the truth?"

Mary's words were muffled by her hand. "No, you didn't."

I waited long before answering her, the shortness of her sentence catching me off guard. "Didn't what?"

She dropped her hand. "You didn't tell him the truth. You never told him once you'd be lying to your aunt."

"Oh, Mary," I breathed. Her faith was a blow I hadn't seen coming. "When I go back to my aunt's, I will have to tell her the truth."

"No, you won't."

I waited again for her to go on before discovering my mistake. "Yes, Mary. I will."

"No, you won't. I've already told my mum you'll be lying to the old witch, certain as certain."

"Mary, I'm very sorry, you can't imagine how sorry, but that decision is already made. I've no choice in the matter."

"You won't do it, I'm telling you."

"Mary . . ." I hesitated. "When my time here is over, you . . . you do understand that I'll be leaving Stranwyne, and that I won't be able to take you with me?"

"No," she said placidly. "I don't understand that. You won't be leaving Stranwyne."

I looked into her comfortable face, utterly bereft of doubt, and felt a chill trickle down my back. The room must have a draft. I turned away without answering and heard the rattle of a cup and saucer on my dressing table.

"Have your tea, Miss," she said happily. "Sleep well." And she trotted off through to her own room, cheerfully slamming the doors in between. I studied myself in the mirror while sipping my tea. If Mary could live a lie, then so could I. Apparently it's what we had all decided to do. I drained the teacup. I had nineteen days.

CHAPTER FIFTEEN

When I opened my eyes, I thought I was flying. My nightgown whipped around my knees as the corridors of Stranwyne whizzed by, dark, dusty, or gaslit and clean, some that were familiar, some I had never seen. I held out my arms to feel the passing air, laughing, the joy of it almost more than I could contain. I flew around the clocks, listening to their many happy ticks, and then zipped through a different door and was lifted right off my feet, floating up a winding set of stairs. And then it was dark, a pearly, shimmering dark, and I could see the stone floor of the chapel far below me, nothing between us but a cool expanse of lovely air.

The parson was down there. He would laugh when he saw me floating; we would both laugh. I stretched out my arms for the stone floor, wanting to feel the rush of wind, but I could not get there. I frowned, waving my hands, but I was held back, and the floor moved farther and farther away from me. I struggled a little more, but even my sight was receding. The shining dark shrank to a pinpoint, and then for a long time the world was black, strange colors twisting one upon the other, writhing through my mind like insects.

When I woke I was cold, aching, on a hard surface that chilled me through, breath shuddering against the nightgown that stuck clammily to my chest. I was on my back in a puddle, and I had no idea where I was. As my sight came back, I perceived shadows on a ceiling, the wet hair on my forehead, the smell of old stone and stagnant water, and a muttering that echoed softly from the walls. I stirred, and the muttering stopped.

"Did my little niece wake up?"

I sat up. I was in the gallery of the chapel, beside the stone rail that looked over to the floor below, and my uncle sat cross-legged just a few feet away, rocking back and forth, twisting fistfuls of his coat. His white beard spread with his smile, and then the smile disappeared.

"I was thinking you might not wake, Simon's baby. You didn't go away?"

"No, Uncle," I whispered.

"That's good. That is splendid. People should only go away when they're too tired. That is what's best. You're not too tired?"

"I don't think so." I was very muddled.

"And if you had gone away you would not have so many years to count, would you, little niece? That would not be so fun."

"No." I sat up farther, shivering in my soaked nightgown, though I wasn't sure if all my trembling was from the cold. "Uncle," I said slowly, "can you tell me . . . why I'm here?"

Uncle Tully frowned. "You got confused, little niece. Sometimes people get confused. They forget. They make mistakes. You forgot about stairs."

I hugged myself, trying to stop the shaking. "I forgot about . . . stairs?"

"Yes!" My uncle's eyes were two points of blue in the dark. "You wanted to go down, and you forgot about stairs. And you didn't want to remember. And then you went to sleep, and you wouldn't wake up. You got confused." He leaned back again, rocking a little. "Sometimes people get confused. That's what Marianna said."

Memory was starting to come back to me, visions of the floor of the chapel. I got to my feet and looked over the rail.

"Don't forget again, little niece!"

Moonlight was flooding the grimy windows, and I saw the stone flags spreading ghostly gray far beneath me, but not so far away as I remembered. I looked at the marbled rail that was beneath my hand, remembering the feel of the same cool stone beneath my bare feet, and of flying, floating to the floor. I backed away, eyes on the rail, and sat down on the edge of a raised stone step, where benches would have once been. Had I really been standing up there?

"And when I pulled you down you went right to sleep, Simon's baby, and I had to get the rainwater. Water wakes people up. Only it didn't this time, and I thought you'd gone away. But I waited, to make sure."

"Rainwater?" I asked eventually. My mind was working slowly. I could not seem to move away from the memory of that floor so far below us, from the believing that I could float there.

"Water from the bucket," said my uncle, "for catching what comes from the ceiling."

I looked at the puddle on the floor, touched my sopping

nightgown, and then smelled my hands. That water must have been there for quite some time. "Thank you, Uncle," I said.

"You got confused," he said again.

"But Uncle Tully . . ." I looked up again. "What are you doing here? Isn't it late?"

"No, no. Not late. It's early, quite early, so early that it was only late thirteen minutes ago."

I took that to mean it was twelve minutes after midnight. I must have slept right through the chiming of the clocks. I had gone to bed at nine, or maybe half past, I couldn't remember. What had I been doing in between? Perhaps I didn't want to know.

"But why were you in the chapel, Uncle?" The irony of the question was not lost on me, since I didn't know why I was there myself.

"For clocks!" he said. "And the ticking. Clock ticking is very nice. You know exactly when the ticks will come, unless you forget to wind them. It is always easy to know what a clock shall do. And it tells you things that are important, like when . . . Are you sad, little niece?"

The horrible truth was only just hitting me, that if Uncle Tully had not been there, listening to what his clocks told him, that my body would now be a broken heap on the chapel floor. And that it would have been no one's doing but my own. A cold emptiness took the place of my other thoughts. I think the feeling was despair. I wiped at my eyes. "It's just that . . . I don't like to be confused, Uncle Tully," I said, "and I'm . . . very cold."

My uncle got up and stood next to me, and then his coat dangled near my face. I wrapped it around my shoulders. It was warm. He sat down beside me, not too near, reached out, gave one of my arms the briefest of pats, and then sat on his hands. He was wearing a long nightshirt that fell below his knees, and his feet were bare.

"I think I should tell her a secret," he said to himself. "Should I? Shall I? I think I shall!" His voice echoed slightly before dropping to a confidential whisper. "Sometimes I get confused."

I couldn't help but smile at him. "Thank you for telling me, Uncle." Then my smile faded as another thought struck. "Do you think . . . that perhaps we might not tell anyone else about my . . . being confused?"

Uncle Tully rocked on his hands. "I don't know, I don't know, Simon's baby. Who do I not tell? Mrs. Jefferies brings the tea, and Lane knows what is right. I could ask Lane. . . ."

"Never mind," I said quickly. I was feeling more alert now, and it would not do to agitate him. Probably the less he thought on the subject the less likely he was to mention it. "But could I ask you to do something else for me, Uncle? Something that is important?"

He leaned forward again, the blue of his eyes bright and intense.

"Could you walk with me . . . to Marianna's room? You know the way, don't you? I don't want to . . . get confused, or . . ." I lowered my gaze, hoping I would not cry. It was difficult to admit these things, even to my uncle. "I don't want to make another mistake, on the way."

"Oh, yes! Yes, yes! That is right. You should go to Marianna's room! That is just so. Come on, then. Come on!"

So I followed after my uncle, the end of his nightshirt flapping against skinny calves as he bounded confidently through the stairways and corridors. When we reached Marianna's door, he stopped, still bouncing up and down on the balls of his feet.

"See!" he whispered happily. "We did not forget at all. No mistakes!"

"No, Uncle." I opened Marianna's door, and saw the key sticking out of the lock from the inside. *I must have done that*, I thought, though I did not remember.

Uncle Tully stepped inside his mother's room, wringing his hands together, turning around and around in his own circle, the right way, of course, as I had done when looking for Davy. The fire was nearly out, but there was a soft glow on the wardrobe and the walls. "You made it clean," he said, accomplishing only a very loud whisper. "That is splendid. That is as it should be." But then unease spread all over his face. "But you are not sitting. That isn't right! It isn't right. . . ."

I dropped quickly into my chair beside the hearth, where I normally sat with my tea before bed, sorry that I was getting my favorite place wet, but more concerned about upsetting the delicate balance of my uncle's comfort. He gazed at me as I sat in the chair, happiness radiating from his face. "Yes," he said, "that is where you sit, where you both sit. That is just the place you both belong. Just so."

I looked back into my uncle's beaming smile. It was Marianna he was seeing sitting in that chair, and the knowledge stabbed me, ripping right through my middle. Marianna would have never betrayed him. "Uncle Tully," I whispered, "may I give you a kiss good night? I forgot to ask . . . the last time."

Uncle Tully frowned and began twisting a section of his nightshirt. Then he came to my chair and suddenly thrust out his neck, eyes squeezed shut as if trying not to see something dreadful. I kissed the place where the prickling beard met his cheek, and he was out the door, arms pumping. Then his head popped back around the doorjamb. "Don't forget playtime, Simon's baby!"

When his footsteps were gone, I shut the door and locked it, hung his coat on the back of a chair, to let the damp spots dry, took the metal bucket from the hearth and shoveled some glowing coals into it. I carried the bucket into the bathing room, opened the rose-petal door, and loaded the little firebox below the water cylinder, first turning the key in the door to Mary's room, though it wasn't likely I would wake her; she truly did sleep like the dead. I twisted the water from my nightgown into the basin and laid it on the hearth chair beside Uncle Tully's coat. Then I sat on the floor, naked but for my dressing gown, waiting for the water to get warm, watching heat ebb from the remaining coals.

When the water was hot, I filled the tub and slid inside, letting the warmth soothe the chill that had not quite gone from inside me, unbraided my hair and washed it, scrubbing every inch of my skin, then scrubbing every inch dry when I was done. I put on a clean nightgown, removed the sash of my dressing gown and carefully made a knot with it around the bedpost. Marianna's bed was warm, the pillows soft, but I did not lie down. I made a decision. If I was going to live a lie, then that lie would not be for me alone. There were eighteen days, and if those days were to be Uncle Tully's last, then by God they would be the happiest I could make them, no matter who I had to hurt, including myself. The trogwynd blew, a soft note that might sing me to sleep. I looped the end of my sash around my wrist, and tied myself to the bedpost.

The next morning I found a trail of pink wallpaper when I ran my finger through the dust on the library wall. So I borrowed an old dress of Mary's — with her permission, this time — and we covered up our hair, tied on aprons, opened the windows, and set to cleaning.

"Lord, Miss," Mary giggled. "What a sight you are!"

I could only imagine. Mary's freckles were lost in a haze of dirt that had settled on her face as we beat the dust from the pillows, curtains, and rugs. When it was almost playtime, I left Mary to it, took off the kerchief and apron, my hair blousy, and walked the moor path to the Lower Village, a basket on one arm and Uncle Tully's coat over the other.

But I veered from the path first, climbing the rolling hills, and found Davy's shallow hiding place. It was empty, but I placed the book about South America beside the little standing stone, draped with a protective cloth and a note tucked beneath its cover, along with a carrot I had pulled from Mrs. Jefferies's garden. Other creatures might get the carrot first, but perhaps not. I found the path again and followed it down to the village, my face warm by the time I reached it, but I was surprised when I got there. Doors were shut, windows shuttered, the dock quiet as I passed. I rang the little bell at the green-painted door, mystified.

After a few minutes, Lane opened the door and left it open, hurrying back out of the room as soon as he had. He was sweaty, dark tendrils sticking to his forehead. "I've left the . . . I've left something hot!" he called over his shoulder.

I came in and shut the door, hanging Uncle Tully's coat on a hook. *Lane must be melting silver*, I thought. I wished I could watch him, but I didn't think he'd like me to. I was unpacking my basket when he came back, wiping his hands on a greasy cloth. They were nearly black.

"Done," he said with satisfaction, then saw what I had set on the table. It was an old sherry bottle, corked. He frowned at it.

"Does my uncle like lemonade?" I asked him quickly. "The lemons came from the boat yesterday, and it's so very hot, I thought he might find it pleasant. But there was only this old bottle to put it in. I found it in the back of the larder. Empty. I brought cake as well." I began folding the rumpled blankets on the little cot where Uncle Tully slept, pretending not to notice the way Lane's shoulders sank in relief at the innocent contents of my bottle. "Where is everyone? There's hardly anyone about on the street."

Lane hesitated for a moment, then shut the door to the hallway carefully, so it wouldn't make noise. "There's been a death in the Upper Village," he said quietly. "Mr. Turner was sick in the infirmary. An old man, probably not long for this world, in any case, but he was found dead this morning, on the floor with a knock to the head. The committees are meeting, to discuss what should be done, and as anyone that wants to can attend such a meeting, I reckon they've all tried. But it's better if Mr. Tully doesn't know."

I glanced at the closed door. "He's in the workshop?" Lane nodded, coming to pick up the bottle, examining it once before reaching up to the shelf for a glass. I remembered Mr. Turner. He'd not liked the sight of me the day I walked by the canal with Ben Aldridge. "But surely he just fell?" I said. "If he was old and ill?"

"Probably. But there were some things missing from the infirmary as well, and a window had been broken. That's serious business. We don't have theft in the villages. Mostly people can get what they need without it. That'll have to be looked into." He paused, swishing the lemonade in the glass. "And just so you know, I've looked into that . . . into what you told me, about the room down from the kitchen, with the candles and the ornaments and such, and . . . I don't think you'll have to worry about that anymore."

"Oh?" I looked up. Lane was leaning back against the table, looking steadily into his lemonade, face flushing beneath the tan. I came to put the cork back in my bottle, though in truth I was only trying to look at him, to see this new color of his skin. Whatever might be causing his embarrassment I could not imagine, but I was enjoying our little pretense too much to risk the asking. So I only said, "Well, if you say it's fine, I'm sure it is, then." With everything else, I'd hardly given another thought to the room of the ornaments and that odd dinner anyway. The biggest threat inside Stranwyne, I had discovered, was myself. "But didn't you want to attend this meeting?"

"No," he replied. "Someone has to stay with Mr. Tully." He was still talking quietly, his voice low, and I was suddenly aware that he was right beside me, very still, and that the door to the hallway was shut.

"You could have left him with me."

"Yes. I suppose I could have." He was smiling, just a little. Neither one of us moved. "It's winding day today. You'll like that."

"I will?"

"Yes."

There was a pause. I stood with my hands on the basket, Lane not four inches away. "I thought winding day was on Thursday," I said.

"Thursday is for clocks. This is different." Then he said, "Are you getting tanned, or are you dirty?"

I looked up to see the gray eyes examining my face, which barely reached his shoulder. "I've been helping clean Marianna's library. For the party."

"I see."

"And I can't find my bonnet," I whispered. His lashes were so dark, and he was staring so intently at my nose that I thought he might lift a finger and touch it. I breathed deeply. I could smell sweat and smoke and metal and . . . Lane. If this was his idea of sugar, it was a very unfair one.

He had just begun to smile again when the door to the hallway opened. I turned quickly back to the basket, heart racing, feeling caught at I knew not what. Lane stayed right where he was, arms crossed.

"Hello," I heard Ben Aldridge say. I turned around.

"Good afternoon, Mr. Aldridge."

"And good afternoon to you." He came properly into the room and shut the door, a little tousled from the wind, I saw, and uncharacteristically unshaven. "You're looking rather well today, Miss Tulman," he said. "I think Stranwyne suits you." Then his gaze settled on Lane. "Mr. Cooper has examined the body and believes it was an accident, and the missing bottles have been found. Not stolen, just misplaced. So no need for Mr. Babcock. Burial this evening." He turned back to me and smiled. "It's almost playtime, is it not?

And I am doubly in luck. Not only has winding day fallen on my day in the workshop, but you will be there to see it as well. May I, Miss Tulman?"

He offered me his arm, and there was nothing to do but take it, and let Lane, his smile gone, follow us into the workshop.

CHAPTER SIXTEEN

Winding day, I discovered, came every thirty days, and was my uncle's time to wind all of his toys one by one, to make sure each was well and in working order. Uncle Tully was bouncing as he walked, beside himself with glee at my presence in the workshop, telling me about each toy in detailed, if rather disjointed, sentences. Ben walked with us, seemingly content though he was ignored by my uncle, while Lane hovered just behind, silent, again the protective shadow. But when I looked back over my shoulder, I saw that the shadows had lightened, the gray gaze fixed on my uncle, a small smile mirroring Uncle Tully's.

I was careful not to ask the wrong questions during our rounds, or to inadvertently touch, until, to my shock and delight, Uncle Tully asked if I would like to push over the dragon. I performed the task with enthusiasm, though not so much as to make another pile of scale painting for myself or Lane, while my uncle alternately plucked at his coat and clapped his hands. When Lane had spun the wheel that stopped the flow of steam and I was catching my breath, dabbing my neck on the sleeve of Mary's dress, I noticed that Ben seemed pensive. He rubbed his whiskered chin as the dragon's whirring hum was reduced to a click.

"You seem displeased, Mr. Aldridge," I remarked. I was flushed and happy.

"Oh, no indeed, Miss Tulman! The dragon is marvelous, isn't it? But the thought has just struck me that perhaps a mechanism that can keep an object perpendicular to the earth, can also keep another object parallel to it, like the fish. . . ."

I left him to his ruminations and watched the peacock spreading its tail, shimmering with turquoise and purple in the gaslight, and I smiled at the towheaded boy — who was not my father after all — spinning the toy top that never quite left his hand.

The toy that was Simon Tulman sat small and thin with salt-and-pepper hair and a large mustache, leaning sideways in a chair with one leg crossed over the other. I had never really noticed him before; he looked nothing like Uncle Tully or the figure of Uncle George. The crossed leg jiggled every now and again, a nervous habit that reminded me of my own tendency to rock on my heels, and he lifted a well-used pipe to his lips. I gasped and Uncle Tully beamed when the smoke blew from his lips. He had serious eyes, I decided, and perhaps sad ones. I asked Uncle Tully to wind him again, and while he was doing that I said to Lane, softly, so my uncle could not hear, "Where does he get the faces?"

Lane glanced once at Uncle Tully, who was talking to himself while he wound. "The porcelain ones are made at the pottery kilns, where they do the figures for the market."

"But is this . . . is it what they really looked like?" I was having trouble looking away from the face of my father.

"Have you never seen a portrait of your father?"

I shook my head.

"There's one in the house. I'll show it to you. But there are the portraits to be used, and Mr. Tully makes sure I don't have the details wrong. He has a very good memory for that sort of thing."

I thought of the life I had felt in the little silver statues in Lane's room. "You carve them, for the mold, and then you paint them?"

"Here he goes, little niece!" my uncle shouted. "Look, look!" The pipe rose to my father's lips. "Simon is thinking of what to do next! He is always careful about what he does next. You should be careful, too, little niece, in case it has not rained again!"

"What is he talking about?" Lane whispered.

"No idea," I replied, eyes on my father, thoughts on a moldering rain bucket in the gallery of the chapel.

"Lane?" my uncle yelled. "Lane! I hear a tick, a tick where it shouldn't be! Lane . . ."

Ready as always, Lane silently held out an oilcan, which my uncle retrieved at a trot, pulling up my father's trouser leg to fiddle with the gears.

"Monday is my uncle's time for trying new things," I said quietly, "and I thought perhaps . . ." But I had to look away, nose wrinkled. It was ridiculous to feel squeamish, but the way the oil ran, and the way Uncle Tully's fingers worked inside my father's leg, it was rather like seeing a surgeon use his knife. I felt Lane's gaze move to me and knew that he was amused. "I thought perhaps I would take my uncle and Davy to the old castle," I continued, "up by the water gate at the head of the canal. Mary says it's just a ruin, but I should like to see it before . . ."

I stopped myself. "Before I go" was a forbidden subject. "Would you come with us? I'd like to make a day of it, for both of them, but if something were to happen, if my uncle . . ."

Again, I left my sentence short, but Lane had known exactly what I meant, on both counts. He said, "You think you're going to get Mr. Tully to hike up to the castle."

"Of course. You think I can't?"

"I reckon you can, actually." Uncle Tully was leaning back now, his beard wide with satisfaction. Whatever had been amiss with my father was obviously corrected. "Oh, I nearly forgot," Lane said, digging down into his pocket. "Is this yours?"

I stared at the plain strip of white satin in his blackened hand. It was the ribbon that had held my nighttime braid.

"You don't usually wear ribbons, do you? But I couldn't think who else it might belong to. It was on the floor of the chapel."

"No, it's not mine," I lied.

"And have you tried the fish yet, Mr. Tully?" Ben said. The question had seemed to burst from him almost unintentionally, and I jumped at the sound. I'd almost forgotten he was in the workshop. "I wondered if the new cap I suggested, if there was less leakage of the air . . ."

My uncle moved willingly enough toward the water trough with Ben as I watched my father's movements slowly wind down.

Lane said, "It's a long walk out to the water gate, you know. There are lots of hills, with boggy patches in between if they haven't dried out. And Davy and I, we have ways of making our own fun up on the castle hill. All that to say, we're likely to get you a mite dirty. But I don't think you'll mind that, will you now?"

"Of course not," I said, lifting my chin. The last time Lane had used that tone I'd gotten more than I bargained for. But the game was different now. And the only thing that truly mattered was making my uncle happy.

I untied my wrist in the chill hour before Monday's dawn, too full of anticipation to sleep, and by the time the sun was peeking over the hills I had tidied myself and again put on Mary's old dress, leaving the corset in the bottom of my trunk. I hurried down to the kitchen for the basket of lunch I had packed the night before. It was a bit heavier than I'd anticipated. Resolving that Lane would have to be the one carrying it on our walk to the castle, I turned from the garden door and carried the basket through the house to the chapel instead. I pushed open the hidden door, ignoring the certainty of Uncle George's glass stare on my back, and stepped inside. The sounds of the clocks came through the walls, striking six of their seven morning chimes as I went down the stairs and began the much shorter, straighter walk through the tunnel to the workshop.

I made slow work of it. The basket was difficult to manage, but in truth, I dawdled, suddenly worried that in my eagerness not to be late that I would instead be far too early and catch both Lane and my uncle asleep. Davy might be there, though. He was an early riser, assuming he had understood the note I left him, and I had the feeling he would understand it quite well. His presence, or lack of it, would certainly confirm his reading skills to me one way or another.

I was thinking this, meandering around the tunnel's only curve, when I caught a glimpse of a man, a small, thin figure in a trailing coat, coming fast from the workshop end of the tunnel. I immediately stepped back again, out of view, stiff with surprise. I was not certain whether he had seen me or not, but I certainly had not recognized him. I waited until I could hear his footsteps, a soft, quick clip on the wet stone, and tried to think of what he might be doing here, and what I might say when he came around the bend.

The footsteps got closer, the clip becoming more of a slap that indicated a run, and then . . . he did not come. The tunnel was silent, and when I dared peek around the bend again it was also empty, nothing but the reflections of gas flickering in small puddles on the flagstones. I leaned back against the wall, heart beating hard in my chest. What if there had been no man? If he was just another phantom of my mind? I set the basket on the floor, hating myself for not being able to trust my own eyes, and moved quietly to the place I thought the man had been.

And about halfway there I saw something I'd not noticed before. The shadowy place between two sconces of gaslight was not a stone wall, but another opening, another branch of the tunnel not even a quarter as wide as the one I stood in, and unlit. I slipped inside and moved as fast as I dared in the darkness, trailing one hand along the damp wall, stepping lightly to keep my footfalls silent, though there wasn't much need. The floor here was dirt, not stone.

After only a moment or so, I heard the creak of hinges come echoing down the passage, and then the click of a latch. I hurried, one hand in front of me, now fully prepared when the passage ended in a door. I felt through the darkness for a handle or a knob, marveling that so far I had felt no fear whatsoever of the man. All I wanted was the sight of a body, to know that my mind had not lied to me again.

And I wanted it desperately. I pushed open the door just a little, and put one eye to the crack.

What I saw, to my shock, was the ballroom. The chandeliers were not sparkling, but a dim daylight came down through the glass cupola far above in the gardens, and there, making his way to the opposite end of the room, was a man. I held in my sigh of relief, and at the same time realized that he was not a stranger at all; I knew his twitching gait. It was Mr. Cooper, the surgeon. Then another mirrored piece of the wall opened, and Mrs. Jefferies's wide body filled the gap, beckoning. Mr. Cooper twitched his way through, and she closed the door quickly behind the two of them.

I waited for a few moments, then stepped into the empty ballroom to examine my door. It was not exactly meant to be secret, I decided — the handle was in plain view below the mirror — it was just . . . unobtrusive, as was the way to the kitchen. I'd never noticed either. But what business could Mrs. Jefferies have with Mr. Cooper?

There could be a medical condition, I supposed, or maybe something to do with the Upper Village. Or perhaps they were having a torrid affair. I shook my head. Whatever their reason, it could be no business of mine. I doubted Lane or my uncle would have been happy to know that Mr. Cooper was sneaking through the tunnels, but I could think of no reason they need know it from me. I shut the door softly and went to retrieve my basket.

"Come along, Uncle! Let's count steps!"

Once again the sun was climbing upward, yellow and hot, though the breeze held a slight promise of something cooler. I'd never known such a stretch of time with no rain, but today I was glad of it. Davy was beside me, his hand warm in mine, the sky was a bowl of blue, and Lane came behind us, carrying the basket and looking none too pleased about it. My uncle huffed and wheezed on my other side as we climbed the first hill, and it was taking all my powers of distraction to convince him that he was having a good time. Though I rather enjoyed that process, too.

"No! No, no!" my uncle was shouting, or as much as he could with his short breath. "It's a day for new things, Simon's baby! New things! Going to the castle is not new. Not new!"

"But you have never been to the castle with me, Uncle," I said serenely. "That is the new part." Uncle Tully appeared to be thinking about this, so before he could think any harder I began counting our steps at the top of my voice. "Seven, eight, nine, ten . . ."

"No, no!" he panted. "Not steps, little niece! It's too late for steps! You haven't counted the first one hundred and eight of them. Count hills! Nineteen hills by the short path, twenty-eight by the long, and when you take the short, it's twelve small and seven big ones, that makes nineteen, and . . ."

"One!" I shouted as we started our descent. "And how many rests do we take, Uncle?"

Uncle Tully trotted down the hill, the inevitable coattails flapping. "Three rests by the short way," he huffed, "five by the long, though Marianna liked six. Marianna liked six by the long. . . ."

"Two!" I shouted, swinging Davy's hand as we crested the next rise, happy to be doing something my grandmother had done, though I did look back at Lane over my shoulder, questioning.

"We're on the short way," he assured me, and sighed.

When we reached the bottom of number nineteen, my uncle sat himself carefully on the blanket I gave him while Lane threw himself down on the grass and lay there. Davy ran ahead, Bertram bouncing patiently on his shoulder. I took off my boots and tried to wipe away the mud — some of the little valleys had indeed been fenny — gave up, tossed them aside, and looked about us, shielding my eyes.

The "castle" appeared to be nothing more than one partial wall and a pile of varied stones on the top of a particularly large hill, the river water dancing below it in the sun. When I looked back the way we'd come, I could see where the river met the canal, a bit of stonework at the junction that I assumed must be part of the water gate, the mechanism that could close off the flow of the river. Beyond that, the hills rolled, fading away to mix with the sky. Stranwyne and the villages were hidden from me.

I turned at the sound of soft muttering and found my uncle sitting cross-legged, exactly as he did in the workshop, bits of fashioned metal he must have had secreted in a pocket already in his hands, being fit and refit together in some mysterious way. Lane lay still in the grass, arms behind his head, eyes closed, the red cap flung aside. I watched a small smile form at the sound of my uncle's chatter, but after a moment the brows came together and the smile fell away, an outward picture of some darker frame of mind.

And for exactly thirty seconds, I allowed myself to wonder what might happen in this moment if I were not Katharine Tulman or even one of those creatures of organdy in the park. If I was just a girl, like the ones Mary told me about — the ones who giggled about Frenchmen and had no responsibilities beyond their own hearth fire — would I go right now and sit down on the grass beside Lane? Or would I stretch out beside him, the sun full on my face, and cushion my head in that nook at his shoulder? If today were only one tick in a room full of clocks, unchanging and unhurried, would he let me make him laugh, put my hands in his hair, take away that lingering melancholy that I could see tingeing the edge of his thoughts?

Lane stirred in the grasses, and I looked quickly somewhere else, anywhere else, fully myself again. Katharine Tulman was not one of those girls. She was the clock, a clock that had lost its key, unwinding in the dark. And she had better make the most of the time she had left. When I looked up, I saw that Davy was up on top of the castle hill now, pulling something large, round, and flat from behind the ruined stone wall. I couldn't see Bertram.

"Not already," I heard Lane say. He was up on his elbows now, eyes on the hill. I turned just in time to see Davy sit on whatever it was that he had retrieved, give a scoot, and come flying down the long grass of the steep slope, the bottom of the hill gentling just enough to slow his speed and keep him from being flung headlong into a rock. My uncle clapped.

"Tell me," I said, raising a brow at Lane, "that is not how you and Davy 'make your own fun.'" But the slow grin on his face told me that it was.

By fifteen minutes before teatime, the sun was lowering and we were walking the hills again, much slower this time, counting backward until we reached the house, where my uncle could forgo the ordeal of walking through the village and take the tunnel to the workshop. I had more bumps and bruises than I could count, though my uncle informed me that I had slid twenty-eight times down the hill, and tumbled over on twenty-two of them. Evidently, steering a disc of polished brass while moving at high speeds down a grassy hill took skills I did not possess. I'd never had so much fun.

"Three, Uncle," I said, swinging both Davy's hand and his. *Uncle Tully must be very tired*, I thought, *to allow me to hold his hand.* "Should you like honey in your tea this afternoon?" My uncle chatted on about motion and wheels and something about spinning — nothing to do with honey — while Lane, the nearly empty basket balanced on one shoulder, held an armful of flowers I'd picked for my room, my mud-crusted boots swinging by their strings from the same hand. I had the most curious feeling then, stronger than my little flight of fancy when we'd arrived at the hill, and the very opposite of my first day in Stranwyne. Instead of moving backward through time, I felt as if I'd moved forward, and to a place that was mine, where all was as it should be. I breathed in the warm afternoon, kicked the grasses with my bare toes, and enjoyed every second of my lie.

I saw my uncle safely to his sitting room with his tea and toast, and hurried back to the house, thinking only of a bath and bed. I was flitting through the half-lit morning room, humming, when someone rose from a chair in the shadowed corner.

"Mr. Aldridge," I gasped, startled. He bowed, his brushed coat and trimmed whiskers making my half-pinned hair and Mary's grass-stained skirt — a condition I'd been entirely comfortable with seconds earlier — feel out of place even among the dirt and the dust sheets.

"Forgive me, Miss Tulman, but I was hoping you might come this way. I wondered if I might crave a moment of your time."

My brows rose slightly. But I came and sat on the chair he indicated with as much dignity as I could muster, placing my dirty boots on the edge of the nearest dust sheet, tucking my bare feet beneath the skirt, the flowers in my lap. Ben cleared his throat, straightened his jacket, and eventually sat opposite me, but then he only cleared his throat again, and remained silent. My spark of curiosity fanned into flame.

"Miss Tulman," he said finally, "I hope you know I only wish to be a true friend to you in every way."

I waited, my back very straight in the chair.

"I'd like to speak to you about certain . . . connections you seem to be forging with the servants."

Now my brows were at their full height. I waited again, but Ben seemed to feel that the obligation to speak was with me. "I'm not sure I understand what you mean, Mr. Aldridge."

Ben sighed. "Oh, come now, Miss Tulman. Everyone knows that you've been rolling about on those infernal wheel contraptions with Lane Moreau. It is forgivable, even harmless, perhaps. But day-long assignations? That is most . . . unwise."

Assignations? All at once my disheveled state took on new meaning, and heat came creeping to my cheeks. I tucked a wayward curl back into place, trying to think how I might explain myself with delicacy. But before I could, Ben took a slip of paper from his pocket and held it out to me. I unfolded it, leaned to the gaslight, and read:

Come to the workshop after breakfast on Monday,
and we shall have a day of play on the moors.
Katharine

Such a twist on my note to Davy was so ludicrous I might have found it funny if Ben's face had not been so grave. But when I opened my mouth to set his mind at ease, I found I had to shut it again. There was no name on this note other than my own, and Davy's ability to read was a secret most likely known only to myself. I dithered, thinking, and wondered suddenly if this rumor had anything to do with Mr. Cooper's visit to Mrs. Jefferies, Lane's aunt. My flush deepened, and I saw that both my color and hesitation had been well noted by Ben. I lifted my head.

"Mr. Aldridge, I am sorry you've gone to such trouble, and regret having caused you any discomfort, but the outing referred to in this note was also attended by my uncle and was meant as a particular treat for him." And with those words any little bit of amusement or even embarrassment I might have experienced gave way to irritation. How was it Ben Aldridge's business, in any case? "Where did you come by this note?"

Ben did not answer. He was leaning forward in the chair. "For Mr. Tully, you say? You say you took Mr. Tully out on the moors?"

"Certainly." It didn't seem that odd to me, but evidently it did to everyone else. "And Davy, too. As well as Mr. Moreau. We had . . . a lovely walk." I was not about to admit I'd been sliding down hills.

Ben got to his feet and walked to the dead hearth, where he stood gazing, apparently, at the soot stains. "Miss Tulman," he said, "I'll ask you to forgive me again if you find me forward, but . . . are your plans unchanged?"

I gathered my flowers and stood, Davy's note crumpling in my hand. "I don't know what you can mean, Mr. Aldridge." I knew exactly what he meant, of course. He meant did I intend to commit my uncle to a lunatic asylum and remove the means of living from more than nine hundred men, women, and children, including Lane and Davy. "My plan is to spend a quiet evening in my room, and to hold a birthday party in thirteen days' time. I hope you will attend. As far as anything else you might be referring to . . ." My back stiffened. ". . . as I have never had any choice in their formation or execution, I do not think it would be accurate to call those plans 'mine.' But you can be assured, Mr. Aldridge, that I will always act in a manner that is prudent for my own future. Good night."

I snatched up my boots and hurried away, out the door and up the stone stairs, not pausing until I was in Marianna's bedchamber, the door behind me locked.

I left the flowers on the dressing table and sat down on the cushioned bench where I could examine myself in the mirror, tilting my head this way and that. I had one or two new freckles, but other than that and some very unruly hair, I was unremarkable, the same girl I had been in London. But it had not escaped my attention that Ben Aldridge had just accused me of an "assignation," therefore implying that I was a girl capable of having such. When I got past my vexation, his naïveté pleased me. I tacked this pleasant lie onto my growing list of fantasies. When the morning came, I would have twelve more days.

CHAPTER SEVENTEEN

I spent my last twelve days not just living my lies, but reveling in them. Ben bore me no ill will for our disagreement, evidently, as he was in the garden the next morning, ready to walk me to the workshop, and at the workshop again in the evening, to walk me back again. I was polite, as always, friendly even, amusing myself by imagining what Aunt Alice or Mrs. Hardcastle might have said had I been one of their lady friends' nieces or daughters. How they would have bandied Ben's merits, pursing their lips over their sugar spoons, weighing his eligibility as a suitor.

I sat up late thinking of dishes that would be sufficiently party-like without stretching Mrs. Jefferies's cooking skills, and Mary made sure my list of needed ingredients made its way to the riverboats. In the workshop, I helped Uncle Tully build a tiny steam train, a miniature of the engine he wished to run back and forth between the villages of Stranwyne. "Little things become big things," he told me incessantly, and on Thursday we wound the clocks, systematically, rhythmically, and in the attempt to coax my uncle's smile, I more often discovered that he had coaxed my own.

With Mary's help, I washed, scrubbed, scoured, and beat every particle of dirt from Marianna's library. Both Lane and Ben came to help move the heavier furniture, and to evaluate what might be needed to make it an acceptable environment for my uncle. But all that had been seen to years ago by my grandmother, from the color of the walls to the box of toys found lurking in the corner, mostly gears and wheels and other metal playthings. I spent several late afternoons polishing each one, rubbing away the old oil and grease in Marianna's bathtub while Mary glued wallpaper back onto the library walls.

On the day I finished the last toy — a now-gleaming boat of tin — I ventured up to the garret in search of extra chairs, and instead found my missing bonnet. It was three stories up, outside a window that did not open, tied prettily by its ribbons onto an old flagpole that could only be reached by way of the roof and a narrow ledge. I broke the window as quietly as possible in the hours just before dawn, dislodging the bonnet with a broom handle, carefully giving no consideration to what I must have done to tie it there. Twice in that week, Mary insisted on dunking me in a cold tub, to "sober me up" she said, and I submitted meekly, though I'd only been happy, with no notion that my actions were strange.

And public opinion or no, I went rolling with Lane in the ballroom, telling myself that he knocked on Marianna's door because he wanted my company, that I longed for him to turn me faster and faster beneath the spectacular lights because I loved to spin, not because of the feel of his hands on mine. And when I caught a glimpse of those dark thoughts on his face, I pretended it was because he would miss me and had nothing to do with the irreparable harm I was going to cause him, cause all of them, when I left. I received two letters addressed in Aunt Alice's handwriting, and fed them both to the fire, unread.

The day before the party I baked biscuits and scones with Mrs. Jefferies, an activity she had reluctantly acquiesced to, I suspected, solely on a request from Lane. But no sour look of hers could weigh down my buoyant mood. She wore her dressing gown again, her usual apparel for the heat of baking, I'd realized, and just as the last of the scones had come out of the oven, Lane ducked through the open kitchen door, a wooden pail in his hand. I smiled.

"From Sam Jones in the Upper Village," he said, holding out the pail for me to investigate. "Or his mother, more likely. Said they were 'for the lady's birthday.' "

I peeked over the edge of the bucket. It was full of whortleberries. "How lovely! But . . ." I looked up from the bucket. "Who is with my uncle?"

"He's gone to his sitting room. I left Ben in the workshop, just in case, but Mr. Tully said good night, so I don't think he'll be going anywhere." Then he spoke very low; I had to lean close to hear. "Are you starting a new fashion, Miss Tulman?"

I looked up into the gray gaze, bemused.

"That flour on your forehead is so becoming, I reckon every girl in the village will be wearing it by next week."

I laughed, trying to wipe my forehead with a sleeve. How I loved this little game we were playing. I nodded toward his pail. "But what shall I do with them, do you think?"

Lane shrugged. "No idea. What do you say, Aunt Bit?"

Mrs. Jefferies looked up from the bowl she was scrubbing, at the two of us standing with the bucket between us, her frizzing hair sticking out all over her head. She muttered something unintelligible.

"What was that, Aunt Bit?"

"I said, 'tart'!" she snapped.

Lane's brows went up, but I merely continued to smile, choosing to assume that her answer was a reference to where the berries should go, and not to my person. Either way, it didn't really matter. "Tarts it shall be, then. Here," I pushed the pail toward Lane's chest. "A gentleman would wash those for me."

He folded himself down comfortably into a chair. "A gentleman," he said dramatically, propping his long legs, one over the other, on the table, "would do no such thing. As my old dad once said, *'Les messieurs avant leurs privilèges.'* "

I glanced at Mrs. Jefferies, who was rolling her eyes, and returned to Lane's rather smug expression. "All right, then, what does it mean?"

"It means," he replied, "that gentlemen take what they can get." And he popped a berry into his mouth, an action I responded to by flinging the flour still on my hands, which was considerable, at his head. He sputtered in a dusty cloud, and we played in a similar way until all the berries I could rescue were inside the tarts rather than him, and both Lane and the kitchen were a ghostly mess.

I went to the washbasin while Lane retreated to the garden to brush off his shirt and hair, and I was humming, still giggling to myself, rinsing off my hands, when Mrs. Jefferies said suddenly, "You remember I said I'd be making it hard for you."

I turned to look at her, my fingers dripping. She had been quiet as a church mouse while the two of us acted so ridiculously. Not participating, of course, but not hindering either. Now she was cleaning the knife I'd used to cut up the larger berries, polishing it slowly with a cloth, and it occurred to me that she'd made not one objection to my touching her things or coating them with flour. I'd forgotten in my distraction.

"You sat right there at my table," she continued, without looking up, "bold as brass, and I told you I'd be making what you'd come to do hard, just as hard as I could. Only I didn't have to, did I, Miss? You've done that all by yourself." She ran her cloth thoughtfully down the length of the knife. One, two, three, four times . . . "How you'll be living with it afterward is beyond me. I don't think you'll be wanting to, that's what I'm thinking."

I dried my hands, telling myself that what she'd said was meaningless, nothing, only vitriol and spite; meaningless, nothing, only vitriol and spite; over and over again, learning my lines like a school lesson. Surely there was not another soul in England that could delude themselves like I could.

"And what's that, then?" she asked, pointing with her knife. I looked down and saw that my sleeve was pushed up, clearly showing a row of green-purple bruises ringing my wrist like a bracelet. I had woken with them that morning, the knots in the sash of my dressing gown pulled tight.

"Oh," I said brightly, jerking down my sleeve, "I just caught my wrist in the door, that's all."

Back and forth went the cloth. "Caught your wrist?"

"Yes. Silly of me, wasn't it? Well, thank you so much for all your help, Mrs. Jefferies. I'll just go upstairs now."

I left her polishing the knife, a small smile on her face, and tucked her words into the back of my mind, where they need not be examined.

Mary waited for me in Marianna's room, but when I sat at the dressing table to unpin my hair it was her face, not my own, that held my attention in the mirror. Her forehead was wrinkled, her eyes downcast, her lips a long, thin line.

"I'm all upset, Miss," she stated unnecessarily.

I turned around to get a better look at her. It could not be the party. Mary had taken her exclusion not only with good grace, but with outright contempt at my thought of inviting her. A young woman of "her position," Mary maintained, did not attend her own mistress's birthday celebration. She was correct, of course, but it could be difficult to tell when Stranwyne's rules matched up with the rest of the world and when they did not. But Mary was standing in silence, and that could only mean something was seriously wrong. "Why don't you just tell me what's bothering you, Mary?"

She crossed her arms and her mouth pressed even tighter. "Well, since you asked me plain, I'll speak even plainer. It's your dress, Miss. It's ugly."

My mouth opened slightly.

"There's just no way to be dipping that one in sugar. It's a shame to wear it after all your trouble, and any good lady's maid would have been making you a new one, and I gave it a go, Miss, I truly did, but . . . I'm thinking you don't really want to be seeing it. Them old linens just wasn't . . ."

"Mary," I said patiently, "if a lady wanted a dress, she would go to a dressmaker's or, at the very least, hire a seamstress. The heavy sewing is not part of a lady's maid's duties." I watched Mary's solemn face committing this vital information to memory. "So in no way have you been remiss in —"

"Does that mean I ain't to blame? Because if it does I —"

"Yes, that's what it means. And second of all, you know perfectly well that I have a gray silk in the trunk that I brought for best."

"But, Miss!" I thought Mary might actually stomp her foot. "It's uglier, I swear on the grave of Saint Michael, it is! I'd see you pinning flowers on the one you're wearing before I'd let you go running about in that. And it doesn't suit! Even you know it doesn't suit."

"Well . . ." I bit my lip. A thought had come into my head long ago, but I had planned on leaving it there. "There is something . . . but I'm not sure I dare. It's not fashionable, or even appropriate. . . ."

Mary's hands were on her hips in an instant. "Show me."

I thought for a moment, then slipped my hand behind the dresser mirror and pulled out the key to the wardrobe. I felt very possessive of Marianna's dresses. They had remained in the wardrobe for so long, and their presence made me feel that she was not so far away. But when I inserted the key and turned, there was nothing to turn. The wardrobe door was unlocked.

I frowned. I'd made sure to lock it after the night I was ill, and found a new hiding place for the key. Mary could have come across the key, I supposed, but I was afraid to ask; I was afraid she would say she hadn't. I threw open the doors, breathed in the scent of lilies and cinnamon, and then Mary was beside me, her pressed lips now a line of grim determination at the sight of those shelves.

"Can we work on them, Miss? To make them fit? Can you sew?" She had a rose-colored silk down and was jerking at the buttons of my worsted before I could answer.

"I think they mostly fit already. But Mary, they must be thirty years old, even more, maybe. If I went out in such a thing in London . . ."

Mary jerked the worsted right off my back. "This is Stranwyne Keep, Miss, in case you haven't noticed where your own feet are standing. What have we to do with London?" She pulled the silk over my head and eyed me critically.

Before half an hour had passed, dresses of every color were spread over the room, an explosion of spring amongst the brooding furniture, and I had been dressed and undressed at least a dozen times. Mary pulled the blue-green gown from its tissue, and it fell in smooth waves from her hand to the floor, shimmering in the candlelight. She had it over my head in a trice, and we both stared into the mirror as I fidgeted.

"I don't know. It would be so foolish. . . ." The dress was more beautiful than I had remembered; I was more beautiful than I had remembered. But my heart sank at the thought of being in a room full of people and discovering myself to be the only one in costume. Mary clicked her tongue.

"The foolishness is in wearing the other one, Miss. If you try to put the gray thing on, I'll throw it in the fire. Just see if I won't. What else is in here?"

"Slippers in the drawer," I said, secretly pleased by her confidence. "And gloves and . . ."

Mary was stepping up onto the raised floor of the tall, closet-like side of the wardrobe to peer at the upper shelves, either unaware of the existence of the stepladder or ignoring it, when she shouted, "There ain't no back, Miss! There ain't no back at all!"

I turned a little half circle, trying to see over my own shoulder. "What are you talking about?"

Mary hopped back down to the floor, pointing into the darkness of the closet side of the wardrobe, motioning for the candle. I brought it and shone the feeble light into the interior. Where the planks that made up the back of the wardrobe should have been, three or four of them were gone, showing instead the panels of a door, the wood the same color as the wardrobe, nearly invisible in the dark. "It's the other connecting door," I said, amazed. "The wardrobe has been covering it up." I climbed inside, holding the candle before me. A brass knob gleamed in the light. I looked back at Mary. "Should we?"

Mary's response to this was both pitying and disgusted. "No, Miss, we should just be putting on our nightgowns and have a proper sleep without thinking no more about it. Go on, then!" She shooed me forward, and I turned the knob. The door swung into the darkness of the next room noiselessly. Mary climbed inside the wardrobe, grabbed my hand, and we clambered through together. "Coo," Mary whistled softly, hanging close on my free arm as I held up the candle.

We were in a nursery, just as dank and cobwebbed as my own room had been when I first came to Stranwyne, though somehow even more desolate. Three small beds were in a row down one wall, their mattresses moldering, and a high iron grate stood before a hearth that was long disused. I looked at the beds, wondering which one my father had slept in. Mary cooed again.

"If I was the ghost of a dead child, I'd choose here to be coming back to. Don't you think so, Miss, 'cause if —"

"Hush, Mary," I said beneath my breath. I had heard rustling when we first entered, but I couldn't hear it now. Mice, scuttling to their holes, no doubt. I took a few steps farther into the room, Mary attached to me like an extra limb, letting the light shine this way and that on tables, broken toys, a dresser, and a rocking chair. I lowered the candle. What I was seeing gave me pause. Unlike the dust that had lain so thick and regular in Marianna's room, whole sections of this floor were nearly bare of it. Mary finally let go of me to peek into a dresser drawer, and I examined the rocking horse beside it, running my fingers over the genuine hair of its mane. It was nearly dust-free. And then, in a corner, I saw something I thought I recognized.

"Good Lord, Miss! Be careful of your dress!" Mary whispered. "You don't want it clean all this time just to dirty it up now, do you?"

I straightened up from my perusal of the floor. What I was seeing was too large for a mouse, and even, I hoped, for a rat. Rabbit droppings. "Has Davy come through our rooms, Mary?"

"No, not that I'm knowing about, Miss. I —"

"And you keep your door to the library locked?"

"Of course, Miss, I told you I —"

"And my door to the corridor stays locked, doesn't it?"

"I think so. What are you . . . Lord, are them things from a rabbit?"

"I believe so. But how he could be getting in here is a mystery to me." We walked the room, but there was no sign of an entrance or exit other than the wardrobe door. I sighed. "Well, there's certainly no harm in it, but all the same, I don't want him coming through our rooms without our knowing. He's very good at hiding."

"That he is, Miss. He had to be, at the workhouse, if you take my meaning."

I had been making my way carefully back to the door, holding up my candle and the dress, but I stopped to look at Mary. "No, I don't take your meaning. Are you saying that Davy was in the same workhouse as you?"

"Oh, yes. Didn't you know that, Miss? He was just a slip of a thing, always trying to make himself small, so he couldn't be noticed. And they'd beat him, Miss, when he wouldn't do as they said, or answer back, or say his name."

I winced. If Mary had been nine years old at Saint Leonard's, then Davy couldn't have been more than four. I started for the door again.

"Mum was trying to help him some, but she couldn't be doing a thing with him, so she showed him to Mr. Babcock, and Mr. Babcock snatched him right up and brought him here to Mrs. Jefferies, and he took to her like fire — Davy, not Mr. Babcock — and so he's been since. She was the one deciding to call him Davy, I reckon. And she seems to know what he's thinking, too. Uncanny, that's what my mum says."

We stepped through the wardrobe and back into Marianna's room, which seemed like a haven of homeliness compared to the deserted nursery. "Well, let's make certain the doors stay locked, Mary, even if we just nip down the hall for a moment. It's no fit place for a child to play, in any case."

Mary waxed long in agreement to this, and when she had finally gotten me ready for bed and tidied up the room to her satisfaction, she ran off to bed herself. I shut and locked the wardrobe in my nightgown, then looked about, trying to think of a place that a little boy would never find a key. After some deliberation I placed the key in the center of an old chemise, rolled it up several times, then stuffed it into the very bottom of my trunk, beneath my corset, reasoning that my underthings should be more than a sufficient deterrent. I tied my wrist to the bedpost and went to sleep, thinking carefully of the blue dress and berry tarts and flour-streaked hair and nothing else. And the trogwynd sang loud that night.

CHAPTER EIGHTEEN

The morning of my eighteenth birthday broke with thunder. I untied myself, leapt out of bed, and threw back the drapes. Instead of the bowl of blue I'd seen every day since my carriage ride to Stranwyne, there was a ceiling of cloud gathered over the moors, low and thick. The grasses swayed a different shade of green in the dimming light, and in a wind that blew from the wrong direction. I smiled with satisfaction. The day was special.

It wasn't until I had pinned my hair and was lacing up my boots that I noticed the door to the wardrobe, sticking out just a bit farther than its fellow. I went to the door slowly, and tugged once on the latch. It swung open, silent on its hinges, showing me the empty space behind. I threw open the lid of my trunk and tossed out the gray silk, some handkerchiefs, and a bit of needlework I'd forgotten before I found the chemise, rolled up like a scroll beneath some stockings. I shook it loose, and the key to the wardrobe fell with a soft thud onto a rose in Marianna's carpet.

But I had no time to consider Davy's nighttime habits; there was too much to be done during the day. How did they manage it, I wondered, those women like Mrs. Hardcastle, holding regular gatherings for hundreds at a time? I was expecting a grand total of five, and every moment was taken, seeing to the last of the cooking and the fires, my uncle's striped cups, cutting flowers, and patching up a stray bit of wallpaper that had not taken to Mary's glue. But I delighted in the minutiae, gloried in every menial task. I wanted them to go on and on, and then the party could not happen, and the next day would never come.

And yet each task was accomplished in turn, and by half past six in the evening the library fire was cheerful, the biscuits and scones, jellies, sweetmeats, tarts, my dilled cucumbers, and a bowl of punch were arranged on a table along the wall, and every surface held a vase of daisies, hyacinth, and roses. The blue dress and matching slippers had been donned, and Mary was arranging my hair while rain, finally making good on its day-long threat, drove like daggers at the windowpanes. I fidgeted on the cushioned bench, nervous, every inch of me aching with remorse in my choice of clothing. Mary rapped me once on the head with her knuckle.

"Be still, Miss, or I'll have to be starting all over again!"

I just fidgeted more. The blue dress was so light and free. I had the uncomfortable feeling I was about to go to a party in my nightgown. "Mary, perhaps I should . . ."

"No!" Mary said, rolling her eyes. She shoved in one last hairpin and handed me a small mirror. "There now. Tell me what you think of that."

I turned away from the larger mirror over the dresser and looked into the small one, gazing over my shoulder at the back of my head. Mary had brought the front pieces of my hair into a loose knot just above my neck, strips of the matching blue ribbon twined all through, leaving the rest of my curls to fall free. Hanging from the many ribbon ends were bits of sparkle, glints of candlelight that radiated in the red-brown. I reached back to touch one. They were crystal pendants.

"Oh, Mary," I said. I'd never dreamed of having such a beautiful thing in my hair. "Wherever did you get it?"

"I made it, of course."

I touched one of the sparkling pendants again, and then dropped the mirror to my lap. "Mary. You didn't get these off a chandelier?"

Mary's eyes widened with innocence. "A chandelier! Of course I didn't, Miss! How could I be doing such a thing?" She busied herself with putting away the hair things, then saw me still watching from the mirror. "Well, they were coming off a lamp, Miss, if you must know. But I say they're looking right prettier where they are now."

I sat still in my chair while thunder rumbled softly, then caught up Mary's hand and squeezed it against my cheek.

"Good Lord, Miss," she said, pulling away. "I never saw a young lady needing so many lessons in how to behave." But I could see from the way her freckles stretched that she was pleased. "And anyway, 'tis your birthday."

She was right. It was my eighteenth birthday, an occasion that for many reasons would never come again. I was going to enjoy it, and never once think about tomorrow. I smiled at her, and went to check the fire before my guests arrived.

But when I came into the library, Lane was there already, standing at the hearth in a clean white shirt, frowning hard into the flames, no soot or paint or sweat stains on him. But I could tell from his stance that something was wrong. He was coiled again, pent up. He looked up at my entrance, as if he had intended to say something, but instead we did not speak. We merely stared, and I knew in that moment that the fullness of time had caught up with me. It was the twenty-ninth day, and our little game of pretense was over. I understood this just as clearly as if the words had been said, and the cold, empty void now spreading through my chest felt very much the way I had always imagined death. He took me in for a long moment, my dress, my bare throat, the pendants in my hair. Then he looked back to the fire, his jaw working in and out.

Finally he said, "I'll bring Mr. Tully up, but then I'm going to go. Until you've gone."

I nodded, and he met my eyes again.

"You aren't angry?"

I shook my head. How could I be angry? I wished he had waited until tomorrow to stop our pretending. Just one more day, for my birthday. But I could not blame him. I never had.

"Here," he said. He raised his arm, and in his hand was a small package wrapped in paper. I came to the chimneypiece and took it, pulling numbly at the knotted string, and when the paper fell away I saw the gleam of silver in the firelight. It was a swan, feathers shining dully from its perch on my palm. The wings were upraised, outstretched in sudden flight, and in my mind I could see the disturbance of water on a pond, a smooth, silent ripple flowing outward to the shore.

"You shouldn't give me this," I said, eyes on the swan.

"Why?"

"Because it's too lovely to waste."

"Waste?" Now he was frowning again. I could not see it, but I could feel it.

"On . . . nothing."

There was silence for a time, until the low voice said, "Do you really call it nothing, Katharine?"

I had heard him say my name once before, in the ballroom, and the sound of it had speared me then, too. And just as last time, my eyes were drawn upward almost against my will. I stared back into the gray gaze, surrounded by it, and as surely as I had understood not five minutes earlier that our game was over, I now knew with just as much certainty that Lane had never been playing a game at all. He had not been pretending, and God help me, neither had I. The room was still with only the sounds of fire and breath, while the entirety of my world shifted beneath my feet. And then he turned and left me, and was gone.

I spent ten minutes alone in the library, ten bitter minutes in which my indulgent games and self-delusions were stripped away, and I saw myself clearly, perhaps for the first time since my trunk had been dumped onto Stranwyne's weed-ridden drive. I closed my eyes, calm in despair, and held tight to the silver swan, feeling it radiate the heat of my own hands back to me. I was losing everything I held most dear, down to what I hadn't even known I possessed. I had thought to save myself, but of all the ridiculous lies, that had somehow been the true one. Leaving Stranwyne, destroying Stranwyne, was going to destroy me instead. There would be no saving of anyone at all.

When the first knock came at the library door, I stood, set the swan carefully on the center of the chimneypiece, and straightened my back. I could at least make this night happy for my uncle, no matter what sort of nightmare it had become for myself. But when I opened the door it was not Lane or Uncle Tully, it was Ben Aldridge, pleasant as always, bearing a bouquet and a bottle. I put on my smile. Pretending had become rather easy for me.

"Miss Tulman," Ben said, "a happy birthday to you. And may I say that you are looking very beautiful this evening."

Earlier I would have been relieved beyond measure at his compliment, mostly because he did not seem to find my choice of apparel shocking or odd; the comment on beauty I would have skimmed over as meaningless. But somehow Ben finding me beautiful was a concept much easier to believe now. I gave him a small curtsy, as if I were one of my uncle's toys.

"Thank you, indeed, Mr. Aldridge," I said. "Won't you come in?"

He came past me, removing a hat still dotted with rain, and I saw that Davy was standing in the dark of the hallway, his eyes on the floor, head resting on the rabbit that was clutched in his arms. Here was someone else I could make happy, even if it was only in a small way. I held out my hand.

"Come inside, Davy. Come on. Nothing to worry about. I have something for you."

He came reluctantly, and I led him around one of the settees to show him the rocking horse that Mary and I, at the last minute and with considerable trouble, had dragged through the wardrobe, cleaned, and pulled into the library. I bent down to his ear, my dress so unrestricted that the movement was easy.

"And you can play with it in here anytime you wish," I told him, "no need to come through my room at night. And it can be our little secret, if you like, like the book, and the hollow."

I straightened up again, frowning a little. I had thought he would be pleased, had so wanted him to be pleased. But the child's body was rigid, his hand stiff.

"Don't be frightened, Davy. Truly. I'm not angry. . . ." Then I looked at the hand in mine more closely. A patch of angry red showed on the area just below his cuff, little blisters in the darkened skin. "You've been burned," I said, bending down again to look at it. "Did you get too close to the stove? Did you show Mrs. Jefferies?"

But the blank look was back on his face, as if he were an empty mold.

"What a great deal of trouble you must have endured to make this corner of the house so comfortable, Miss Tulman," Ben said loudly. He was examining a watercolor of the moorland in the candlelight, the bottle and flowers still in his hand.

"Forgive me, Mr. Aldridge, I've forgotten to take your things." I left Davy staring at the rocking horse and hurried around the settee to take Ben's hat. Ben held out the flowers to me, and I recognized the wild beauty of his cottage garden.

"These are for you, of course, though I see I've only managed to bring you something you've plenty of." He smiled at the vase beside him, overflowing with Mary's decorative arrangements. "But this is something I dare say you don't have." He held out the bottle. "Claret, from the year 1802."

"It's French," I said, examining the label. "Wherever did it come from?"

Ben's grin broadened. "I found it, hiding in a sheltered recess of my dear old aunt's cottage. Put there for medicinal emergencies, I am sure." He winked. "Shall we open it? I can think of no better occasion. . . ."

A knock on the door stopped my reply. I set the flowers on the table, the blue satin swishing as I crossed the room. At the first crack of the door Uncle Tully shoved his way inside, jerking the latch from my hands, nearly knocking me down in his rush for the safety of the familiar room. Lane filled the rest of the doorway then, and I could not meet his eyes. He had done exactly as he said he would. And now he would leave, and I would never see him again. I wondered if my uncle could hear my broken parts inside, as he had with my father; I wished he could fix them.

"Lane, Lane!" my uncle was calling. He turned around and around in his own footsteps, clockwise, of course, looking at the library. "Come and look! Isn't it splendid, is it not right? Look at the . . ." Then, for the first time his bright eyes focused fully on me. He went still, and then he began to walk, his pace uncharacteristically slow across the rose-covered carpet, until he stood right before me, just a little too close. He leaned to the side, took a deep breath, and for a moment I thought he was going to kiss my cheek.

"Lane!" he yelled suddenly, very close to my ear. I jumped. "She smells just as she ought! Not like engine oil, but just as she ought!"

Ben chuckled and my uncle beamed, and then Mrs. Jefferies pushed past Lane and came huffing into the room, wet and obviously upset, but I had eyes only for her nephew. The tension was back in his stance, the sense of readiness to spring, his gaze leveled at the bottle of wine still in Ben's hands.

"God in heaven," Mrs. Jefferies was saying. "What do you think you're playing at?"

I tore my attention from Lane to see her small eyes narrowed at me, hands on hips, her lace cap lying limp and damp on her head. She was not just wet, I realized; she was soaking. Then her head turned straight to the settee, as if she'd heard a call, and whatever annoyance might have been on her face dissolved into instant relief. She barreled across the room to crush poor Davy into her dripping body, and my uncle charged with just as much purpose to the trunk in the corner of the room, where he threw back the lid on the box of toys. I stood where I was, bemused, until Lane's low voice came from just behind my shoulder.

"Let me explain," he said. "Aunt Bit has been running about the garden in a right state because she couldn't find Davy. She says Davy has stopped talking to her, and she's going to peck like an angry hen at anything that comes near her for the rest of the evening because of it. And you look so much like your grandmother standing in this room that I think it's enough to give anyone who knew her a start. And, I gather, that you have somehow managed to smell like her as well, a scent that is in no way like engine oil."

"It's the dress," I said quickly. "And how do you know what my grandmother looked like?" I was afraid if I let him stop talking he would go.

"Because I carved her face, remember? I know every curve of it. She was a child, but it's not that different."

I looked away again, wondering if that meant he knew every curve of my face as well. Uncle Tully had the toy boat out of the box and was doing something to it with a screwdriver, bright eyes eager as he chattered on about various combinations of the number eighteen. Ben squatted beside him, drawn like a moth to his flame, while Mrs. Jefferies was looking into Davy's unresponsive eyes, saying things to him I could not hear. I turned to the hearth, my breath coming short. There were many things to say, and perhaps only an instant to say them. The silver swan sat on the chimneypiece, wings raised, as if it were attempting to fly away. I raised a finger to the ridge of shining feathers.

"You must have worked for a long time to make this," I said. I felt him coil up again. He could not have known I would recognize the little statue to be of his own creation, and I could not explain why I did know it. But it was very important to me that before he left, he knew I understood. "When I look at it, I can feel it trying to fly."

"You would like to fly, I think. That is why it's yours."

Mrs. Jefferies's voice chopped through the room like a dull axe. "When are we getting to eat some of this? It's all stone cold, I'll warrant. And your fire needs tending. And can't you see this child is famished?"

I turned away from the swan, too numb even to be annoyed. It would be later that I would cry. "It's all meant to be cold, Mrs. Jefferies, and of course Davy may have something, and you as well."

Davy truly did look miserable. I came to the table and picked up a plate for him, but Mrs. Jefferies snatched it from my hand. "I'll be doing that," she snapped.

"Shall we open the wine?" said Ben, coming across the carpet. My uncle was still absorbed in the workings of the boat. I smiled, grateful for the interference.

"Yes, Mr. Aldridge. That would very nice." I turned to Davy. "Where is Bertram?"

Davy looked quickly around him, but his pet was only a few feet away, calmly gnawing out a hunk of chair leg. I lifted a napkin that had been draped over a plate of lettuce and greens and gave it to Davy, who favored me with the first, slight show of a dimple as he bent down to set the plate on the floor.

"Can I offer you a glass?" Ben said to Mrs. Jefferies as he pulled the cork.

"Never touch the stuff," she muttered, heaping her plate.

"Mr. Moreau?" he inquired over his shoulder.

"No," the low voice said.

Ben turned his back to the rest of the room. "Then it's just the two of us, isn't it, Miss Tulman?"

I looked at him curiously as the red-purple wine poured, with his brown suit and his boyish face with the side whiskers. Ben Aldridge was quite the gentleman. The gentleman that had walked me to the village and back and forth to the workshop, and had been jealous — yes, jealous, I decided — when I spent my time with another young man. I shook my head. How absurd to have only just opened my eyes. Properly encouraged, Ben might have rescued me from Aunt Alice. And I might not have even minded. Not that much. But I had ruined that as well. Now his saving would only be another kind of servitude; he could never compare with what I could not have. I stole a look at the long dark figure watching us from the hearth, still and tense, like a cat ready to spring as Ben handed me the wineglass.

If I were Ben Aldridge's wife, I could lie to Aunt Alice without fear of repercussions. There would be no danger of starvation on a

London street. But surely even I could not be so selfish as to saddle a man with a wife that was not in control of her wits. Or could I? If I could lie to my aunt, then Lane and Uncle Tully might not have to leave their home, not for a very long time. Or ever, if Mr. Babcock was correct. What would I sacrifice for that? Quite a lot, I decided.

"To your very happy future, Miss Tulman," Ben said, lifting his glass.

I smiled at him from beneath my lashes, feeling slightly ill as I did it. "Thank you, Mr. Aldridge." The expression coming at me from the hearth was disapproving, but I was careful not to look at him again as I sipped the wine. I'd never had claret, and could not say that I had acquired an appreciation for its taste, but Ben need not know that. I took another large sip. "May I help you to a plate, Mr. Aldridge?"

Eating took away some of the room's tension, I noticed; it gave both hands and mouths something to do. When I came back from taking my uncle his customary tea and toast, Ben handed me a dish of my cucumbers and we sat close together on the settee. I gave him my best false smile and ate every cucumber while I listened to him talk, feigning interest in his new position in London, and the house he hoped to acquire there.

I finished the wine, little pendant crystals tinkling as I tipped back my head, while Ben went to sit on the floor with my uncle again, observing with enthusiasm as Uncle Tully played with the boat. The room was very warm, stuffy even, but I smiled as I dabbed my temple with a napkin. My uncle was so happy; the sight of it made contentment ooze all through me. Lane still stood at the fireplace, not eating or drinking, and not leaving, either, just watching me like a statue of some gray-eyed Spanish god while wind and rain battered the windows.

And then several things happened at once. Ben jumped to his feet and took a step back, startling the room. He was staring at Uncle Tully's boat, which now bore some kind of mechanism with a spinning wheel in its middle. The boat was balancing perfectly, impossibly, on the point of its keel, falling neither right nor left on the carpet. Uncle Tully clapped his hands.

"Isn't that just so?" he shouted. "Isn't it right? For eighteen, and just as before. All just as it was before. . . ."

The door to the corridor burst open, and Mary Brown ran in, her hair wild and chest heaving so that she could hardly speak. She closed the door as quietly as possible behind her and leaned on it.

"Men!" she shouted in a whisper. "Downstairs! Two of them, Miss, wanting Mr. Tully. And one of them's the magistrate!"

CHAPTER NINETEEN

It took ten heartbeats for my mind to sort out what Mary had said. The magistrate. Uncle Tully. Aunt Alice. Letters, unread, burning to ash in the fireplace. The time of reckoning was not in some distant future. It was now. I got to my feet, still sweating, keeping one hand on the settee for support.

"I told them I wasn't knowing any Mr. Tulman and took off running but they followed," Mary panted. "And I think they heard me coming up the stone steps. If they did, they'll be finding their way in a lamb's shake —"

"Lane!" cried Mrs. Jefferies, but he had already moved to my uncle's side. Uncle Tully was shrinking against the wall, clutching his coat at the sight of Mary, while Ben stood with his hands at his sides, still transfixed, apparently, by the balancing boat.

"Come on, Mr. Tully," Lane was saying. "Playtime is over now. . . ."

"No!" Uncle Tully protested, now thoroughly panicked. "No, NO! It's isn't time, it isn't . . ."

"Lane!" Mrs. Jefferies pleaded. "Please . . ." Then she spun desperately about. "Where's Davy gone? Where . . ."

I hurried across the room and knelt before my uncle, Lane scooting over to make room for me. "Uncle, look at me." I waited until the blue eyes were able to fasten on my face. "That is Mary Brown over there. I told you about her once, do you remember? She likes toys very much. Don't you, Mary?"

Mary blinked like an owl at Uncle Tully, then nodded enthusiastically. I waited for my uncle's eyes to come back to me. "Take your boat into Marianna's room and show it to Mary. Wait for me there."

Uncle Tully's bright eyes were solemn. "I should wait?"

"Yes, Uncle."

"I think they're coming, Miss!" Mary hissed, her ear to the door, and my uncle's gaze darted fearfully to Mary.

"Should I do what the girl tells me?"

"Yes." That was an unexpected boon.

"Is this when the men come? Should I go to the tunnel if the girl tells me?"

I stared back into his serious face. "Yes, Uncle. But go to Marianna's room first. Do you understand?" My uncle nodded, picked up the boat, its wheel still spinning, and took Mary's arm as docilely as if he had done so all his life. They hurried away together through the connecting door, my uncle's coattails flapping.

"She got him ready," I heard Mrs. Jefferies whispering, "Great God above, Miss Marianna got him ready. . . ."

Yes, Grandmother, I thought, closing my eyes. *You got him ready so long ago because you knew it was inevitable. I hope you can forgive me for what I must do now.* Thunder rumbled, shaking the silent room. I hoped they could all forgive me, someday, for what I was about to do. I opened my eyes and tried to stand up, but had to grab the back of a chair to keep from falling. For a moment, the roses on the floor had gone out of focus. I felt sick. Lane took a step toward me, and then a male voice, a stranger's voice said the word *light* right outside the door. I straightened my back, still holding on to the chair, neck and forehead damp with the effort. The hinges creaked, and the library door opened.

Two men stood in the hallway looking in at us, their top hats and greatcoats speckled with rain. One was tall and clean shaven, the other much shorter and with the wiriest, bushiest blond beard I had ever seen. The tall one took off his hat.

"You'll pardon us, I'm sure," he said, "but no one answered the door, and we've had the most extraordinary time finding a servant."

No one spoke for a moment, and then Ben Aldridge stepped forward with his genial expression.

"Come in, gentlemen. We are very glad to welcome you. And do accept our apologies for your trouble. I am Mr. Aldridge. Have a seat by the fire."

"No, thank you, sir," said the man with the bushy beard. His voice was clipped, sharp. "My name is Lockwood. I'm a magistrate of this county, and this is Mr. Thomas Purdue, attorney-at-law. Take us to Mr. Frederick Tulman immediately, please. We've business that cannot be delayed."

An uneasy silence permeated the room. Mr. Lockwood turned his beard from face to face, studying each of us in turn, while the tall man, Mr. Purdue, eyed the proliferation of flowers. "Are we . . . interrupting something?" Mr. Purdue asked eventually.

"Come now," said Mr. Lockwood, ignoring the question. "We've traveled a long way through moor and storm, and I for one intend to do what we came for. We've a charge of lunacy to deal with here." His shrewd gaze moved to the food table, where Bertram was now perched, head down, finishing off my cucumbers. *That is exactly how they will look at my uncle*, I thought, like a specimen in a glass, an exhibit at the zoo. It made me angry.

"If you would take us to Mr. Tulman, please," said Mr. Purdue, his tone more apologetic, "we shall have the business over with as little trouble as may be."

"And who has levied such a complaint, sir?" I said a little too loudly. The eyes above the blond beard moved to me, and now I was the specimen. I had a vague notion that something about me was odd, something about no corset and a chandelier, but my mind would not grasp it.

"That information is confidential at this time, Miss," Mr. Purdue was saying. "The charges in this case are brought with the utmost regret, and only for the safety of the patient, of course. The party placing this charge has been promised complete anonymity."

"Oh, come now," Mr. Lockwood said again. "Look at the lot of them, Thomas. Like a den of thieves. Every soul in this room knows what we've come for. Why else did that slip of a girl take off like a jackrabbit? So, let's get on with it, shall we? We've been outrageously delayed, and if we don't leave in half an hour there will be no one awake to unlock the gates at Dr. Whitby's. At this rate the . . ."

Mr. Purdue responded to this, and then Mrs. Jefferies began babbling nonsense while the magistrate's beard moved up and down, and up and down, words blending together in a meaningless chorus. But I wasn't listening. I was clutching the back of the chair as if I would break it off, not just angry now, but shaking with it, consumed with rage. Alice Tulman lacked the courage to even use her own name. And these men had obviously already made up their minds, or she had made it up for them. Because my uncle had a different way of thinking, a view of the world they did not understand, and money that others wished to spend. For this they would lock him in a cell without even a proper examination. Lock him up like specimen.

And then, all at once, with none of my ordering or logic or even a moment of real consideration, I knew that none of that was going to happen. I didn't care if I lived out the rest of my life on a street corner, or picking rope in a workhouse, or died in a hedgerow. Aunt Alice's greed would for once go unsatisfied. Next year, next month, even tomorrow would have to come as it would, but that magistrate was not going to lay the first finger on my uncle. My voice rose over the hubbub.

"Excuse me, gentlemen, but I'm afraid you have made some sort of a mistake. There is no one in this house in need of your services. We have no lunatics here."

The noise died, and no one spoke, though I did see Mrs. Jefferies's mouth drop from the corner of my eye. I clutched harder at the back of the chair, driving splinters beneath my nails.

"Perhaps you have come to the wrong address? And if you are late, then please, do not let us delay you for a moment. Can I have someone show you the way out?"

I was still shaking, burning with fury, and I felt rather than knew that Lane now stood behind me. I stared back at the men across the room, and Mr. Purdue's face, very slightly, seemed to change its shape.

Mr. Lockwood removed his eyes from me and turned to Ben, whom he had evidently decided was in charge of this outlandish affair. "Sir, if you could kindly tell us where Mr. Tulman is, I would be —"

"Frederick Tulman is a respectable gentleman," I said very clearly, so they could understand. "In fact, some say he is on the verge of a peerage."

"That's right," said Mrs. Jefferies.

"No doubt it will come through in a year or two, but in the meantime . . ."

"Katharine." The voice came low from behind me, and my thoughts faltered at the sound of it. "Katharine, stand up straight. . . ."

". . . but . . . in the meantime, Mr. Tulman is just as sane as I am, no matter what my . . . no matter what Aunt Alice might have . . . might say about it. . . ."

"Are you, by any chance, Miss Katharine Tulman, young lady?" said Mr. Lockwood. I blinked at him. "Hmph," he said, "I thought you might be." He sighed and turned to Ben. "There's no use playing the gallant, Mr. Aldridge. If Mr. Tulman is here, let's see him at once and have this business over with. We've a very competent doctor waiting in —"

"But she told you," said Mrs. Jefferies, "there ain't a thing wrong with Mr. Tully . . . Mr. Tulman."

"Uncle . . . Mr. Tulman isn't at home," I said slowly. My head was spinning, and I was so hot, I could hardly breathe. "Mr. Tulman . . . went on a trip, a very long trip. . . ." An arm snaked around my middle, and I felt a body against my back, the only solid thing in the room.

"There seems to be some sort of confusion here . . ." Mr. Purdue was saying.

"I'm not confused about anything, young man," replied Mrs. Jefferies. "How about you?"

I could feel the nightmares creeping on the edge of my mind, and my fingers were burning; they were on fire. I was sweating with the pain of it. I clung to the arm around my middle.

"We want to see Mr. Tulman about a charge of lunacy . . ."

"Stand up," the voice was whispering in my ear. "My God, Katharine, stand up. . . ."

". . . not for himself, of course. The charge of lunacy is . . ."

The fire was on my legs now, too, crawling upward with pricking feet.

". . . against his niece, Katharine Tulman."

Lunacy. Against his niece, Katharine Tulman. I remembered now. Katharine Tulman saw things that weren't there. The arm tightened around me.

"Good heavens, John," said Mr. Purdue, "she's raving now. . . ."

"She's drunk," said the low voice. I tried to brush away the fire. It hurt, like bugs, little stinging bugs. . . .

"She's raving, I say."

Hands were trying to hold on to mine, but I had to get the bugs away, to brush them off. They were hurting me, crawling up my neck, making my breath come short.

"There now," said Mr. Lockwood. He was very close. "Let me have her, son, so she can be kept from harm. . . ."

"No!" I yelled, though I could hardly breathe. "Let me . . . make them . . . stop. . . ."

I opened my mouth again, but there was no more air. I reached out an arm, and then an earthquake began in my own body. I shook, violently, overpowering the restraining arm, and I hit the floor hard, my teeth clacking together beyond any control. I tasted blood, and heard my name, and voices, and somebody shouting, "Doctor!"

Then a man yelled, "Look at the animal!"

My eyes flew open and through the shuddering world I saw Bertram on the table among the sweetmeats and the tarts. His legs dragged oddly behind him, his mouth white and frothing, as if he'd been eating cream. A pistol appeared from Mr. Lockwood's jacket, leveled, and a brief flame spurted from its end, etching the air long before I heard the explosion of the shot. And when the sound did come, it came from very far away. I closed my eyes, and felt myself sink into a pit.

CHAPTER TWENTY

I was trapped in a box, weighed down so I could not move or see or hear, only think, and even my thoughts were vague and disordered. The weight pressed on my chest, there was no air, though there was pain in my very center, both burning and sharp, and I could do nothing against it, not even groan or curl up my knees. I could only know that it was, and endure. When the silent hurting became more than could be borne, the heavy box around me flipped and was turned back again by forces that were not my own. I thought maybe I was vomiting, but that, too, was beyond my control. And my pain ebbed, the weight in my chest eased, and there was quiet, a deep, tired quiet, where nothing existed but darkness, myself, and my box. I lay still inside it.

After a time I heard things, noises creeping to me: the squeak of a floorboard, a door latch, water in a glass. I heard the rough sound of Mrs. Brown, and the answering voice of a man I did not know. And I heard my name, many times, said low and soft to my ear. My breath came deep and content, and very slowly, I slipped away.

When I woke, Marianna's room was full of gray daylight, the kind that only comes from an afternoon soaked in heavy cloud. There were one or two candles lit against the dim, but the rest of the room was in gloom. I studied this for a few moments, then the pink fabric canopy draped far over my head. When I had examined it thoroughly, I moved my gaze again and discovered Mary, her round eyes red-rimmed.

"What happened?" I asked, but I was weaker than I realized. Mary frowned and scooted forward, leaning close. I tried to speak louder. "What happened to me?"

"You had a fit, Miss," she whispered, "in the library, while the magistrate and the solicitor was here. They would've been taking you away right then, only you fell on the floor and shook so, and then the rabbit had a fit, too. Then you went still and we thought you was dead, but he poured black stuff in you and made you puke and . . . you was lying there so still. . . ." She took my hand and patted it. "We've sent to Milton, but the rain is so bad the doctor ain't come yet."

I tried to piece together Mary's story with the incoherent pictures that I thought were memories, but I was so tired. I shut my eyes.

"Don't go to sleep again, Miss! Can't you speak a bit more? Can you take some water?"

Mary's distress made me instantly guilty. I opened my eyes again and with much effort asked, "Who is 'he'?"

"What, Miss?" Her freckles were screwed up in concentration as she strained to listen.

"You said he made me . . . made me . . ." I was hoping she would understand, because the words were almost all I could manage.

"Oh!" Mary's face brightened with understanding. "Him is him, Miss," she said confusingly.

I sighed, and went to sleep.

When I woke again the windows were dark, there was fire and candle, and I realized that it must have been raining before only because the sound was now gone from the room. Mary's mother sat asleep in my chair, mouth hanging open unceremoniously as she snored, but other than that and the hearth crackle, the room was very quiet. Experimentally I moved my arms, relieved to feel a little life in me, sat up, waited for my head to clear, and swung my feet over the edge of the mattress. I padded unsteadily to the bathing room, noting that I was still in my grandmother's dress, now thoroughly crumpled, shut the door, and when I returned Lane was in the shadows, sitting on the far edge of Marianna's bed.

I did not wait to notice whether Mrs. Brown was still asleep or to think of more proper clothing. I was not sure how much longer I could stay on my feet. I climbed into the bed in the blue silk and snuggled down beneath the portion of the coverlet that Lane was not pinning down with his weight.

"How do you feel?" he said.

"A little tired," I whispered. I was exhausted.

We stayed that way for several minutes, Mrs. Brown snoring, Lane utterly still, me settled deep into the pillows. But it was my body that was weary, not my mind. My mind was adding and subtracting, trying to order a set of jumbled events into a logical row. Lane. Party. Marrying Ben and saving my uncle. Magistrate, a man with a twisting face, fire in my insides, and flame from a pistol. Pain and then stillness. Words in my ear, and, I think, a hand in mine. How I wished I knew what had been real.

"Am I ill?" I asked finally.

"You were poisoned," Lane replied.

I frowned, trying to understand this idea.

"Mr. Cooper agrees," he continued. "But we're waiting for Dr. Metcalfe from Milton. And we've sent for Mr. Babcock. The rain has swollen the river, and some of the moor road is washed out. But it's stopped now."

I nodded, though I wasn't sure he could see that in the flickering dark and with the blankets pulled up to my chin. I thought of what Mary had said. "Did you make me . . ." I struggled for a more genteel word. ". . . make me get rid of it?"

"I gave you ipecac and made you vomit."

"What sort of poison was it?"

"Mr. Cooper doesn't know."

"But how did I . . . Where was it?"

"Bertram ate the cucumbers, and he got sick, too."

I remembered the world shaking, and the explosive sound that had been so long in coming to my ears. "Did someone shoot Bertram?"

"Yes. Mr. Lockwood thought he was rabid."

I closed my eyes. "Where is Davy?"

"Aunt Bit can't find him."

"Does she know where to look?"

"Yes, I told her."

"He'll come back," I said, though I was not sure it was true. I could hear Lane's breathing, hard and fast, and then I understood that all his calm words had belied the fact that he was angry, very angry, in a fury only just held in check. I took my arm from the blankets, reached across the bedclothes, and found his hand. He let me take it, letting out a long, pent-up sigh. The familiar warmth made me think that some of my dreams had been real. "Where is my uncle?" I asked him.

"Hidden. Purdue left, bad roads or no, but Mr. Lockwood is still here. We're putting him in the Upper Village until he can leave safely, but I don't think he'll go even then. We told him Mr. Tully was upset by what happened and is ill as a result, and that you were ill and still are, but the man's not an idiot. The rain has kept him indoors, but that's over now. He'll be about tomorrow, asking questions. Ben is with Mr. Tully at the workshop, and we've men looking out. He'll get Mr. Tully into the tunnels if Mr. Lockwood comes around. Mr. Tully doesn't . . . Aunt Bit told him you were tired from your birthday, and that the bad men were gone away. He doesn't know."

Ben was keeping my uncle hidden. If I married Ben Aldridge, he would help me continue that process, I was certain of it. I looked to the dark shadow sitting on the edge of my bed. I had to do it. I would do it. For Uncle Tully, and for him. I felt empty inside. Lane swung his feet onto the bed and lay back against the pillows, one arm behind his head, our hands still between us.

"You lied for us," he said.

"Yes." I shut my eyes again, to better feel his closeness.

"And what will happen to you now?"

"I will be cut off when my aunt finds out."

"Can you come back here, if that happens?"

"There will be no 'here' if that happens." I listened to the fire spitting sparks at the hearth.

"You weren't drunk at the party."

"No, I don't think so."

"Have you . . . ever been drunk?"

I thought carefully before answering. If I spoke honestly, then there would be nothing left for him to know but the truth, that Mr. Lockwood had good reason to take me away. I took a deep breath. "No. I never have."

He did not speak for a time, and when he did, the low voice was very quiet. "How often does it happen?"

"I don't know." My stomach was writhing, having to admit these things. "Sometimes."

"Why didn't you tell me?"

"Better to be drunk, than . . . than . . ." I left the thought unfinished. "But they still have to think it. That I was drunk. They can't know, I don't want any of them to know."

Lane sat quiet, thoughtful, the tightness of his hand unchanging in mine. "Someone sent those men here to take you," he said. "And someone poisoned you. Why both of these things?"

I opened my eyes again. "I don't know. I don't understand any of it." Strangely, I'd accepted all the facts presented to me without once considering that someone, someone who knew me, must be responsible for them. "Do you know . . . who?" I asked.

"I was hoping you did."

And then, like fitted cogs that intermesh, my thoughts came together, and I did know who. There was only one person who hated me so thoroughly, and would have done anything, I believed, to keep me from ruining Stranwyne. "It was Mrs. Jefferies," I said. I felt Lane stiffen.

"What do you mean?"

I remembered the sheer spite in her eyes the night before my birthday, when she had said I would not want to go on living. And she had known I would eat those cucumbers. "It was her. She poisoned me."

"You're wrong."

"Who else, then? You? My uncle? Ben Aldridge?"

"We need to talk about Ben Aldridge."

"Yes," I said. "We do."

He caught my tone, and turned on his side to better look at me, brows down, the gray eyes level with our interlocked hands. "Why?"

"Because . . ." I looked away. "Because I've thought of a way . . . to fix this."

"Have you now? Took you long enough."

"And what does that mean?"

"It means that Ben Aldridge would marry my aunt Bit if he thought it would get him closer to Mr. Tully."

And I would marry Ben Aldridge in the blink of an eye to keep Lane and my uncle safe at Stranwyne. The thought made me glad and sick at the same time. Someone, at least, could be saved, even if it wasn't myself. When I found the courage to look up again it was to an expression I knew well: dark, brooding, and with a thunderstorm brewing, a look I'd seen many times in my first days at Stranwyne. I tensed, as if anticipating a blow.

"Do you really think," he said to me, "that you can run off to London and be Ben Aldridge's wife, and that somehow, in some miraculous way, that everything will come out right in the end?"

I did not answer.

"Ben Aldridge might protect Mr. Tully for the sake of his toys, but do you honestly think that he will take that much care of you? Do you truly think . . ." His words were rising like the wind. ". . . that you can leave here now, and that nothing will change? That everything will just go on being the same as it ever was?"

I had nothing to say. Keeping Stranwyne unchanged was the very best I could hope for. I could feel his clouds growing thicker, churning.

"Well, it will not be the same, Katharine. Not for all of us . . . Not for me."

I lay very still. His words made tiny fractures run all through my insides, like the minute cracks on the parson's face. My uncle would be free, and Lane, and the people of the villages would have their homes. This I could give them, and whether Lane knew it or not, it was an infinitely better gift than my shattered self. He sat up suddenly. "You're going to do it, aren't you?"

"Yes," I whispered. I felt ashamed, though it was all for him and Uncle Tully. But I had not been prepared for how fast or how violently his storm would break. Lane had flung away my hand and was on his feet before I had drawn breath. He leaned over the bed, his fists sinking down into the mattress.

"Well, go on and do it, then, Miss Tulman. I won't be stopping you. As you told me once yourself, there's nothing here at Stranwyne that actually belongs to me. Enjoy that fine new house in London, down to your last miserable bloody breath!"

I was hurt, exhausted, heartbroken, and poisoned, and all at once, in a flaming temper. I spat out the words. "If you are so eager for my misery and death, Mr. Moreau, why don't you consult your aunt? She could offer you some excellent advice on the subject, I'm sure!"

The look that was his response to this made me wish I was dead already. He straightened into a shadow I could only just see, melting away, and then the door to Marianna's bedchamber slammed, shaking the room and the pictures on the walls. I buried my face in the pillow.

"Well. It's been nothing but smooth sailing around here since you walked through the door, Miss, that's certain. But a hot temper is a good thing, in my book. People don't die when their blood's up."

I turned my tear-streaked face toward the hearth, where Mrs. Brown's eyes were bright and snapping, not a trace of sleep in them. I tried to remember the last time I'd heard her snore, and couldn't.

"A piece of advice to you, Miss. One and one don't always add up to two, and you can't be making it do so. And if I was you, I wouldn't be eating the first cucumber, or anything else for that matter, 'less it comes from my Mary. There. That's two bits for you, and all for the price of one."

I turned my head back into the pillow, right into the wet spot my tears had left. Mrs. Brown spoke from close beside the bed.

"Here, Miss. Have some soup, then. You're as pale as the linens."

I looked up at her in surprise, then at the bowl in her hand, and shook my head. She smiled.

"And that's the first sign of sense I've seen from you, Miss, if you don't mind me saying." She sat on the edge of the mattress, a bowl and spoon in her hand. "But I can swear that there ain't been a touch on this but my girl's own hand, and it came straight from my cottage, every bit. Been keeping it warm for you, too." She offered up the bowl. "You will have to eat, Miss."

I looked into her round, plain face and decided that if Mrs. Brown was an assassin, then the world was no fit place to live in anyway. I sat up, and let her feed me.

CHAPTER TWENTY-ONE

When I opened my eyes, the trogwynd was lowing, eerily soft, and Davy stood next to my bed. The fire was out, the room was black, and his face was the only thing I could see, illuminated by a wavering light that set his features in motion. The windows of his eyes were shuttered, telling me nothing, and one small hand was extended toward me. I took it without hesitation, without question, and we moved in silence, both of us barefoot on the carpet, in a pool of flickering glare that came from a lantern held in Davy's other hand, the hand that was burned. Mary Brown slept by the hearth, and the wardrobe door stood open. Without letting go of my hand or disturbing his light, Davy leapt lightly inside and turned back to look at me, waiting. I lifted my foot, and stepped inside the wardrobe.

Through the door and across the rotting rug of the forsaken nursery he led me, sending mice scuttling for the shadows, and on the far end of the room a piece of the wall swung open. I saw that it was not a wall but a door, paneled and papered to look just as the rest of the room, as the doors to the ballroom had been, and then we were in another bedchamber, picking our way through rubble where the ceiling had given way to damp. Out to the corridor of the portraits, the light briefly trailing its beams over the face of my guardian, Davy took me, ghostlike, to the stairs and then downward, into the lower reaches of Stranwyne.

Around and through, his hand guided me, past the kitchen and into the room of the ornaments — there was no fire there now — and out the door to an unkempt corner of the garden, mist and moonlight setting it aglow. The rusting door of the iron-and-glass greenhouse creaked, and my feet touched potsherds and crumbling leaves, edges of broken panes glittering sharp, as Davy set down the lantern to pull an iron ring attached to the floor. A trapdoor opened, and he picked up the lantern and put his dirty foot on a stone step that led into the earth. For the first time I resisted, but when he turned and looked up at me, pleading, I realized that the round cheeks and long-lashed eyes I'd seen so many times were not really a child. They were only the mask of a child; beneath the exterior, Davy was like an old man. I took his hand again, and descended.

This tunnel was narrow, low, and wet, built mostly of dirt with some reinforcing wood and stone, smelling strongly of earth. I went at a crouch, my unbound hair brushing both the roof and the walls, feeling for the first time the weakness of my body on this strange journey; my legs shook long before we reached another set of stairs. The steps led up to a hole in the ground, and Davy held aside a screen of hanging vines to let me crawl out, gasping, as I was finally able to stand upright. We were in a garden, the white walls of a cottage rising very close, light spilling from all of its windows.

He let me rest for a moment, among flowers that swayed on long, untended stems, then the grip on my hand became tighter, and he pulled me silently to the door. We entered an ordinary cottage, not very tidy, and with an odd smell in the air, sweet with an underlying bitterness. Clothing was strewn about here and there, the hearthstone needed scouring, and unwashed dishes were scattered upon the table. One of the windows was propped open with a boot, and then I knew where I was. This was the cottage of old Mrs. Daniels. Ben's cottage.

"Davy," I whispered, speaking for the first time, but he only tugged on my hand and hurried me to the stove. The bittersweet smell was stronger here. Davy set down the lantern, took both my hands, and laid them on a pot that was covered in a sticky brown resin. I protested at the unpleasant touch, but he lifted my hands and had me smell the strong odor, the same that was already in the air.

Then he opened a cabinet, almost frenzied in his hurry, and took out empty glass bottles, handing them to me one by one, removing the tops and putting them below my nose to note the corresponding smell. "What is it?" I asked. He turned the bottle so I could see its label. LAUDANUM. Then he took my fingers and put them in a dish of brown sugar. He held my fingers up to my nose, then put them against my own lips. I tasted the sugar and caught a hint of the odor I had smelled. It was vaguely familiar. Like Stranwyne's tea. "I don't understand," I whispered.

But he only picked up the lantern and pulled my hand again, taking me to the back of the cottage where another door led into the earth, though this time with wooden steps instead of stone. We stepped down into a cellar and, as we descended, there was another smell, different from before, acrid and horrible, what I had smelled once before on Ben Aldridge, only many times stronger. I put my hand over my nose, and then we were at the bottom of the stairs and inside a small workshop. It was much more rudimentary than my uncle's, even I could see that. There were a few tables, bottles, and tools, and, to my surprise, the boat my uncle had been playing with at my party, on its side now, the new wheel in its middle.

But even as I took all this in, my eyes were drawn to a workbench in the center of the room, where a replica of my uncle's fish lay propped in the air across two metal stands. It was larger than the original, and without any of the realistic touches provided by Lane's painting. A panel hung open on its side, showing its cog-and-gear guts.

Davy brought me to the workbench and held up the lantern carefully, as far from the fish as was possible, took my hand and placed it on the metal skin. He ran my fingers along the sleek body, asking me to feel all the way to the machine's metal snout. And I found the difference. There was a joint where my uncle's had none; the head of this fish was a separate compartment.

I tried to move his lantern hand closer to better see, but he held the lantern away and, instead, placed my fingers into small pile of fine, cotton fluff. He had me take a piece of the fluff and put it to my nose, but I pulled my face away. It stank, like the cellar. I looked to Davy again, asking as silently as he might have, and with the fluff still in my hand, he led me to a corner, so extremely careful with his lantern that I had to crouch down to see.

There was a jagged hole in the dirt floor, nine or so inches deep in the middle, splaying out for perhaps two feet in width. I touched blackened scorch marks on the wall stones. His large eyes solemn, Davy took my hand with the fluff and had me set the cotton in the center of the hole. He turned his arm, showing me the burn on his wrist, let me ponder this for a moment, then led me back to the workbench, placed my hand on the metal snout of the fish, back to the cotton fluff, and then back to the fish.

My forehead wrinkled. I knew Ben was intensely interested in the workings of my uncle's fish, particularly in its method of holding depth. But why build this one with an extra chamber? And if Davy was trying to show me that this cotton had somehow caused that hole in the floor, and the burn on his arm, then was the cotton somehow like gunpowder? Did the cotton explode? I looked again to his lantern, this time in alarm, and then a door closed above us in the cottage.

Footsteps moved, a fine mist of dust raining down from the ceiling that was also the cottage floor. Davy's hand left mine, and he shrank instantly beneath the workbench, his lantern chasing the shadows that had gathered below it. A moment later the light was blown out, Davy could no longer be seen, and I stood where I was in the darkness.

The footsteps were hurried. I heard water being poured and then the clink of glass and plates. It sounded as if Ben were tidying up. I slid down to sit in the dirt on the floor, my legs no longer able to support me, the horrible odor in the workshop not just a smell but a taste in my mouth and a burn in my lungs. I wondered if I had the strength or the courage to climb the cellar stairs, and how I might explain my presence without implicating Davy. Perhaps I should join the child under the workbench? Or perhaps Ben would leave the cottage without coming to the cellar at all.

The cellar door opened, and light poured down from above. I glanced at the workbench, relieved to see that the darkness beneath it was still impenetrable, and when I looked up again, blinking, Ben Aldridge was on the stairs with his own lantern and his usual grin.

"Miss Tulman," he said. "I am honored. And I had thought you confined to your bed."

He came farther down the steps, dragging a large wooden crate with his other hand. I opened my mouth, but could find nothing to say. I used the table behind me to pull myself upright.

"Please," he said, "don't trouble yourself." He tossed the crate onto the floor and set the lantern on another workbench, well away from the cotton. "I do apologize for the smell. It's terrible, I know, but other than that, how do you like my little workshop? It's nothing to your uncle's, of course."

"It's very nice," I said slowly.

"And this?" he asked, stroking the spine of the fish. "Lacking the more attractive aspects of the original. But a much more functional machine, to be sure."

"What is it for?"

His eyes crinkled, and he hoisted his crate onto the workbench. It was full of sawdust. "Tell me, Miss Tulman, how are you feeling? Any lasting effects from your party?"

"I am . . . tired."

"But not too tired for a jaunt to my cottage in the middle of the night? Not that I mind, Miss Tulman. And not that I don't know exactly who brought you here."

I had completely forgotten it was the middle of the night. The journey from my bedchamber had had such dreamlike quality, so much of my life lately had had such a dreamlike quality, it was just now dawning on me that all this was real.

"But really, Miss Tulman," Ben chided, "you truly are a sight. Quite wild. What would Mr. Lockwood say to such behavior? As a friend, let me advise that you can scarce afford any more oddities at this point. That man is ready to cart you away."

My brows came together. "But I was poisoned, not . . . Mr. Lockwood will know I was not . . ." I couldn't bring myself to say it. "Mr. Cooper will have told Mr. Lockwood so."

"But what about your other escapades?" Ben came around the workbench to stand right in front of me, his boyish face inches from my own. I looked away. "About nighttime ramblings and self-inflicted wounds, and a certain balancing act in the chapel?"

I did look up at him then, this time in horror.

"Those are not the acts of someone capable of maintaining her own welfare, Miss Tulman. And I'm sorry to tell you there has already been a document signed to that effect, and by our surgeon, Mr. Cooper. Mr. Cooper states that while you have extended periods of lucidity, such behavior as this, and the unfortunate episode you suffered right before Mr. Lockwood's eyes, are all symptoms of a chronic mental condition, indicating that you are a danger to others as well as yourself. He didn't mention poison, I'm afraid."

I was thoroughly awake now, but with the thrills of fear I'd come to associate with my nightmares. Mr. Cooper didn't mention poison. Of course he did not. For all he knew, I was about to take his home away from him.

"Can you deny that you did these things, Miss Tulman?"

I could not deny it, and somehow Ben knew. "They'll tell him it's not true," I countered.

"Who will?" His face was very close.

"Mary, and . . ."

"I don't think her opinion will hold much weight. And if you were going to mention a particular young man, I think a servant to whom you've show a certain . . . licentiousness of behavior would be quite likely to lie rather than lose the privilege of your favors, wouldn't you agree?"

I looked up into the lines around those cheerful eyes. "Does the paper say that, too?"

"Of course."

"But Mrs. Jefferies, the people in the village —"

"Will not choose to defend the person who is responsible for removing them from their homes."

"Will you tell them it's not true?"

"No."

My gaze focused on the fish behind Ben's shoulder. Ben wasn't going to help me. He had never wanted to help me. I thought of Aunt Alice's stories of asylums, and my heart beat harder. I had no way to defend myself, and an asylum was exactly where the magistrate was going to take me. Then I caught sight of Davy, sliding like a snake from beneath the workbench to begin a silent move toward the cellar stairs. I lifted my chin, keeping Ben's eyes on me. "You wrote to the magistrate."

He smiled. "When you finally catch on, your mind works apace."

Davy was up three steps. Ben Aldridge was going to have me committed. Hopelessness flooded my chest, chilling, making me shiver. Seven steps. Why would he do this? Twelve steps, and Davy was away. There wasn't even a speck of dust from the ceiling. I was alone. "Why do you hate me?"

Ben's smile faded. "Oh, my dear," he said. "I don't hate you. You are quite an interesting, pent-up little thing. It was just your misfortune to stand between me and what I want." He shook his head. "I gave you every opportunity, you know. Again and again I asked if you would go to your aunt, and you were so . . . inflexible. I couldn't let you take away what I so desperately needed, which was unfortunately tucked deep inside your uncle's head. It's rather ironic, you know, that at the eleventh hour, I got what I needed anyway."

"You got what you needed?"

"Oh, yes. But it's too late to turn the clock back now." He sighed. "I am sorry for you." He stepped over to the workbench and his crate. "But as for that child," he continued, "that child is not trustworthy, and he is disobedient. He will pay for that." He looked back at me and smiled. "I don't enjoy being crossed, Miss Tulman. As I'm sure you will have noticed by now." He lifted the fish carefully into the crate.

"Will it explode?" I asked, trying to turn his mind from Davy.

Ben's face was so pleased I was startled. "Why, how clever of you, Miss Tulman." He laughed. "Yes, it certainly shall explode, unless all my experiments are wrong. Did you see my little accident over in the corner? Only a tiny bit packed in a medicine bottle and the force was . . . gratifying. Moisture, I believe, will be the key to its safety. Or let us hope so anyway."

I watched him take a dripping cask from a large barrel of water, where it had been soaking, and gently pack the cotton fluff tight inside the wet wood. He wedged the wet cask into the crate, then picked up my uncle's boat, saw me looking, and gave the little wheel a spin.

"A gyroscope, Miss Tulman. A simple concept, though in this instance, applied in an utterly new way. That is true genius." He tucked the boat into the crate alongside the cask and the fish. "Did I not tell you we live in a fantastic age? An age where nothing is impenetrable, and where ideas can be rewarding, indeed. But I am overdue and must therefore bid you adieu, my dear."

He laughed once at his little joke, then took three long steps across the room, grabbed the hair at the nape of my neck, and kissed me, hard on the mouth. "You deserved that," he said as he shoved me away, all his laughter gone. "You shouldn't have looked so pretty on your birthday. Thank God there are more of you in Paris."

He picked up his crate, very cautious not to bump it, and had a foot on the first step before he looked back at where I stood, still stiff with shock, the back of my hand over my mouth. "The village committees are meeting with Mr. Lockwood this morning, Miss Tulman. Very soon, actually, as dawn has broken, and I daresay that will be the proverbial nail in your coffin. I don't have any of the cucumbers you love so well, but that bottle of claret is just there beneath the workbench. Had the devil of a time with the dosages, never did get it right, but judging by your reaction before, there should be more than enough left to do the job. There are far worse things than death by opium, Miss Tulman. You might prefer it to the indignities of Bedlam." He favored me with the boyish grin I had so come to associate with Ben Aldridge. "Au revoir." The steps creaked, the door to the cellar shut, and I heard a key turn in the lock.

I sat down on the floor again, in the awful smell and mist of dust from Ben's movements above, the lantern light wavering, thinking of death by opium. There were opium dens in London, I had read about them in the newspapers. Men — sailors, many of them — hooked like fish by the pleasures, but who could not stop, even when their raving dreams drove them mad. Laudanum was made of opium, and that had been in the bottles upstairs. I could hear Ben smashing them now. And hadn't medicine gone missing from the infirmary, the night the old man had died? Mr. Cooper said it had been misplaced, but Mr. Cooper had also signed a document denouncing my sanity. Bottles of laudanum, and sugar with the bitter, slightly familiar taste . . .

And there, sitting on the dirt floor of a cellar in my ruined dress and almost certainly on my way to an asylum, I experienced a rush of undiluted happiness. Katharine Tulman was not insane, never had been insane. She had not even been poisoned. Katharine Tulman had been drugged. I thought of the bottles of laudanum, boiling, leaving the potent brown residue in the pots, sticky opium that could be scraped away and mixed with sugar. And Davy knew of it and knew how to enter my room through the wardrobe, to come from the nursery and turn the inside latch — no need for a key — to replace the sugar for my nightly tea.

And then I thought of footsteps in the corridor, my things moving, disappearing, the portraits changing, my bonnet tied to the flagpole. Davy, who could move so quietly, hide so well, and who knew all the ways of the house. How had Ben coerced him? But I knew that, too. All Ben had to do was threaten the rabbit, and Davy would have felt he had no choice. I remembered the odd, blank look, and the way Davy had tugged my hand, pulling me away from Ben's cottage when I had been offered tea. What guilt the miserable child must have suffered, and the risk he had taken to try and tell me, to show me, by bringing me here.

But why force Davy to do these things? Ben had wanted to keep me from going to my aunt, to keep Uncle Tully at Stranwyne, but he was leaving now. With Mr. Lockwood asking questions, Uncle Tully was in just as much danger from Aunt Alice as he'd always been. Ben said he'd gotten what he needed. But what had he needed? What had he wanted so much?

I got to my feet, brushed off my hands, and rummaged as quietly as possible through the workshop while the movements carried on upstairs. I found nothing, nothing but the bottle of opium-laced claret beneath the bench, as Ben had said. Every paper was taken, the fish, the boat, and the cotton gone, even most of the odor had dissipated, or at least I could no longer smell it. I sat down again to rest, closed my eyes, and instead of sorting what was in front of me, sorted through what was in my head.

Ben Aldridge had said he was going to Paris. He was taking Uncle Tully's little boat with him as well as the fish, the boat with its new spinning mechanism, the gyroscope. And then I remembered. On winding day, Ben had mused that perhaps the dragon and the fish worked in the same way, and now the boat balanced on its keel, the same way the dragon balanced. What if they all worked by gyroscope? I remembered the way Ben had leapt to his feet at my party, spellbound by the boat. If he understood how Uncle Tully's fish worked, how did that help him? But Ben didn't just want a fish that worked. He wanted a fish that would explode.

My eyes flew open, and I held my breath. I could see the fish swimming beneath the water as it had in the canal, its empty snout full of the volatile cotton, silent and unseen but for a small trail of bubbles, holding its course, holding its depth, and when it hit something solid, say the hull of a ship, the explosion that would follow. Ben had said that France was making new ships made of iron, impenetrable to cannon fire, but what had he said only a few minutes ago? That nothing was now impenetrable? And he wasn't going to London, he was going to Paris, where the nephew of Napoléon was now the president. Where the ability to sink every ship in the English navy would be worth a mighty reward, indeed.

And it was for this he would destroy me. I looked up at the silent ceiling, the cottage above me now still. Ben was gone. I thought of my father, the sea closing over his head as his ship journeyed down to the depths. And what about Davy? Davy had betrayed Ben, and Ben knew it. What would Ben do to him? *Anything*, I thought.

I jumped to my feet, grabbed a box of tools, and dumped the contents all over the workbench, the clatter grating in the quiet. I held up the lantern, searching, and it was the work of a moment before I found something that would serve my purpose. A small, thin chisel.

CHAPTER TWENTY-TWO

It took longer than I had anticipated to pry the pins from the cellar-door hinges. But once I had them out, the whole door slid away from the lock and scraps of wood I had used for props and went thudding to the floor planks. I ran full speed through the empty cottage, barefoot, muddy, and in my filthy blue dress, out the front door and down the sun-dappled path. I had to find Davy.

I burst through the little white gate onto the High Street, and was almost immediately yanked back by a strong grip on my arm. I squealed until I saw that the grip belonged to Lane.

"Where is he?" I panted.

"Who?" Lane shook his head. His hair was loose and tousled, his chin unshaven. "Never mind. Come with me. Now." He half ran down the street, dragging me with one hand, his rifle in the other. "Should have known you'd go there," he was muttering, "I should have known. . . ." He seemed angry and pained all at once, and I had no idea what he was talking about. I gave a sudden jerk, tearing my arm from his hand, and took a step back.

"Where is Davy, and where is Ben Aldridge?"

Lane turned and put both his free and his rifle hand up, as if I might startle like a pigeon. Or no, I thought, it was the same way he looked at my uncle, trying to ward off a tantrum. "Calm down," he said, very gently. "Come with —"

I stepped back again. "Where are they? Have you seen them?"

"You have to come with me, now. Please . . ." The gray eyes were darting right and left, and it occurred to me that it was getting on into the morning, and the street around us was deserted. Then I remembered the magistrate and the committees. I took another step back, hand on my throat.

"Are they coming for me?"

"Yes. Mr. Lockwood already came, but you'd . . . thank God you were gone. Let's go to the tunnel, and I'll take care of you. I'll get both you and Mr. Tully out, I promise." He held out his hand. "Just come with me. Please . . ."

"I am not insane."

"Katharine . . ."

"I am not!" I shouted. "I understand now. It was opium, because of the fish. . . ." I knew from the look on his face that I sounded exactly like what I was declaring myself not to be, but I had no more time. "I can't go without knowing where they are."

"If I tell you, will you come?"

I looked at him warily. "Yes."

"I passed them not fifteen minutes ago, on the way to the Lower Village, with a cart of things for Mr. Tully. Ben was going to keep Davy away, until all this was . . ."

But that was all I heard. I was already running, fleet as a deer for the Lower Village.

I was all the way to the canal wall before he caught me; fear for Davy lending me a speed I would have never guessed I had. Lane's long arm got me around the waist and jerked me right off my feet.

"Shhh," he said in my ear as I tried to kick his shins, a move not nearly as effective as it would have been with my boots on. "Stop! Let me help you. . . ."

And then I saw the boat coming down the canal. "There!" I yelled. Lane must have seen them, too, because his grip on me loosened.

Almost the entire boat was visible, a testament to the amount of rain we had received; the canal must have been running nearly to the top of the wall. Ben stood in the stern with the tiller, the white smoke of the steam engine puffing, the boat moving fast, one hand on Davy's collar as the child cowered on top of the wooden crate from the cellar. I thought his cheek might be bleeding. Ben saw us looking up at him and took his hand off the tiller, grinning as he waved. Then he glanced once at Davy and back at us. Before I could comprehend what I was seeing, he grabbed Davy in both hands, lifted the child up, and heaved him over the side. The small body made a slow arc through the air.

Lane gasped behind me, Davy hit the water, and I heard someone screaming. The screaming was from me. "Can he swim?" I yelled. "Can he swim?" But Lane had already dropped me and the gun and was at a dead run for the slope where the banked earth met the canal wall, clambering up to reach the level of the water.

I looked up into Ben's angelic smile, shining down on me from above. If I had been hot with fear and anger before, now I was dead cold with it. Eyes still on Ben, I bent down and snatched up the fallen rifle. I'd never shot a gun. I didn't even know if this one was loaded, but I knew enough to pull back the hammer. It clicked into place. I raised the muzzle, aiming at the boat that was running closer and closer to the edge of the wall. I could see Ben very clearly, and that crate of cargo that had been more precious to him than my life or Davy's. The smile left his face, replaced with puzzlement, and perhaps a bit of curiosity as to what I might do next. I pulled the trigger.

The gun jerked back hard, knocking me down, and at almost the same instant, bafflingly, the boat above me exploded, pieces of wood and iron boiler spewing upward, sending a force of air over my body and a pulsing ball of flame to the sky. I felt a grinding thud in the ground beneath me as what was left of the boat struck the canal wall.

I left the rifle where it was and tried to stand, confused and with my ears ringing. Water and tiny pieces of boat rained from the sky. Lane scrambled up from where the blast had knocked him down and began climbing the bank again. I ran, crawling up the rising land after him, and when I got to the canal he was already in the water, diving below the pieces of burning wreckage floating here and there on the surface. There was no sign of Ben. Or Davy.

It was a long time before Lane came out of the water, dripping and empty-handed. He ran his hand once through his hair, wringing out the wet, and we did not speak, just half walked, half slid down the bank together. My thoughts were unwound, leaving me loose, beyond functioning. We walked to the low place in the land, at the base of the canal wall, where Lane's rifle lay on the ground beside the path. He looked at the rifle, and back to the top of the wall.

"Gunpowder?" he said.

"He had a kind of cotton, that he said . . . would . . . explode. But I didn't . . . I didn't think . . ." I couldn't say any more. What had I done?

"But why? And Davy? Why?"

I knew the answer to his questions, but I had no more speech. I watched the gray eyes, blank as they stared up at the canal, suddenly narrow in concentration. I followed his gaze. Thin lines of wet were streaking down the wall, making dark stripes against the stone. Near the top, where they originated, a crack now ran through the mortar, trickles of water seeping from it.

"Katharine," Lane said slowly, "I think Mr. Tully is in the tunnel. Go quickly, and take him to the chapel. And if you hear Lockwood or the men coming to the chapel, go back in the tunnel and shut the door. But just wait on the other side of it, don't run back toward the workshops. Do you understand?" He turned to me. "Hide, and take care of Mr. Tully until I can come for you. I think I've got to close the water gate and drain the canal, just in case. Do you understand? Can you do it?"

I nodded.

"Go now," he said, and pushed me gently toward the workshop, waiting to see me on my way before picking up the gun and sprinting off toward the upper end of the canal. I hurried down the canal path. How I wished he didn't believe I was a lunatic.

I was still far from the green-painted door when I saw someone small slip inside it. I ran harder and found wet, bare footprints, child-sized, drying on the paving stones. I threw open the door and burst into my uncle's sitting room.

"Davy!" I called. "Davy!"

My feet made soft, quick slaps through to the hallway, but the gas in the workshop was unlit, my uncle's menagerie a collection of bizarre, black shapes in the dark. I searched the hall again and opened the door to Lane's room.

"Davy! Where are you?"

The boiler room and foundry were also empty, no smell of coal smoke, none of the engines running. I dashed back down the hall to the tunnel door, and flew down the stone steps. "Davy! Uncle Tully? Where are you?"

My voice echoed as I called, again and again, my limbs beginning to shake as I ran down the tunnel. I thought my legs would give way, or that I might be sick before I stopped, and then I saw a small figure just before the bend in the tunnel, stock-still and dripping in the gas glow.

"Davy!" I yelled, but I saw that he was ready to run if I came too near. I slowed. "Are you all right?" I said, trying to sound calm, though I was fighting my panting breath, and my stomach, and tears. "We couldn't find you. Thank God you can swim!"

His large eyes were down, and he did not acknowledge me. I stopped while still several feet away and went down to my knees on the floor stone, so he would know I would not try to chase him, and so I could rest. "I want . . . to . . . tell you some things. Will you let me?"

I waited, the seconds ticking one by one in the hiss of the gas-lights, until Davy took a few halting steps forward. He stopped, still well out of my reach. He was such a lonely little figure, standing there without his rabbit, bereft, and with a cut on his cheek.

"I want . . . to tell you," I said slowly, "that I understand what you were trying to say in the cottage. You did . . . very well. You showed me everything I needed."

He looked up then, and I could see him clearly in the glare, from his darkened, wet hair to his muddy pants and shirt. And his eyes were unshuttered, dark expressive pools. I saw remorse and fear and grief that made me ache, and there was hatred, too, not for me, but for the one who had made him hurt those he hadn't wanted to.

"I know," I whispered, "and I am sorry. And I'm not angry, not at you." I held out my hands to him. "You are not to blame. Do you understand me? It's not your fault."

He took one step toward my hand and stopped. A distant rumble vibrated through the tunnel, and we both looked to the stone ceiling. I had thought it was thunder, but instead of fading the rumbling grew louder, nearer. I stood. I could feel the shaking in my feet.

"Run," someone told me, the voice echoing.

My head swiveled, looking for who else might be in the tunnel. The rumbling grew louder. Had the voice been in my ears or only in my head?

"Run!" the voice commanded, high and flutelike, but full of fear.

I turned to Davy, staring into the two black eyes, and then the gaslights flickered, and went out. The wrench of splitting wood ricocheted down the tunnel, and a then a wind, and a thundering roar. I ran through the dark, hands out, reaching for Davy. My fingers had just brushed the collar of his shirt when I was struck violently from behind, and the world became a black chaos. I was tumbling, spinning, hitting floor, ceiling, or wall, I knew not which, and there was no air, no breath, no control. I hit something hard, and the turmoil changed direction. My lungs burned, water was in my nose, and I slammed against something solid, a heavy weight pressing me to it harder and harder, squeezing the life from my body.

When I knew I would die the solid thing gave way, and I was thrown with a rush into a murky pool. I rolled, slowed, found something beneath my feet, pushed upward, and broke the surface of the water, gagging and spitting, pulling in gulps of precious air. Daylight spilled down from the glass-and-iron cupola above me, a roar replacing the water in my ears.

I was in the ballroom, but I was thigh deep in a brown lake of muddy water and debris. The grand stairs were a waterfall, and when I looked back I saw the piece of wall that was the tunnel door floating off to my right, the doorway itself now a spigot. "Davy!" I tried to yell, coughing, but I was alone, the rushing water deafening as it continued to rise.

I turned around, my skirt clinging, trying to comprehend. The tiny crack in the canal wall must have opened, perhaps the whole wall had come down. And if Lane had not reached the water gate, if he hadn't closed off the flow, then not just the canal but the entire river would be emptying into the valley that was the Lower Village, and the lower end of Stranwyne. I moved, pushing my way through the current to the other door, the one Mrs. Jefferies had opened, but I stopped before I'd gone far. The water was now halfway up the door, past my waist, and the door opened into the ballroom. I would not be able to pull it open against the weight of all that water. I spun about, looking for escape, saw none, and panicked anew. I could not swim.

I tried to catch hold of the broken door to the tunnel, thinking to climb on top of it like a raft, but it moved away from me in the swirling current. I flailed after it, but the dress tangled around my legs and I could not stay upright. A wooden box floated past and I got my hand onto it just as the water lifted me from my feet. I clung to the floating box, nothing solid beneath me, breathless with fear, and when I licked my lips, I tasted saltiness. At least some of the moisture there was not from Stranwyne's canal or even the river, but was my own blood.

I kicked, trying to keep the box lid well above the surface so it would not fill, feeling cool currents come up from below my legs. The stairs were still a waterfall, though a much shorter one now; the water would soon be above the opening. I thought of Davy, hoping he had been swept down the main tunnel to the chapel, where he could escape, and about my uncle. I prayed he'd never been in the tunnel at all.

I was more than halfway up the ballroom walls, the beautiful chandeliers coming within touching distance, the mirrors now reflecting a nightmare. I was so tired, and my head hurt, not from any cuts, but from my ears; they were aching from the inside, the air trapped by the rising water becoming a painful pressure. I gritted my teeth, got my feet on the nearest chandelier, and pushed hard to position myself beneath the cupola. How odd, the detached part of me thought, that I would work so hard to live the few minutes longer that glass dome would give me. I was going to drown like my father, only I would do it staring upward through glass, watching pink roses sway in the sunshine. I pushed again, finally grabbing the corner where the ceiling met the dome and pulled myself and the box inside it. I had five, maybe six more feet.

And then the pain in my head and ears grew so intense that I screamed. I kicked at the glass with my bare feet, and then I thought of my box, but I could not hit it hard enough against the thick glass without losing my grip. New, warm blood ran down from my nose. I thought to just let go, to let the water in my lungs and stop the hurting, and then a new thought struck. I flung the lid off the box, reaching blindly inside, and found, still dry of all things, the rolling skates. I got one in my hand and hit the glass.

Nothing happened. The pain in my head was excruciating. I beat the glass harder, over and over again, agony giving me strength. A piece chipped out, long cracks racing outward, and when I hit the glass again, it broke. Air escaped, whooshing past my head, the pain in my ears eased, and water gushed from the hole into the garden. I let go of the box and grabbed hold of the iron window frame, broken shards sinking into the hand that did not hold the skate, and knocked out what remained of the glass. I pulled myself through, the rushing water now a help rather than a hindrance, and sank, gratefully, into tangled rosebushes and mud.

I crawled up to the next terrace, where the earth was firm, and lay there, panting. The lowest terrace was a running river, a new spigot now pouring from the open pane to join it. I felt the rain-softened grass on my cheek, and the dirt beneath it, taking note of each breath, feeling the sun as it dried the water on my skin. Then I got to my feet, stumbling as I climbed up each level of the garden until I came to the circular drive.

I opened the front door, my steps moving faster, leaving a wet trail, taking the same route I had my on first day at Stranwyne. I ran through the clocks, shouting Davy's name, fumbling with the door to the chapel. When I got it open, I ran to the far wall and then dropped to my knees. Water was leaking all around the edges of the hidden door, wetting the stones and seeping in pools over the floor. But the hidden door had opened into the tunnel, not out of it, and that tunnel was now full, the door held irrevocably shut by the weight of the water.

It was Mrs. Jefferies who found me there, I don't know how much later, on the chapel floor in a muddy heap, the blood dried on my forehead and cheeks. When I told her what lay behind the hidden door and explained what I knew, she cried and I cried again with her, our shared pain echoing from the stone. And when we couldn't cry anymore she put my head on her soft lap, sitting in the puddles that leaked from the tunnel, stroking my soiled hair with a pudgy hand. In ragged gasps, I told her about Ben Aldridge and opium and Davy, and firing the gun and breaking the glass, even what I thought she'd done to me, all in a haze of exhaustion and grief. Again and again I asked her, "And where is my uncle? Where is Lane?" She patted my back as her own breath shuddered and called me "duck" and said she didn't know.

When I was nearly asleep, she lifted my head and helped me up from the floor of the chapel, walking me to Marianna's room. I was calm by then, so tired that I was mostly beyond thought, and there, in Marianna's bed, was Uncle Tully, in his black coat and with the pink coverlets pulled up to his beard, asleep. He did not wake, even when I stood next to the bed.

"Let him sleep," said Mrs. Jefferies, her voice hoarse. "It's good to be forgetting." And then, very gently, she took the rolling skate from my hand. I had not known I was still clutching it.

It took two bouts in the tub to get the mud and smell of the river off me and my hair. Mrs. Jefferies soothed as she scrubbed, even while sometimes she cried herself, and I took comfort in the fact that I was not alone in my misery. She rubbed salve on my forehead and the cuts on my hands before pulling the nightgown over my head and putting me in Mary's bed. I didn't know where Mary was either, and the deep part of me that could still feel something, twisted with a new fear. I fell asleep with the late afternoon sun shining from the curtains, Mrs. Jefferies's hand on my head, the sense of water and mud flowing over my body, though none were really there.

CHAPTER TWENTY-THREE

I sat up in Mary's bed, early rather than late sun pouring through the window. All night I'd dreamed of noise, of the rushing of waterfalls, the ringing in my ears that came with an orange ball of fire, and the flutelike voice, begging me to run. I got up quietly, a bit unsteady, put on one of Mary's dresses, braided my hair, and tied it up in a kerchief. I sat for a moment on the edge of the bed, weak and tired, looking into the small mirror Mary had hung. The cuts on my forehead and hand hurt, and my shoulder was stiff, colored with various shades of green and purple. I was bumped and bruised in smaller ways all over, inside as well as out, but more than anything else I was aware of a heaviness inside me, a burden of weight that I did not think would leave me soon. And it was no one's fault but my own. I had fired the gun, exploded the boat that cracked the wall. If Davy was gone and Stranwyne ruined, there was no one but myself to blame. I tiptoed through to Marianna's room.

The heavy drapes dampened the effects of the sun, but even in the dim the first thing I saw was broken china, thousands of pieces on the dressing table, all of the teacups Mary had brought for my use from the kitchen. I touched a gritty shard.

"They was sticky," said Mrs. Jefferies from the hearth chair, "little bits of sticky all on the inside, so you wouldn't hardly notice, 'less you was looking."

Not just the sugar, then. Even my cups had been coated with the stuff. "So you smashed them," I said.

Mrs. Jefferies folded her hands. "I saw him with the green-striped cup, that devil. That first day you took tea with Mr. Tully in the workshop. Let him put that cup right on the teacart, all nice and helpful, and didn't think a thing of it. Your sugar has been poured out, too." I left the broken cups and went to the bed to look at my sleeping uncle. Mrs. Jefferies said, "Lane was coming up last night, but I told him you was sleeping. We had a chat and I set him straight on a thing or two before I sent him off. And Mary Brown was on the floor for a time, but she took off early. Needed at home, I'm thinking."

"Is all the Lower Village flooded, Mrs. Jefferies?"

"Yes, it is, Miss."

"Then Mary doesn't have a home to go to."

She sighed. "I'm thinking not."

The pink coverlet rose with my uncle's intake of breath. The workshop was gone. I remembered my dream the night I bit my hand, the nightmare of destruction Ben's opium had given me. And I had been the one to make that nightmare a reality. I adjusted the covers and then straightened my back. If this disaster was of my doing, then so must the remedy be. "Mrs. Jefferies, I think I need to go to the Upper Village."

"As you say, duck." She got up heavily and waddled over to stand beside me. "But we'll be feeding you first, or the wind'll take you."

"My uncle is sleeping very soundly. Will he be all right if he wakes, do you think?"

"I'm thinking he'll stay right here, Miss. I'm thinking he won't want to leave this room."

I turned to look at her, taking in her red and swollen eyes. "Were you able to sleep at all?" But she only put her arm around me, her mouth a sad line, and I leaned my head on her frizzing hair. "Thank you, Mrs. Jefferies," I said.

We stood together on the path, on the last rise above the Lower Village, and gazed down on a small sea. The canal had been consumed, and though the occasional peak of a thatched roof was visible, and the church steeple, it was a world made of water. The workshop and the smokestacks were missing. Riverboats torn from their moorings sailed serenely where the streets should have been, one of them upside down, and I saw the black-and-white carcass of a cow. I thought of the figure of my father, and my grandmother, all washed away, and wondered why everything had to die by my hand.

"Let's go, Mrs. Jefferies," I said. It was time to start making amends.

The Upper Village was a madhouse, as I thought it might be, and I did not forget that the people now running back and forth on its streets had been ready to put me in one. I lifted my chin and nodded at any who stared. I could smell the flood from the High Street, the stench so like the inside of the ballroom where I had nearly drowned that it gave me a thrill of terror deep in my stomach. Mrs. Jefferies followed me to the church, a small but curious crowd gathering in our wake, and there I found the greatest noise and hubbub. I pushed my way inside toward a knot of shouting men, their arguing close to becoming a fight.

"Excuse me, gentlemen," I said, though to no effect. "Excuse me!"

"Hush it!" yelled Mrs. Jefferies.

The arguing men turned about, and a gradual silence fell.

"Thank you, Mrs. Jefferies," I said, my voice now echoing in the sanctuary. I saw Lane in the crowd, his gaze piercing me from across the room, and Mr. Cooper, and next to him, Mr. Lockwood. Mr. Lockwood's jacket was gone, his sleeves rolled up, and he had mud up to his thighs. I walked slowly through the crowd of staring men, stepped up on the dais, and sat myself down in the parson's chair, surveying the group. "I see the head of our Upper Village committee, Mr. Cooper, is here, but who is head of the Lower Village?"

Mr. Cooper would not meet my eyes, but a man in a mud-spattered shirt who I had never seen before stepped forward. I managed to smile at them both, a gesture Mr. Cooper could not see.

"If I could also have the parson, and you, Mr. Moreau, up here for a few moments, I would be very grateful. If the rest of you gentlemen would be so kind as to wait for ten minutes, I hope to have some instructions for you then."

The quiet dissolved into a buzz and hum as the group I'd asked for moved toward the dais. Mr. Lockwood came and stood with them, silent, feet apart, arms crossed. I tried not to look at him. Lane hung back a few paces, watching both me and Mr. Lockwood over the heads of the other men. He was coiled up again, I could see that.

Probably because he had no idea what I might do next. Small wonder.

"Gentlemen," I began, "I wish to find out what's being done for the people displaced, and for those injured." I turned to Mr. Cooper. "How many are injured?"

Mr. Cooper twitched. "I'm . . . sure I don't . . ."

"Not many, Miss Tulman," Lane broke in. "A few bumps and cuts, one broken arm, and there have been three deaths. Most of the villagers were . . ." He paused.

"In this chapel," I finished for him, "discussing me. Yes, I quite understand, Mr. Moreau. That is fortunate, in hindsight, is it not?"

There was some shuffling of feet. I caught Mr. Lockwood frowning as the parson spoke up. "There were a few still in the Lower Village at the time of the flood, Miss, but they were able to climb on the thatch and were taken out by boat."

"I see. Thank you." I turned back to Mr. Cooper. "And who has died?"

Mr. Cooper stammered something unintelligible, and the parson rescued him. "A Mr. Bell, who was manning the gasworks."

"Was he from Upper or Lower Village?"

"Upper, Miss."

"Then his family is not displaced?"

"He had no wife or children, Miss."

"And there is also Ben Aldridge," came Lane's low voice. "He was in one of the boats. And there is a child."

"Yes," I said quietly. "Thank you, Mr. Moreau." I took a deep breath, and turned again to Mr. Cooper. "So, it seems that the infirmary is not particularly in use. How many beds are there in the infirmary?"

"Twenty," he finally managed.

"Good. We will use all of them, and by tonight we should be able to take perhaps fifteen families at the big house. I will see to that. And let's not forget that Mr. Aldridge's cottage is empty. We can put at least two nice-sized families in there. Is Mrs. Brown about? Or her daughter?"

"They're both down at the square, finding people beds," Lane said.

"Good. Mrs. Brown will be in charge of placing families with others in the village that might have room. I shall tell her so myself. And, Parson, I shall want a list, the name and number of all the families that have lost their homes. Is that understood? Bring it up to the big house as soon as may be."

"Yes, indeed."

I looked to the head of the Lower Village. "I'm sorry, sir, but I don't know your name."

"Mr. Waycroft, Miss."

"How many of our supplies were destroyed by the flood, Mr. Waycroft?"

"Everything that was down there, Miss, though the Upper Village carries the bulk of things."

"Have we any working boats?"

"A few, though not all."

"Then that is a priority. Put together a crew of men to round up and repair the boats, so the supplies will not be interrupted. Can we get them to the river?"

He bobbed his head, and I addressed the group.

"Is the water level rising, falling, or is it remaining the same, gentlemen?"

No one answered immediately. "It's dropped about three feet since yesterday, Miss Tulman," Lane said. "But has held steady since."

"I see. Have we any notion of how the Lower Village might be drained? We have underground places that must be emptied immediately. . . ." I stopped for a moment, while various phases of bemusement passed over the row of faces in front of me. The thought of the water-filled tunnel was almost more than I could bear. Mr. Waycroft spoke up.

"My understanding, Miss Tulman, is that the canal was made to be closed off and emptied, in case of repair. If we could empty the canal, and then cause the floodwater to drain into the canal, possibly by digging ditches, we should be able to lower the water level, at least."

I smiled at him. "Mr. Waycroft, please see if any others think this might work, or if we have anyone else that might have expertise in such a matter. If you get a consensus, then you have my permission to begin work immediately." Mr. Waycroft bobbed his head. "Now, is there anything I haven't considered, gentlemen, or that might need my attention immediately?"

There was a chorus of shaking heads, though Mr. Lockwood's stance was unchanged. His eyes were boring a hole through me. I looked away from him, and stood.

"Then I will see Mrs. Brown and to my own preparations. Parson, would you please speak to those that are waiting here in the church and make my instructions known?"

"Gladly, Miss Tulman." He smiled broadly at me. "I'll see to it at once."

"Thank you, sir." I gave him a curtsy and I walked away through the crowd, head up, Mrs. Jefferies sailing in my wake. I only hoped none of them knew that my knees were trembling.

And they trembled periodically for the rest of the morning, my hands with them, though not from fear or nervousness, but for reasons I did not understand. I sat with Mrs. Brown in the infirmary, quivering fingers hidden in the folds of Mary's skirt, and between the two of us we concocted a plan to provide housing and provisions, and to wring as much order from the situation as was possible. Mary joined us, crushing me with one brief, fierce hug about the neck, then came back to the big house to help Mrs. Jefferies search out the most suitable rooms for temporary housing.

The lowest wing we found to be partially flooded, the corridor to the ballroom standing in water and showing an even higher mark on the walls, and I wanted no one near Marianna's rooms — to spare my uncle — or anywhere near the chapel, which I considered a tomb. But in the end I was able to send word to Mrs. Brown to increase the number of families sleeping in Stranwyne to twenty. In most cases the rooms were not much, but there was at least a roof and a fireplace.

The rest of the afternoon was spent making pot after pot of soup, none of which I could eat, and while the fourth pot boiled, my entire body began to quake from the inside out. I made an excuse to Mrs. Jefferies, left the kitchen quietly, and as soon as I was in the corridor fled to the room of the ornaments, where I could cower on the yellow settee and be alone with my tremors. Fourteen minutes ticked away before my fear of sinking back into my nightmares ebbed. I closed my eyes, trying to rest, and remembered our neighbor in London, a man who would shake when short of his daily requirement of whiskey and beer. Perhaps my body was craving the missing ingredients in my tea. Or maybe my grief and guilt were just so intense that I was sick with it.

It was full dark when I left the last scrubbed pot upside down on the dishcloth, pushed open the kitchen door, and went outside, every inch of me aching with weariness. I'd been thinking while I scrubbed, planning my coming days, and the thought of what I must do next left me bleeding inside, a slow trickle that I knew would never let me sleep, no matter how tired. The garden was alive with moon shadow and night whisperings, and then I saw that one of the shadows was Lane. I heard his feet coming to me on the gravel, watched as the tops of his muddy boots stopped in front of mine. I kept still, eyes on the ground, dreading my next bout of pain.

At length he said, "Last night I was told, in no uncertain terms, that if I ever said a cross word to you again, the devil would burst from the ground, grab me by the ankles, give a good yank, and drag me straight back with him."

I smiled in spite of myself. "Your aunt is very . . . enthusiastic in her likes and dislikes."

"True."

"She told you . . . everything?"

"Yes." The wind eddied through the garden, setting leaves and stalks in motion. He let the breezes die down before he said, "Opium, then?"

I nodded.

"And at the party, you got too much?"

"I think so . . . yes." I still had not looked him in the face. He thrust his hands in his pockets and sighed.

"You did well today, at the village. After you left, Lockwood had Mr. Cooper backed in a corner, waving that signed paper in his face until the man shook like a fly on a string." He paused. "We found Mr. Bell from the gasworks, but . . . that's all. The way the current was moving I guess Ben could have gone down to the river, before the wall came down. I didn't see him when I was diving, but the water was murky." I watched the toe of Lane's boot move a piece of gravel back and forth. "Aunt Bit said that . . . you were with him."

He was speaking of Davy now. I could hear the grief in his voice, and it tripled my own. I nodded again, silent. We studied the cabbages in the dark.

"I went to the rose garden," he said finally, "and saw the broken glass."

I didn't answer.

"You're hurt," he said, reaching for my cut hand.

"It's nothing." I crossed my arms, and said quickly, "I want you to know that it wasn't his fault. Davy, and the opium, I mean. He didn't want to. Ben was . . . he was making him."

Lane put his hands back in his pockets, and I listened to the long, slow release of his breath. His anger seemed to have the ability to change the air. I could feel it on my skin. But he only said, "And you're certain that he wanted that fish to explode, and that he was taking it to Paris?"

"Yes. The stuff was like cotton that hasn't been spun, and it had blown a hole in the floor of the cellar. There was a cask of it on the boat. I suppose that's what . . . And Ben told me once that France was making ships encased in iron, ships that could not be sunk with cannon fire."

Lane ran a hand through his hair, thinking perhaps, as I was, of how the iron boiler of the steamboat had flown into the air in pieces. "My father," he said slowly, "he used to talk all the time about the war, and the sea battles between the British and French. If France had had ships that England couldn't sink, or if they could've sunk all of England's, then . . ."

Then this garden would have belonged to France. All of Britain would have belonged to France, and Europe with it. I understood it well. I remembered Ben's look of satisfaction when he'd said that ideas could be rewarding. "I think he was expecting to be very rich, indeed," I whispered. And then I shuddered. That other look of satisfaction had come unbidden to my mind, when Ben had kissed me and then thrust me aside, just before his almost friendly suggestion of my suicide. The tension I could sense in the shadows before me suddenly intensified.

"Did he hurt you?"

I shook my head, and the shape in the darkness came nearer, until I could smell the river water and silt and the unmistakable scent that was Lane. He reached again for my hands, and against every wish of my being I took one small step back. He stopped and went very still.

"I see," he said simply.

I closed my eyes. How I wished I'd never come to Stranwyne Keep. Mrs. Jefferies had been right. I had been the one to make it difficult. I had ripped myself into tiny pieces, and a hundred years at

Aunt Alice's could have never hurt me so badly. But my course was now set.

"When Mr. Babcock arrives," I said, measuring my words, "he will manage the arrangements for repairs."

I could feel the gray gaze on my closed eyelids. "And then you will go," he said.

"Yes. I'll do as he asked from the beginning. I'll go back to my aunt and tell her as many lies as I can think of. It won't last for long, but I will make it last . . . for as long as I can."

"Katharine," the low voice said.

I opened my eyes. I couldn't help it. The wind gusted around my back.

"I would have taken care of you. Both of you."

I looked back into his shadows, at the dark brows and unshaven chin, and knew with the same unyielding certainty as on the night of my birthday that Lane was telling me the truth. He would have cared for us as long as we needed him, and not only for the sake of my uncle. He would have done it for me. "I know," I whispered. "I know you would have. And now, let me do the same for you, and for Uncle Tully. There's nothing more important than keeping my aunt away from Stranwyne Keep."

Instead of answering, he came nearer, near enough that I could hear his breath, feel the cool of the darkness change with his warmth as a hand came near my cheek. I took a step back, my insides splitting in two, and then took another, and another before I broke into a run for the kitchen. When I put my hand on the latch, I heard him coming after me, fast on the gravel. I yanked open the door, not wanting him to make it any harder than it was, not wanting him to see me cry, but my gaze went straight to Mary. She was pressed flat against the kitchen wall, eyes round amid the freckles, her chin jerking frantically toward the hearth. I turned, and up from the smoky shadows rose Alice Tulman.

CHAPTER TWENTY-FOUR

I stood absolutely still, my breath cut short, the shock of seeing my aunt in that moment, in that kitchen, like a physical blow. Lane ran up behind me, grabbing my shoulder as if he would turn me around, but he stopped, and I could feel him near my back, tense and unmoving. He dropped his hand.

"Katharine," Aunt Alice said.

She could put many meanings into my name. She could say, "You shock me," "You disappoint me," and "You are a worthless excuse for a person," all with two simple syllables. It was efficient of her, really, and jarring compared to the way I had last heard that word spoken in the garden. But it brought me back to myself. We had lost, everything was lost, but despair would have to be dealt with later.

"Aunt," I replied. "What a surprise to see you here."

"I'm sure," she purred.

I came into the kitchen and untied my kerchief. "Please, do sit down, Aunt. You must have had a tiring journey."

She took in my state of dress, and then Lane, dirty and wild-headed, filling the darkness of the doorway to the lintel, and lowered herself back into the chair. I saw she was sitting on the very edge of it, to save the purity of her traveling costume, and I vowed to keep her there as long as possible. It gave me pleasure to imagine her with an aching arse. Lane shut away the night noises of the garden and came to stand beside me, arms crossed.

"Aunt, this is Mr. Moreau. Mr. Moreau, this is my aunt, Mrs. Tulman. Mr. Moreau is my uncle's . . . apprentice, Aunt."

Lane inclined his head slightly, and Aunt Alice just deigned to do the same. Mary was still jerking her neck at me, this time toward the corridor. Evidently she had something to say.

"And I suppose you have met Mary Brown, my maid. And hello, Hannah. I had not seen you there." On the hearth stool in the corner was poor Hannah, Aunt Alice's personal maid, whom I'd always suspected of lasting so long in my aunt's service because she was so very good at cringing. She gave me a weak smile.

"Dear Katharine," my aunt said, straightening the lace at her sleeve. "You are quite friendly with the help here. How pleasant. But I must admit I am concerned by your appearance, my pet. You seem to have been in some sort of accident. It was truly kind of you not to write and tell me all about it. Obviously you wished to spare me worry on the subject."

I'd forgotten the cut on my forehead. I smiled at her. "I am always happy to spare you any discomfort, Aunt. And indeed, I do wish that you could have written to me . . ."

Aunt Alice raised a carefully plucked brow.

". . . so that we could have been best prepared for your comfort now." I glanced again at Mary, who I truly thought might injure her neck, while Lane's appraising gaze moved back and forth between all of us. "Excuse me for one moment, Aunt. Mary and I will just discuss the preparations for your room."

Mary was out the door like a shot, and I ignored my aunt's indignation to follow, Lane coming just behind. Mary pulled us both down the corridor as soon as the kitchen door was shut.

"What to do, Miss, what to do? I was coming down to get you and what do I find but her ladyship in the kitchen!"

"All right, Mary. I know." A stampede of village children came down the hall then, seven of them breaking around us like a wave as they played a game of chase through the corridors. If Aunt Alice was listening at the door, I hoped their noise might mask our conversation. "We'll just have to put her in my room, it's the only decent one in the house, and —"

"But Miss! It's Mr. Tully! He —"

I turned to Lane. "Is there anywhere else he would be comfortable? He can't be near her. . . ."

"Miss!" Mary was nearly jumping up and down with impatience. "I'm trying to tell you Mr. Tully won't talk. He won't even move, Miss! I was checking on him this morning, and then this afternoon, and I thought to myself, 'My, how he's sleeping!' But now he's just lying there, staring and staring, and . . . I think he may have," her voice dropped to less than a whisper, "*soiled* the bedclothes, Miss!"

I stared at her, then looked to Lane.

"I thought he was sleeping earlier, too," Lane said, and so had I. Had he really not left that bed all day? My feet moved, taking me straight to my uncle, but Lane put out a hand.

"No. Deal with her." He glanced toward the kitchen. "You're the only one that can. I'll go to Mr. Tully."

I bit my lip. He was right. "But what could be wrong with him?"

The gray eyes looked full into mine. "You know. The workshop is gone."

Now that all I wanted in the world was to save my uncle, everything I did seemed bound to destroy him. "Mary," I said after a moment, "run down to Mrs. Jefferies's cottage and tell her what has happened. Between the two of you find somewhere for my aunt to sleep and fix it up as best you can. I don't care if there are six children in there already, just make it at the opposite end of the house from my uncle. I'll keep her in the kitchen as long as possible. And tell Mrs. Jefferies to bring breakfast to the drawing room at seven sharp. To the drawing room, mind you, and have a fire built there."

"I'll do that," Lane offered.

"We don't want her wandering the house if we can help it. Perhaps we can feed her and she'll go." But I knew this was not so. My aunt smelled blood, and she was ready to spill it. "And let's keep Mr. Lockwood away, too, if we can. No one but the three of us, and Mrs. Jefferies, is to know where my uncle is, is that clear? If they cannot find him, they cannot take him. Are we clear?"

Mary nodded, saucer-eyed, and started at a trot back the way she had come.

"I'll come up as soon as I can," I told Lane, and took exactly one step back toward the kitchen before he reached out and took my face in his hands. Before I could think or even speak, he had his lips on mine, my head held so tight that I could not have gotten away if I'd wanted to. But I didn't want to. My arms wound around his neck, my fingers twining into his hair, and faintly I heard Mary's snort of "Lord!" come from somewhere down the hallway. His hold on my face gentled, and he let go of me first, reaching back to untangle my fingers.

"Go, now," he said, and put his lips once to my forehead. It was like a benediction, in case that chance should never come again.

I watched him sprint away to my uncle, my breath coming hard, and when he'd disappeared into the darkness of the corridor, I turned and found Aunt Alice in the doorway to the kitchen. Her mouth wore a tight, pinched little smile, a smile that told me just how much she'd seen, and just how much she was going to enjoy taking everything away from me. I lifted my chin, and she let me brush past her, back into the kitchen.

"I was just telling my dear niece what a free and easy way you have here at Stranwyne. It's all so very friendly, indeed."

Mrs. Jefferies was in the kitchen now, evidently of the opinion that I needed protection from my aunt more than Mary needed help with a bedchamber. She'd come straight from her cottage in her dressing gown and with her hair half-pinned.

"Of course it is!" Mrs. Jefferies huffed, busily removing dishes from my aunt's reach. "Our little Katie's a right friendly girl!"

She patted my cheek as she passed, and I tried not to grimace. Bless her, but she was not helping my cause. Aunt Alice simpered, her small eyes on me.

"So it seems. I am so looking forward to informing Mrs. Hardcastle and the other ladies of the very special friends you have made during your stay. I'm sure they will enjoy hearing of it very much."

I met her gaze with equanimity. The children from earlier were somewhere above us now, jumping up and down on the floor, little bits of dried onion skin floating down from the braids on the ceiling to decorate my aunt's hair. I picked up her teacup. "Do you still take two lumps in your tea, Aunt?"

"Yes, Katie dear."

I put in three and stirred vigorously before she could do anything about it. I hoped Ben Aldridge had doctored them. I set the tea in front of her, piping hot, and said, "Toast, Aunt? I could build up the fire." I could see that she was perspiring, her fringe of curls clinging to her forehead.

"No, thank you, dear. You are too kind."

I came around the table as unobtrusively as possible, and handed poor Hannah a cup of her own while Aunt Alice perched on the edge of the chair, brushing onion skin from her skirt. Hannah sipped quickly, before my aunt could decide to take it away.

"Katharine," Aunt Alice said suddenly, "where is your uncle?"

I saw Mrs. Jefferies go stock-still at the washbasin, and then look to me in alarm. I smiled sweetly at my aunt, sat down at the table across from her, and changed my expression to one of concern. "You are probably not aware, Aunt, that there has been a . . . catastrophe at Stranwyne. I'm afraid that's why we were not prepared to receive you properly. The entire lower portion of the estate has been flooded, and the people there displaced."

"Oh?" she said. "The servants were displaced, were they? How dreadful."

"Yes. Some are even staying in the house now, temporarily." The children upstairs squealed.

"And just how many servants were displaced, Katharine?"

I folded my hands in front of me. "All that lived there, Aunt. And my uncle is, of course, very distressed and tired from the execution of his duties. He is . . . ill, as a matter of fact."

"Ill? Then perhaps I should go to him now, to see if there is any relief I could offer him."

"No need for that!" Mrs. Jefferies interjected. I held in my sigh.

"You are always kind, Aunt. But he is resting at the moment, and it would be harmful to disturb him, I'm sure."

Mary burst through the door, remembering, rather late, to drop my aunt a curtsy. "Your room is ready, Miss, uh, Ma'am," she said, panting.

"Thank you, Mary," I said quickly. "My aunt is undoubtedly tired and will wish to retire at once. We shall have breakfast in the drawing room at . . . eight o'clock, Aunt." I decided to give myself a one-hour margin. "I shall send Mary to fetch you. And Aunt, I do wish to warn you that some of the lower portions of the house are in water, as I referred to earlier, and other parts are now sheltering the displaced, and other places are possibly . . . unsafe. So I wouldn't wander about, if I were you. And if you should hear things in the night — odd noises, howling, screams, and such — please do not distress yourself. But do lock your door, Aunt, merely as a precaution, I assure you. Good night."

Aunt Alice's eyes were wide. I bobbed her a quick curtsy and left the kitchen, waiting in the shadows until Mary had taken both my aunt and Hannah away, somewhere down the corridor in the opposite direction. I would not risk Aunt Alice seeing which way I turned to go to my rooms.

Upstairs, my uncle's blue eyes were wide and unseeing, staring into the canopy. "Uncle," I whispered. "Uncle Tully?" He blinked once. I took his hand and put it on my cheek, but when I let go it dropped like a stone to the bedclothes. He was wearing my nightgown, I saw, and Lane had somehow managed to change out the linens. The others were in a pile by the door.

"I'll try wrapping him," Lane said, "but that works when he's upset and thrashing. I've . . . never seen this."

I nodded. "Tomorrow I will try to make my aunt go and convince her to leave me here. But this . . . will not be successful. Most likely I will have to go with her, and she will start the proceedings to take Stranwyne, if she hasn't already. I'll give you all the money she gave me to come here, and you and Mrs. Jefferies, you'll have to take Uncle Tully away somewhere and hide him."

"Come with us."

I shook my head. "I'm only another mouth to feed until someone finds work. If she'll keep letting me do the accounts, then I can change the numbers, and if I can change the numbers, I can get you money. It's what I was going to do for myself . . . before." That "before" seemed like an age ago. And I would have to make very sure Aunt Alice believed that I hated, detested, and despised keeping those books. After what she had seen in the hallway, she would need new ways to punish me. "Keep in touch with Mr. Babcock," I said, "and

I'll do the same. He'll pass the money along. Otherwise none of you will have anything to live on." Mr. Babcock would be on the side of whoever was helping my uncle, I was sure of that.

"I don't know if he will live," Lane said, "if he has to leave here."

"He has to."

He looked long into my face. "And you will live with that . . . woman."

I took a deep breath. "Yes. I have to."

CHAPTER TWENTY-FIVE

I stayed with Mary that night, the two of us squashed into her little bed, and when the sun rose, so did we, I think without either of us having slept at all. The trogwynd had blown until just before dawn, as loud as I'd ever heard it. I could only hope my aunt had not closed her eyes either. Mary helped me dress in silence, pulling my corset strings tight, slipping the worsted over my many petticoats and smoothing my hair. By a quarter till seven, the mirror showed the girl I had been when I first came to Stranwyne. Though I knew I would never really be her again.

"Good-bye, then, Miss," Mary whispered. I hugged her tight before I left.

When I entered the drawing room, I found that Aunt Alice had anticipated me. She was sitting before the cold hearth one hour before her time, the early sun shining through the pink of the drapes, and with Mr. Lockwood by her side. I looked from my satisfied aunt to the distressed Mr. Lockwood, my last hopes shredding.

"Ah, Katharine. Good morning. You know Mr. Lockwood, I gather."

"Miss Tulman," he said, and stood hastily to offer me a chair. I had no idea what conclusions he might have drawn about me or my current situation, but the robust, businesslike man now struck me as thoroughly cowed.

"Thank you, Mr. Lockwood." I took the seat opposite my aunt, and we all looked at one another. Lane, now clean and shaven, came with an armful of kindling and stopped at the door, surveying the group.

I turned to Mr. Lockwood. "I am very glad to see you well, and that you were not caught in any of this terrible flooding."

"Yes. Though I hear you were, Miss Tulman. A most remarkable accident. I am very pleased to see you looking so healthy and well." He placed particular emphasis on these words. Lane came across the room and began laying the fire.

"Mr. Lockwood has been telling me that there are hundreds upon hundreds displaced on the estate, Katharine. How extraordinary that there would be so many. We shall have to find suitable places for them to go as soon as may be, shall we not?"

A lump of wood crashed hard into the hearth, causing Aunt Alice to jump.

"I rather think that decision will be up to my uncle Tulman, Aunt."

Mr. Lockwood looked uncomfortable.

"Mr. Lockwood has also been telling me, my dear, about the strange circumstance that brought him to Stranwyne. My, my, but you have been having a busy time. Small wonder if she found no time to write, wouldn't you agree, Mr. Lockwood?"

"Well . . ."

The fire was crackling, and Lane was only busying himself now, unwilling, evidently, to leave.

"But it is a rather lovely old place." Aunt Alice looked happily about the room. "Sadly neglected, of course, but men never think of such things." She reached over and placed a delicately gloved hand on Mr. Lockwood's. "It takes a woman's touch, don't you think?"

My eyes widened. Aunt Alice was truly playing all her cards. I looked to the fireplace. Lane did not need to see or hear any more of this; I didn't trust his temper. "Thank you, Mr. Moreau. Would you tell Mrs. Jefferies that we're ready for breakfast?"

Lane inclined his head, gazing at me for a long time as I pled with my eyes for him to go. He moved reluctantly toward the door.

"Katharine has such a way with the servants," my aunt whispered loudly. "They just seem to give her whatever she wants."

"Miss Tulman," said Mr. Lockwood, the bushy beard turning my way. "Let's stop the shilly-shallying. I am going to have to see Mr. Tulman. We both know that."

Lane was in the doorway beneath the stairs, and he stopped again, his back rigid. "I'm afraid that is impossible, Mr. Lockwood," I said.

"And why is that?"

"Because my uncle is quite ill."

"Ill or no, Miss Tulman, I will be seeing him."

My aunt's eyes went demurely to her lap, the little pursed smile on her lips. Lane's long body melted away through the door, and I knew he was running, getting ready to move my uncle. "I truly believe that seeing my uncle would be a grave risk, Mr. Lockwood. Are you sure you don't wish to wait a few days, to be certain?"

"Certain of what?"

"Why, the nature of his disease, of course. Perhaps you aren't aware, Mr. Lockwood, that our resident surgeon is concerned about an outbreak of typhus?"

"Typhus? I saw nothing of . . ."

"Such diseases often follow flooding." I smoothed my skirt. "But perhaps you are right, perhaps it is nothing but a cold. Or cholera."

"Cholera? Really, Miss Tulman, I . . ."

Mrs. Jefferies came in then, with her lace cap on and a tea tray clattering over the various rugs. We watched her come in silence, and then turned as one to the door. It was not just the tea cart jangling, there was a rattle from the drive as well. A carriage rolled past the front door, which in less than thirty seconds was thrown open.

"Hello! Hello, all! A thousand apologies for my late arrival." Mr. Babcock threw down his hat and came hurrying across the room, tossing a satchel to the floor beside my aunt's chair. "Miss Tulman," he said, leaning forward to kiss my hand. "Enchanted, as always. And Mrs. Tulman." He turned to my aunt and bowed his oddly shaped head. "Keeping a stiff upper lip, I see. And you are, sir?"

"Mr. Lockwood, this is Mr. Babcock, the Tulman family solicitor," I said. My aunt gave me a dark look, reminding me that he was not her solicitor. I ignored it. "Mr. Lockwood is a county magistrate, Mr. Babcock."

"Of course, of course," said Mr. Babcock, pumping his hand. "A pleasure, sir. An infinite pleasure. Ah! Breakfast!" He settled with a slight thud on the settee that contained Mr. Lockwood, and took the cup handed to him by Mrs. Jefferies. "A tower of strength as always, dear lady," he said to her.

Mrs. Jefferies set the tea tray on the low table at the center of our little gathering, and Mr. Babcock slurped his tea with an enjoyment that seemed to preclude all other thought. "Just before you arrived, Mr. Babcock," I said, "I was telling Mr. Lockwood and my aunt about the outbreak of disease we are experiencing on the estate."

"Were you indeed, Miss Tulman?" The shrewd eyes met mine over the teacup. Mrs. Jefferies paused briefly in her ministrations.

"Yes," I replied. "It is most unfortunate."

"Cholera or typhus?" Mr. Babcock asked. My aunt raised an eyebrow.

"Mr. Cooper isn't certain," I said firmly.

"My niece is so considerate of my health," said Aunt Alice. "She feels it would be unwise for Mr. Lockwood or myself to even be in the same room with Mr. Tulman."

"These country doctors," said Mr. Babcock, helping himself to a roll, "always looking out for epidemics and whatnot, when likely it's all down to nothing but a bad bit of beef."

I closed my mouth and looked hard at the little lawyer. "I think," I said slowly, "that it would be wise to follow Mr. Cooper's recommendation, Mr. Babcock."

"Tosh, young lady. I am surprised at you. No reason why Mr. Lockwood shouldn't have a peek at Mr. Tulman, and if Mr. Tulman is indeed ill, the assistance of his family might be appreciated. Do you have him in Miss Marianna's rooms, then? That's as good a place as any for being ill."

Mrs. Jefferies dropped a plate to the floor and it shattered, feeling as I did, no doubt, the depth of Mr. Babcock's betrayal. He was giving my uncle away, handing him over to Mr. Lockwood. I would never have believed it possible. I banged down my cup and stood quickly, looking down on my aunt's triumph and Mr. Lockwood's concern. Mr. Babcock chewed his roll.

"Then I will just let him know to prepare for visitors," I said icily. "But please do finish your breakfasts, and then Mrs. Jefferies will show you the way up. Mrs. Jefferies?" She looked up at me from the floor, where she was collecting the broken bits of plate, tears rolling from her eyes. "Take them by way of the clock room. I think that's fastest, don't you?"

She opened her mouth once to protest, but then only said, "Yes, Miss."

I left the drawing room at a dignified pace, and as soon as the door was shut, I ran.

When I flung open the door to Marianna's room, my uncle was in the same attitude as before, staring at the canopy. Lane looked up from the bag he was stuffing.

"They're coming," I said. "Ten minutes at the most. Does he have any clothes up here?"

"All in the workshop."

"No matter." I shoved the soiled linens under the bed while Lane scooped Uncle Tully into his arms, but my uncle chose that moment to show his first signs of life in hours. He yelled like a banshee, flailing so hard and suddenly that Lane dropped him back on the bed.

"Hush, Mr. Tully. It's all right, everything is —"

He struggled and wailed, one of his wild arms striking Lane's face. He didn't appear to be seeing what was in front of him.

"I'll have to drag him," Lane said, raising his voice over the noise. "I won't be able to carry him when he's doing that!"

"Uncle!" I shouted, coming around the bed. "Uncle Tully, look at me! Do you remember what Marianna said?"

He went instantly still, and I got in his line of sight, so that his eyes could focus on me. I had no idea what Marianna might have said, but surely she had said something to benefit the occasion. "Yes," he said slowly.

"Such behavior is not good, Uncle, even when you are frightened. It is not splendid, isn't that so?"

"Yes," he whispered. His lips were dry and cracked.

"Lane and I are going to take care of you. We want to help, do you understand that? Now, I'm sure you are hungry, and thirsty, and that you haven't had your playtime, or your toast and tea. Take my hand and come with me."

And he did. He was weak and tottering, but he took my hand firmly enough while Lane held his other arm. We started across the room.

"What is thirty-four times twelve, Uncle Tully?"

"Four hundred and eight." He took one step and then another, his skinny legs sticking out of my nightgown.

"Four hundred and eight times nine?"

"Three thousand six hundred and seventy-two. There was water," he said shakily. "I saw water. . . ."

"Yes, Uncle." We were entering Mary's room, though she wasn't in it. "You will have to build new things now. Eighty-eight times naught?"

"N-naught. New things, little niece?"

"Oh, yes, think of all the lovely new things to build. All brand-new, and right out of your head."

My uncle's face lightened, he was moving quicker, and some of my fear had actually begun to ebb when we entered the library and he spied the box of toys. Uncle Tully jerked away from both of us and charged for the box, flinging it open.

"Uncle, no. Not now! Tea first, and toast, remember?"

"We had it in here before," he said stubbornly, rummaging through the box.

"Yes, but not this time. This time we —"

"The boat is gone away! It was just right, and now it's . . ."

Lane was speaking low into my uncle's ear, trying to pull him upright. There were voices coming down the corridor.

"Uncle, please!" I pleaded. "Thirty-five times fourteen?"

"Gone! It's gone! No, NO!" he shouted, his face turning red. "It's not George's, or Simon's! It's mine! Mine, mine!"

"Ah, here we are," I heard Mr. Babcock say.

When the library door opened, I was clinging hard to my uncle.

CHAPTER TWENTY-SIX

"Sad," Mr. Lockwood mused, leaning back into the settee in the drawing room. "Very sad."

"Truly," said my aunt. "The fall of a great man."

I wished my gaze could do anything I wanted. I wished with one look I could drop my aunt into a puddle of mud, or perhaps dung, or boiling oil. And Mr. Babcock, I wished I could flay him, or twist his thumbs. . . . Mr. Babcock drained his third cup of tea.

"So, Mr. Lockwood," said Mr. Babcock, his large jowls shaking, "is it your opinion, sir, that the head of the Tulman estate should be declared incompetent?"

"I don't see how it cannot be so," said Mr. Lockwood, studying his hands. He, at least, was not enjoying this process. I could almost forgive him for shooting Bertram. "Mr. Tulman is in no fit state to make decisions of finance or to provide for his own welfare. It is my opinion, sir, that he must be institutionalized, for his own safety."

"Ah," replied Mr. Babcock, "very judicious of you, I'm sure, very prudent. But that particular decision will be made by the next head of the estate, will it not? If Mr. Tulman is declared incompetent, the estate passes downward." Mr. Babcock smiled and turned to my aunt. "Is that not correct, Madam?"

My aunt inclined her curled head, her tight smile threatening to burst its bonds. "But as the heir of Stranwyne is not of age, Mr. Babcock, I, of course, will have to stand in that stead." She leaned toward Mr. Lockwood. "It is a great burden, and one I feel keenly, I assure you."

Then her hard little eyes moved from Mr. Lockwood to me, and my aunt and I reached an understanding. My position had been made all too clear. Not another penny would pass my way in her lifetime, or ever, if she could help it. I looked into my teacup, and began drafting an advertisement in my head. *Young lady, well educated — no, perhaps moderately educated — seeks work as . . .* I had no idea what I could seek work as. I realized Mr. Babcock was talking.

". . . and as such is a sentiment bravely felt and bravely spoken, my dear lady. I commend you! But it is a burden, I am happy to tell you, that you will not have to bear."

I looked up, wondering what Mr. Babcock could be talking about. My aunt's smile did not falter.

"You are probably not aware, sir, that the heir of Stranwyne is merely a child. He will not come of age yet for several years."

"Ah! You will forgive me for contradicting you, Madam, but the inheritor of Stranwyne has come of age. I'm sure I have the paperwork here somewhere . . ." He began rooting through the satchel he had brought while my aunt frowned, craning her neck to try and see each paper that was ruffled. Mr. Lockwood sat back and crossed his arms as Mr. Babcock prattled to himself in an infuriating manner.

"Sir!" said my aunt, finally exasperated. "I am quite certain I know the age of my own son, no matter what sort of paper you might have in your bag!"

"Oh!" said Mr. Babcock, looking up from his searching. "Mrs. Tulman! Your son! I am . . . well, I am most discomfited, dear lady. But what an embarrassing mistake you have made! Surely you were not under the impression that Robert Tulman is the heir of his uncle?"

Something akin to paralysis fell over the drawing room, and the striking of the clocks came faint through the walls. I counted them. One . . .

"You ridiculous little man!" hissed Aunt Alice. "What do you know about it?"

"Really, Madam!" Mr. Babcock perched a pair of spectacles on his nose, *tsk-tsk*ing as he searched through the papers. "I know quite a bit, as a matter of fact! Your son, Robert, is second in line to the estate."

Two . . .

"My son, Robert, is the only one in line for the estate, sir!"

Mr. Babcock chuckled. "Oh, I think not," he said amiably, eyes on the shuffling papers. Mr. Lockwood crossed his legs.

Three . . .

"Now, let's see, ah, yes! George Tulman, born fifteenth February of the year 1800, third son of Martin Tulman, eldest child, Robert . . ."

Four . . .

". . . and then we have Simon Tulman, born October . . . October, what was the day, what was the day . . . third day! Yes. October, year 1798, second son of Martin Tulman, eldest daughter, Katharine . . ."

Five . . .

". . . and then we have Frederick Tulman, born January, year 1794, eldest son, becoming legal inheritor of said Tulman estate ninth November, 1814. Sad day . . ."

Six . . .

". . . and do hereby declare . . . yes, yes . . . as said Frederick is without issue or progeny, henceforth . . . that brings us to . . . logically . . . and therefore . . ."

Seven . . .

"Ah! Bringing us to Miss Katharine Tulman, eldest grandchild of Martin Tulman, who according to her grandmother's will came of age on July eighteen, thereby making her the heiress of her uncle and the Stranwyne estate."

I blinked once as Mr. Babcock looked over his spectacles. Eight o'clock in the morning. My aunt leapt to her feet.

"The Tulman estate is entailed, you bloody fool! Only males may inherit!"

"Dear me, Madam." Mr. Babcock mopped his head with a handkerchief. "Please arrange yourself. Your loss of composure is distressing Mr. Lockwood."

Mr. Lockwood drank his tea as my aunt sat down hard in her chair, her face murderous. More papers appeared from the satchel.

"Forgive me if I should have explained this sooner, Mrs. Tulman, but the entail on the Stranwyne estate was broken by Marianna Tulman three days after the birth of Simon's eldest child." He leaned forward apologetically. "And here, I am afraid, is where I must admit myself to be most mortified. Through the negligence of a faulty clerk, long-since sacked, this paperwork was only proved in court this past week, when, as you know, Miss Katharine Tulman came of the legal age, as stipulated in the will signed by Frederick Tulman, year 1835 . . ." Paperwork was piling into my aunt's lap at an alarming rate. ". . . long, of course, before he was declared to be incompetent, clearing the way for a female to inherit, which is, quite clearly, this young lady, here."

My aunt was staring at her lap in confusion, her face blanched.

"So," Mr. Babcock said, turning to me, "now that you are of age, my dear, you spare your aunt a mighty burden. The income and debts of this estate are yours, along with the difficult choices concerning your uncle's future. As well as the allowance from your father, of course . . ." He went back to digging in the satchel. ". . . as stipulated in his will, from the year . . ."

"Wait," I commanded, finally spurred from my stupor. "What allowance from my father?"

Mr. Babcock peered over his spectacles, for once, I think, caught by surprise. It was an event I'd wager did not happen often. "Your allowance from your father, my child. The interest on his income earned by trade, the bulk of which you have inherited as well, of course, having no siblings, and now that you are of age."

I gaped at him, and then we both looked to my aunt. Unbecoming blotches of red dotted each cheek.

"Oh, dear me, Mrs. Tulman," said Mr. Babcock. "Your memory is as faulty as my clerk's, I fear." Mr. Lockwood smiled.

"Excuse me," I said. I stood, and walked out the front door.

I sat right down on the front step, feeling the sun burn my face and watching the breeze blow the grasses. Mr. Babcock's horses, carriage, and driver were biding their time a little ways down the drive. *Someone should show them the way to the old stables*, I thought. Perhaps there might even be hay. I would tell Lane or Mrs. Jefferies. Then my eyes moved from the carriage and I observed a family of hares on the hillside, grazing above the black hole that was the tunnel. If Davy had been here, we could have caught him one of the babies to raise.

And then it occurred to me that the tunnel I was looking at was mine. The stables were mine, the rabbits and the grass mine; the step I sat on was mine. My uncle would never have to go anywhere else. I never needed to go anywhere else. I took a breath, and discovered I needed another, and another. I covered my face. I could not seem to breathe properly at all.

The door opened behind me, and Mr. Babcock came out. I could hear the squeakiness of his shoes. Or perhaps it was his knees. With difficulty he placed himself on the crumbling step beside me.

"Well, well, Miss Tulman, great fun! And nearly two decades in the making! The best kind, of course. Nothing like it!" He waited for a moment, then continued when I did not respond. "I have left your aunt perusing paperwork that she appears to find distressing. Truly, the language of the legal profession can be difficult to comprehend."

I could not make a sound. He dug in a pocket and handed me his handkerchief.

"Did you really not know about your father's money, my dear? Did you think you had nothing?"

I nodded, dabbing at my eyes.

"And therefore thought I was asking you to choose a wretched life beneath your loving aunt's thumb! My apologies, Miss Tulman. I was in a hurry. I assumed. It is a lesson to me."

I turned to look at his balding head and worked up the breath to speak. "You don't have a negligent clerk," I told him. "You would have suppressed every bit of that paperwork, and my grandmother's wishes, had I not been . . ." *How had he put it before?* ". . . sympathetic."

Mr. Babcock smiled slightly and shrugged. "Perhaps I would have. But it is your grandmother's wishes that have always been my guide, and your grandmother's wishes have always been to the good of your uncle. No disrespect to you, of course."

"But what made you . . . How did you know where my . . . sympathies lay? I think I gave you no encouragement last time."

"Never forget that the law has eyes, Miss Tulman, eyes everywhere! I tend to know which way the wind blows at Stranwyne."

Which meant Lane and Mrs. Jefferies wrote him letters. I looked back at the waving grasses. "I think you must have loved her very much."

The voice beside me softened. "She was ten years my senior and this long time gone, and yet never have I forgotten her. I hope you understand, my young heiress, that always, no matter what, I do my utmost for the house of Tulman."

The sound of glass breaking made both of us glance back at the house.

"Mr. Babcock," I said. "I think I shall need your advice very soon, on several matters, some of which are . . . quite beyond me. You will stay the night? Would tomorrow morning be convenient?"

"Yes, indeed! I shall stay for several nights, I think. We have quite a mess to mop up, my dear, quite a mess!"

Something else breakable shattered. I handed Mr. Babcock his handkerchief and got to my feet. "Would you like to come inside with me, Mr. Babcock? I am going to tell my aunt to leave my house."

"I think it would be wise, my dear. She seems to be breaking your ornaments."

CHAPTER TWENTY-SEVEN

The removal of Alice Tulman from Stranwyne was a messy business, ending with a forcible escort to the carriage by Mr. Lockwood, poor frightened Hannah cowering at her side. I pointed out to my aunt that making herself an unwelcome addition to my household was not in her own best interest, as I was now the arbiter of her monthly allowance, but jealousy and spite are not always wise. I instructed Mr. Babcock to keep my aunt's allowance the same, adjusting only for the yearly rise in expenses, and to inform her that if she wanted more she need only ask me. And as I was confident she never would, I was also quite confident I might never see her again.

Mr. Babcock and I stood on the rise above the flooded Lower Village, and he muttered and *tsk*ed and blew his nose, and then we walked back to Stranwyne and together laid out a scheme for rebuilding. We turned our attention first to restoring housing, doubling the output of the pottery kilns until the foundry, engines, and gasworks could be rebuilt. The canal was closed off and enormous ditches dug to siphon off the water, but it was weeks before the ground truly drained, and months before every family had a cottage. It was decided to move the site of the Lower Village closer to the Upper, above the repaired canal wall, to prevent a repeat of recent disasters, and merge the two into one. I pored over every aspect and detail of these plans, pleased to be rebuilding what I had once thought I would destroy.

I also made Mr. Babcock aware of the other events at Stranwyne, a talk that lasted far into the night, and in true Mr. Babcock fashion, this conversation resulted in a visit from the British government. Mr. Wickersham arrived on a December afternoon and sat with me before a fire in the little morning room, a room I had set aside for my own use, and one of the first to receive the benefits of my father's money. The walls were not crimson or pink, but pale green, the curtains a shade darker. Mrs. Jefferies had piled the chimneypiece with evergreen and berries for Yule.

Mary brought in a gyroscope my uncle had recently built, gave both it and a small curtsy to Mr. Wickersham, and left the room with her nose wrinkled, eyes riveted to the small pocket watch she carried. I'd not seen her expression so intent since the day I had found her in Marianna's bedchamber, feeding the fire with pieces of my worsted. Mr. Wickersham spun the gyroscope, a tiny wheel in the center of a small, shaped flower, watching the petals open and close as the little machine balanced on his palm. He listened as I explained everything I knew about the workings of my uncle's fish and about the cotton fluff that had exploded so powerfully as to blow up the boat and crack our canal wall.

When I had finished, he said, "And you say the original fish, Miss Tulman, was not found in the ruins of your uncle's workshop, but is likely buried somewhere in the mud, or washed into the canal?"

I inclined my head. The same was true for Ben Aldridge, though neither one of us said it. I glanced once to my right. Mr. Wickersham's companion was a thin, nameless little man with ink-stained fingers, scribbling into a tiny book at a furious rate. He dipped his pen and, alongside words, I caught a glimpse of a drawing of my face, quite recognizable. The man tilted the book ever so slightly away from me without interrupting his pen.

Mr. Wickersham let the gyroscope wind down, set it on the table, and slapped his knees. "Well, I do thank you for your time, Miss Tulman, and for the service you've done Her Majesty's —"

"Mr. Wickersham," I said. He had begun to stand, but sat down heavily again at my interruption. "Surely you are going to tell me whether any of my suppositions are correct?"

"Correct, Miss Tulman?"

"Was Mr. Aldridge planning to blow up ships, sir?"

Mr. Wickersham sighed, and put his elbows on his knees. "Aldridge was not even his name, Miss Tulman. The man was born Charles Benjamin Arceneaux, son of a Frenchwoman who went by the name 'Aldridge' while in England — to avoid local prejudices, one might suppose — and a Royal Naval officer of the name Daniels. Under none of these names, however, was this man a graduate of Cambridge, or any other institution, or employed in any sort of teaching position in London."

I looked back at Mr. Wickersham's copious mustache, thinking of so many lies, heaped one upon the other, like coins of brass. "And the ships, Mr. Wickersham?"

"Yes, yes, Miss Tulman, of course he was planning to blow up ships. Or at least, to sell the ability to do so. That threat is now neutralized, for which every sailor in Her Majesty's fleet thanks you."

"Mr. Wickersham," I said. He paused in a half crouch, sighed, and sat down again. "I would like to know why Ben Aldridge did not . . . dispose of me."

Mr. Wickersham looked at me keenly while the pen scratched. "You are asking me why you weren't murdered in your bed? You would have found that a more logical solution, young lady?"

"Of course."

The man stared at me a moment longer and then chuckled. "We could also ask why he didn't merely steal the fish, Miss Tulman, sail away before the thing was missed, and have the contraption studied by an expert at his leisure."

I nodded. I had thought of this, too.

"As you are obviously not a fool, I shall be frank with you, Miss Tulman, and depend upon your discretion. There were letters going out in the post, I understand. Three of them, at different times, and written completely in French."

I frowned. Mary had mentioned this to me long ago, though it had never crossed my mind since.

"And though Mr. Moreau is the only professed French-speaking literate on the estate, it appears that he was not the author of these letters. They were left anonymously, and right at sailing time, and, most unfortunately, Mr. Moreau was never able to read one."

Davy, I thought, a twinge of sadness temporarily diverting me from Mr. Wickersham's words. "So you are saying that you believe Mr. Aldridge wrote these letters, and that therefore someone else was involved in his plans. Someone who was perhaps French."

"Someone, or perhaps many someones, planning to pay your uncle's workshop a visit. If one extraordinary and valuable idea was present inside it, then why not two, or three, or even four? It would have been imperative, therefore, to have the workshop and your uncle in place and intact, as hidden and private from the world as they'd always been. And, I must say, that your dead body would have been rather likely to attract more attention from the outside than less of it, Miss Tulman. But if you were to be proven insane . . . well, in that case, you would merely be the unfortunate victim of illness, unremarkable, and any tales you chose to tell about Stranwyne likely to be discounted."

I had almost stopped listening, thinking of men like Ben descending on the estate. I leaned forward in my chair. "Mr. Wickersham, is my uncle safe at Stranwyne?"

"There is no longer a workshop, Miss Tulman, so I think these men will likely believe that the honey has left the hive. And let us remember that Mr. Aldridge himself was attempting to leave in the end, whether from a change in the game or a magistrate that was more penetrating than he could wish, I do not know. But in return for your question, my dear, I will ask you two. Are you aware, perhaps, that the current leader of France, Louis-Napoléon, is none other than the nephew of the tyrant Napoléon Bonaparte?"

I felt my brows come down. "Yes, I'm aware of it."

"And are you quite certain, Miss Tulman, that last June Mr. Aldridge made the statement to you that the emperor of France expects his ironclad ships to sail very well?"

"Yes, that is almost verbatim."

"Then please consider, Miss Tulman, that in June of this year the nation of France had an elected president. Not five days have passed since Louis-Napoléon dissolved his parliament and declared himself to be Napoléon the Third, emperor of France. Vigilance, my dear, would not be out of order for any of us." He stood and bowed quickly, giving me no time to speak. "A very good day to you, and again, many thanks from Her Majesty's navy."

Mr. Wickersham strode from the room while the man without a name finished his last bit of jotting, gave me a bob of the head, and hurried out after him. I watched the hearth flames, thinking.

"Are they gone, Simon's baby?"

I turned to see my uncle's bright blue eye peeking around the doorjamb. "Yes, Uncle. And you did splendidly. You let him hold it for . . ."

Mary's head popped into the doorway, and she held up the pocket watch. "Four, Miss!"

"Four minutes," I continued. "Last time you only waited for three."

"Five comes next," my uncle sighed, coming cautiously into the room to take his mechanical flower. "Big things can be little."

Or sometimes little things can be big, I thought, my mind on Mr. Wickersham.

"Twenty-eight!" Uncle Tully shouted suddenly. "Twenty-eight to playtime! If you come to the workshop in twenty-seven, you shall be early, little niece, and in twenty-nine you shall be late!"

I smiled. "I will be there in twenty-eight, Uncle."

And that was the first day that Lane did not come to the workshop.

Marianna's library had become the workshop, temporarily at least. It was full of tools, benches, whirring, ticking, my uncle's chatter, and new burn holes in the carpet. But I did not think Marianna would have minded that. On Wednesdays, Uncle Tully allowed Mary to join us, and she brought him salvaged pieces from the flood to play with and reassemble. It was Mary's day when my uncle's newest project became recognizable: a child-sized clockwork arm connected to the gears of a long-legged rabbit. Lane set down the wax he was carving and said, "I can't make that face for you, Mr. Tully."

My uncle's mouth went slack, as if Lane had pronounced a sudden predilection for the green-striped cup. "You can't?"

"No, Mr. Tully."

I watched them both cautiously, and when my uncle showed his first hint of agitation I said, "You like to remember numbers in your head, don't you, Uncle?"

He frowned. "Yes, but . . ."

"You don't always write them down to look at, do you?"

"No . . . I . . ."

"Well, I think Lane would like to remember Davy in his head, too. Without looking."

"Oh!" My uncle's face brightened. "He likes to remember in his head! That is just so. Lane always knows what is just so." He picked up the clockwork arm and the bright blue eyes fixed themselves on the gray ones. "But what about . . . rabbits?" he whispered very loudly. "Do you like rabbits to be in your head or outside of it?"

"I think outside will do just fine, Mr. Tully," Lane replied, his smile as much for me as for my uncle.

I'd been glad to see it. With the rebuilding for him and the planning and management for me, the care of my uncle, a house full of people waiting on the completion of their cottages, and Mary's watchful eye, it wasn't often that he managed to take my face in his hands, as he had once before. Though he had managed it. He could be rather ingenious that way. When I brushed my hair at night, I looked at the silver swan on my dressing table and no longer saw the upward escape of flight. I saw the act of alighting, of settling softly in. But lately he had struck me as restless, and sometimes I would catch his gaze wandering, looking at things I could not see.

And then one evening he knocked on the bedchamber door and asked Mary if I would like to go rolling. I couldn't imagine what he meant, the polished floor of the ballroom still being mud-covered and ruined, but when I saw the long, wide hallway that led to the upper garrets, the floor newly polished, and the skates, cleaned, oiled, and dangling from his hand, I could not hide my delight.

We raced — no telling what the villagers still in the house below thought of our noise — while Mary, ever vigilant, watched from the garret steps. He wouldn't let me win, as I thought a gentleman might have, and only laughed when I complained, telling me that I had no complaint, as he'd never been a gentleman. But I could also see that he had something on his mind. When I slowed after our sixth lap, laughing and trying to catch my breath, he turned to me and said, "Mr. Cooper came to see me today."

I waited for him to go on, but there was no other noise than our wheels on the passing floor. And then I saw something I had only ever seen once: a tinge of pink beneath his skin. I stared at the new color as he skated on, hands in his pockets, until we were at the farthest end of the hall, away from Mary.

"Mr. Cooper came today and . . . he asked my permission to marry Aunt Bit."

I blinked. As good friends as Mrs. Jefferies and I had become, I had never thought of her as . . . marriageable. Of course, I'd never thought of myself that way either, not before Stranwyne. But I'd not forgotten Mr. Cooper's signature on the paper denouncing my sanity, though in light of the threat to his home, I had struggled to. The gray eyes were on me, waiting, so I said, "Well, what does Mrs. Jefferies say about it? Isn't it rather sudden?"

He slowed to a stop and ran a hand through his hair, and I watched, enthralled, as his skin flushed further. "That's . . . why I'm telling you this, actually. Aunt Bit says she's going to come to you herself, and . . ." He lowered his voice. "The truth of it is, this whole thing's been going on a long time. I didn't know until you said something about the room with all the ornaments and the crystal and such. I knew she'd borrowed that silver wolf — or I knew it after she told me she had — but . . ." He sighed. "I reckon she was trying to impress him, and they had to meet away from the village, so . . ." He shrugged. "Aunt Bit says Mr. Cooper has a taste for 'fine things.'"

My eyes widened. I remembered Mr. Cooper's twitchy gait down the tunnel, and Mrs. Jefferies opening the ballroom door when they knew we were all going to the castle, and the silver wolf on the table in the room of the ornaments, with a supper laid out before the fire. I thought of that night, and felt my hand go to my throat.

"Oh, no."

"Oh, yes," he replied.

"And I just sat there on the settee, waiting and waiting. . . ."

"While they peeked through the window, their supper going cold."

I stared back into Lane's appalled face. The situation was ridiculous and horrifying all at once. A long moment passed, and then I giggled, Lane smiled, and seconds later the bare walls rang as we laughed. Mary shook her head at us, her face showing disapproval from the stairwell as Lane took my hand, pale cream in his tan, and pulled me forward to skate the other way down the hall while I tried to catch my breath.

"You're going to hear the whole thing straight from Aunt Bit in the morning," he said. "She's shaking in her boots about it. Feeling guilty, I reckon, but . . . I thought you could use a bit of warning, for God's sake."

"Well, I thank you for that," I said. "I wouldn't want to hurt her feelings, but I'm not certain I could have kept my countenance had she . . ."

But then I stopped, both rolling and speaking, suddenly aware of everything that might be causing Mrs. Jefferies to suffer guilt. Mr. Cooper had signed that paper and given it to the magistrate not just for himself and the villages, but for Mrs. Jefferies, possibly even at her urging. In fact, now that I thought of it, I was certain he had signed that paper at her urging. Lane stood still, watching my understanding dawn, and as always he waited, letting me decide.

"All that is long done and gone," I said. "I'll tell your aunt so myself in the morning. I will wish her joy."

"Thank you," he said quietly, and put his lips to the back of my hand that was still in his. "You are more forgiving than I am."

The next morning I did exactly as I'd said, kissing Mrs. Jefferies's teary cheek, wondering only then who Lane had not forgiven. And the afternoon after Mrs. Jefferies's visit was the second time Lane did not come to the workshop.

The third time he did not come I said nothing. The fourth time I left my uncle with Mary and went to find him. He was in the little hollow, sitting beside the mound of dirt that was Davy's grave, the upright rock now serving as a headstone. Lane had gone into the tunnel and found Davy himself, as soon as the water had dropped far enough to wade, a day I wished I could not remember. It was nearing February now. Late afternoon clouds sat low on the land, the air dusky and sharp with cold, though the hollow dulled the worst of the wind. I sat down next to Lane, huddled in a blue-and-green-patterned shawl, listening to the trogwynd sing high and then low, eerie and inhuman, a sound I had come to love. I had not heard its music for a long time, not since the night Aunt Alice was here, just before I'd discovered that Stranwyne was mine.

I stayed quiet for many minutes, sensing the black mood beside me, and then I said, "I think about Davy often, you know. And I think that he talked all the time, just not to people. I think he only talked to Bertram."

"Why do you think that?" the low voice asked.

"Because when he told me to run that day in the tunnel, his voice was clear, not gruff or disused. And do you remember the first day I came to Stranwyne, when I was so anxious, and frightened, and running from clocks?" I was pleased to see a faint smile. "I wandered into the chapel, my nerves wound tight, and a laugh echoed all around me. Then I caught sight of Uncle George in the mirror and let out a scream you should have heard all the way to the workshop."

He laughed softly.

"I think Davy was just up in the gallery, or in the little hallway behind it, playing a game with Bertram. He laughed because he could. Because he was alone. I imagine he did the same in this place, as well."

Lane pulled the red cap from his head and twisted it, turning it over and over with perfectly coordinated fingers. "I wonder . . . if you can have any idea just how angry I am."

I looked at him carefully, at the dark brows and the gray eyes that would not meet mine. I was used to Lane's bouts of temper. They were like a gunpowder flash: hot, powerful, and soon over. But this was different. What I had taken to be restlessness and absence of mind, I now recognized as slow-burning coal.

"I am angry at all that mud down there that was my home," he said. "And I am angry at this pile of dirt beside us, which should not exist. But mostly I am angry at Ben Aldridge, and I am angry at myself, for not hurting him when I had the chance."

I pulled the shawl closer. "Ben Aldridge is dead."

"That gun," he replied as if I had not spoken, "should have been in my hand. I should have shot him then and there. If I had, none of this would be happening. I knew Davy could swim. A little."

I put my hand on his arm, surprised to feel the tension beneath my fingers. "You didn't even know he had done some of those things, not at the time . . . you . . ."

"Aunt Bit has someone to take care of her, and Mr. Tully has you and Mary, and he's so much better at getting used to things than he was. You run this place as if you always have, and you're wealthy now, with a thousand different choices than before." The cap twisted and writhed. "No need to make you the scandal of London."

I stared at him, a little unnerved. Likely I was the scandal of London already, if my aunt Alice had anything to do with it. But what did I care about that? The only person outside of Stranwyne whose opinion I valued was Mr. Babcock's, and he had only ever referred to Lane as a "fine young man." I was making my own rules at Stranwyne. I squeezed his arm. "What are you talking about?"

He got up instead of answering, three springs taking him upward to the edge of the hollow where he stood in the icy wind, hat in hand, looking out over what used to be the Lower Village. His next words were only just spoken and would have never been heard had the wind not blown them to me. He said, "And I have never seen the sea."

I didn't know what to do or to say, could not think of what might ease this dark frame of mind. Then I saw that his back had gone rigid, the coiled-up posture I knew so well. I got to my feet. "What's wrong?" I said. "Is someone there?"

He turned down the little slope, coming back quickly to where I stood at the center of the dell. "No, nothing's wrong. Go inside now. You're cold."

"Come with me." Again I put a hand on his arm and again felt the tightness of the muscles, this time possibly to the point of pain. "Come, and I'll get you some tea."

He shook his head. Then he bent down, took my face in hands, and placed his lips once to my forehead. The wind hit my back like a wall of ice.

"You'll do well," he said, more to himself than to me. "Go back to the house now, Katharine. Go on."

I stood my ground. "Aren't you coming?"

"No. Not just yet. Hurry on, then. Mr. Tully will be waiting."

But I did not hurry. I moved slowly, brow furrowed, looking back once to see him up on the edge of the dell again, bareheaded and arms crossed, the catlike readiness still present in his stance.

Later that evening I heard a tromping on the stairs and then Mrs. Jefferies — now Mrs. Cooper — was banging on the door to Marianna's rooms, yelling as if the place were ablaze. I jerked open the door in my nightgown.

"He's gone," she said.

We stood together in the doorway to Lane's room, a small place, closet-like, in the same corridor as the kitchen. I'd tried to give him better but he would not take it, saying he did not like so much space. The cot in the corner was neat, the blankets smooth, the worktable where he carved swept clean of its wax and plaster shavings. The clothes pegs stood bare and the red cap was gone, though the smell of him was still there: metal, paint, and Lane. I stared at the empty room, stricken, experiencing a shock as mind-numbing as when I'd watched Ben's boat fly to pieces in a ball of flame. The trogwynd wailed, and Mrs. Cooper sniffed. There was nothing else to say.

I sat in my chair until late in the night, listening to the wind, watching the silver swan gleam with hearth flames, my father's cautious gaze looking down from the portrait Lane had hung for me in my room. I had locked my doors again, with no explanation to poor Mary, to be alone and savor the bitterness of my pain. I searched my memory for the things I must have done wrong, and could only conclude that the trouble was deeper. The trouble was me. What Aunt Alice had always insinuated about me was true. Why had I ever thought differently? I must have deluded myself just as surely as before Mr. Lockwood came. I thought of the words that had passed between us in the hollow, all the reasons why Lane felt he wasn't needed. All the reasons why he could go away and be free of me, without guilt.

And then I got angry, the deep, cold kind, the kind that made me calm. No matter what my faults, Lane's behavior was inexcusable. He should have spoken; surely I was due that. And in the hollow he had said that if he'd shot Ben Aldridge, then "none of this would be happening." Shooting Ben Aldridge would not have resolved any dissatisfaction with me or even a mere wanderlust. This was not logical. I did not like that.

I pulled on my dressing gown, lit a candle, and dried my cheeks with the back of my hand. I would search Lane's room, open every drawer, look under the bed. And if that failed, I was going to Mrs. Cooper, late hour or no. I hurried to the bedchamber door, head full of this plan, my progress only halted by a hard, chilly something beneath my bare foot. I looked down. In the ring of candle glow, lying on a carpet rose, was a key. It had been pushed beneath my door.

I picked it up, turning it over and over in my hand, running a finger over its ornate casting. It was a clock key. Had it been there earlier, when Mrs. Cooper came? It could have been, but we'd both been in such a state. I shut Marianna's door behind me, glanced once at my guardian, and stole softly through the corridors and down the many stairs, until I was in the room of the clocks.

The gaslight was on here, no need for my candle, the ticking a comfort to fill my head. I searched the maze, running my fingers over shining wood and sparkling glass, looking for a clock that had no key. I found it after one deafening cacophony that proclaimed the half hour, on the floor in a back corner, small, with a walnut case, a silvery swan with raised wings etched on its door glass. Now I knew where he'd seen the swan, I thought, though the one in my room had so much more life.

I got on my knees and opened the clock case slowly, my heartbeat now louder than the ticking, and in the back, behind the swinging pendulum, I could just see a small slip of paper. Careful not to disturb the clock's rhythm, I slid the paper out. It was blank but for five letters on its back, inked in Lane's hand: PARIS. I sat back on my heels, tears pricking my eyes. I did not understand.

I climbed the stairs to my corridor, one painful step after another, and when I reached the top, my uncle stood in the hallway with a candle, his thin, pale legs sticking out below his nightshirt. He was looking at the portrait of my guardian, and his white beard turned at my approach.

"I'm not sleepy!" he announced in full voice.

"I'm not either, Uncle," I whispered. "But let's speak more quietly, in case Mary is." Uncle Tully went back to his examination of the portrait. "Do you like that picture, Uncle?"

"Oh, yes!" he replied, nose nearly touching the paint. Then he remembered and whispered, "Oh, yes! And Lane has gone away, little niece."

"I know it, Uncle." I studied the shadows collecting at my feet. "Do you want me to bring you something warm to drink?"

"Oh, yes! I mean, no. I mean, no, it's not the forever kind of going. Yes, that's what he said. Not the forever gone away."

I looked up, trying to sift my uncle's words. "Did Lane tell you that, Uncle Tully?" I should have known. He might leave without informing me, but he would never have done such a thing to my uncle.

"Yes! He said that sometimes people go away because they must, not because they want to. Because sometimes things are not splendid, or right."

Like me, I thought. Then I saw that Uncle Tully was plucking at his nightshirt. He fidgeted so much that I reached out and gently took away his candle.

"I think I shall tell you a secret, Simon's baby. Should I?" He bounced on the balls of his feet. "Shall I? I think I shall!" He whispered loud and slow. "I saw the man."

"What man?"

Uncle Tully beamed. "The man who holds the toy!"

A picture of Ben Aldridge with my uncle's fish came to my head, and I felt my insides flinch. "What man who holds which toy?"

"The flower, little niece, the flower!"

I let out a breath.

"I saw him, but he didn't see me, and neither did the other man. The other man didn't ask to hold the flower, so I didn't have to do five." Uncle Tully looked relieved. "And they didn't want me to see, so I waited, very quiet, until Lane came and then they all went away. The man didn't mind that Lane saw him. The other man likes to write things. But he didn't want to hold the flower."

My mind was already in motion, clicking fast like a new-oiled machine. Mr. Wickersham had held the flower. He could only mean Mr. Wickersham, and his nameless, scribbling assistant. Mr. Wickersham had been in the house, tonight, in the clock room with Lane. "How did you know they didn't want you to see them, Uncle?"

"Because they hid! Behind the clocks! People who hide behind clocks do not want to be seen. . . ."

In the clock room, not wanting to be seen, where Lane had left me a word: *Paris*. There was another click in my head. *I should have shot him then and there. If I had, then none of this would be happening. . . .* Lane was not going to Paris to be away from me, he was going to Paris to look for Ben Aldridge.

I let out another breath, the force of my realization like a blow. Of course the English government was not going to trust the safety of their navy to one girl's word about a missing body and a missing machine. What tosh Mr. Wickersham had told me in the morning room. And who better to send? Lane was young, unmarried, spoke French, knew my uncle's fish, had known Ben Aldridge. I sighed at the flickering candles I held, one in each hand, my logic like a balm. Lane had been upset beside Davy's grave today, angry, wound to the point of pain. He was guilty that Davy was gone and wanted to make his amends. I could understand that. Hadn't I been trying to do the same for the past six months? But he had also been torn . . . because of me.

I closed my eyes, the welling relief of understanding a stark contrast to the depth of my emptiness. Why not just tell me where he was going, what he was doing? Even this afternoon, when we were alone in the hollow? Then I thought of Lane's stiff back as he looked over the edge of the dell. What, or rather who, had he seen? The piece of paper that said *Paris* crinkled between my fingers and the candleholder, the weight of the clock key heavy in my pocket. Perhaps this knowledge was dangerous? Perhaps he had told me the only way he could. And surely he must have known that Uncle Tully would repeat his words.

I opened my eyes and found my uncle's face just a few inches from my own, his expression perturbed. "You are too silent, Simon's baby. I do not like silence. It leaves empty places in my head."

"I'm sorry, Uncle. Did Lane say anything else? About going away?"

"Oh, yes!" Then he whispered, "Oh, yes. He said that sometimes people go away, and sometimes they come back."

Lane had said they come back.

"Does that make you happy, too, Simon's baby?"

I looked into the two bright eyes that were searching for my happiness. "Yes, Uncle. Very much so."

"Sometimes they come back. Lane always knows." He sighed and pointed to the portrait of my guardian. "She came back."

I had decided who the portrait must be many weeks ago, but I'd never asked, not wanting to be wrong. "Did she, Uncle?" I whispered.

"Oh, yes! Marianna was very tired, then. But you are her before she was tired, aren't you, little niece?"

Oddly this made perfect sense to me. I smiled. "Would you like to go listen to the clocks, Uncle? Until we're sleepy? Tomorrow is the day for new things."

"Ticking is very good. Clocks should always tick, so they can tell you when."

I blew out one of the candles, left it on the floor, and we started down the hallway together. I wondered how many ticks until a ship sailed for France, and when the wind might blow that ship back again. I wondered if I could make the clocks tick faster, if time would do the same. The idea pleased me so much that I said, "Perhaps we should wind them up, Uncle Tully."

"Wind them?" Uncle Tully seemed shocked. "Oh, no! No! It's not the day, little niece! Not the right day! You have to wait for the right time and turn them the right way. The other way is backward. Marianna said we have to wait and turn the right way, Simon's baby. That's what is best."

I took his hand. "You're perfectly right, Uncle."

AUTHOR'S NOTE

The Victorian estate in *The Dark Unwinding* was inspired by England's Welbeck Abbey, where the reclusive fifth Duke of Portland built a mile-long tunnel for his carriage and a vast ballroom and library that were both completely underground. By 1870, he had erected his own gasworks, iron-and-glass stables, marble-floored cowsheds, painted every room of his sprawling mansion pink, and regularly encouraged his employees to roller-skate. The Duke's massive building projects depleted his family fortune, while at the same time providing work, food, and shelter for an estimated 1,600 men over a twenty-year period — men that might have otherwise died in poverty with their families. Madness or benevolence? History has never quite decided.

ACKNOWLEDGMENTS

No author writes a book alone. The only real surprise is that just one name ends up on the spine. A myriad of people have given their weekends, their workdays, their homes, gone out on a literary limb, and generally exercised never-ending patience and understanding to help make this book happen. The following are just a few members of my tribe. You all have my love, respect, and thanks.

First, the wise, supportive, talented, and infinitely dear critique partners that were willing to read my drafts, and then read them again, and then read them again, and most importantly, tell me what was wrong with them: Genetta Adair, Hannah Dills, Amy Eytchison, Rachel Griffith, Rae Ann Parker, Courtney Potter, Linda Ragsdale, Ruta Sepetys — thank you for your friendship, endless cheerleading, and your cabin's creative mojo! — Howard Shirley, Angelika Stegmann, and Jessica Young.

My smart and savvy agent, Kelly Sonnack, who was perfectly aware she was signing on an unproven writer with one book that was way too long and significantly lacking in commercial appeal: Why, oh, why did you do it, Kelly, and where would I be if you hadn't? Your guidance and belief have made all the difference to my career, and I thank my lucky stars for it.

My lovely and talented editor, Lisa Sandell, who combines beauty, grace, and the ability to correctly use the word *who* to devastating effect: Thank you for your wisdom, patience, and incredible insight, and for taking such a huge chance on me! The book has reached a new level because of you.

To the editorial, production, marketing, sales, and publicity staffs; Book Clubs and Book Fairs; the design and foreign rights teams; and all the others that worked behind the scenes in ways I'll never know: You gave me something to be proud of, and then sent it out across the country and the seas. Thank you.

The Society of Children's Book Writers and Illustrators: Thank you for giving me inspiration, knowledge, and a really big award. You showed me that I could think of myself as a professional long before I actually was.

The Sue Alexander Most Promising New Work Award selection committee: You strapped me to the catapult of change. Things moved pretty fast from there.

My offspring, Christopher, Stephen, and Elizabeth, who didn't mind all those times Mom was out of town, lost in deep, deep thought, or just super excited about really nerdy things: Thanks for turning out okay in spite of me.

And last, everlasting love and appreciation to Philip, who built balancing boats, drew schematics, played with gyroscopes, learned everything there ever was to know about a gasworks at any period in history, described lever switches, researched canal building, and cooked up volatile and foul-smelling explosives in our basement. And all just for me. What more could a girl want?

ABOUT THE AUTHOR

Sharon Cameron was awarded the 2009 Sue Alexander Most Promising New Work Award by the Society of Children's Book Writers and Illustrators for her debut novel, *The Dark Unwinding*, which was also awarded the SCBWI Crystal Kite Award and named an ALA Best Fiction for Young Adults selection. When not writing, Sharon can be found thumbing through dusty tomes, shooting a longbow, or indulging in her lifelong search for secret passages. She lives with her family in Nashville, Tennessee. Learn more at sharoncameronbooks.com.

MORE DANGER AND ROMANCE AWAIT IN KATHARINE'S NEXT ADVENTURE,

A SPARK UNSEEN

When Katharine Tulman is awakened in the middle of the night by a kidnapping attempt on her uncle, she realizes that Stranwyne is no longer safe for them. After fleeing to Paris, Katharine soon finds herself embroiled in a deadly maze of political intrigue.